CROWFALL

Praise for the Marathi original, *Tya Varshi*

'There are some incidents in this novel that touch the heart and others that demonstrate the writer's fine eye for detail. The prose is largely free of decorative devices. Yet when similes, metaphors and extended descriptions come, they hit the mark with fine precision.'
—Anuradha Potdar, *Navshakti*

'While the writer's contemplative handling of issues like the creative process, violence, annihilation, loss and death add substance to the novel, her sense of irony prevents it from tipping over into sentimentality.'
—Sushama Karogal, *Pratishthan*

'*Tya Varshi* sets the world of artists and their art in the larger world of self-serving politicians, land-grabbing builders, the media and the man in the street, creating a vivid portrait of Mumbai.'
—Anant Deshmukh, *Lalit*

CROWFALL

SHANTA GOKHALE

PENGUIN
VIKING

An imprint of Penguin Random House

VIKING

USA | Canada | UK | Ireland | Australia
New Zealand | India | South Africa | China | Singapore

Viking is part of the Penguin Random House group of companies
whose addresses can be found at global.penguinrandomhouse.com

Published by Penguin Random House India Pvt. Ltd
4th Floor, Capital Tower 1, MG Road,
Gurugram 122 002, Haryana, India

First published in Marathi as *Tya Varshi* by Mouj Prakashan 2008
First published in English in Viking by Penguin Books India 2013

Copyright © Shanta Gokhale 2013

ISBN 9780670086948

Typeset in GoudyOlSt BT by R. Ajith Kumar, New Delhi
Printed at Replika Press Pvt. Ltd, India

www.penguin.co.in

This is a legitimate digitally printed version of the book and therefore might not
have certain extra finishing on the cover.

For Jerry
without whom this translation would not have happened

1

That day again. The day Siddharth didn't turn up, twelve years ago. How time flies. Even when nothing else happens, time flies. She had once overheard Anna tell Ai the time for that had gone; and she had wondered where. She had also wondered how time was a girl when it went and a boy when you were getting late. Funny language, Marathi.

She smiles at the memory, looking out of the window. When she isn't busy in the kitchen, when she isn't reading, when she isn't sitting in a darkened auditorium watching a play or a film, she looks out of this window, watching the light of the world fade away. That it should fade and disappear is inevitable. That Anima should watch silently feels equally inevitable.

There is a world set in her window frame. A gulmohr leans over from the left. Its brown bark is gradually turning black in the gathering shade, the rough ridges on its trunk losing definition. The few tired leaves left on its branches turn lifeless from bottom up. Beyond the tree is the rusted gate of the large, deserted maidan; and beyond that a cluster of cheery house lights. From amongst them rises the skeleton of a new twenty-storey building, growing inexorably every day. Only a few cars pass down this road. As they race by, their headlights swing into the window frame for a few brief seconds and then die out. The house lights beyond the maidan are recent company. Earlier there was only darkness.

Anima had sat here, like this, on that day too, but filled with a gnawing unease, her insides dark and dry like the trunk of the gulmohr. Versova was at peace, but the city was not. You could never be sure where trouble would flare up and why. Gangs of men roamed the streets,

1

their chests puffed out. Hunters, impelled to blood by some primeval instinct. The quarry, alert, went about its work, moving on cat-burglar feet, hugging shadows, its eyes averted from other eyes. At such a time as this, they were out there—Arif and Siddharth. They were roaming the city, unconcerned about the hunt. The hunt wasn't part of their life. They were on shore for this brief while. Land held no dangers for those whose fierce battles were with the sea.

The evening had stretched out long and dark while Anima's ears yearned for the sound of the key in the latch. The time was long past when she should have heard it. Anima's throat had gone dry and cracked. She had lifted herself out of her chair and had been in the kitchen with a glass of water when the bell had rung with a trill of Bhairavi, the raag of endings. Siddharth had had the bell custom made. Had he forgotten to carry his key after all? Anima had rushed to the door, the water in her glass slopping a trail behind her.

Arif, and behind him Anisa, her head bent. Arif's shirt was smeared red, his face white. Arif and Anisa had stood outside and Anima had known why. She had said, 'Why don't you come in?' The crack in her voice was of the quake inside her. They had come in and with them had come a cool puff of breeze. They had sat down, silent. Anima's eyes had flitted around Arif's blank stare. Then he had spoken. Then he had stopped speaking. A cab was waiting downstairs. Arif had gone down to bring Siddharth's shredded body up with the driver's help. Anima had looked at his face, still the same, and she had died within.

Over the next twelve years, this day has returned remorselessly, with the same shapes darkening to night in the frame of this window, except for that other—the empty skeleton of the twenty-storey building in the distance. These days a naked bulb hangs from a long wire in one of its upper rooms. Anima's eyes are fixed on its light when suddenly she arrives at a decision. I must stop writing my diary from today. Today is now. This minute. I must free myself of its shackles, from the rigid self-made rule that a few lines must be written every night. Drop a day and guilt takes away sleep. The oppression of it. Tired, bored, but you must write. Write. Who for? Who is going to read that drivel? People with children write in the hope that their children will read. Family history will live and grow. But who will read the daily notes of my life? Stop fooling yourself that you're writing for yourself. Perhaps you did, in the beginning, to vomit the grief in your stomach. It was even a way to keep the conversation with Siddharth going. But when the sharp edge of grief had dulled, why then? The ego stepped in, didn't it? You started pontificating on the political events of the day. You started reporting conversations overheard on your commute, with sociological analyses attached. Weren't you secretly thinking that someone would discover your diaries decades after you were gone and exult in their revelations of life in these times? Like some latter-day *Smritichitre*?

Get over this foolish temptation of trying to forge a link with the future. Fifty years from now attention spans will have shrunk to zero and diaries written by some ancient woman about an ancient life might make no sense at all. Anima gets up and dispels the darkness of the room with a flick of a switch. She takes four long strides to the wooden wardrobe–cum–chest of drawers that Anna had had specially made for her as a wedding present. She opens the right bottom drawer, pulls out the secret drawer built into the back and draws out the twelve notebooks, all of the same size, resting within. They chronicle her life from the January of 1993.

Anima carries the notebooks to the centre of the room. The ceiling lamp sheds maximum light here. She fetches a cane waste-paper basket and sets it down beside the heap. She sits before it on the floor, cross-legged, a pair of scissors in her hand. She picks up the topmost notebook, the first in the series. Salman Khan smiles up at her from its cover. She resists the temptation of opening it. If she begins to read it, she is lost. She tears out a thin sheaf of pages from the notebook, shreds it into ribbons and stuffs them in the cane basket. As succeeding sheaves of paper enter the jaws of the scissors and are shredded, the tearing and shredding fall into a natural rhythm. She accompanies the rhythm silently with a childhood tongue-twister about the aunt who cuts up the uncle's work papers with a pair of scissors and stuffs them into a waste-paper basket. '*Kakune Kakanche kamache kagad katrine kapun karandit komble.*' As a child she used to have a vivid mental picture of the aunt. She sat on the floor like Anima now, but fatly. Her eyebrows clashed above her nose and her hair was pulled to the top of her head in a Narad Muni knot. In Anima's imagination, the story continued beyond the rhyme with the aunt rising and dancing ferociously on the heap of shredded paper in the basket.

Anima's work picks up speed. She has shredded six notebooks. She fetches another basket from the bedroom and varies the beat of the aunt-and-uncle rhyme, so that sometimes the scissors snap together on the first beat and sometimes on the last. After the eighth diary, she brings out the bath bucket from the bathroom. Finally, the twelfth diary goes into the bucket, Shah Rukh Khan's dimpled smile and all.

For a few moments Anima sits exhausted, looking intently at the two baskets and the bath bucket filled with mountains of paper. She takes a tentative breath, allowing it to feel her insides as it comes up. Any regret? A faint twinge of pain? No? Nothing at all? Let's test this. Let me do the dangerous thing. She plunges her hand into a basket and pulls out some random pieces of paper. Each of the shreds carries just a few legible words. She reads them. One shakes her slightly. Anna. But even that name produces only a brief shooting pain. Siddharth's none at all. It's like muscles that die in a myocardial infarction. When the infarction happens, the whole chest cavity is a single epic pain. The muscles die. Medication will not bring them to life. But those that are still alive return to work. And soon it is as if the others never existed.

When Bachchu Kaka had his myocardial infarction, he almost died. With Anna's untiring nursing, he managed to hang on.

Anima gets up. Does a few luxurious stretches, mutters, 'Free at last', fetches a large, old pillow cover, stuffs the contents of both baskets and the bucket into it, drags it to the door and deposits it outside for the garbage man to take away. About to close the door, she wonders. Shall I keep it in the house and give it to the garbage man when he comes in the morning? But then shuts the door resolutely, changes into her nightclothes and gets into bed.

Sediments rise. The days and nights after Siddharth's monstrous death. The distorted faces that peopled her dreams. Changing faces, always distorted. No sleep. No hunger. Get up. Pace from this end of the room to that, wide eyes blank. Sit down in a chair, wanting never to get up. Anisa's visits in the day. Sharada and Shekhar dropping in to be with her. Feroze's concerned calls. Haridas's insistence—'Stay with me for a few days. You'll feel better. Or let's see a film.' But then night fell, with just her nightmares to fill the house.

One sleepless night she picked up a razor blade and walked to the bathroom. She shut her eyes, the blade at her wrist. The blade didn't move. She shut her eyes tighter. The blade would still not move. The strength drained out of her. Her hand went limp. The blade slipped out of her fingers and fell to the floor. Anima stood rigid. Then collapsed, howling.

She sat the whole night on her bed, her knees pulled up to her chest. Am I feeble in mind? Is my will so weak? Do I not love Siddharth enough? Isn't desiring death when your husband dies the ultimate definition of love? Why did I hold back then? Could it be that the will alone is not enough? Do you need physical courage as well? Do I not have that? Where do those girls of fifteen and sixteen who hang themselves from fans with their dupattas find it? They write farewell notes to their parents, pull up chairs to stand on. They are about to do something they've never done before, but they go the whole hog. What pushes them? Despair? Fear of the future? What did Yogesh fear when he put razor to wrist? People had always raved about his work. Finally there is just one answer. Some people want to die. I don't.

So live. It was then that Anima bought her first notebook. Her entry on the first page was a description of Siddharth's death as told to her by Arif that evening, and every other evening, with growing helplessness, when she repeated her questions. 'They came down the road. They would have let us pass if we had moved aside. But we continued to walk as before. They didn't like that. They stopped us. They grabbed Siddharth's beard. "What are you, hanh? Hindu or Mussalman?" Siddharth said, "A human being." They went mad.

They threw him down. I flung myself on him. They picked me up and threw me aside. "We'll attend to you later," they said. I hit my head on something and became unconscious. When I came to, they had gone. And Siddharth . . .' At this point Arif's wounded gaze would slide to the floor. His story would always end here. And once again the hope in Anima's eyes would die.

She wrote all this in her diary. And added: as a child, if I didn't like the way a story ended, Anna would change it for me. He would narrate the new end with such conviction that I would believe it. It was not in Arif's hands to change the end of this story.

Cut them down they said
The Allah-hu-Akbar men

Surve's *Shigwala* and my Siddharth. Murderers of different religions but linked by inhumanity. Would she ever have dreamt that a poem she had read, with exclamations of aesthetic delight, would come so terrifyingly true in her own life? How could you have stood before those animals and called yourself a human being with such stupid courage, Siddharth?

Six months later Arif and Anisa packed their bags. They had found themselves a place in Jogeshwari. Anima had pleaded with them not to leave. 'We're all here for you.' But Arif had shaken his head sadly. 'There's a monster let loose amongst us. He's never going to go away. Like Bakasur, he will keep returning to devour innocents. I should have been their target, but they got my noble friend. Nobody is safe now. Not even those who have let the monster loose.'

Arif and Anisa left. The city had been torn apart. The gash of that partition now ran between Anima and Anisa's homes that had once faced each other.

Reading her diary description of Siddharth's death became Anima's solace. She would read it before facing each new day. It was now her life with her lover-husband. Over time, as she absorbed the shock of his death, its meaning expanded. Siddharth's death became the death of Jews in Germany. It became those left dead by the partition of India.

The death of a mahatma on 30 January 1948. Thousands of Sikhs in Delhi in 1984. The two thousand murdered in Gujarat in 2002. Corpses were piling up. Amongst them was one Siddharth. A single droplet in an ocean of the killed. How much longer was she going to cradle his death in the palm of her hand, against her wet cheek?

2

Ashesh doesn't quite know what has woken him up. He is in the hazy state between sleeping and waking. Was it the dream? One black tunnel leading to another and another, with him holding on to their slippery sides trying to get out? Was it a sound? Did the bed shake? Could it have been a quake?

Ashesh lies with eyes still closed, wondering; then sinks back into sleep. But the next moment his eyes fly open and he freezes. His sheet is jumping. His heart thumps. The sheet trembles, jumps. Only one part. He kicks it off. His right hand. His right hand is jumping, disconnected from the rest of his body, from his will, like something possessed. Ashesh watches it for five minutes, fifty—he isn't sure—then grabs it with his left hand and holds it down. It grows still.

Ashesh frees the hand warily. It lies motionless by his side. He raises it, lowers it, closes and opens his fist. It's working. Ashesh's tense body relaxes. He bursts into a sweat, gets up, walks to the kitchen, legs trembling, swallows a glassful of water and walks out on to the veranda.

It's a long veranda, both corners screened by madhumalati creepers. He does not love potted plants. But he loves privacy. He lowers himself into the cane rocking chair and rocks himself gently. He tries to laugh. His lips don't part. They're still dry. Haridas would have laughed. 'You really tore your arsehole there, didn't you? Hypohypesthesia.' One of Haridas's concocted words. It means a condition of irrational anxiety.

Whenever Ashesh wakes up in the middle of the night, he plays a game with himself. He tries to guess the time. He feels the weight of the silence and the density of the darkness to gauge it. His guess now is five minutes past three. He screws up his eyes to look at his watch. Dead right. Most times he is. No surprise there. But when he isn't, he feels angry. He can lie in bed for hours afterwards wondering why. Anima says it's the effect of bachelorhood. 'You'll soon start talking to yourself, you'll see.'

Ashesh switches on the light. At once, the canvas standing on the easel leaps at him with a blank stare. It has been wordless for days. He has looked into its depths with pleading eyes, but not a single image has surfaced. It has remained a two by one and a half feet of desert. The canvas is not at fault. He is. His imagination has deserted him. That thing called inspiration hasn't shown up. He's like slashed and burnt earth—no shoot or sprout in sight. He stands looking at the canvas with empty eyes, his mouth set. In the old days he'd have panicked. Pack-up time, he'd have told himself. Who said you're an artist? Get yourself an art teacher's job in the old school in Surgaon.

He doesn't despair quite so easily now. He has come to terms with the waywardness of the creative spirit. He is willing to wait.

Haridas once had a pet dog. Not by choice. It presented itself at his door one day and Haridas fed it. Then fed it the next day. When the dog felt secure in his ownership of the man, he began to reveal interesting shades of his personality. You put a dish of food before him and said, 'Eat.' He turned away and gazed into the distance. You coaxed and cajoled him. He remained disinterested. Then you said to yourself go to hell and moved away. At once he pounced on the food with relish. Creative ideas are like that. You don't plead with them to come. You pretend you can live happily without them. Then they steal upon you like thieves. Just be alert to grab them by the hair when they do.

The empty canvas has begun to oppress Ashesh. He's tired. Fed up. He must take it off the easel. Stand it down, face against the wall. Why force a relationship that isn't happening? Take a few days off. Go to Matheran, to Feroze's bungalow. Forget you're an artist.

Ashesh switches off the light gloomily. The canvas looks innocuous in the semi-darkness, but wait, something's happened. Two thick diagonals have appeared on its face—one across the upper left corner, one across the lower right. Ashesh looks at them and then around, surprised. It's the light of the street lamp. His window bars have blocked it, casting the shadows.

Ashesh is suddenly alert. Something is happening in the space between the shadows. He's straining to catch what it is. Something is struggling to rise in his mind. It's coming. Yes, he can almost see it. Then it's gone. Lost. His mind goes totally blank. His shoulders droop. He throws himself into a chair, but springs up in alarm. The shadows are there today. Tomorrow morning they'll be gone. This space in which an image was trying to insinuate itself will be irretrievably lost. It must be preserved.

Ashesh looks at the tubes of paint on the stool next to the easel. His mind prompts his hand to act. His hand picks up a tube of black. He squeezes it on to the palette and dips his brush into the ooze. With the loaded brush he lightly paints in the shadows of the window bars. Now he grows calm. The first marks have been made on the canvas to guide and restrict him. Anything that goes on to the canvas now will have to relate to them, to the way they are deployed, to their colour, their form, their texture. He sighs, satisfied. He cleans his brush carefully, returns it to its place. Tired, he lays his body down on the bed and falls into a deep sleep.

Ashesh stands on the veranda sipping his morning cup of tea, looking at the half-broken body of the building across the street. In an hour or so, the hammer-men will emerge from their cane shelters in the building compound, scrub their bodies under the outdoor tap, drink the tea brewed by their women on improvised three-stone fires and climb the building to hammer it down. The massive walls of the building will shake under the impact but they will not give way immediately. The workers will fall into a rhythm. Lift hammer up, swing it back over the head, bend knees to balance the load on the arms, jerk the body up, bring the hammer forward to crash against the concrete slab. Again the knees will bend, again the hammer will swing back over the head, again it will come down on the slab in an arc. A few bits of masonry will fly up. This through the whole day and the next and the day after and who knows for how long before the building is rubble.

The building was built by an ancestor of the present owner to last seven generations. It would have had at least another fifty years of life had the present owner not sold it to the developer. The owner had only been waiting for Mr Dholakia on the first floor to die. Mr Dholakia, the Gandhi hater, had been Anna's regular sparring partner. Whenever Anna visited Mumbai, the two would fire up at least one evening in political debate.

It's been a fortnight since Dholakia died and the developer's hammer-men moved in. For two weeks, the neighbourhood has found it impossible to work with those remorseless hammer blows. Even with doors and windows tightly shut—and no way to breathe—the noise has been percolating into every home. There's only one way you can deal with it. Accept it. Absorb it into the rhythm of your life.

Ashesh stands sipping his tea and, with it, the silence, before the hammer-men arrive. He runs his forefinger around the rim of the ceramic mug, taking pleasure in its roundness. He touches the drip of tea running down the side to feel its wetness. The half-moon in the sky is pale but still alive. Its pallor could be taken as a sign of defeat against the advancing sun, or survival in its face.

Ashesh breathes in the warm aroma of the tea. Women's precise fingers have plucked the leaves, infusing his cup of Darjeeling with the delicacy of their touch. He brings a similar delicate precision to the way he brews it. Making the first cup of tea is a cherished ritual in Ashesh's morning routine. He uses Anna's tea pan. Puts it to boil on the same right-hand burner that Anna preferred. When the water begins to boil, he puts in exactly three-quarters of a teaspoon of tea leaves, followed by two quick, simultaneous actions. He turns off the gas with his right hand and puts a lid on the tea pan with his left. The water must not be allowed to simmer even for a moment after it reaches boiling point, nor must the aroma be allowed to escape after the tea leaves go in. Wait for exactly five minutes, lift the tea-pan lid, strain the amber-gold liquid into the ceramic mug and, unadulterated by milk or sugar, carry the tea out to the veranda. It's time then to simply be. Ashesh, tea, silence.

The last drop of the tea has been sipped. Ashesh walks into his bedroom to tidy up his bed. One look at his sheet takes away all the energy his tea has given him. He looks at it as though it could be hiding a snake. Is it moving? Was that a dream? No. He saw it with wide-open eyes. Kicked off the sheet. Saw the hand—his hand—jump. He turns away from the bed and hurries into the living room. He draws a book down from the topmost shelf of the book rack near the door. *Your Health: Symptoms and Treatment*. He turns the leaves swiftly, looking for 't-r-e-m-o-r-s'. 'Tremors' isn't listed. How's that? Don't people have tremors? How can this book have nothing to say about what his hand was doing last night?

Ashesh mulls over the problem. A thought that's been trying to push its way to the forefront of his mind finally finds an opening. Involuntary trembling. Isn't that a symptom of Parkinson's? He begins to turn the pages of the book again with a heavier hand. His mind has jumped ahead to an extreme thought. Parkinson's would be the end of his painting. Or not. He is thinking of the time when they were all at his place and the conversation had turned to Benode Behari Mukherjee's blindness. How could he have painted after he went blind? They had all asked themselves which impairment scared them the most. Ashesh had said Parkinson's. Sharada had laughed at his fear. 'Thirakwan Khan Sahib's hands trembled constantly in his last years,' she said. 'But when they touched the tabla, they became agile and produced the most complex rhythms. Without breath there can be no music. Kumar Gandharva was severely short of it with just one lung. But he used it to evolve his powerful, original style of singing. Gangubai Hangal lost her original voice. She trained her new gruff voice and continued to sing.'

Ashesh looks up Parkinson's. 'A disease of the nervous system also known as paralysis agitans. The condition is rare in people under the age of fifty.' H'm. Rare doesn't mean unheard of. 'It is more common

in men than in women.' There you are. 'The first symptoms include
tremors in the hands, arms and legs.' As I thought. 'In the later stages
the muscles of the body begin to stiffen.' So even twiddling my thumbs
will be impossible. 'Tremors are generally worse while the patient is
resting.' There! 'They tend, however, to disappear during sleep.' What?

Ashesh reads the last line over and over again. He leans back in
his chair, takes a clean, folded handkerchief out of his pyjama pocket
and wipes his sweaty forehead. He picks the fat health volume off his
knees and sets it down on the floor. Putting his hands behind his head,
he hums Sant Tukaram's abhang.

Bliss upon bliss
Bliss ripples on the deep pond of bliss

He hums it in the traditional tune. Jijabhau's tune.

There's bliss and bliss. Hard of hearing, Kamala Attya next door
listens to old songs at full volume on her radio and breaks into audible
ripples of bliss. But her ripples are confined to things within four
walls—she has made a perfect batch of puran polis; somebody in the
family has been promoted. Jijabhau's spiritual bliss breaks walls and soars
upwards to touch the sky. Music has that power. It creates its own space
with the throw of voice, intensity of emotion, density of meaning, the
primeval power of note and beat. The painter is trammelled. His space
is given. All his acrobatics must happen within it. He must use sleight
of hand to convert a two-dimensional surface into an illusionary three.
Or protest against the compulsion of pretence and exaggerate the two-
dimensionality of the surface. This surface has only two dimensions. I
accept this limitation. The limitation challenges my imagination. To
face the challenge is to retain the purity of painting.

Twenty years ago Ashesh had followed in the footsteps of his gurus
and created abstract works that emphasized the flatness of the picture
space. Ai used to call his paintings a mess. Then he became interested
in depth, in the play of light and shade. He spent years with space,
light, shapes and colours. He let himself go with colour. His palette

turned vivid. Then Nasreen left the country and he abandoned colour. He turned to drawing with pencil, charcoal, crayon, ink. That was also when the human form entered his work. By the time he reached out for colour again, the human condition had captured his imagination completely. The pictures that followed were not vibrant with colour. The men and women in them, their environments, their living spaces, the objects surrounding them, were translated into shades of grey and brown. Yet he sought to emphasize their separateness from 'real' life, painting frames within the picture frames to underline the 'pictureness' of his pictures. It was a deliberate act, unlike last night's when he had allowed an accident to enter his art through the bars of his windows.

Ashesh turns to the canvas and starts. He has never used such an uncompromising black before. Suddenly his palms are cold and there's sweat on his forehead. He ignores these signs of panic and forces himself into a still, quiet concentration. He listens for the faint whisper that had stirred in his mind last night, narrowing his eyes to concentrate on the space within the two black diagonals. What image, what idea had that space prompted? It wasn't a human form. It was something else. He gets up and moves towards the canvas. The doorbell rings. His movement is broken. His shoulders droop. He is empty.

Reshma enters like a whirlwind. In the next thirty minutes she will sweep, swab, wash, clean, cook and run to the next job. She has four children to feed. Plus another—her husband—if his fancy brings him home. Ashesh is expected to remove himself from her path during her operations. He dresses quickly, slips into his chappals, calls out to her as usual, 'Close the door behind you when you leave,' and steps out of the house. His mind is filled with two black diagonals and a grey unease.

There's very little traffic in the lanes and by-lanes of Gamdevi. Out there on Hughes Road the traffic runs like a river in spate. But on this street it's just the occasional car—long, sleek and washed—sliding noiselessly out of the gate of a bungalow to purr away down the road. Ancient trees, weighed down by dense foliage, flank the street, cooling old two-storeyed bungalows with their shade. There's still abundant space here for the breeze to play around. It plays now with Ashesh's straight, fine hair, ruffling it lightly. He smoothes it down, but soon realizes there's no disciplining it in the circumstances and lets it be.

Ashesh walks briskly. His eyes are fixed ahead but see nothing except two diagonals and the space within. He descends on to Vaccha Gandhi Street then turns left on to Pandita Ramabai Road. His eyes seek out, through habit, the figure of the man who sits on the step of a shop up ahead. He's tall and humped. His head is bent so low over his work that the end of his nose practically touches it. Ashesh has named him Framroze.

Framroze is doing what he does every day—sewing scraps of fabric together with the intense concentration of a man on a mission. When passers-by put coins or bread or biscuits before him, he doesn't raise his head from his work. But if you give him cotton sewing thread or bits of fabric, he will look up. Anima did that once when she was staying over at the Gamdevi house. When he saw what she had put before him, he had raised his head slowly and looked at her with cloudy eyes. Then he had picked up her gift with a wrinkled hand and stuffed it into his bundle.

His clothes look soiled today. But there are times when he is scrubbed and gleaming. Who bathes him is a mystery. But Ashesh knows who cuts his hair. It's old Shankar the barber, probably the same age as Framroze. Shankar still makes home visits as before, carrying his kit with him, to cut hair, shave chins and administer brisk head massages. He used to do that for Anna in the old days. You just sent him a message and he'd come. Then the two had their routine conversation.

Anna: 'How are you, Shankarrao? All well on Mt Kailash?'

Shankar: 'Yeah, sure, but them devotees are a pest. Give me this, give me that. No contentment.'

Anna: 'I tell you, Shankarrao, you must learn to conjure up holy ash from your sleeve. That'll thrill them. See how it rains money in your house then.'

Shankar would laugh and concentrate on cutting what was left of Anna's hair. The massage followed. Ashesh can still hear its oily *pit-pat, pit-pat* on Anna's head. Framroze too must have been Shankar's client in his better days. There's an ease between them that comes of habit. Shankar cuts Framroze's hair while he sews. But he turns his head exactly as the pressure of Shankar's hands indicates. The hairstyle too must belong to Framroze's early days. The hair is combed forward and the ends flicked up to look like the foaming crest of a wave poised atop Framroze's high forehead. Shankar picks up his kit wordlessly and moves on to his next job. There's no giving or taking of money.

Ashesh turns left again and his pace slows automatically. This is Laburnum Road. It is his favourite. Flanked by its old laburnum trees, totally covered by hanging clusters of yellow flowers in May, so thick that they cast a lemon light on the ground, the road is most specially marked by the historic building that stands at No. 19. Radiant symbol of peace, it is also the birthplace of the rousing cry, 'Do or die.' For Ashesh, to spend a few moments each morning looking at this elegant bungalow is to begin the day auspiciously. His mind at peace, he then turns into Tejpal Lane, walks around Gowalia Tank garden and sets off for home.

Somewhere along the road he feels a hard something underfoot. It is a pod of gunj seeds. The gunj is the minimum unit used by goldsmiths to weigh gold. He looks around for the tree that has dropped it, but can't recognize it amongst the others. Back home he runs his thumbnail along the seam of the pod, eager to see and feel the textures and colours within. There it is—a velvety, green-yellow case with four compartments. Nestling snugly in each is a polished red seed with a black eye. He cannot look long enough at that plump, saturated red—the colour of a parrot's beak. He cannot feel enough the satin smoothness of each globule. Finally, Ashesh closes his fist over the seeds and drops them one by one into a glass bowl, there to find their way, small and brashly bright, amongst his collection of amethysts, mother-of-pearl and delicately veined agates.

Ashesh has been dialling Anima's number repeatedly and finding the line engaged. Finally he's through.

'Who were you talking to this long?'

'Sharada. About her concert. It's on Saturday.'

'So?'

'She's planning to sing something of her own.'

'That'll be the end of her.'

'She's worried. But excited.'

'Good. Just a request . . .'

'You will visit Ai again next Saturday, right?'

'Well, yes. Yes. This is a tough painting. See, I'm giving you ten days' notice. If it's your young friends' Saturday, there's time to make some adjustment.'

'It's not my young friends' Saturday. But this is simply not on, yaar. Last time you made some other excuse. And I ended up listening to Ai's griping about you. You better give me a really good excuse this time. Difficult paintings don't impress her.'

'My show's coming up in six months. That should impress anybody.'

'Not Ai.'

'Go on, deal with her. She complains even when I go. "You come but don't say a word." You'll go, won't you?'

'Do I have a choice? I'd go every fortnight, but I'm not the son—I'm the daughter. A dark-skinned daughter at that. A daughter with opinions.'

'Shut up. Just go.'

'Right. Now as a brother you want to make solicitous inquiries after me? Like how have I been, etc.'

Ashesh laughs. Anima sighs.

'So I'm fine. I withdrew my case last week. I'm erasing the past. This thing's been going on for ever. The lawyer's pockets are getting heavier, mine lighter.'

'I told you long ago.'

'Sure. But I'm not an escapist like you. I believe one has to fight. But I'm tired, that's all. So tell me, are you coming to Sharada's concert? Forget it. I don't know why I expect decisive answers from you. Do you have a loving message for Ai?'

'Tell her I'll definitely come next month.'

'How? Your show will be only five months away then.'

'Then say I asked about her health.'

Anima hangs up.

Ashesh stands before his canvas. These black triangular shapes. There are only two ways to deal with them. Paint them out of existence. Or respond to their challenge. Ashesh takes a few steps back from the canvas. Then a few steps forward. He inclines his head to look at the canvas from a different angle. The black has barred all routes to the usual shades of his palette. There's only one colour that can checkmate black. Red. But Ashesh does not have the courage to use it. At least not at this moment. In his opinion, only one artist in the city uses red with conviction. Haridas.

Ashesh hurries to his CD shelf. He wants music that will rouse him, something that outreaches itself, but still lands on the final beat of the rhythmic cycle with aplomb. He chooses Krishnarao Pandit singing Raag Todi. There's no beating about the bush here. The first note he utters is the beginning of the song. The note is just there, deadly precise.

I cajole my beloved
I don't know why he will not listen
His unconcern distresses me so
My darling get up, come to me

The singer elaborates on the first couplet in slow tempo in his powerful voice, conjuring up a vision of ancient trees, their enormous trunks carved with complex patterns. Waterfalls cascade off cliffs, clouds thunder, lightning flashes from skies that darken from ink blue to blue-black. The singer rises to the high notes of the next couplet. The tempo becomes urgent. Ashesh sees a blur of images. The plea in the words becomes his plea. Looking at the canvas he feels them.

Your unconcern distresses me
My darling get up, come to me

Ashesh plucks his gaze from the canvas. When the hand stalls, the brain can sometimes give a hand. Ideas, thoughts—these too must be allowed their place in art. Ashesh sits still, thinking of the colour black. Thinkers of the visual world have had many things to say about it. Krishnarao Pandit's volcanic voice in his ears drags a few of them up from deep within his memory.

'Black demands respect.'

'Black leaves no place for compromise.'

'Black does not please the eye, nor titillate the other senses.'

'The colour black is not for sale. Black never prostitutes itself. It does not play with your feelings. It is at all times nothing more or less than an agent of the intellect.'

Ashesh takes a measure of the black triangles on the canvas. As he gazes at them, he grows calm. He knows that he will accept this challenge. He will dare to set foot on the new path that the colour opens up before him.

3

It is Saturday. The koel, in the rain tree across the road, fervently practises his five-note call. There's a hint in the air of the changing seasons. Sharada will sing Raag Basant this early spring evening. As she slips the cover off her tanpura, a doubt scratches the top of her mind. Her prevalent mood cannot be called bright, whereas Basant is pure joy. How will she sing it? She pushes the thought away as romantic nonsense. It is not written anywhere that Basant cannot be sung sombrely. There's that too in spring. The sprouting of the new comes with the decay of the old.

Sharada tunes the tanpura. Holding it up, she lays the stem close to her cheek and is soon absorbed in the resonance of the two notes that its four strings produce. *Pa-sa-sa-Sa.* She spends a few minutes getting into the melodic frame of Basant. She sings a succession of long-held notes that define the raag before singing the song she has chosen to elaborate it.

In the durbar of heaven
sing together all you divine denizens
sing the praises of spring

The fewer the words in a song, the more exciting their elaboration. Praise be to the glossy new leaves of the rain tree. Praise be to the koel that sings. Praise be to the scent of the flowers that the woman hurrying down the road wears in her hair. Praise be to the quick, capricious, clear-blue season of optimism.

Sharada sings, but grey clouds still drift in from the edges of the blue. No matter. A raag may express all the moods there are. Equating a raag with a mood reduces its potential. There is no reason why Sharada cannot allow her unease to cloud her rendering of Basant. So be it today.

As she lays down her tanpura, doubts come flooding in. She is going to sing her own composition. She wishes she had the poet Narayan Surve's thumping self-confidence.

I am a worker, a flaming sword,
Noble Literature! I am about to sin against your canon.

She is too firmly trapped in the rules of the guru–shishya tradition to feel she has the right to break free. Shekhar has a name for the classical musician's caste: Ear Touchers. Pronounce the guru's name, touch your ears with humility. Miss a note, touch your ears with shame. Miss a beat, touch your ears in abject apology. And she, ear toucher if ever there was one, proposes to sing her own composition this evening. Her guru's face is before her—thin-lipped smile frozen hard. 'We hear you sang your own composition, Mrs Sakhardande. You also sang the noon raag Sarang at twilight. Flung away the blinkers of mouldy tradition, did you? Bravo!'

By the time Shekhar returns from his walk, Sharada has lost spirit and will. He strides across to her, straightens her shoulders, slaps her lightly on the back. 'The composition works. Don't think. Just sing.' Sharada glances at him gratefully. This is all she wants, just that much support. She raises her tanpura and sings.

> I have seen black Time, my friend, I have seen black Time today
> A shower of black fell from the skies
> and fear filled my heart
> I have seen black Time today

It was two weeks ago on a morning like this. Sharada was preparing to practise Raag Bhairav. She held the first note in the lowest octave to clear her voice, before moving into the melody. Soon she was lost in its massive structure. Shantanu woke up. He came out rubbing his eyes and lay down in her lap. She moved the tanpura a little to make place for his little head. He smiled up at her, put his thumb in his mouth and closed his eyes.

Sharada worked around the nishad in the lower octave with as many variations as she could think up, and was about to touch the komal dhaivat note, when a cacophony of cawing exploded outside. She turned her head. Frantic crows zigzagged across the window. Her komal dhaivat was lost in their cawing. Sharada stopped singing. Shantanu half opened his eyes. The crows continued to caw. Sharada watched. Shantanu's lips puckered. Sharada patted him, held him close. The cawing continued. It would soon stop, she thought. 'Come, sweetheart, let's get you your milk.' Shantanu was watching the crows, his eyes fixed on the window in a fearful stare. The crows zipped right and left and circled dementedly. Shantanu began to cry.

Sharada laid the tanpura down and held him tight to her chest. She rose, still holding him. With her free hand she put milk and sugar in his tumbler. She tried sitting him down next to her at the table, but he wouldn't loosen his little arms from around her neck. He wouldn't even sit in her lap. She was desperate. The cacophony of cawing rose and fell. Just when it seemed to be subsiding, it rose again. It was as though all the crows in the city had gathered around her home.

When Shekhar returned from his walk, he said crows were falling dead under the old rain tree. He stepped out on to the veranda. 'I've never seen anything like it. They are falling from the sky, dead.' Sharada carried Shantanu out on to the veranda. Shantanu broke into hysterical weeping. Another crow fell from the sky. Sharada pushed back the scream that rose to her lips and ran into the bedroom holding Shantanu to her. Shekhar stood in the veranda watching the sight. Each time a crow fell, the others' cries reached a crescendo. Blinded by fear and grief, they dashed against the veranda. One came flapping in. Shekhar cried out and quickly slid the windows shut. He hurried into the bedroom and slammed the door behind him. But the lament of the crows continued to pierce through the heavy wooden door.

Sharada and Shekhar sat frozen on the bed. Images of Hitchcock's *Birds* rose before Sharada's eyes. The revenge of the birds against humankind—entering their houses through doors, windows and chimneys, tearing lumps of flesh out of their bodies, gouging out their eyes. Mauled bodies lying around. Sharada shivered.

At last it grew quiet. Shantanu stopped whimpering. Only the helpless cawing of an occasional crow was heard. Shekhar returned to the veranda. The bodies of the dead crows had vanished from the street. Only a scatter of feathers was left. A few crows tiptoed around them, their cawing guttural, as if gargling blood.

The doorbell rang. Sharada opened the door. It was Shekhar's driver, Kripashankar. Father of four children, he lived in the shanty colony abutting the railway line. 'Did you hear the crows?' he asked excitedly. Sharada nodded. Shantanu's arms were still wound tightly around her neck. Kripashankar laughed. 'What? You were scared? It was Nakhatesahib's grandson,' he said to Shekhar who had come up behind her. 'The boy has a gun. Not real bullets. Bird killer. Doesn't make a sound. Just "thuk". Clever fellow. He told the watchman to put grain under the rain tree and killed the crows as they flew down to eat it. He killed many. He can now be his grandfather's bodyguard. For free.'

Later, when Sharada was making Shekhar's tea, a line had flashed into her head, complete with melody and beat.

I have seen black Time, my friend, I have seen black Time today

The melody was in Shuddh Sarang, sixteen beats, medium tempo.

4

To: Ashesh Joshi, Anima Joshi, Feroze Banatwala, Shekhar Sakhardande, Atul–Anju Dodiya, Sudhir–Shanta Patwardhan, Gieve Patel, Sakina Mehta, Sara Epstein, Maria Carlotti, Shankar Hariharan

Subject: Sema Al-Radi

I've just read on the net that our friend Sema is fighting leukaemia in Beirut. It's been two years since she mailed any of us. We were worried about her during the American assault, wondering what a quiet, peaceful artist like her does in times of such violence. I know now. There's a link with the news story about her leukaemia to an essay she wrote two years ago. You can see the link below later, but here's a short extract of the essay. Some of us talk a lot about the violence that's going on here, and how our work should reflect it. But what is our violence against what's happened in Afghanistan and Iraq?

I'm a potter, sculptor, painter. In my work I have tried to touch upon the lives of people, their relationships with each other, with nature. But doing my work has become increasingly difficult during the events my country has passed through in the last twelve years. To sing of dark times in dark times, as

Brecht proposed, is not as easy as it sounds. At the moment I am in Pakistan, preparing for my show. A journalist here asked me, 'Why is it that your paintings don't have anything to say about the thousands of children who have died in Iraq, about the destruction of centuries of cultural treasures that filled the museum that was bombed, about the sanctions that were inflicted on Iraq for twelve years before that?'

My answer to his question was this: 'I was in Baghdad during the first Gulf War. I started writing a diary. I made notes about how we were living our daily lives with bombs exploding over our heads. We were living as best we could, working as much and as well as we could, keeping our heads down.

'This diary was later published. I had expected America to reel under the shock of what they had done to us. Twelve years from that time, when my country's blood has already been sucked by sanctions, another assault is happening. What can we do that is different now from what we did then? Once again twenty-two million people are struggling to survive, heads down. Before this we had a dictatorship. That has been uprooted. Now we have an alien aggressor and occupation in its place. What can they do for us? What can artists do when the world is taken over by monsters? All I can do is look within myself to gauge how much humanity is left in me; to ask myself what I can still do of what I did before, when I knew myself to be human. Do I have in me some traces at least of the creative power I once had? Let me gather what is left and continue to do my work.'

These are fundamental questions of creativity in times of maiming and death. We have never faced anything like them, have we? We've never had to examine our work in that ultimate context. What are we when we say we are artists?

But I'm rambling.

Haridas sends the mail and sits staring at the computer till the screen flashes 'message sent'. His thoughts are about Bush. This man can kill millions who don't belong to his country and some of his own too in a futile war, but is supposed to be 'pro-life'. What does his 'pro-life' amount to? A foetus in a woman's womb is an act of God. To take its life is to abrogate God's work. Then what about the killing of millions in Iraq who have grown from foetuses into running, chattering children? A fancy phrase takes care of that. They are not killed. They are 'collateral damage'. They also lie on 'the axis of evil'. Bush isn't abrogating God's work in deciding who is evil. He is doing God's work upon earth.

Bush and his men must have been Brahmins in their past incarnations. The twice-born with the natural right to kill the once-born. They killed his father. His mother has barely survived. She is dry and wrinkled, every wrinkle a mark of aggression on her body by those who have the right to assault.

The 'sent' message has long since disappeared from the computer screen. Haridas senses a small movement behind him. Girji has set his mid-morning glass of milk beside him. She has come like a shadow, and gone like a shadow. She too is like his mother—survivor of life, that most dangerous thing.

5

Ashesh's feet are nailed to the ground. It is difficult to tell how long he has stood there. One hour? Could be two. In that time, however long it is, he has grown uneasier by the minute. He is fed up of this canvas. Mildly angry even. He wants to opt out of this torture. Who the hell is going to force him to bear it? He's his own master. He is free to decide what he wants to paint. He wants to pick up his brush, paint over these demonic triangles and start afresh.

Ashesh picks up a brush and frowns at his colour tubes. In despair, he throws himself into his chair. Which colour has the power to obliterate black? And what if that elusive image presents itself again one day?

No. Take the canvas off the easel and put another one up. Another canvas, another painting.

He gets up. He lifts the canvas off the easel, stops, puts it back again. He is truly angry. He picks up a tube of black, mixes it with white, dips his brush into the grey and lets his brush decide where it wants to go. The brush paints a vaguely round shape. It becomes a painter. Ashesh doesn't interfere. The brush marks the round shape to bring a face into being. A floating head. The eyes stare white out of smudged sockets. Below them the mouth is split open.

Ashesh watches the face emerge. He has seen this face before. Not specifically this one, but many like it. He mixes more black and white for more shades of grey, paints faces next to the first, till they crowd each other. The area between the black diagonals fills with faces, leaving no space to breathe. They are similar and yet different, unlike Mardhekar's 'I am an ant, he is an ant.' These faces are not ants. They are vividly human, each face unique with its own story. He thinks of Auschwitz. And he thinks of chained human bodies, before Auschwitz, transported in crowded holds of ships, to be enslaved on foreign shores. The canvas grows heavy with faces.

Ashesh washes his brushes, wipes them and puts them away in their mug. He stands still for a few moments and then walks stiffly to his chair like a wound-up toy. His mind is free of thought. His heart is free of emotion. His body is free of movement. It is nicely tired. His eyes close.

He is woken up by the loud *paw paw* of a truck's bulb horn. His eyes open reluctantly and he pushes himself up into the real world. The horn blares again. He ambles on to the veranda, surprised that a truck should be parked there. He sees no truck, but the horn goes off again. His ears tell him it is blowing outside his door. What nonsense! He hurries to the door. Haridas stands there holding a colourful object with a bulb horn attached. He brings the object close to Ashesh's face and blows it.

'Stop being childish,' Ashesh yells. Haridas follows him into the house blowing the horn. He looks at the object in his hand dramatically. 'Childish? You misguided soul. This is a piece of art. The work I did at the art camp.' Haridas dances the object above his head in triumph. 'This is what I did in Goa. In between fish and feni. What did you do?' He throws a sarcastic look at the canvas. 'Fought with the Kaliya serpent some more.'

Ashesh smiles drily at Haridas's high spirits.

'Thinking and more thinking has constipated you. You must include fibre in your diet. That's your problem. Look at me. It comes out naturally. You paint and you're relieved. But I'm just a brush man. You are the thinking artist, man.' Haridas blows the horn again. Ashesh takes the object from his hand and is surprised at its lightness.

'You thought it was wood, hunh? Fibreglass.' Assuming the tone of an adult explaining a simple thing to a child he adds, 'People have stopped painting in the outside world, see? This is today's medium.'

The object is a more or less rectangular piece painted parrot green. In the centre is the horn—bright pink, not rubber as it appears to be, but some light plastic material. Around it is a border of creepers and flowers. At the bottom of the frame, inscribed in bold purple letters are the words: OK. HORN PLEASE. MOTHER–FATHER'S BLESSINGS. A thick, gold-painted chain is hooked to the top of the frame for hanging. It is a brash object but so perfectly crafted that Ashesh can't take his eyes off it.

'You want it outside your door?'

Ashesh declines the offer with a smile and a shake of his head.

'It's your big chance for some publicity. The *Mumbai Observer* wants to interview me about the Goa camp. They'll ask what I did there. I'll say, "You want to see what I did? Go to Ashesh Joshi's house." A photo in the papers will follow. Think.'

'So you've managed to get to that new paper?'

'Excuse me. They have got to me. They've hired a female titbit to "cover" culture. Her half page is called "Kulture Khichdi".'

'Does that mean you'll be at the top and a recipe for khaman dhokla below?'

'Why not? The titbit is nice. Big eyes. Big boobs. Voice is a little husky. Sexy.'

'The hunt is on?'

'Hunt? Only subtle signals.'

'Sniffing?'

'Son of Surgaon, get your sur right. You sniff at fine wine before you savour it. Are you coming to Feroze's on Sunday?'

'Why?'

'It's his birthday. Let's go. I'll give him this. He may not accept it. But at least he'll appreciate it, unlike you. Plus I'll get to see a few lines on his canvas unlike yours.'

Ashesh grabs Haridas's shoulders. Pushing him towards the easel, he stands him before the canvas. 'Now talk.'

Haridas looks at the black-and-grey work closely. 'Thank God you're free.'

'Is that all?'

'Isn't that enough? For now? This isn't going to stop here. It's only the beginning. Black doesn't let go of you that easily.'

The friends stand before the canvas. They stand looking deep into it. Haridas has said what Ashesh already suspected: this is a new beginning.

Haridas leaves. As usual, a gaggle of children crowd around his red Mercedes. They stare curiously at the object in his hand as he walks down to the car. He passes it around for them to take turns blowing it. He looks up at Ashesh with a false smile of apology before driving away.

6

Feroze Banatwala's house has become a railway station after his mother's death. Anybody can come, spend time, have tea, leave. Jijabhau is there to look after their needs. Feroze need not bother about playing the host while he's around. He can keep to his studio, paint, read, snooze. Jijabhau is the real host of the establishment. Feroze is the master of the house only in name. When Burjor Uncle drops in, he often sits with Jijabhau in his room, has tea, asks if Najoobai has visited, says goodbye and leaves.

While Feroze's mother, Freny, was alive, the house, its residents and its visitors were strictly regimented. Her stern eye controlled not only Burjor, Feroze, Pavaiah and Janamma, but also every object and fixture in the house. How she did it without ever raising her voice was her secret. As a child, Feroze had imagined her standing in the middle of the house, even before she had had her first cup of tea, and looking at everything animate and inanimate with warning eyes. After that, for the rest of the day, nobody dared loiter, shirk work, sit on their fat arses or jabber. The art teacher at school had once asked Feroze's class to draw a picture of their mother. Feroze's mother stood with clenched fists on her hips and big, angry eyes. Her eyes were so big they swallowed up her face. The art teacher had told him in a sweet voice that a mother is the fount of all love and the child who doesn't see that gets only two out of ten. No matter. Feroze had been used to getting even zeroes for his work because, while the rest of the children painted bananas green or yellow, he would paint his in other colours, including purple.

Burjor is Freny's only brother and a bachelor. He had lived in this home for many years. At the age of thirty-five he declared, 'I'm old enough now to live on my own.' It wasn't that he had been eager to move away. He had desperately wanted to escape the innumerable objets d'art that dotted Freny's home. For, as his girth increased, a battle for space had ensued. Burjor had once confided to Feroze, 'What do you think she'll say if I sit on one of her precious objects one day? By mistake?' Finally he had bought himself a tiny flat in Colaba—furnished with one bed, one table and one chair—and found supreme happiness.

Freny had straddled two worlds. One was her balwadi in Ganesh Nagar, which contained no furniture at all, and the other was her six-bedroom bungalow on Altamount Road where furniture and objects collected by her parents from Europe, China and Africa crowded every available bit of space.

After he shifted to Colaba, Burjor's visits to the Altamount Road house decreased gradually till soon they were reduced to three visits a year—on Jamshedi Navroze and on his sister's and nephew's birthdays. He was resigned on those three days to taking on the chin Freny's battery of observations about his irresponsible obesity, while he polished off her dhanshak and kebabs. When he wasn't eating, he'd remain standing in fear of her objets d'art. Then Freny would say in cold anger, 'Why are you standing there like the Khada Parsi, Baji?' So Burjor would inch sideways like a wary crab between the carved teak stools topped by china, porcelain and ceramic figurines towards Feroze's studio where he could relax. On one such day, Burjor had thrown himself into a chair where Feroze had just set down his palette. When Feroze cried out a warning, Burjor had sprung up to reveal a backside that was vividly coloured like a baboon's. With no possibility of his getting into a pair of Feroze's trousers, he had waited till dark to go home. 'Body painting's in fashion, no, dikra? Good.' Then he had added as an afterthought, 'Girls don't follow me for my mug but for my seductive backside, maybe, hunh?'

After Freny died, her home, brought up under strict rules of discipline, became suddenly orphaned and went wild. Pavaiah, who had been bound to her rules for decades, felt gloriously free and wanted to be even freer. While she was alive, Freny hadn't given him and his scarecrow wife, Janamma, even a second's respite. At every moment of the day, her objects were to be free of dust. Even the smallest speck was not acceptable. But she had bequeathed to them in her will a pension so grand that even their most hallucinatory dreams could not have encompassed such a sum. It was enough and more to keep them in luxury back home in the village and Pavaiah was dying to be gone.

Janamma had brought up Feroze. She had been his ayah in childhood and a foster mother later, softening the harshness of his biological mother's discipline. It was a wrench for her to leave him. But Pavaiah stood in the garden, pawing the ground, afraid they'd miss the train if his wife took much longer over her tearful farewell. Finally he unlocked Janamma's skinny arms from around Feroze's neck, practically dragged her to the waiting taxi and stuffed her in. After they left, Feroze continued to hear them moving around the house all night. The next morning he had locked up the house and left for Matheran.

Going to Matheran was a jump from a recent sorrow into an older one for Feroze. Many pleasurable and painful memories bound him to Sylvania, the bungalow Hoshi Uncle had left him. In childhood Matheran had meant gorging on sour berries plucked in the wilderness at the back of the house, giving himself acute stomach aches. Teasing Tehmi to tears. Learning to play chess from Hoshi Uncle and one day checkmating him. Eating bhakris roasted by Pandurang's wife, Shevanta, by lantern light in their hut. Cleaning his teeth every morning with the aromatic powder Shevanta made and returning home triumphantly with Hoshi Uncle's gift of a jar of Monkey Brand black tooth powder only to have Freny throw it into the waste bin with a disgusted, 'Hoshi taddan gando chhe.'

In late adolescence Matheran had meant being driven crazy by Tehmi's smile and golden skin. Being tongue-tied in her presence. Not taking the slow train or hired horse up the slope, but climbing all the way to the gate of Sylvania tucked away in a jungle at the other end of the hill town and coming to a dead halt right outside, panting, not so much because he was tired but because he was nervous and excited. Stepping into the spacious colonial bungalow—hidden by tall, dense trees—still breathless, smiling weakly at Hoshi Uncle's good-natured jibe, 'Losing breath climbing such a small hill at your age, dikra? Not a good sign.' And then Tehmi flying in from somewhere to throw her arms, gleaming with golden down, around his neck, turning his legs to boneless extensions.

Feroze had carried his confusion in Tehmi's presence well into adulthood. The only difference was, with his newly acquired social poise, he was better able to suppress its outward signs. He had even learnt to hug Tehmi expertly and give her a peck on the cheek in greeting, but always fearing that she would feel the thumping of his heart against her body and wonder. He had decided he would declare his love and propose to Tehmi as soon as he had sold his first painting. It was all right to marry your mother's first cousin's daughter and Freny was fond of Tehmi. But Tehmi went before his first painting was sold. Her cancer hadn't given her much time between detection and death.

The doctor had described it as a galloping cancer, and it swept her away. No drugs could stop it. One day Tehmi had felt the food stick in her throat and a month later she was gone. The shock had sent Hoshi Uncle into his own shell. There he had created a secret world where he must have seen and heard much that people outside couldn't. It showed in the occasional smile that slid over his drooping lips. Six months later, he too died. In his sleep. He had willed Sylvania to Tehmi. Now it was Feroze's. But the new master hadn't visited it for years afterwards.

Pandurang came running out when he saw Feroze at the gate. Dressed in a spotless dhoti, a long shirt and a white cap set at a slant, he was a vital part of Sylvania. Feroze drew much reassurance from his presence.

'Bag?' Pandurang asked, glancing at Feroze's empty hands. Feroze shook his head. 'I'll make do with what I have here.' Pandurang's face shadowed over. 'Frenybai is gone. Too sad. She was a mother-god to the poor.' He pulled up the end of his dhoti and dabbed at his eyes. Sipping the hot, lemon-grass-scented tea that Pandurang had made for him, Feroze said, 'Pavaiah and Janamma have gone back to their village.'

'What now?'

'Find me someone like you. Or you come.'

Feroze glanced at Pandurang's embarrassed face. 'It's all right. I know you won't come. It's like asking these trees to uproot themselves.'

Pandurang burst into an open laugh. 'True. I'll leave this place only to go up there.'

He scratched his head, hawked, took his time and said, 'There is someone. A cousin. He was robbed in Bombay. He went back to the village. But his children are still at school and college. How much can he make on farming, Ferozedada? He's willing to do anything for his children's education. See if you want to try him out.'

That was Jijabhau, the man who has turned Feroze's house into a home again. His hospitality brings Feroze's friends to his place as a halfway house to events in South Mumbai. Painter and film-maker friends come from Thane and Kandivali and Dahisar. They eat, sleep and carry on.

Jijabhau is a Warkari. Naive man of God. Wouldn't hurt an ant. He used to sell vegetables on the streets of Mumbai. One evening he returned from his day's work to find his room locked. The neighbours said, 'Your partner has sold it. Didn't you know? You didn't get a share of the price? What will you do now?' They had stared at him in disbelief. He had to be the only creature in the city not to have grown wise to its crooked ways after ten years of living there.

Long enduring and tenacious, Jijabhau had pushed himself for months. Sold vegetables all day. Lined up outside public toilets in the mornings, lain down on the footpaths at night. But there were ownership fights there too. He was driven away, sometimes by thugs who owned slices of pavements and sometimes by the police. Occasionally he got beaten up. Finally he returned to Chakan, his head bent low in shame. His elder son had asked, 'What about my college?' He was one year short of a bachelor's degree in commerce. Jijabhau had had no answer till Pandurang sent him a message. 'If you're willing to do housework, go to Mumbai. Ferozedada needs an honest man. The money will be good. You'll be happy.'

Jijabhau had never done housework before. He was acutely nervous when he rang Feroze's doorbell. Between ringing and the door being opened he had thought a dozen times of disappearing. Such a big house. How would he manage? But the minute Feroze opened the door and said, 'Come, Jijabhau, come', he felt he had come home. Even after Jijabhau arrived, Feroze continued to get his food from Goolmai in Tardeo. But soon Heerabai came. She swept, cleaned, washed and cooked. Jijabhau had proved naive in his own transactions, but was very particular with Feroze's.

Feroze's life has again acquired form. Among Hoshi Uncle's books in Matheran he had found an excellent, abridged translation of the Mahabharata. The night he finished reading it, he saw Krishna in a completely new way. The following morning he had made a rough sketch of this Krishna. He was going to be the central figure in a large painting, crowded with detail. Feroze was brimming with ideas by the time he got back to Mumbai.

He is working feverishly, making cartoons of different sections of the painting. It's going to be a large one. During the day Jijabhau watches him from a distance. In the evenings, he retires to his room to sing bhajans with his Warkari friends.

7

Anima is angry with Ashesh. It's become a habit now—using work as an excuse to avoid Surgaon. After Anna went away, they had decided they would take turns on Saturdays. He kept to the schedule for a while, though not without a fuss. But after she was sacked from the school, he took to shoving the entire responsibility on to her. Anima is 'free' now. She has no 'work'. He's the one who has all the work.

She could have read Amitav Ghosh today after running through her chores. She'd started on the fifth essay last night, but snapped the book shut after the first paragraph. This wasn't the best bedtime reading for her. This was Ghosh coming to terms with the 1984 massacre of the Sikhs in Delhi. Why wake up her ghosts reading an essay that had helped him settle his?

Anima had put the book aside but hadn't been able to put aside the turmoil that even those first few lines had created in her. It had been thirty years since that event and the butchers who had turned thousands of women into widows overnight were still free men. No justice yet for the fatherless children who must now be her students' age. Had they been able to regain their faith in this country and its people?

How did she feel, her students had asked her hesitantly one Saturday. Had she not wanted to see her husband's murderers hanged? She had thought about it and for the first time realized that not for a moment after Siddharth was killed had she wished good or ill upon his killers because they simply hadn't seemed real enough. 'See,' she had tried to explain, 'these people weren't people. Who they were, how they looked, were they called Dilip, Keshav, Sanjay? None of that mattered. They were a mob and a mob is just that—a mob. The inciters of mobs cite history, religion, community—anything to convince them that killing innocents is justified. But before the world, the inciters defend their acts as an outburst of spontaneous emotion. Justice finds it difficult to punish mobs.'

The youngsters were livid. Kartik said, 'How can that be allowed? Justice is justice. It can't change with circumstances. As a victim you should have demanded justice.'

The wry smile on her face was because of the circumstances under which this group of young students had first come to her. They had been the liveliest of her final-year batch. They had rushed to her house when they heard the news of her sacking. Vaishali and Radha were weeping. Mangesh and Rahul stood looking glumly at the floor. Every muscle in Kartik's body was tense. He demanded, 'Why?'

'I read out something to you in your last lesson . . .'

Vaishali said, '*Gatha Saptashati*, wasn't it?'

Mangesh smiled. 'The language was vaguely Marathi, but it sounded so strange.'

'I'm afraid a student's mother found the poems offensive. She complained that I was reading out obscene things to tender young children.'

'Meaning us? Tender young children?' The girls' eyes dried up in laughter.

'But that's no reason to sack a senior teacher,' Kartik exploded. 'Anyway what was obscene in those poems?'

'You need to ask the mother. Or the school trustees,' Anima said. 'They put pressure on Principal Kolte. The mother and the trustees wanted to know why this teacher should read out things that weren't part of the history syllabus.'

'But we got so much more history out of those extra things you did with us. Why should we suffer because of one woman's idiocy? What kind of democracy is this?'

Anima held up a finger. 'No school claims it is run on democratic principles.'

'You're not going to take this lying down, are you, ma'am? You're going to fight, aren't you?'

'Yes, I am. Let's see how things turn out.'

'We'll win. No two ways.'

The students had sat with her for a long time after that. This was Anima's first meeting with them outside the classroom. They talked of many things. After that they had continued to drop in at her place once in a while. They spoke to her of their doubts, ideas, hopes, ambitions, loves. At some point they decided it wasn't right to drop in casually and take up ma'am's time. They would meet one Saturday a month instead and spend the evening together. Gradually Anima stopped being their teacher and became a friend. One of them would make tea or coffee and order snacks. They lounged around, thought, leafed through her books. She grew to treasure those Saturdays with its discussions, debates, quarrels and impromptu readings. Sometimes life's big questions came up for debate and everybody grew solemn.

Anima had expected the pleasure to end with time. Her young friends would leave for universities and jobs in other places. But by a happy chance, they had all gone to college and found jobs in the city and the monthly Saturday meetings had continued. The students were of an age that Anima's children would have been had she and Siddharth been able to have them. The thought coloured the evenings.

Anima stuffs the book of Amitav Ghosh's essays into her handbag with the foolish hope that she might be able to read it on the train. But there's a stampede. The number of people commuting to and from Surgaon and beyond has been increasing by the day. From early afternoon, the return trains start flooding with human bodies, bringing with them the assorted smells of sweat and favourite perfumes. These days the paunchy

and the lean, the stunted and the tall exude seductive Brut. As if this
were not enough, the man next to Anima has plastered his hair with
Loma. She is surprised. Loma, which turns grey hair into muddy brown,
is still in the market as an instant dye. Never mind. Even Loma would
be easier to tolerate if the man wearing it would sit properly. But he's
the spreading type. As soon as he is seated, his legs begin to part and
his hand begins to play hide-and-seek with her right thigh. Anima
knows there's no escape from wandering hands till a woman has lost
every hair on her head and every tooth in her mouth.

Anima is in the habit of carrying a long, thick pack needle in her
handbag to control active hands. She has gifted one each to Vaishali
and Radha, with a live demonstration of how to use it. After years of
practice, she herself has become a master of the art. The drill is set. If,
like today, the groper is sitting on your right, you grip the needle in your
left fist, point turned right. Cross your arms, the left pressed under the
right. Train the point of the needle at the nearest part of the groper's
anatomy—in this case Loma's flabby left arm. When the train sways
pretend to lose your balance and crash into the said arm. Before the
groper has the chance to enjoy the pleasure of contact, a searing pain
has gone through his arm—source unknown. And before he recovers
from the stab, the needle has been sheathed.

Anima follows the drill now. Loma shouts in pain. People stare at
him. He stares at her. Her face is innocent. Her gaze is fixed straight
ahead. Loma mutters a loud obscenity and retracts his body. At any
other time, Anima might have ignored the obscenity. But today her
brain is addled with the overpowering fumes of Loma. So she turns to
him and says loudly so everyone can hear, 'If you have problems with
crowds, why don't you travel in your Mercedes?' This is the line gropers
normally throw at women who dare to complain. Not only has Anima
deprived him of his line, but she has flung it at him with added sting.
People laugh. Loma's chagrin knows no bounds. He has allowed a mere
woman to get the better of him. It's like handing over his marbles to
her. Could a man be more pathetic, more laughable than this? Loma
sits wordlessly beside her, his face a mess of emotions. He doesn't know

what's going on in the world. In his entire career of groping women in buses, trains, shops and temples, he has never before met one who has hidden spikes, like a porcupine.

Anima may now look out of the window in peace.

These days the city never seems to end. But when it does, you get miles and miles of flat, arid land on this route. Then a group of hills shows up, squatting on the horizon. A sprawling hill pushes up above them, its peak a narrow needle. Anima has an old relationship with this hill. A thrill travels down her spine each time she sees it. Scenes from the annual Mahalakshmi fair begin to dance before her eyes and the deep monotone of the tarpa hums in her ears.

When the needle peak of Mahalakshmi Hill recedes and date palms appear, you know you are near Surgaon. Toddy, coconut and date palms are the region's resident trees. They were Ashesh and Anima's childhood challenges. Come climb, they said. The bruises of answering those challenges have remained as memories on Anima's skin.

Like her skin, the trunks of palms tell stories of their age. As the palm grows, it sheds its fronds, leaving a deep ring behind. Count the ridges circling the trunk to read the history of the tree. Observe the long clusters of green dates nestled close to the trunk and you know the fruit will turn a plump orange, tight with pulp and juice, in a month's time. Anima's tongue, even at the age of forty-seven, salivates shamelessly.

It's time to rise. Anima twists her torso a little to get her sweaty back unstuck from the back of the seat and pulls her blouse down. Mr Loma contracts in fear. You never know when porcupines will strike. She raises a derisive eyebrow at him and moves to the door.

At Surgaon station the heavy, sweet fragrance of mogras floats high above all the other smells. Little children scurry up and down the platform carrying baskets of leaf cones filled with black sour berries. Young men top paper-cone servings of fried gram dal spiced with finely chopped onion, fresh coriander and a squeeze of lemon. Outside, brown, rough-skinned chikus with their surprisingly soft, sweet pulp are piled high beside translucent love apples. Together they constitute the Surgaon scent.

Anima ambles down the station road sniffing the air, smiling. Even today she misses old Shantaram's gruff call, practically ordering one into his horse carriage for the ride to the Joshi bungalow. His mouth was off-kilter like his cap, but his talk was straight. He went years ago. Now his son drives an autorickshaw, drawls like a film hero and drinks half his earnings.

Anima doesn't take Shantaram's son's rickshaw, though he invites her in. She needs time to prepare for the meeting with her mother. Walking will give it to her. But it's hot. Holi is still two weeks away, but what passes for winter in Surgaon has already fled. Drops of sweat fall from Anima's frizzy, tightly bound hair to the nape of her neck like Chinese torture. In the old days, summer would begin precisely on the day after Holi like somebody had switched it on.

Anima checks herself. Over the years she has grown sceptical about this thing called memory. Does she really remember the change of seasons or has she merely picked up what older people say? Memory's a damned dangerous thing. Who knows what part is imagination and what part fact in the things we recall. A novelist imagines people and events but memories of personal experience colour what she creates. And how reliable is that? Our recall of the past is neither coherent nor complete. We are aware that we have an incomplete story. But we must tell a complete one. So we fill in imagined details. Unconsciously, of course. But even if we did it consciously, we would refuse to admit it. Listeners must believe it's the truth, whatever that is.

When Ai talks about Anna, she claims her memories are exactly the way things happened. But Anima listens to them as stories. In the last ten years, her stories have changed. For a long time the details remained constant while the tone of the telling changed, changing meaning. Now the details too are changing.

It has been different with Anima. She has frozen every detail of Siddharth's being in her memory. But she can no longer have a conversation with him. His killing killed the values for which they had lived. Their shared life ended abruptly. The world in which she had to piece her life together again was not the world he knew. The walls of their home are a different colour now. There is a different cover on their bed. New cotton has been stuffed into their mattress, filling out the familiar hollow of his body on his side. It has been painful not to continue living in the world he knew. Yet she needs Siddharth's memory, even in its frozen state, to accompany her through the rest of her life.

Ai too is destined to have Anna with her till the end of her life. So she has had to create an image of him that she can live with. She began by gradually erasing the memories that were too burdensome to carry. It is now her story, shorn of everyone else's. She is the chief protagonist, the heroine—a tragic heroine as it happens. She compares herself to Kasturba. She, Sindhu Joshi, too has had to endure a lifetime of neglect like Mother Kastur.

'In that too, Anna was Gandhian. He expected me to follow all his principles, however extreme,' she said to Anima. 'When Ashesh wanted to marry that Mussalman girl? Did it matter to Anna? I couldn't touch food or water for a whole day due to the shock. But your Anna? He scolded me for putting emotional pressure on Ashesh. Was I doing that? I was just doing what I thought was right. Luckily Ashesh understood that. He even took responsibility for changing his mind so Anna wouldn't be upset with me. If he had done what you did, I'd have killed myself. You at least married a Hindu, though from a lower caste. Small mercies. I wouldn't have put it past you to have run off with a Mahar.'

All in all, in Ai's story, Anna had never loved or respected her, nor felt concern for her. That's why he had upped and left so easily. The explanation has made life endurable for her. Anima tells herself often enough not to grudge her that.

Anima decides not to quarrel with her mother over Anna today. It might help reduce the tension that has been building up between them over the last few meetings. Anima is near 'that' peepul tree now—the one in which, Rama had whispered, evil spirits lived that came out at night. She had always had implicit faith in his stories and had been petrified to walk past it even in the daytime. When Anna saw her fear, he took her to the tree one new-moon night. Standing below it, he asked, 'Where are they—the evil spirits?' Her jaw was locked with fear.

But her mind was ticking fast. It prompted her to hurriedly say, 'No spirits. I can't see any. Why don't we go home?' Anna had laughed and picked her up. How warm and secure she had felt against his shoulder. Where could Anna have gone, and why? Bachchu Kaka, she and Ashesh had asked themselves this for ten years. There could be no release for them from the pain of the question till they had found the answer. Bachchu Kaka was particularly hurt. He and Anna had shared a school bench. How could Shankrya have gone off without telling him? Everything had been going so well for him. He had some money at last. He'd built himself a home. The town Brahmins' anger against him had lost its edge. Or perhaps his growing eminence in the legal field had made it awkward for them to show it openly. They knew 'all sorts of caste and no-caste people' still drew water from his well. The polluted ones still had entry into his kitchen. But why let it affect them? Why ostracize him? It was his well and his kitchen. As long as they did not eat and drink in his house, they should allow themselves to move with the times, be liberal. So Shankrya, without compromising his values, had come to be accepted as an honoured citizen of the town. Why then had he suddenly abandoned it all? Why was the remainder of this sum a zero?

Anima looks around attentively as she walks. In this region of chiku orchards, a shiny, glass-fronted mall has gone up on the main road. Surgaon was never the quaintly charming place that you think small towns are. But its dusty dhoti has, in the last few years, been paired with a striped tee shirt, a cap turned back to front and a cell phone in the hand. The jungles around it are not as densely dressed as they used to be and the sun is no longer stopped from striking directly at its head.

Fortunately, beyond all these transformations, the sea remains the same. It is still the full, surging Arabian Sea on whose waves the Portuguese, the French, the Dutch and the English came riding to set up their colonies. Looking out at that sea, Anna had once said to Anima, 'Ours has been a strange history. Yes. All these alien people came and settled here. But we let them come, didn't we? Was that hospitality, laziness or a narrowness that wouldn't let us see beyond family, clan and personal property? Was it wrong to let them come and stay? I don't know.' Anna had taken her hand in his. 'The whole thing is so complex. Read our history when you grow up. Read other people's histories. Compare. Ask questions. It might help you to see why we are what we are today.'

She was twelve or thirteen then, with a healthy hatred of history. Kings, dates, wars—how were they complex? If you parroted them, you got seventy or eighty per cent. But Anna's words must have stuck in her mind. For when the time came to choose her major at college, she knew it had to be history.

Anima has arrived at the red-tiled bungalow that Anna built with such love and care. He had thought hard before settling on a name for it. Plain 'Home' without qualifiers was his decision. Not our home, your home or anybody else's home. Just 'Home'. Separated from possessive pronouns, it yielded shades of meaning that could match your mood of the moment or the light at the time of the day. A picture changes under different light conditions. When a singer holds a note long enough, you begin to hear all the halftones and microtones that are normally hidden in its amplitude. For Anima, the solo 'Home' has a web of associations that includes Anna's form and face. A name may not mean much when lexically defined, but amongst other things it reflects the name giver's idea of life.

Anima was born many years before Home was built and Ai used to love doing an exaggerated take-off on how she was named. Back then she did such things.

'We were living in Chaubal Chawl when you were born. Your father and Bachchu Kaka were sitting on the common veranda in front of our rooms. Anna stroked his nose and said, "We must give her a name that will not be a burden to her. A small, quick name. Nothing that labels her with as yet unknown attributes. Call her Suhas and she might turn out to be a whiny. That kind of thing." So I said, "Why not call her by attributes we can already see? Kurupa?" He was wild.

You were the most beautiful thing on earth! Bachchu Kaka said, "Call her Annu. No name can be smaller and quicker than an atom." Four vertical lines creased Anna's forehead. "Annu? Whose fission will one day destroy our planet?" Bachchu Kaka said, "No. Annu whose fusion will create stupendous amounts of constructive energy." I wanted to run to a dictionary to look up fission and fusion, but stayed. You couldn't put it past those two to give you some Warli name while I was gone. I only murmured, "Not Annu, please. The 'nn' is too hard for a girl's name." But who cared what I said? Those two had forgotten all about naming you. They were engaged in a face-to-face over some book on the making of atom bombs. Anna sat like this, Bachchu Kaka like this and their faces looked like this. You were in your cradle, crying and still nameless while Bachchu Kaka was saying, "The man's research is totally dishonest. Why should we take him seriously at all?" Anna said, "Honest or dishonest, he has put his finger on a question that must be decided. NOW. Fission or fusion?" They continued like this till Bachchu Kaka remembered you and said, "All right. Forget Annu. Call her Anu." Anna said, "And what's that supposed to mean? We want a short name but not a meaningless name." Then he muttered, "But I like names that begin with 'a'." After stroking his nose some more, he leapt out of his chair shouting, "Anima!" I objected. The name reminded me of enema. Bachchu Kaka clamoured, "Meaning, meaning?" Anna smiled smugly. "Go look in the dictionary. Not the Marathi. The *Oxford*." The *Oxford* added to our knowledge: "Anima: the part of the psyche which is directed inwards, in touch with the subconscious." "Maybe," I said. "But it's still too close to enema. I'll call her Nima.'"

How did that lively, storytelling, laughing woman change into what she is today, Anima wonders painfully, but knows that the answer lies in Anna's going away.

Anima enters the gate of Home and takes a deep breath before moving into the house. She climbs the steps to the veranda and enters the spacious living room where shadows have begun to slither in from the corners. A slanting beam of weak light falls across the floor from the doorway. Ai sits in that beam, with motes dancing around her. She

senses Anima's coming but does not look her way. Anima puts a hand
on her shoulder. The shoulder does not respond. Anima walks through
to the back veranda, down four steps to the bathroom. She washes her
hands and feet and turns into the kitchen. She takes a bottle of water
from the fridge and drinks straight from it in big gulps. 'You still won't
drink from a glass, will you?' Ai is standing behind her. Anima smiles
to herself at having provoked a reaction. She lifts the covers of the
two pots on the cooking platform. There's methi in besan and plain
dal. Next to it is a small bowl of peanut chutney and next to that a
large bowl of sheera. She'd have seen two pots less if Ai had expected
her, not Ashesh.

'Plain dal because he likes it with rice, ghee and lemon. He said
he'd come.' Ai sighs with deep pain. They sit facing each other at the
table. Ai does not look at her when she speaks. Anima gazes at her
refined features. Her once-clear skin is now slightly blemished. A few
hairs have sprouted at the corners of her thin-lipped mouth. Her neck
is all hollows and bird bones. She is sixty-nine. 'Why didn't he come?'

Anima says work. If she overstresses the word, a stormy argument will
follow. The messenger of bad tidings must learn to preserve her neck.

'Work is a convenient excuse when there's no genuine reason.' Ai
is angry. 'Of course, even if he had come, he'd have sat around like a
clam. I put so much thought into deciding what to cook for him. I make
things that he likes. But will he ever say the food's nice? Never. When
he's been and gone my mind's like a cyclone. Why is he like that? Am
I his enemy? Is it because I forbade him from marrying that Mussalman
girl? Does he still hold that against me after all these years? He should
have ignored me. He had Anna's support.'

'Has Mrs Karnik sent my banana flour? I've clean run out.'

'There are enough girls amongst us if you want to marry is all I said. I
said that to you too. But you did what you wanted. He could have done
the same—married his Mussalman girl.' Anima is tired. 'Mussalman
girl' hurts her ears. 'I sit here talking to you, but not a word out of your
mouth. You're his elder sister. You never thought to demand an answer
from him. How can you treat your mother like an enemy?'

'Her name is Nasreen.'

'Whose?'

'The girl Ashesh didn't marry.'

'So? Who she is means nothing to me.'

'But she has a name. She's doing very well. She's highly regarded in Europe.'

'I am not interested. All I was bothered about was my son's welfare.'

When Ai is angry, she has a way of retracting her lips that makes her teeth look longer. It reminds Anima of Ambu Aunty whose frizzy hair she has inherited. Ambu Aunty's teeth stuck out so much that they were practically parallel to the ground. The family says they had diminished her chances of marriage. Single and lonely, Ambu Aunty found herself a vocation. She became possessed by a goddess on all family occasions. The family called it 'Ambu's little farce' and kept a watchful eye on her while a marriage or thread ceremony was going on. The moment she began showing signs of possession, she was whisked off to a faraway room—there to go into a frenzy of whirling, her hair flying, her teeth protruding more than usual, her eyes staring. Some people would stand around to cluck soothingly at her till she stopped whirling and broke into a sweat. When Ai did her take-off of Ambu Aunty, everybody, including Anna, would roll on the floor, feeling terribly sorry and guilty at the same time.

The smell of raat rani wafts in on the breeze, soothing Anima's ruffled spirit. 'Come, let's take a turn in the garden,' she suggests. But Ai sits motionless. 'I am so alone,' she says. Anima glances quickly at her mother, anxious and moved. She looks feeble. Her voice is weaker.

'Aren't you feeling well?'

'Nothing's the matter with me.' The answer comes quick as a whip. She is proud of her health. She's never had to swallow a tablet or take an injection in her life except for a while because of the complications after Ashesh's birth.

Anima gets up. 'Come, Ai. Let's go out to the garden.' She holds her hand out to her mother. Her mother does not take it. Instead, she hoists herself up with the help of the chair. Anima sees that her legs are slow to steady. She follows Anima into the garden and immediately sits down on the bench. Before them stands the Gandhi mandir that Anna built with the house. 'You don't have to worry about my health,' Ai says. 'Dr Bhaskar drops in to see me every day.'

'Who's Dr Bhaskar?'

'He's come here to work. From America. His parents live in Palghar. They're old. He's come to look after them.'

'So what does he do in Surgaon?'

'He gives free health care to the adivasis all over the district. He feels deeply for them.'

'He comes to see you? That means you are not well.'

'Why should I not be well? But I'm alone. The kind man thinks he should visit me.'

Anima takes a deep breath. 'You know you don't have to live alone here. I have a place . . .'

'I will not live in my son-in-law's house.'

'But your poor son-in-law . . .'

'All sorts of people come and go in your house. I've lost the habit of putting up with all and sundry.'

Anima bows her head. She's quiet for a few moments. 'Come, let's go in,' she says.

Dinner is brought to the table. Ai breaks the uneasy silence. 'You're silent. But something's brewing in your mind. I can see it.'

'The vegetable is delicious. Did it come from next door? I haven't been to see Shantaram for ages. When I hear the buffalo lowing to be milked in the morning, I'll know I'm home.'

'When the buffalo lows? Not when you see your mother?' She pauses. 'Has Bachchu Kaka been to see you lately? He frowns when he sees Dr Bhaskar here. Let him. I know what it is to be alone. Does either of you care about that?'

'Ai, please. Don't I plead with you to come and stay with me every time I'm here? I just did that.'

'Has Ashesh ever asked me?'

'He lives alone, Ai. And he's not the type to say it.'

'He should come and stay here. He only makes daubs on paper. He can do that here.'

Anima is silent. This conversation has no end.

'If he won't come here, let me live the way I want to.'

'Do we stop you from doing that?'

'You wouldn't dare. If you did, you'd have to take responsibility. So let's just agree. You live your life, I'll live mine.'

The grandfather clock is preparing to strike. It whirrs, coughs and strikes eight in its low, resonant tones. Before its echo fades away, Ai says, 'There's lots of Anna's stuff in the steel cupboard upstairs. Books. Files of newspaper cuttings. I don't want to be responsible for all that now. Take it away.'

'But I'd stored all the stuff neatly in his room.'

'I've moved it.'

'Why?'

'Am I in the dock? It's my house. I'll do what I like here.'

'But of course, Ai. I only asked why you did it.'

'Because I've given the room to the doctor to run a free health clinic. Anna would have been happy to have his room used for good deeds.'

Ai gets up to wash her hands. Anima guesses from the emphatic way in which she pushes her chair back that she wants no further questions on the subject. But the chair topples over and Ai's legs grow unsteady without support. Anima springs up to help her but stops.

Upstairs, Anima opens the steel cupboard and sits on the floor to look through its contents. There's dust on everything. Anna's spare pair of spectacles is covered with it. She picks them up and wipes the lenses with the end of her sari. She sees Anna's light-brown eyes in them. She remembers how they looked on the day he heard about Siddharth and rushed to Mumbai. Tears had solidified in them and over that glazed surface had flitted shadows of pain, helplessness, compassion. When he held her to his chest, she had heard a heart grown erratic. She had glanced at his face. His ruddy skin had gone pale. She had loosened the tight circle of his arms around her and sat him down in the settee.

She had sat beside him, his head against her shoulder, stroking what was left of his wispy hair.

He must have begun to die inwardly after that. One day Anna had risen at dawn and disappeared. While Ai had gone into a shell, Bachchu Kaka, Ashesh and Anima had searched for him in the unlikeliest places, crazed by grief and bewilderment. A year, two years, then three years passed. In all that time, Ai had not said a word about his going. Initially, they thought she was in shock and didn't pester her with questions. At last they gave up the search out of sheer exhaustion. But the hope of finding him some day would not die. Even now, their eyes flit through crowds automatically, looking for his familiar face. Even now, they scan news of men from nowhere doing good work in remote places, and, with deep dread, news of unidentified bodies found in wells and on railway tracks.

Seven years after a person is reported missing, the law declares him dead. (Why seven? Why not six? Or eight?) Legally Anna died after seven years. His property, shares, bank deposits which had always been Ai's, now went to her legally. Anna's will said they should. But that did not mean Anna was really dead. Anima has still not abandoned hope that he will reappear one day.

Anima draws a file out of the cupboard. She had loved filing Anna's articles, neatly sticking cuttings on A4-size sheets of white paper with the name of the newspaper and date of the edition inscribed at the top. Anna had been an advocate. That is where his money and prestige came from. But what he had poured his soul into were these newspaper articles in English and Marathi. He had an unshakeable faith in the power of words. If society is to change, words are the only instrument to bring it about. Words make people introspect, think rationally. Without that, the diseases that are rotting the vitals of our country—corruption, blind faith, casteism, subjugation of women—will never be cured.

Anna's idealism always upset Bachchu Kaka. If words had that kind of power, we should have been the world's kindest-hearted, most uncorrupt and tolerant people, he said. Enlightened words had flooded our literature for centuries. Even today there was no ebb to the production of words. As for written words, how many of us were even literate, he demanded. In a country that had preserved illiteracy like a prized heirloom, it was sheer stupidity to expect society to change with the power of the written word. Anna listened to Bachchu Kaka's diatribes with a smile and continued to believe.

Anna would be busy fighting cases every waking hour of the day, but somewhere in the corner of his mind an article would be taking shape. He would soak up the sociopolitical air of every new town he visited. He would talk to the local people, ask searching questions. When he returned, his typewriter would go clickety-clack all night like the woodpecker in the bakul tree. As a child, the rhythmic sound of his typewriter was Anima's lullaby. When she was sleepy, she would creep into Anna's room, throw her arms around his neck, then lie down on the floor and fall asleep. When he finished his article, he would carry her to her bed.

Anima flips through the articles in the file. She stops at one. 'The Ceaseless March of a Corrupt Society' by Shankar Narayan Joshi. Anima reads.

We have been a free country for seven years. Far from improving governance, we see its continuous decline before our eyes. There is shoddiness everywhere. Government workers are punctual only by error. However, they are punctilious in their observation of the unwritten rule that they must leave office before working hours are over. The citizen who visits a government office for urgent work must waste valuable time attempting to divert the staff's attention towards himself from the vitally important things they are engaged in gossiping about. There are those who hold that the indifference of the government employee towards his work is the result of the growing power of unions. It has taken away the fear of punishment from the workers' minds. This might even be true to some extent. But in the opinion of top-ranking officials, the real reason for the lethargic uninterestedness of clerical staff stems from the irrational disparity between the living standards in cities and the salaries they draw.

More than the lack of interest of clerical staff, however, good governance is damaged by the string-pulling, nepotism and gifting away of government posts and contracts to the undeserving that happens at every level. By the grace of a chief minister some deputy magistrate suddenly becomes the additional district magistrate, superseding a hundred men his senior. The moment a middle-school teacher's husband becomes a minister, she becomes a professor in a college. A man who marries a government official's daughter finds himself happily raised from clerkdom to officerdom. Hundreds of people pull strings to get into small jobs without being qualified for them. Higher-ranked officials do not restrict their largesse to their kith and kin. It is enough to belong to their caste to receive jobs that far exceed one's worth. If this is the case with appointments, the case with promotions is no different. If you desire a promotion, the sure-fire way to get it is to say yes when your boss says yes. As against this, if you inconvenience your boss by your honesty, if you refuse to bend the rules that govern your work, you can be sure you will be dislodged from your seat and transferred forthwith to a punishment post.

The next paragraph is devoted to facts and figures of funds embezzled in every district of the state. Anima is astonished. Although Anna's language sounds a little old-fashioned now, what the article says holds true even today. The date at the top of the cutting is 4 March 1954. How strange! The fourth of March was also the date on which Anna disappeared in 1994. For forty years he had suffered the knowledge of his beloved country rotting from within. One day, his daughter's husband was murdered in the name of religion. Did it drive him to despair? Did he lose his mental balance temporarily? Had it become impossible for him to see things in a larger perspective that went beyond his individual life? Was it during those moments of weakness that he had run away, abandoning his work and those he most loved and cared about?

But that couldn't have been true. Nobody had seen any signs of despair. Bachchu Kaka would have been the first to notice. There is only one answer that makes it understandable. He must have had an idea—a scheme that he wanted to put into action. Perhaps its nature prevented him from revealing it to anybody. He must have been afraid that his loved ones would exert emotional pressure on him to stop him from going away.

The clock downstairs strikes ten. Anima stands up. She pulls all the files out of the cupboard, dusts them, ties them up in an old bed sheet and puts them beside her overnight bag. In the morning she stands silently, looking at her mother. It irritates Ai.

'What are you looking at?'

'Ai, lock up this house and come and stay with me. Please listen to me,' Anima holds her mother's hands and speaks in an urgent voice. Her mother disengages her hands. 'Don't go on about the same thing. I've said no. Here. Take this sheera. I made it for Ashesh. Give it to him. Who'll eat it here?'

Anima looks at the Gandhi memorial. 'I'll take these scriptures next time.'

'Make it soon, please. Who knows when this thing will come down?'

'Come down? Why should it?'

'How many years will it stand under sun and rain? It's bound to collapse one day. I don't want to carry that inauspicious event on my head.'

In the train Anima returns to what Ai said, trying to understand its meaning. She doesn't understand. As a matter of fact, she admits to herself that she has stopped understanding Ai altogether.

8

Horn OK Thank You!

Last month, industrialist and art connoisseur Shirish Sethi held his annual ten-day art camp at his sprawling bungalow in Goa. Five young and five senior artists participated. Janaki Patil in conversation with Mumbai's well-known artist Haridas, one of the senior participants at the camp.

Haridas. He has no surname. But he has made a name for himself all over India and abroad.

Haridas has no home town either. He claims every place in every part of the world is his home.

He lives in a small, tiled cottage in one of Mumbai's old wadis, but he drives a red Mercedes. These days the driver's side of the car bears a painted elephant, the outcome of a recent dream he had in which he saw himself riding into a jungle on an elephant, wearing a gold-bordered turban.

We are sitting in an exclusive restaurant in South Mumbai. This too would appear to be Haridas's home. He knows all the waiters by name, and everything he does brings smiles of appreciation to their faces. For example they smile appreciatively at his clothes today. He is wearing a Bengali dhoti and a voluminous embroidered jhabba, about whose virtues he volunteers the following information: 'It allows the air to circulate freely and me to look elegant at the same time. We must do such things for the media, mustn't we, or what would they write about?' The joy he takes in mocking the media is boundless. Unfortunately, his sartorial choices are not the purpose of this article. His work in the camp at Goa is.

'I have heard that the host of an art camp has the first right over the works produced there. I have also heard that, of the ten works produced at the camp, your piece was the only one that Shirish Sethi did not offer to keep. What, in your opinion, might have been his reason?'

Haridas's answer is to draw the said work from his large designer sling bag and lay it on the table. It is an elaborately decorated bulb horn of the type trucks are fitted with. 'It works,' he says and squeezes it. People at the other tables look startled. The waiters snigger. Haridas's face is wreathed in the contented smile of one who has broken an unwritten rule of exclusive restaurants. It becomes apparent that he is not only a visual artist, but a performing artist as well. Being the centre of attention appears to be high on his agenda of things to do. He looks with quizzical absorption now at the object of his creation and asks himself, 'Why did Sethi not like this? Could it be because he has not evolved fully as a connoisseur of art?'

At first sight the thing under discussion, painted with loud-coloured creepers, flowers and an inscription, strikes one as pure kitsch. This raises a question. 'Could you explain why this object should be called a work of art at all? Is it a work of art only because you—a reputed artist—have made it? Or do you claim it possesses qualities that set it apart from truck horns?'

'Why should my work be expected to look or be any different from the regular truck painter's work?' Haridas asks. 'I would suggest the contrary. Why can his work not be called a work of art?'

If one is tempted to believe on present showing that Haridas opposes hierarchy in art, one only has to remember the times when he has expressed a very different view. When he held his widely unappreciated 'All White Show' a few years ago, his much-quoted retort to critics who panned it was, 'An artist is not a truck painter to paint the same creepers and flowers year after year. That poor man needs to make a living. I need to experiment.'

When one points out the disparity between that earlier opinion and the one he affects now, the performing artist does an elaborate yawn behind an elegant hand and says, 'Is there anything more boring than consistency? If we always think the same thoughts we will always do the same work. How tedious that would be.'

This puts a stop to all further questions except the inevitable last one. 'What are you working on now?'

'These days I spend time looking at Arun Kolatkar's collection of poems *Bhijki Vahi*.'

The answer has its desired effect. How can Kolatkar's wonderful collection be 'looked' at? Haridas is suddenly serious. 'When you read Kolatkar's poems you see them. They are pictures. He paints in words. He creates powerful images. It is fascinating to see what he sees.' Then, after a pause, he adds, 'Best of all, the poems are full of fantastic women—Laila, Helen, Isis. Sheer bliss!'

Haridas laughs loudly, pleased at the twist he has given to an uncharacteristically serious answer. The people at the next table are preparing to leave. They cannot resist stopping at our table to look more closely at the horn.

'That's how a work of art draws attention to itself.' Haridas grins.

It must be admitted that it does. It is difficult to take one's eyes off the Haridas horn. Its shape, proportions, flamboyant colours, fibreglass lightness, and the very concept of mounting a truck horn in this fashion, are products of an artist's imagination. They extend our ideas of what a work of art is or can be.

9

Haridas toys with the idea of wearing a lungi to Feroze's place. Jeans squeeze you in. He has just bought himself a pair of Madras lungis for the hot months ahead. One is checked blue and yellow, the other green and maroon. Lungis are bliss in summer. Their only drawback is the freedom with which sweat can travel in rivulets down your thighs. At home you can wipe the sweat off with the lungi itself. You can't do that in company. Women think you are making obscene gestures.

But the new lungis will not do. He has forgotten to soak them to take the starch off. He will have to wear the old batik one. Old cloth absorbs sweat more efficiently. Marli is standing right behind him.

She takes the old lungi from his hand and irons it with quick strokes. He taps her cheek in gratitude. Her mother, Girji, cooks for him and Marli sweeps and cleans. When her work is done, she follows Haridas around. She stands next to him when he's painting—handing him his brushes, his wiping rags, his tubes of paint and whatever else he needs. He mutters to her while he paints. He doesn't ask her if she understands. He likes to have her around.

Unlike Ashesh, Haridas likes people to come and go when he is painting. His house guests, generally artists from here and abroad, hold serious conversations with him while he works. Sumitra Basu from the new seven-storeyed apartment block on the main road drops in to watch him work. She is a diploma holder from a Kolkata art school, but hasn't held a brush in her hand since the day she got married. She does not have the space, the silence or the encouragement to paint in her house. Also, she has children. So whenever she can, on her way to or from the market, she stops by Haridas's house and greedily watches him paint.

Haridas tops his batik lungi with a colourful sleeveless vest and leaves. He looks at his Mercedes and decides not to drive. He wants to feel close to people. He has his horn with him. He will offer it to Feroze as a birthday gift. If Feroze turns it down, he will give him the recently published *Krishna in Miniature Painting*. Feroze has become avidly interested in Krishna.

Sitting on a platform under the banyan tree, Ramprasad points to the horn. 'What's this you've got?' No resident or resident's friend who enters Hengewadi during Ramprasad's waking hours can escape paying up at his tollbooth with conversation. He has ironed their clothes for fifty years, starting with two paise per garment and going up to the current two rupees. After half a century of sweaty work, he has earned the right to sit around doing nothing. It is difficult for the residents to grudge him a few minutes of conversation. So they generally add a few minutes to their schedule to accommodate the inevitable pleasantries. Unknown people entering the wadi must also submit to a check—tell him where they are going. He considers it his right and his duty to know. The pictures of Sai Baba and Goddess Lakshmi that he has nailed to the banyan tree bless him from behind their frame of aerial roots for the sentry work he has taken upon himself.

Meanwhile his eighteen-year-old nephew Manmohan, to whom he has handed over his business, has recently begun his career as the resident istriwallah. In Ramprasad's entire career, nobody has had occasion to complain about his work. Manmohan is expected to carry on this unblemished tradition. He is young. Ramprasad does not think it wise to trust the new generation, so he keeps an eagle eye on him while he irons.

Haridas is obliged to answer Ramprasad when he asks, 'What's this you've got?' So he settles down on the platform next to Ramprasad and places his work of art in his hands.

'I made it in Goa. Do you like it?'

'It's okay.' Ramprasad sounds doubtful.

'Keep it if you like.'

'What will I do with it, sa'ab?'

'Blow it. Other people blow trumpets. You can blow a horn.'

Ramprasad laughs torrentially, thereby avoiding responding to Hariprasad's offer. Painter sa'ab is a strange man but straight. He must take care not to hurt him.

An elderly couple walks into the wadi. Ramprasad casts an angry glance at them. 'These people are buying a flat in the new building.'

Haridas is surprised at the irritation in his voice. 'What's your problem if they are? I should have a problem. That building is going to block my light and air.'

'They're Sindhis.'

'So?'

'They're from there.'

'Where?'

'Pakistan.'

'Sindhis left Pakistan when it became Pakistan. Because they were Hindus. Like you.'

'Like me? Not like you? Who are you then?'

'If you knew who I was, you'd be very unhappy.'

'Come on, sa'ab. You're not a Mussalman, or an untouchable. You have Brahmin friends. Why should I not be happy?'

'Never mind, Ramprasadji. I could be anybody. But Sindhis are Hindus.'

'We don't accept that. What kind of Hindus could they be, living amongst Mussalmans? Their bodies smell different. See. I'm older than you by many years. Before our country became independent, Gandhi, Nehru and all those people misled you.'

'How?'

'How? With their talk about all religions being the same. They didn't believe in caste, think about that. That's going right against our scriptures, against what our rishis and munis practised. They say these Sindhi people lived like brothers with those Mussalmans.'

'You mean you don't believe Hindus are Hindus no matter where they live?'

'Of course I don't. That's why we always prohibited Hindus from going to foreign lands in the old days. If they still went, we put them through penance when they came back. Otherwise they were not Hindus. Now look at these Sindhis. Where all have they not been to make money? They are polluted. How can we accept them as Hindus? We don't do that in our family. We are devotees of Ram. Shri Ram even rejected Mother Sita for the same reason.'

'She wasn't in Pakistan?'

'She lived with Ravan in Lanka. Ravan wasn't a Hindu. Okay, he was a devotee of Shiva but he wasn't a Hindu. When he took the form of a raven and abducted her, he touched her, didn't he? Then? Didn't that pollute her? Naturally Shri Ram exiled her. Touch pollutes. In our family we keep away from these Sindhis. Understand?'

'Yes, I do.'

'Good. You have to go now. I have taken up too much of your time today. But these are important things for the future of our country. Where are you going today?'

'To a friend's.'

'The gora aadmi? The Englishman?'

'I've told you before. He's one of us. A Parsi.'

'How is that one of us?'

'Indian.'

Ramprasad laughs in relief. 'Oh, Indian? That's different. Many people are Indian. We must accept that.'

Haridas stands up. Outside the wadi, he hails a cab. He puts the horn beside the driver when he gets in. 'Do please blow that when you need to.' A cabby's life is full of risks. One of them is not knowing what kind of a nut is going to be your next fare. 'Fear nothing and nobody,' Haridas says. 'Blow with a generous hand. This is not your common or garden horn. This is art. Blow it once and you won't want to stop.'

Wary of Haridas, the cabby blows the horn tentatively, just to be safe. If the passenger is one of those loose-screw fellows, he might just hit you on the head with something. But this passenger turns out to be chatty. Soon the cabby is narrating the story of his life to him, from Jaunpur to Mumbai. Haridas is full of curiosity. The journey from Prabhadevi to Altamount Road is long. Along the way he makes many sympathetic noises. At the end of the journey the cabby says, 'Thank you, sir.' As a sign of gratitude, he blows the horn once more. 'I like this thing of yours. Otherwise it's the same old cab and the same old horn.' As he takes the fare he even asks, 'How long will you be, sir? I can wait if you want to go back.'

'No. I don't wait for anybody and nobody waits for me.'

This line strikes the cabby as thought-provoking. 'You've said an important thing, sir. I will think about it for the rest of the day.' The cabby salutes Haridas, turns the cab and drives off.

On Feroze's birthday all his relatives turn up for lunch without invitation. During the rest of the year, one or two drop by on a Sunday to see how Freny's boy is getting along. Feroze orders dhanshak, kebabs and brown rice from the Ratan Tata Institute every Sunday. Heerabai makes an excellent kutchumber of tomato and onion. The amount of food ordered for two would render even half a dozen lunchers immobile.

But more must be ordered because more might come, and whoever drops in before lunch stays for lunch. That's the way of the house.

On Feroze's birthday, however, Jijabhau considers it improper to fob relatives off with the usual fare. He has persuaded Heerabai to learn how to make chicken farcha, bhindi par eedu and saas ni macchhi from Frenybai's cousin Ratibai who lives in Pune. One or other of the female relatives may always be relied upon to contribute the dessert—dal podi or custard. Jijabhau is happy when the table groans.

Haridas has been dropping in on Feroze's birthday even when Freny was alive, but just to greet, give and go. Now he comes for lunch. Besides being extremely fond of Parsis in general, he is fascinated by their idea of racial purity, guarded jealously for seven hundred years while living away from their original homeland. They adapted to local ways in externals like dress, food, language and social customs. They have no qualms in breaking bread with people of other religions. But marriage has to be within the community to keep the race pure. Haridas, who instinctively rebels against all forms of orthodoxy and ideas of purity, still feels drawn to Parsis for their sheer love of life and generosity of spirit.

As Haridas enters Feroze's living room, he hears his uncle Burjor's cannon voice going off. 'Dikra, at least as your social responsibility—' He breaks off when he sees Haridas. 'Come, come, come. The great artist. You all know him, neh? See today's *Mumbai Observer*. Huge photo, this big, wearing a dhoti, like a Bengali babu. *Ketlo handsome laage chhe.*'

'Please allow me to blow my own horn,' Haridas says, raising his work of art and going *paw paw*. This raises roars of laughter. Haridas loves it. Parsi laughter is as much part of Parsiness as the long nose. Everybody wants to blow the horn. It goes around and each time it is blown, there's another roar of laughter. Feroze's face displays a mild, all-purpose smile. Only when Haridas puts the horn in his hands and says 'Happy birthday' does the 'ee' of his smile turn into an 'o' of surprise. He hands the gift back to Haridas, returning to the smile. Meanwhile everybody has noticed that Haridas is still standing. There are three empty chairs at the far end of the huge living room, but he must be saved from walking the distance. So Noshir of the thin, pale face and large spectacles rises, pushes him down into his own chair and slopes off to the other end.

'You tell me, Haridas,' Burjor picks up the broken tail of his earlier lecture. 'Shouldn't your friend here marry? Are you artists forced to take an oath of bachelorhood before you're allowed to touch a brush? "I'll die but will not marry!" He's got this huge flat. What's his problem?' Burjor leans heavily to one side and draws out a newspaper cutting from his trouser pocket. 'See. The *Indian Express*: "Today the Parsi community stands at 70,000 members. The death rate in the community is three times the birth rate. Thirty-one per cent of the Parsi population is over sixty years of age. If the community dwindles at this rate there's a danger of it becoming extinct by the year 2090."'

Jehangir laughs out loud. 'Then we'll be stuffed for museums.'

Najoo makes a little-boy face. 'Mamma, what is this animal?'

Jehangir makes a mamma face. 'It's a Parsi, my pet.'

'That's not funny, you two.' Soonu laughs but is angry.

'Of course it's not funny,' Burjor says quickly. 'I think it is tragic. That's why I'm trying to put some social responsibility into my nephew's head.'

'Get off his back. It's his birthday. Think first of your social responsibility. That poor Meher is still pining for you and you . . .'

'I'm going straight to her from here. This Burjor isn't one to shirk his duties. I was only trying to bring this one around to my way of thinking.'

Burjor leans forward. The movement of his body creates a small turbulence amongst the objects on the side table. One object falls to the ground. He lifts his eyes heavenwards. 'Sorry, Freny. But see? Nothing broken.' Jijabhau hurries in on cat's feet and replaces the object. He sets the lunch table soundlessly.

The obstructed flow of Burjor's persuasion continues, '. . . so Feroze dikra, what I'm saying is, we'll find you a strapping young Parsi woman. Marry her. You'll get home-made dhanshak. You two can make a dozen dikra–dikris. In return I will marry Meher and see what I can do. Is that a deal?'

Feroze's smile is intact, but he moves his hand and says, 'No.' His hand is almost transparent. His eyes are the colour of honey. They shine with amusement.

'You think this one will ever marry?' says Soonu. 'You need to say at least four words for that: "Will you marry me?"'

'Sad. That's how the Parsi man is.' Burjor drops his shoulders dramatically. 'Women are no better. Won't marry. Why? Because they want independent flats. No living with boy's parents. Independent flat in Mumbai equals two digit lakhs, sixty–forty white and black. Not everyone is Tata or Godrej. No flat, no marriage. So where will children come from? The sky?'

Jijabhau signals that the table is laid. They rise like a flock of cranes and settle at the table. There is silence after that except for the sound of eating. It is only when the Parsi Dairy Farm kulfi is polished off that Shireen says, 'Burjor, *ave ainyathi siddhu Meher paase jaeene* propose to her. Then go home. You aren't a Tata–Godrej but you have a flat.'

'Done. But on one condition. That you'll let me tell a Tata joke.'

Everybody groans. The catch with Burjor's jokes is that he forgets the punchline. Listeners remain suspended between anticipation and laughter till they realize it's not coming. But today, Burjor won't be dissuaded because he thinks he's got a really good one. A deal is struck. He gets to tell his joke and takes Shireen as witness to the proposal. She could also give a helping hand if Meher faints. There's another condition. The minute he realizes he's forgotten the punchline, he must raise his hand and release the listeners from suspense.

Burjor moves forward in his chair to tell his joke. This dislodges Feroze's glass on the right and Najoo's plate on the left. The glass is empty but the plate upturns its load of chicken bones into Najoo's lap. With a resigned sigh, Najoo returns the plate to its place, gathers up the bones in her napkin and places the whole mess back on the plate. This operation over, Burjor clears his throat and begins.

'Ten devout Parsis standing in a row on the beach are busy praying. One by one, nine finish their prayers. The tenth remains where he is, still muttering. The nine are upset at the thought that the tenth wants to appear more devout than them. They wonder what he could be praying so hard about. They inch forward to eavesdrop. And this is what they hear . . .' Everybody round the table is looking at Burjor, mouths open in anticipation. Burjor looks lost for a moment, then says brightly, 'Now you guess what the fellow is saying.'

Najoo looks exasperated. 'He's forgotten again. *Haath upar kar ni!*'

Noshir intervenes quietly. 'It's a joke from the last century.' The tenth Parsi is repeating just one line through clenched teeth: "Sisterfucker, you gave it all to the Tatas, and nothing to me."'

Burjor is thrilled. 'You guessed right, dikra. Very good.'

'It's an old joke.' Noshir shrugs.

'And it stinks,' says Soonu.

Burjor laughs uproariously to cover up for the bad press.

They rise. Time to go. Shireen reminds Burjor of his part of the deal.

'But I didn't tell the joke. The joke is in the punchline. Noshir told it. Noshir, you go and propose to Meher.' There are howls of protest and noisy byes as they leave.

Feroze sighs, throws himself into an armchair and closes his eyes. Haridas steps into his studio. There's a huge frame up on one side, covered with three pieces of canvas joined together. A stepladder stands before it. This is going to be the last and most difficult of Feroze's Krishna series. When Haridas comes out, Feroze has fallen asleep. Jijabhau gets him a cup of tea.

'Is your bhajan meeting on this evening, Bhau?'

'Yes, yes.'

'May I come and listen?'

Jijabhau is embarrassed. 'Of course. I'll tell you before we start.'

'No need. I'll hear you.'

Much later, solemn voices rise from the far end of the house.

When I saw your divine form
happiness filled my heart . . .

Haridas walks out of the living room into a dark passage. He turns left into the kitchen at the end of the passage. Jijabhau's room is on the other side of the kitchen. Haridas inches the door open soundlessly. The muted light of the early evening sun slants into the room from the western window, throwing into relief the lines on the faces of the four men gathered in the room and the texture of the black sacred powder marking their foreheads. Haridas slides to the floor near the door and joins the refrain of the invocatory bhajan.

Our Vitthal, he is beautiful
Our Madhav, he is beautiful

The sprightly dhumali beat on the mridang fills the room with hope and joy. They sing:

You are the mother of compassion
You are the shelter of the poor

followed by,

I will serve you with all my soul

and finally,

His beautiful form stands on a brick.

The poetry of saints has lived on people's tongues for seven hundred years. Tukaram's abhangs, once drowned in the river by envious men, floated up and spread through the length and breadth of Maharashtra. A cherished treasure, an unbroken tradition of devotion, the very foundation of people's lives. These four men belong to that tradition. One is a porter at the railway terminal, one a vegetable seller, one a peon in a government office and one the sole pillar of a Parsi artist's household. They sing the final five prayers and their voices rise in the ecstatic culminating chant of '*Vitthal-Rakhumai*'. They rise and touch each other's feet—each one a devotee, each one Vithoba.

When Haridas comes out into the living room, his mind is churning with ideas. Feroze has woken up. Haridas does not wish to talk. He lifts his hand in farewell and lets himself out of the house.

10

Anima's eyes haven't moved from the protuberance of the woman's stomach. The woman is sitting across from her and Anima is staring at her stomach. Every time the train stops with a jolt, Anima's concern for the baby rises. It is sure to be fine floating in its shock-absorbing amniotic fluid. That's the miracle of the way a woman's body is constructed—built to protect the embryo from the knocks she takes in life. Anima has not experienced the magic. The pain of waiting ended with Siddharth. Then she thought bitterly, good we didn't bring a child into this jungle.

When the train jolts to a halt at Bandra, the woman gets up and hurries to the door. A horde of women makes for the compartment. As they rush in, the woman manages to slither out. Anima twists her neck to watch her cutting through the crowd towards the exit. Why does she take these risks at this stage of pregnancy?

'You want to know why?' the woman might say if she heard Anima's unspoken question. 'My man's at home sleeping. Drunk. When he gets up he'll beat me. I'm going to my mother's to keep the baby safe.'

'You want to know why?' the woman might say. 'The man tells me the child isn't his. Take it to your lover boy. I don't have a lover boy. I'm going to ask my old employer for work and shelter.'

'You want to know why?' the woman might say. 'When I got pregnant, he went after another woman. Now he's brought her home. My brother says leave him. And where will I stay? In his small hut with his wife and kids? I'll stay with him for a bit, then go back. Learn to live with the other one.'

Anima turns the woman's voice off and closes her eyes. When she opens them again, a woman in her early thirties has squeezed into the pregnant woman's place. She has opened a book and is poring over it. Anima leans forward most impolitely to look at the title. The world of books operates under a cultural system that accommodates such curiosity and includes the tradition of not returning borrowed books. Anima's curiosity is entirely justified. If she has read the book the woman is reading, they'll have an interesting conversation. From such a conversation might even spring a friendship.

The young woman is aware of Anima's curiosity. She smiles sweetly and says, 'The Time of My Life by—'

'Krishen Khanna.'

'How do you . . .'

'I'm from that world.'

'Sorry?'

'My brother's an artist. He gave me the book two years ago for my birthday.'

'Brother?'

'Ashesh Joshi.'

'Oh.' There's a long pause. 'I bought it because it is about the old art world—friendships—Padamsee, Souza, Husain . . .'

'Are you an artist?'

'No. I edit a so-called art section.'

'Newspaper?'

'Mumbai Observer.'

'You're not Janaki Patil of the Haridas article, are you?'

The woman looks surprised. 'Yes.'

'We loved it. Didn't get taken in one bit by his drama. But don't let me keep you from your book.'

Janaki bends over her book again but, on second thoughts, closes it.

'I'd like to interview your brother some day.'

'Have you ever come across one?'

'One what?'

'An interview? He doesn't have what it takes. He doesn't talk much.'

He is very private and doesn't do flamboyant work.'

'I try to do serious stories. Whenever I'm allowed to.'

Both women get off at Churchgate.

'Where are you headed?' Janaki asks.

'Sharada Sakhardande's concert.'

'Are we in a Hindi film? This is the second coincidence.'

'You too?'

'Yes.'

They walk down Marine Drive. They could have taken the Oval Maidan route to Chavan Centre. But walking along the Arabian Sea at sundown is a chance not to be missed.

'The evening light is so lovely,' Anima remarks. 'Like a mother's touch.'

'The imagined mother.'

Janaki's voice is dry.

'Many mothers have a tender touch,' Anima defends her sentiment.

'So I hear.'

'They've endured much but love the world.'

'So I've read. Never met one of them.'

'Meet Sharada's mother-in-law.'

'You mean you know Mrs Sakhardande?'

'She and her husband are part of our group.'

'Will you introduce me to her?'

'You want to interview her?'

'Perhaps. But I also want to learn from her. I heard her in Kolhapur. I loved her music. Of course . . . that is . . . if she has the time.'

'Have you learnt before?'

'With this voice? Haven't dared. But I want to try.'

The third-floor mini auditorium in the Yashwantrao Chavan Centre is already quite full. Sharada's popularity has been growing steadily. Her last concert was at the Dadar Matunga Cultural Centre where she had performed only for an hour and a half before a flautist took the stage. Even then a crowd had gathered around her at the end to congratulate her. They had been captivated by her powerful voice and style. A connoisseur told her he had called his wife halfway through her bada khayal to drop everything and come.

Anima looks around the little hall. Shekhar is sitting right up front, next to Madhavrao Sabnis, a disciple-devotee of Sharada's guru. Farther down is Urmilatai Mahajan who taught six-year-old Sharada her first basic bandish which described the qualities of Raag Yaman. She had been pleasantly surprised by the little girl's innate sense of tune and rhythm. In a corner at the back of the hall sits Haridas. He is wearing a Peshwa-style twelve-string shirt over voluminous pyjama trousers.

Anima settles down next to Shekhar with Janaki on the other side. 'Janaki,' Anima introduces her to Shekhar. 'She wants to learn from Sharada.'

Janaki smiles at Shekhar. He returns the smile, showing his small, straight teeth. She notices that his eyes are light brown and his other features well placed and suitably proportioned—ears aligned, chin firm, no major mess-up. 'What do you do?' he asks Janaki.

'I work for the *Mumbai Observer*.'

'Janaki Patil?'

'Yes,' she answers, surprised.

Anima cuts in hastily, addressing Madhavrao on the other side. 'How are you?' Madhavrao moves his head in quick half arcs down right, down left, like a ding-dong doll to say he is well. He prefers not to speak.

Anima turns towards Janaki and whispers, 'Sorry I cut in. He's read the interview. He can't stand Haridas. Didn't want to upset him.'

Sharada's accompanists arrive on the low, brightly covered platform, their tablas and tanpuras in hand. She follows to a scatter of applause. While the announcer introduces her, she sits with eyes closed. The accompanists tune their instruments.

The listeners sitting expectantly before Sharada are an invitation and a challenge to her creativity. That's how it is in Hindustani music. No score, only the notes of a raag as framework and songs of three or four lines set to rhythmic cycles of varying numbers of beats. The songs are skeletons on which Sharada will improvise flesh. At this moment she has no idea how big the song will grow. She will know only as the notes pour out of her in response to her musical ideas, the audience's involvement and even atmospheric features like light, air and how the audience is seated. She has years of practice and a few concerts behind her, but that is no guarantee that her singing today will soar. If it does, she will give deep but transient pleasure. The emotion she will pour into the words; the imagination that will prompt her play with notes, words and beat; and the musical ideas with which she will elaborate the theme will fill the air, then fade away. The audience might say of the concert later, 'She sang well,' or 'She has a beautiful voice,' but the details of her work will be lost.

If her music does not soar, the audience might be, at least partly, responsible. They must be alert, participate actively in the creation of the music with their informed responses, knowing that the music on that day, in that space, at that hour, is being created exclusively for and with them. Sharada looks for signs of pride in the body language of the audience that should come from knowledge and sensitivity.

The tanpuras are tuned. Sharada folds her hands and bows her head in humble greeting. She is dressed in a ruby-red silk sari. Her neck and ears are adorned with pearls. Her eyes shine.

Sharada closes her eyes again, silent for a few moments. The drone of the tanpuras fills the air. She slides her opening 'sa' imperceptibly into their 'sa'. The two notes blend so perfectly that it is difficult to tell the instrument from the human voice. The opening notes tell the audience which raag she is presenting. 'Poorvi,' the murmur goes around. Recognizing a raag is like being on the road home to your village. Recognizing a song is like arriving there. Sharada has chosen to sing 'Charan paarasat'. It is not a song often sung; but those who have heard it before know that the composition by the Sufi saint Nizamuddin Auliya sets up a clever play between words and rhythm to deepen meaning and emotion. The fast-tempo composition that follows praises the beauteous form of Lord Ram. The Sufi and the anonymous Hindu poet, who have both poured their devotion into the mighty flow of Hindustani music, unite in Sharada's shimmering rendition.

Poorvi is not an easy raag to unfold. The singer must guard its personality from encroachments by Paraj, Gauri and Bihag in its lower reaches and Puriya Dhanashree in the upper. But the dangers do not exist for those who have sat with their gurus, year in and year out, getting the melodies note-perfect. Sharada touches the pancham unerringly, only as lightly as she must and stays on the lower nishad only as long as she should. Building the raag note by note, her Poorvi acquires the glint and gleam of a precious stone.

Winding down the sombre Poorvi in a slow release of end notes, Sharada allows a few moments to pass before leaping into the bliss of Basant. The shadows of the morning have lifted. Her voice sparkles, her taans run swift, the audience sits up with new life. They sway in time as they enter the play of word and beat, the unexpected tihais worked out with mathematical ease and the smooth glissandos. The third tier of the raag elaboration, the fast-tempo tarana, takes off with its rapidly enunciated sound syllables. One powerful, sinuous taan, an unexpected tihai and the tightly wound skein of notes loosens, spills and slowly unravels into silence. The applause is thunderous. It will not stop. Sharada acknowledges it with bent head and folded hands, but her eyes turn surreptitiously towards Shekhar with a question. Anima catches the look and follows it. Shekhar encourages Sharada with his eyes. She looks at Anima who does the same. The applause has petered out. Sharada's expression grows serious. She speaks with deep humility.

'I now present a song in mid-tempo. It is my own composition. It came to me in Marathi. So it is not in the Braj dialect of Hindustani classical songs. It came to me in Raag Sarang. So it is not in an evening raag. Yet, I will dare to sing it at this hour, because I must. It is newly made and raw, so I shall sing it for a few minutes only. I beg your tolerance and hope you will accept the composition with generous forgiveness. I will end the concert with a tappa in Raag Bhairavi.'

Sharada's voice begins with a hum and expands to full volume as she holds the first note with a hint of a nervous tremor. She allows her voice to grow stronger before she begins to unfold the notes of Shuddh Sarang. Growing confident, she leaps into the song, singing it in its entirety—refrain and stanza.

I have seen Time, dear friend,
I have seen Time

The audience is silent, suspended in disbelief, not knowing how to respond. Shuddh Sarang in the evening is one thing, but these words . . . Time. That is death. A song about death. That is inauspicious. Classical music must not be about such things. Their silence seems to give Sharada's voice a sharper edge of pain so that every word is etched in space. Anima is struck by how perfectly the notes of Shuddh Sarang match the mood of the song. The raag belongs to the white heat of the midday sun. The words speak of small black lives quivering and freezing into stillness. The audience senses the intimacy of melody and word. An involuntary 'wah' escapes somebody, more like a sigh than an exclamation of aesthetic pleasure. Even as the listeners try to find a balance between habit and acceptance, Sharada ends her experiment, leaving a throbbing sense of incompleteness in the air.

The listeners are lost. Shekhar begins to clap. Anima and Janaki join in. There is some more scattered applause, full of uncertainty. Sharada's face shines. She thanks the audience sincerely for their tolerance. 'I'm not going to try your patience further,' she assures them with a mischievous smile and moves into the first words of the Bhairavi tappa. She sings of the beloved, of his constant presence in her life without which she is nothing.

Within a moment the listeners relax. They have found their place. They know this music and its sentiments. This is not an ambush. The beat is Pushto. It moves with the gait of a camel. The long, exquisite glissando at the end of the first line brings out spontaneous 'wahs'. The audience loses itself in the swirling taans of the tappa and the tender emotion in Sharada's voice. Her eyes turn again and again to Shekhar. He returns her gaze. They exchange private smiles. He is the man of the song. He is that beloved, that friend, that lover in whose being lies her highest happiness. And what does one do with a beloved's not-being? The thought strikes Anima and her throat constricts as a wave of loneliness floods her.

The tappa ends. It has moved the audience. Some gather around Sharada to congratulate her, carefully tiptoeing around her experiment with murmured nothings. But other than that, she sang her pure gharana, in her guru's style.

Anima signals to Sharada over the heads of the crowd to say she will call the next day. She and Janaki leave together. Anima's mind is full of Siddharth. A life that quivered and froze. My beloved, my lover.

In the train Janaki asks, 'What did you think of her composition?'

For a long time, Anima says nothing. Janaki is uncomfortable. She says tentatively, 'There's no place for the bhayanak and the bibhatsa in our music, is there?'

When Anima replies at last, it is as though she is talking to herself. 'There was a time when the bhayanak and the bibhatsa had no place in poetry either. Now it does. Poets decided poetry could not be just hasya, shringar and bhakti. It had to speak of other realities. If composers of classical songs feel the same way today . . .'

'Connoisseurs and critics will not accept it.'

'Who knows? It's all a question of habit.'

A long while later Janaki says, 'But the words . . . after a concert, what we take home are the melodies. Today the words are coming too.'

11

Sunday is Janaki's day off, but the offness doesn't begin till late afternoon. Before that, she washes the week's clothes, spreads them out to dry in every spare bit of space, draws money for the following week from the ATM and does her shopping. Today she must buy flowers for Sharada. She's been pestering Anima for an introduction since last Saturday's concert. Finally it has been fixed for this evening, five o'clock.

Shekhar opens the door to them. He's in shorts and a sleeveless tee.

'Please excuse my Sunday best.' He grins. Anima says to Janaki, 'This is for your benefit, okay? I've seen him in worse and less.'

The living room is more space and less furniture. What furniture there is has style. The general colour scheme is off-white and olive green but there are discreet spots of red scattered in places like the cushion covers and the painting from Ashesh's abstract period. Sharada falls in with this scheme in her Adyar sari of green bordered by turmeric yellow.

'Janaki, *Mumbai Observer*, came for your concert last Saturday, heard you first at the Deval Club, Kolhapur, went crazy over your music and wants to learn from you,' Anima does a formal introduction. Sharada smiles but shifts her eyes quickly to the floor, embarrassed at the open admiration in Janaki's eyes.

They settle on the durrie.

'From whom have you been learning?'

'Nobody.'

'Blank slate,' Anima offers.

'Bathroom singer?'

'Not that either. At home it was . . . and here again . . .'

'So what makes you want to learn?'

'My mother used to sing . . . they say.'

'They say?'

'They say. I want to know if I've inherited anything.'

Anima gazes at Janaki. Sharada nods.

'Would you like to come in please?'

Sharada leads them into a small side room. There are two tanpuras, a pair of tablas and a harmonium here, all in their cloth covers. They sit down. Sharada pulls the harmonium forward. Taking off its cover, she says, 'I'm going to play the notes of the scale. Try and sing them after me.'

'I'll try.'

Sharada, judging the pitch of Janaki's voice, places her finger on the kaali chaar key for the first note 'sa'. Janaki begins way off the note but adjusts her pitch till she gets there, more or less, before losing breath. Sharada plays all the notes in the scale one by one. Janaki follows approximately till all the notes are done. She is deeply embarrassed at her tunelessness.

'You are using a false voice,' Sharada tells her.

'False?'

'It's a top voice. It comes from the throat, not from the chest cavity and stomach. You'll have to work hard to find your true voice. How much time will you have for riyaz? Do you have the space? Landlords and neighbours don't take kindly to beginners in classical music.' Sharada's smile holds an encouraging warning.

Janaki is silent. The contours of Sharada's body are round. Her voice too is sweet and round. But there's no roundness in what she says. That is straight. Janaki hasn't thought about the questions she has posed. Mrs Khanna, her landlady, is a fun-loving widow. But Janaki isn't sure she will be amused by her paying guest's early morning voice training to hit the right musical notes. Janaki is lucky to have found a room in Mrs Khanna's sea-facing flat at Worli. She doesn't want to jeopardize it.

The phone rings while she is lost in thought. Shekhar brings the handset over to Sharada. His eyes are like flakes of ice. 'Haridas,' he says curtly. Anima glances at him sympathetically as he hurries away. Just the name Haridas curdles and sours his refined features. It is seven years since the time Haridas had taken possession of Sharada's body and mind, but it still hurt. In those spellbound days Haridas only had to suggest what Sharada should eat and drink, what colours and textures of saris she should wear, for her to happily submit. The only suggestion she had rejected, even while she was in thrall, was to change her guru. Haridas was of the opinion that women should learn from women gurus. Give up Pandit Kinikar, he had told her. Go to Sumati Sharangpani. But Sharada had stuck on with Pandit Kinikar because that was the music she wanted to sing.

The two years of bondage to Haridas had been painful for Sharada's parents and friends but specially for Shekhar, who admired her music, respected her as a person and had fallen in love with her. The world knew that Haridas was an incorrigible womanizer. Her friends could not understand how she could be so blind.

Yet there was reason for her blindness. Haridas had opened her eyes to the world of art beyond music. She had grown close to his friends—Feroze, Anima, Ashesh. These friends in turn had begun to listen to her music. Their response to it became important to her. And one day, Anima had mustered up the courage to say, 'I hope you aren't expecting a long-term relationship with Haridas.'

'Of course not,' Sharada said and laughed but without conviction. Then Haridas met a French musician and got involved with her. He said to Sharada, 'She plays the harp. You'll like her. The two of you could even do an east–west encounter. Wouldn't you like that?'

Sharada's insides had been torn apart. She had tried not to let it show on her face; she did not know if she had succeeded. Her friends rallied around her. Shekhar felt profoundly sad. He proposed to her. She said she needed time.

Sharada's music changed after the Haridas episode. It became richer. With the passage of time, she came to terms with herself. Her visceral muscles had relaxed. She accepted Shekhar's proposal. Her only condition was that he must believe she now felt only simple friendship for Haridas. Shekhar had instantly said, 'Of course I believe you. It's evident. You have many common friends. You'd want to . . . we will naturally meet them. That's not a problem. But,' he had added, 'I must also lay down a condition. You must not expect me to indulge him. Don't expect me to cut him slack because he's a great artist. To me, if a man is corrupt, his work is corrupt.'

On the phone Sharada is saying, 'Yes, that'll happen in time . . . I don't know. I'm not anticipating anything before I meet him.' She ends with a neutral thank you.

'What was he saying?' Anima asks.

'Liked the concert. He has reservations about the new bandish. He said rice served straight off the fire is tasty but a bandish is tasteless until it's had time to mature. Wanted to know what Guruji was going to say.'

'Did you read Janaki's piece on him?'

'Yes. Good. His famous lifestyle ignored for questions about his work.'

Janaki makes a face. 'I asked only one question about his work. Even then the boss said we don't want "intellectual" writing. Our readers won't get it.'

'Did he call to thank you?' inquires Anima.

'Yes.'

'And did he suggest you meet some time?'

'Yes, that too.'

'Watch out. He eats women.'

'I know.'

Anima looks at Janaki for a few moments, then turns to Sharada.

'So have you thought about Guruji?'

'It's going to be an ordeal by fire. I'll be cursed.'

'Let it happen and be done with it. Stand your ground.' Anima reaches for Sharada's hand. 'A day comes when artists must leave the guru's shelter. If that day has come for you, just face it.'

'That's not how it is, Anima. How can I explain?'

'What's there to explain? I see Ono in you.'

'That's a different culture.'

'Yes and no. They are as traditional as we are.'

'Who are "they"?' Janaki wants to come in.

'The Japanese. This novelist Kazuo Ishiguro . . .'

'The Booker Prize winner?'

'Yes. But that was for a later novel. This one's about painters, the society they live in and all that.'

'So who's Ono?'

'Ono is a young artist. He lives in the guru's gurukul with the other disciples. They are expected to have total faith in their guru's world view and paint his subjects in his style. A point comes when Ono can't accept this. The guru's pictures are romantic depictions of beautiful geishas and colourful nights spent drinking sake. But Ono sees another, more disturbing world around him. He paints this world. His paintings upset the guru but he dismisses the work as the energy of youth expressing itself. Ono protests it has nothing to do with energy. This is how he thinks, he says. He doesn't believe an artist should be forever sunk in the contemplation of beauty. We live in difficult times. The artist must look around and give value in his work to what he sees. The guru explodes and tells Ono to leave the gurukul.'

'And?'

'The room in which the conversation takes place has been darkening. Ono lights the lanterns one at a time. That is his chore in the gurukul. Then he leaves.'

12

Dear Janaki,

I have just found out that you are working for an English newspaper in Mumbai. I knew what was happening with you when you were in Madras. You never asked me how. There was a person I used to send you letters through once in a while. I don't know whether you read them or threw them away. I wrote from a mother's heart. It can't stop feeling for a child. The man in Madras gave me your Mumbai office address. I will write to you whenever I can, my dear. It is my solace in the hell that I live in. It gives me strength to know that someone of my flesh and blood is living with self-respect. Even if she is angry with me, she is mine. Why did you leave the Madras job? Is the new job better? I hope you are eating well. Don't neglect yourself, my pet.

Ai

Janaki stares at the computer, chin cupped in her palms. She doesn't see the computer. She sees nothing. She is waiting for the stream of memories to start. Each time there's a letter from her mother, they come as photographic stills. Her mother's face. Her terrified eyes. Her body contracted into itself. Janaki in the background. Not the Janaki she sees in the mirror every day. She is a different person, her face distorted with hatred. He stands before them, the object of her hatred. His massive hand grips her mother's arm. He drags her into their bedroom, showering her with obscenities. She comes out later, a little less human. Janaki, watching, is choked with revulsion, like an overfull gutter, at this woman who allows her humanness to be gouged out of her, lump by lump.

When it ends, Janaki expects to return to herself, to crumple the letter into an angry ball and fling it away.

But today the memories don't come. Her mind is a blank, numbed by the abjectness of her mother's letter. She finds no trace of the familiar revulsion. Has time done its bit? If her mother were to stand before her now, would she shred her with her tongue or . . . what? What would she do?

Somebody shakes her arm. 'Where are you?' Suryakanta from Marketing is looking at her with mild surprise. 'I said come for lunch, twice. But you're like all spaced out.' She notices the letter in Janaki's hand. 'Sorry, yaar. Problem?' Janaki folds the letter and slips it into its envelope. 'Of course there's a problem,' she says getting up. 'I'm paralysed by the thought of the oily cutlets in the canteen. What kind of life is it for them to sit on chipped plates—burnt and oozing oil— pretending to be lunch?'

'Who said anything about cutlets? I have a free meal for two at the Golden Dragon. How's that?'

'Why me? Is Rishi trekking in the Himalayas?'

'You because Rishi has trekked out of my life.'

'Oh?'

'Yessss. We've ssssplit.'

'You split in March and again in May.'

'This is for good.' Suryakanta swings her hips, packed tightly into a pair of jeans, in haughty anger as she leads the way. Janaki grins at the thought of how she's going to look at the Golden Dragon sitting with this piece of today. Perhaps she should get herself some smart clothes. One of these days.

13

A new hoarding, roughly ten feet by five, has gone up at the corner of the junction, exhorting the whole square, as it were, to do its bidding. Sharada lets her eyes wander over it as she waits for the red man to turn green on the traffic lights. At the centre of the hoarding stands a political leader in a crisply starched white kurta pyjama. He has pink lips—the hoarding painter's flight of fancy. Ranged around him like buzzing flies waiting for a ride on a buffalo's back are several gentlemen named Pednekar, Bhagwat, Bhure, Gangan, Boite, Sheikh and suchlike. They wear triumphant smiles. The leader's right hand is raised, four fingers folded in, the forefinger jabbing the blue sky angrily. Inscribed at the bottom, in bold green and saffron letters, is the order: 'Come, march to Shivaji Park.'

On the pavement below it, a ragged child is beating up a younger, even more ragged child with a supple twig. As soon as the signal turns green, Sharada hurries across the road and instinctively grabs the hand that holds the twig. The child looks at her with moist, hollow eyes. A fly alights on the corner of his open mouth. He jerks his head to shake it off. Sharada's grip around the child's sticklike hand is as tight as the child's on the younger child's hand. The younger child stares at her with dumb hope.

'Why are you beating the poor thing?' Sharada asks the older child sternly. The older child says in an expressionless voice, 'Aunty, he won't sing.' His mouth hangs open after he has spoken. It is made that way.

Sharada is still holding the older child's hand, uncertain what to do with it. She sees how idiotic she must appear, standing on the corner of a square looking blankly at two children, who in turn look at her in silence. She must say something. Or do something. Fed up with waiting, the older child intones yet again, 'Aunty, he won't sing.' He looks at her and explains, 'He won't sing to get money. He won't sing to get food.' The two children stare at her again.

Sharada is embarrassed. The older child probably expects her to tell the younger one, 'You must listen to your elder brother. You must sing.' The younger child probably expects her to free him from the older child's control. She can do neither. She should never have meddled. Passers-by stare at her. They probably expect her to set up a cry: 'This child has stolen my purse.' They will then help her beat up the child to extract the truth and the purse from him. Her palms grow sweaty. Her grip on the boy's wrist loosens. He worms his hand free. Defeated, she pats him on the head and says, 'Don't beat him. He's so small.'

'If he doesn't sing, they'll beat him.'

She doesn't ask who 'they' are. She wants to escape as fast as she can. She gropes in her handbag, pulls out a couple of coins, pushes them into the younger child's hand and says, 'Tell them he sang.'

The older child says, 'They are watching.'

Sharada hurries away. Behind her the younger child howls again. She keeps walking. Her mind is in turmoil. Why did she give him money? She should have bought him pao. The beating might have hurt less on a full stomach. Soon she hears two voices, raised in song—one strong, the other tearful.

Tumhare hain tumse daya maangate hain
Tere laadlon ki dua maangate hain
(We are your own, we beg you, have pity
We pray for blessings for your loved ones)

The song takes Sharada back some thirty years to her aunt's house in Pune. It was the summer vacation. Aunts and cousins were playing antakshari on the terrace, under a bright starlit sky. The last letter from the previous song was 't'. Shalinitai began to sing, '*Tumhare hain tumse . . .*' The refrain was sung, the first stanza was sung. According to rules, she might have stopped then. But Tai continued. Sharada's eyes streamed with tears. The song rose to a final crescendo. Tai sang the last two lines.

Bacha ho jo roti ka tukada dila do
Jo utara ho tan se woh kapada dila do
(Give us leftover food
Give us discarded clothes)

Sharada had burst into uncontrollable sobs. Her aunt slapped her back lightly and said, 'Really, Leela's daughter is too sensitive.' Sharada did not understand what the English word 'sensitive' meant. But she gathered it was not a good thing to be and quickly rubbed her eyes dry.

Sharada climbs up the ramshackle stairs to Pandit Keshavrao Kinikar's rooms. There is an iron ball in her stomach. Pandit Kinikar lives in a two-room unit of the Umrao Chawl in a lane behind Kohinoor Mill No. 2. The door is open. Guruji stands at the window. He remains standing with his back to her even after she has entered. The expanse of the mill land spreads before him. Mill workers once laboured here in three shifts, spinning and weaving twenty-four hours of the day. The mill is now razed, the teeming workers rendered jobless. Guruji has seen those days from this window. Now he sees these. His seventy-year-old back—straight as a toddy palm—is rigid, as though prepared to receive a sudden blow.

Behind him, Sharada pulls out the durrie from under the cupboard and spreads it noiselessly. She lifts the tanpura from the corner and silently sets it down horizontally. She waits, making herself as small as she can. Guruji is still at the window, apparently lost in the view outside. A puff of breeze enters and with it a dried leaf flutters in and settles on his shoulder. Guruji continues to stand absolutely still. Only his fingers intertwined behind his back move imperceptibly. Sharada has seen Guruji's anger take many forms, but never this. What must she do in these circumstances—keep standing like a statue, or fall at

his feet and ask for forgiveness? She cannot do that. She did what she
did knowingly. To ask him to forgive her would be hypocritical. She
continues to stand.

She shifts her weight from one foot to the other. If a way is not found
out of this impasse, she is afraid she will burst out laughing. Just then,
Madhavrao Sabnis walks in on furtive feet; catching sight of her, he
freezes. His customary expression of devotion turns to confusion at the
sight of her. He half smiles at Sharada in greeting and hurries forward
to touch Guruji's feet. This is not easily done, because Guruji's feet
point towards the wall. But he does what he can. He touches them
from the side and moves back.

Madhavrao had once been Guruji's disciple. He poured his soul
into singing and was tenacious. But just around the time he was
beginning to realize that mere tenacity was not enough for producing
a true shadja note, he was diagnosed with cancer of the throat. On
hearing the news, Haridas had said, characteristically, 'God sometimes
intervenes to reduce discord in the world.' Now Madhavrao just about
manages to produce a speaking voice. It seems to come from a throat
covered in sandpaper.

Madhavrao is a chaste man full of goodness. He thinks his voice
annoying, so he does not say much. If he agrees, he nods and smiles.
If he does not, he hangs his head. He worships Guruji. He believes,
without a trace of doubt, that such a singer has never been born before,
and never will be again. For the past thirty years he has accompanied
Guruji on the tanpura at every concert. On these occasions, his face
lights up with such guru-love, that people's attention is often diverted
away from the singer to him.

When Madhavrao touches Guruji's feet he does not bend, touch
and straighten up as others do. He prostrates himself. When he rises,
his eyes are invariably moist. He feels no embarrassment. He pulls a
handkerchief out of his pocket, gives his eyes a thorough wipe, and
even snorts into it on occasion. He then stands aside with a smile
full of bliss, awaiting Guruji's order to sit. On this day, he has been
denied prostration, and the order to sit has not come. Moreover, he is

perplexed at Sharada's presence. So when Guruji finally turns around and signals to him to sit, he gesticulates and arranges the lines on his face into the question: how can I sit when it appears to be Sharada's time for a lesson? Guruji makes another sign to him to sit. 'There's no lesson today,' he says. Sharada starts. For the first time, Guruji looks at her and says, 'You too may sit.'

'There's no lesson' is the first part of her punishment. She guesses that Madhavrao's presence means more will follow. She realizes she is still standing. Guruji says, 'Sit down, please. You're perfectly self-sufficient now. You should not need my permission to sit.'

Guruji's voice becomes nasal when he makes cutting remarks. Sharada's palms have been sweating. Now her heart begins to pound. She is not afraid of what Guruji will say next. What she is afraid of is that she will suddenly lose her respect for him. Where will that leave her? So far she has managed to justify even his most irrational outbursts, his arrogance in dealing with people, his paroxysms of rage against Pandit Raghuvir Sharma of their own gharana. She has told herself that nobody understands Guruji's greatness. He has never got over the grief of losing his wife at a young age. His ideas about music are too idealistic for today's world, et cetera, et cetera. But lately, doubts have begun to creep in.

'Did you attend Sharadatai's concert, Madhavrao?' he asks. Madhavrao looks intensely uncomfortable. He knows Sharada has done wrong. He has been disturbed about it ever since he heard her composition at the concert. He has also known that he will be asked this question. He is a simple man. He nods uncertainly in answer to the question, not seeing, what Sharada sees, that Guruji is laying a trap for him. She does not wish to see him being used in this game. Guruji should tell her what is in his mind and be done with it. But he will not. Sharada looks at the floor.

'Yes, I heard you were there,' Guruji says softly.

Madhavrao nods again.

'What did you think?'

Madhavrao is trapped between the devil of saying he liked the concert and the deep blue sea of saying he did not. He flails around.

Guruji says, pronouncing every word clearly, 'Pandit Raghuvir Sharma was overheard telling someone that Sharadatai is the only star amongst my disciples. The rest is darkness.' Poison has gathered on Guruji's lips. The glint in his eyes suggests that the poison has a sweet taste and a tender touch. Pandit Sharma's name has this effect on him. Guruji's concerts attract a few true connoisseurs. Pandit Sharma's concerts attract the world. In Guruji's opinion the reason is this: 'He is handsome. I am ugly.' On occasion he has added a gloss to this statement. 'In our country fair skin is worshipped. We submitted to the British. We made Pandit Nehru our prime minister. If we had chosen Vallabhbhai Patel, the future of our country would have been different. But Vallabhbhai was dark. His nose was large.'

Madhavrao's eyes are fixed on Guruji. What should he think? Is Sharadatai the only star or is she not? How should he shake his head? Guruji returns his look with curiosity and a sweet smile. Sharada feels suffocated. She is not sure she will be able to resist the urge to get up and leave if Guruji doesn't vent his bile soon. If she leaves, there will be no way back. She will have lost a great guru and taken upon her head the sin of hubris. Guruji says thoughtfully, 'I am told that Sharadatai did not sing full-throatedly as we do. She modulated her voice. What is your opinion about the present trend of voice modulation?'

'My . . . my . . . opinion?' Madhavrao is reduced to stuttering. Even assuming he has opinions, Guruji has never sought them before. Even now, is he really expected to give his opinion or will Guruji answer his own question as he often does? Guruji speaks.

'There is, isn't there, a fundamental difference between popular songs and classical music? We are not expected to tickle the listener's feelings as the pop singer does. The listener is your fellow-traveller, or at least he is expected to be. When you sing, your arduous practice, your honed skills, your faith, your tradition—you are gifting him the product of these invaluable things that he doesn't get from his daily routine. Your attempt is to elevate his mind—something that the materiality of the here and now does not do. It is not an easy thing to do. That is why you put in years of practice. Only those who wish to escape hard work do sensational things. Like singing their own songs, composing their own raags or singing raags outside their time frame to create a sensation.'

At last, Guruji turns to her. 'You don't need those great old composers Sadarang-Adarang any more. You've demonstrated your individual creativity. Your ideals are no longer those of your guru and your guru's guru. Your ideal is Pandit Raghuvir Sharma. He has flitted wantonly through all the gharanas, sucking here, sucking there, composing his own raags, his own songs. If you wish to follow his ways, you're free to become his formal disciple. It is a disease that afflicts our nation, to despise our own and run after the alien. Grab and use is what people respect most these days. How can you escape it? Let's celebrate it then.'

Guruji is choked. Sharada looks at him with wet eyes, thinking, this man has suffered unknown hardships to acquire the knowledge he has; and although he has not given with as generous a hand as he could have, he has given me enough to last a lifetime. What did he expect when he was passing on this treasure to me? That I would sing his music in his name. So I do. But how can I convince him I do? How do I tell him that my confidence in doing something different comes from the fullness of his music in me? How unfair it is that he should think people enjoy my music because I use gimmicks to please them? How do I tell him that the audience did not care for my experiment that evening? That it made them uneasy, that such experiments are not designed to add to my popularity; if anything, they will do the opposite.

Guruji's face suddenly grows soft. He sighs and meets Sharada's eyes directly. 'People say we must change with the times. I believe this should not apply to a timeless art like music. It is possible that my mind is mildewed. I am nearly seventy. You are barely thirty-five. You tell me then. What was your idea in singing Shuddha Sarang in the evening?'

Sharada knows this path is strewn with mines. Since Guruji has put a direct question to her, it would be impertinent not to answer. But to answer would be an arrogant admission that she thinks differently from him. Sharada takes a deep breath. 'I didn't do it just to be different. When the song came to me it came composed in Shuddha Sarang. It so happened that I had this concert coming up. So I felt tempted to try out the song before an audience, that's all.'

'Merely because you felt tempted, you thought you would . . .'

'Not just that. I also thought that Carnatic musicians don't adhere to rules of time and season. The Carnatic system and the Hindustani system have emerged from the same source. We have borrowed several raags from one another. When I attend Carnatic music concerts, I do not suffer loss of enjoyment because a raag has been sung out of its time or season. We too have made compromises with time rules.'

'We have? Compromises?'

'We don't have too many night-long concerts because people don't have the time. So we sing raags meant to be sung in the middle of the night much earlier. If we've stopped associating raags rigidly with sunrise and sunset for practical reasons, it shouldn't matter greatly if one sings a raag that is right for the mood and the meaning of a song, at a time that is deemed wrong.'

'Did you place this thought before the audience?'

'No.'

'So how did they respond to this innovation of yours?'

'It did not go down well with their listening habits.'

'Their listening habits? Or their faith in the rightness of tradition?'

Sharada says nothing to that. But to herself she says, people who once listened exclusively to dhrupad began to enjoy the khayal when they got used to it. Dhrupad was once tradition. Khayal was the innovation. If only some historian had recorded the stages by which that transition was made and received, we would not be arguing about this now.

She does not know how Guruji has interpreted her silence. After a while, he says quietly, 'You are a free person, free to do what you wish. We live in the age of individual freedom. But if you want to continue with such experiments, please do me the favour of not naming me as your guru.'

He says this and rises. Madhavrao and Sharada also rise instantly. 'I have to go out for a while now,' he says. Madhavrao and Sharada glance at each other. Guruji never goes out, although several uncles, aunts, cousins and others from his huge extended family live in the city. He stopped visiting his relatives after his wife died. So when he says he has to go out, he is saying to them, please leave. Guruji's parting line is: 'Give a thought to what I have said and make up your mind. You need not come here till you've decided which way to go.'

Madhavrao and Sharada descend the worn-out stairs of the tenement building. The ripples from Madhavrao's perplexed state of mind lap against Sharada as she walks beside him. He clears his throat many times but not a word emerges. She herself is in a daze. Sing the way I tell you to or I am not your guru. This is the essence of what Guruji has said. Think about it and only then come to me. Think? That I have no creative freedom, that I am duty-bound to sing traditional songs in the traditional way? That if I wish to step out of this rigidly defined tradition, I must do so without a guru? What space does that offer me to think and decide?

Madhavrao and Sharada are on the street below. Madhavrao must face the last test. How is he to say goodbye to a disciple who has offended his guru? With a smile, as though nothing unusual has happened? Or with a stern face that will make it clear she did wrong? Madhavrao does neither. There is no smile in his heart for it to emerge on his face. There is no sternness in his nature for it to enter his voice. Looking utterly miserable, he says, 'So sorry, so sorry,' a few times in his sandpaper voice and hurries away with lowered head.

Sharada stands below Guruji's rooms in the slanting sun. Her feet will not move from the spot. She raises her head to look at his window. He is not there. She feels orphaned.

14

The spacious auditorium of the college in Vile Parle is full. The new two-storey art gallery, self-deprecatingly called Shosha, located on the main road near the college, has established itself in the two years of its existence as a gallery with a difference. Galleries generally exhibit and sell works by their stable of artists and a few others. That's the sum of their activity. Shosha holds what it calls an art bazaar twice a year to display works by a range of miscellaneous artists. Old and young, established and new, abstract and figurative, traditional and contemporary—you can see them all there. The general public is familiar with bazaars. You can stroll through a bazaar. A bazaar represents choice. It offers the possibility of finding an unexpected something that will catch your fancy. The bazaar is a place where you meet other shoppers, discuss each other's buys or the day's news. A bazaar is a place where you need not buy but merely window-shop. The general public which has been to Shosha's bazaars finds the place familiar enough for it to walk in for its regular shows too. Not only does the public come for them, but also looks forward to writing its unminced opinions in the visitors' book at the entrance.

Shosha also has a scheme to help the man in the street buy art painlessly, with one down payment and easy, interest-free instalments. During the period they are paying their instalments, they are allowed to take their work of art home for the weekend. Shosha takes the responsibility of transporting it safely there and back. During the rest of the week, the work is hired out to head offices of middle-range companies. The benefits of this arrangement are threefold. Buyers benefit because their instalments are interest-free. It is possible for the seller to give them this benefit because he makes many times more than the interest in weekly rent from the companies who hire the work. The hiring companies benefit because they do not have to pay the price of the work that gives their image a boost; and they get different paintings every six months or so, breaking the monotony.

Vikram Shah, the young businessman-owner of Shosha, benefits by the increased footfalls in his gallery leading to higher turnover. The artists win a bonanza of benefits. Not only do their paintings get sold at the right prices, but the increased viewership for and sheer reach of their work makes their signatures more widely known.

Vikram Shah's way of conducting his business is the result of his long-cherished dream about art. He dreams of a day when commuters on Mumbai's locals will discuss paintings as enthusiastically as they do Hindi films. Towards this end he also holds art-appreciation workshops in his gallery. This year he has taken one more step towards realizing his dream. He has organized a one-day seminar on 'The Many Views of Art' for the lay person. Shreyas Kubdekar, a popular lecturer in Economics at the college and a close friend of Shah's, has promised to fill at least half the house with students. Shah is happy because students are as 'lay' as you can get.

Seminars on art are a dime a dozen, but each is driven by the interests of a clique of artists and critics. Shah knows that the uninitiated have no interest in the internal politics of the art world. They simply want information about the world of art and why painters paint the way they do. With a view to inform the audience, Shah has invited speakers from across aesthetic ideologies and ages. The speakers have agreed to be there, with many reservations. The questions that have bothered them are: Who is Vikram Shah? Or rather, who the hell is Vikram Shah? Where has he suddenly sprouted from? How can an art gallery be called Shosha? How can a serious thing like art be sold in a bazaar? Why is the seminar being held in a college in the eastern suburbs of the city of all places, instead of somewhere in South Mumbai?

Everything about Vikram Shah and his seminar smacks of charlatanism, but the speakers have come, persuaded, in no small measure, by the trimmings around Shah's invitation. Shah has offered them a handsome fee in addition to providing air-conditioned transport to the venue and back. He has also organized cocktails at a five-star hotel near the airport for the speakers, artists and collectors. What has drawn artists, critics and the press to the seminar is the promise that something spicier than the usual mealy-mouthed discussions on dead-horse issues is likely to happen.

Anima has reserved two seats beside her for Janaki and Ashesh. Janaki will come directly from work and he, when he can. Anima is astonished at the crowd. The faces around her belong not just outside the usual suspects of the art world, but far beyond its farthest extensions. When Janaki takes her seat beside Anima, she asks with a lopsided grin, 'Are we at the right place?' The answer comes from behind. 'The Shosha seminar? Yes, this is it.'

Anima and Janaki turn around. Anima sees an unfamiliar young man with bright, lustrous eyes. Janaki sees a faintly familiar face.

'Janaki?' the young man says eagerly. 'Don't you recognize me? Prakash. Jadhav. I used to come to Kolhapur in the summer holidays. To my grandfather's. Hambirrao's.'

Janaki does remember. Her face lights up. 'What brings you here?'

He answers in his Belgaum lilt, 'I went to art school here. Remember I used to draw? I knew since then that I wanted to . . .' He is eager to tell her all. Janaki takes fright. This is neither the place nor the time for unabridged life stories. She nods violently, smiles and obstructs his flow. 'Shall we meet after the seminar?' That's the only escape she can think of at the moment. But when he nods enthusiastically, she realizes what she's gone and done.

Janaki recalls vividly Prakash's thumbnail, grown long to do nail etchings, for which he received much praise from the townspeople. When he sat staring at Rankala Lake, people would say, 'After all, he's an artist.' Being an artist, he would hasten home and not draw what he had seen, but paint rivers, hills and sunsets which he considered the more appropriate subjects for art. Janaki was granted elder-sister status in his life. As befitted this role, she too joined in praising his river-and-hill paintings. Hambirrao, his grandfather, had been a drawing teacher in one of the better-known high schools in town. His special skill was drawing large portraits in charcoal from small photographs. The shading of facial lines, eyes and drapery was done with such finesse that you felt his subjects would start talking to you any minute. His portraits of

Gandhi and Nehru hung in the front room of his house. Beside them also hung framed magazine covers of women by Dalal and Mulgaonkar. He had more of these covers stored away in a large trunk.

When Prakash visited his grandfather in the summer vacations, he would pull out the trunk and copy as many Dalal–Mulgaonkar women as he could. Hambirrao was thrilled with the likenesses his grandson turned out. He would take them around town and give them away free to anybody who asked for them. 'Take them while they're free.' He would laugh with pride. 'Soon you'll have to pay through your nose for Prakash's work.' And so it came about that many dingy front rooms in homes around town were lit up by imitation Dalals and Mulgaonkars. One of Prakash's Mulgaonkar maidens hung in Janaki's home too. The woman had plump pink cheeks, large fawn eyes and hair knotted in a loose bun at the nape of the neck. She was dressed in a diaphanous blue sari and tight choli through which the nipples of her perfectly rounded breasts pointed invitingly. Janaki's father would look at this young woman in a way that revealed its meaning to Janaki much later.

'There he is, in time and all,' Anima exclaims, waving to a man of medium height, perfectly made nose and fine hair, who is just entering the auditorium. He nods in acknowledgement of her raised hand. So this is Ashesh Joshi, Janaki thinks, looking at him with some curiosity. He walks towards them in a straight line, looking straight ahead. He wears a shirt with tiny red and blue checks, a well-cut pair of grey trousers and floaters. Introductions over, Ashesh tells Janaki he liked her article on Haridas.

'It was hardly an article, just a snippet.'

'A snippet of this size on art in a Mumbai newspaper makes it an article.' He laughs as he turns towards the stage which has become suddenly active. Janaki notices that one of his front teeth overlaps the edge of the other.

Vikram Shah walks on to the stage with a humble namaskar. He stands before the mic, looks around with easy warmth and begins to speak. The mic coughs and screeches. 'I forgot to pray to it,' Shah says with a grin. There is laughter all round. People take to Shah immediately. Then, without further ado, he invites reputed art critic Suresh Pancholi to the stage to speak about the purpose and structure of the seminar and to moderate its proceedings. Handing over the mic to Pancholi, he comes down to take a seat near the door in the front row.

'The purpose of this seminar,' Pancholi begins, 'is somewhat different from the usual. Vikram Shah is a successful businessman, art lover and a man with what he calls a mission. I would call it a naive dream. But Shah means to make it real. His simple wish is to spread the knowledge and love of art amongst people who would be art lovers if only they understood what it was all about.

'The art world has changed too rapidly in recent years and become too closed-in for the lay person to understand what is happening. Shah realizes that the schism between what is generally seen as a beautiful painting and what critics praise as good work has been growing wider. Further, because we have entered the globalized world with such enthusiasm, narrower schisms have sprung up within the art world itself. In art as in life we are living at many levels and in different times. It is for this that Vikram Shah has felt the need to take an all-encompassing look at art today, in the presence of the lay public.

'Artists face many questions today. What is and should be the connection between today's art and today's world? Is the growing power of the art market a good thing or a bad thing for the making of art? And the old, old question that continues to hound artists—what is Indianness? Does an artist need to make a conscious effort to achieve it or do we assume that any work an Indian artist does is automatically and by definition Indian? At the root of this question is another. How do we define Indianness in the context of the globalized world if we still need to do so?

'It is the organizer's hope and desire that this seminar will throw light on these issues. He has therefore invited speakers, artists and critics, who belong to different though not necessarily opposing schools of thought. The seminar is structured as follows. Four speakers will be on stage to make preliminary statements that will be open to comment by invited artists and critics on the floor. The discussion will then be thrown open to the audience at large. Vikram Shah has charged me with the responsibility of conducting the seminar. May I therefore request the four speakers of the day to come to the stage please? We have with us today Sadashiv Bapat from Pune, Ashutosh Sen from Kolkata, the senior Mumbai painter Jairaj Santoshi and one of today's leading young installation artists, Kruttika Jathar.

'I shall call upon Jairaj Santoshi to speak to us about his art. He was one of the half-dozen artists who went to Paris and London after Independence. While the others settled in Europe, Santoshi returned home at the end of the fifties. Thereafter he developed his own style of abstraction where you might see sky, mountains and sea or you might see only colour, line and texture. His palette has always comprised muted shades of pastel colour. Jairaj Santoshi on the ideas that feed his art.'

Those who had heard Jairaj Santoshi before knew what he was going to say. He fulfilled their expectations. 'I believe that art, whatever form it takes, is essentially a spiritual journey. It is about transcendence. I have never felt the need to make my work a mirror of contemporary society. Human life and its transactions here on earth are by definition transient. What is eternal is the expanse of the universe and its mysteries. I believe the purpose of my art is to explore that and find expression for the discoveries I make in my humble way. How is a man, puny and inadequate as he is, to comprehend the infinities of the universe? The ancients have told us infinity may be seen in a grain of sand. I see the universe in a drifting leaf or a scampering crab on an endless beach. I paint the veins and fine mesh of dried leaves. I paint the tiny patterned holes in the sand that crabs scamper into. I paint the nuanced shades of rain clouds piled high on the horizon . . .'

Santoshi's long, white hair blows around his neck. His silk jhabba ripples in the breeze stirred up by the overhead fan. His voice is soft, his diction crisp. His speech lulls the audience into acquiescent listening. When it ends, there's a sharp shower of applause.

The audience pours out into the foyer for tea, falling into groups like patterns of glass pieces in a kaleidoscope. In a group in the far corner, Sadashiv Bapat who is scheduled to speak next is already saying a great deal. The eyes of the young men around him are transfixed on his animated face. Prakash is weaving his way around the different groups in search of Janaki. He spots Anima and guesses that Janaki, who was sitting next to her, must be somewhere around her. Joshi sir and Banatwala sir are also there. Prakash had been in art school when some alumna had persuaded the dean to invite practising artists to interact with final-year students. This would not only be of immense help to the students as they got ready to step out into the real world of art, they told the dean, but it would also add glory to his name as the man who tried to do something new and different for the art school. The dean had welcomed the idea. He had instantly sent out letters of invitation to reputed artists in the city to come and talk to the students. Some of them accepted and came, Padamsee sir, Joshi sir, Banatwala sir amongst them. However, a few weeks later, the dean saw that the artists barely gave him the time of day. Not only did they not give him the respect he deserved, they gave too much to the students, which was a sure way of putting ideas into their heads. What hurt the dean most was the complete lack of interest that the media had shown in his innovative programme despite his having sent press notes to every paper. Thus, much against his will, he had been compelled to close down the programme.

Prakash hovers around Anima's group. 'Excuse hunh, but where is Janaki?' he stutters. Somebody in the crowd knocks into him causing his right hand to plunge into Anima's teacup. It confuses Prakash. He says 'sorry-sorry' to Anima, not once or twice but again and again like a wound-up toy. Anima puts her teacup down and waits patiently for him to wind down. Then she grabs his wet hand and gives it a good scrub with her handkerchief. 'Now let's do one thing,' she says gently. 'Take this tea to the counter there, see? Leave it there and bring me another cup, please. Get a cup for yourself as well. Janaki is also somewhere there. She's gone to get herself tea.'

Prakash spots Janaki as he walks carefully towards Anima balancing two cups of tea. He hands Anima's cup to her and turns back. 'Janaki,' he calls out, hurrying towards her. 'What are you doing in Mumbai?'

'You tell me first what you are doing.'

'I told you already. I'm an artist. Passed out from art school two years ago.'

A middle-aged woman standing near them turns around to look at him with interest. She has the air of a senior queen in a royal household. She wears a long-sleeved, embroidered blouse and a fine sari the colour of latte. The end of the sari is drawn over her head and stays mysteriously put. A string of large, lustrous pearls hugs her neck.

'Your turn.'

'I am . . . a journalist.'

'Don't tell me. Which paper?'

Janaki mumbles, '*Mumbai Observer.*'

The senior queen quickly turns her eyes on Janaki. While appearing to continue her conversation with a man, made entirely of grease head to toe, her ears are busy picking up what they can of Janaki and Prakash's conversation.

'You mean you're the Janaki Patil who's written about Haridas sir? This must be his twelfth interview in the last year. How does he manage it? But you're something, hunh!'

'How?'

'Would anybody have thought that Janaki Patil of Kolhapur would shine in a big Mumbai paper? It's great for me. I'm doing a joint show with three fellow alumna in a new gallery. You'll give us publicity, no?' Janaki is instantly wary. 'Two of the chaps are known a little. I'm the most unknown. A little publicity would get us a trickle of visitors. An artist is nothing without the media, no? One critic said he'd write but I can't afford his rate. You'll do a perfect job, knowing me so well . . . my childhood, my grandfather. I'll bring my portfolio over to show you. I used to do portraits, you remember that? I could do them blindfold even now. But critics aren't interested in portraits. So guess what I'm doing? Abstracts!'

Janaki looks at him helplessly. 'Prakash, that's not how it works. The editor decides what, when and about whom I should write. Sometimes the owners decide. They like big names in their paper.'

'Chhah,' Prakash is disgusted. 'This is a mess. You need the media to make a name; but the media will not look at you unless you are a name.'

'Sorry, Prakash, but I promise to see your show.' The crowd has started moving into the auditorium. Janaki shuffles after it. Back in her seat she glances at Prakash. He looks crestfallen. 'Don't let it get you down,' she says kindly. 'Today's big names had a pretty rough time before it got better.'

'It was different then,' Prakash says shaking his head. 'We are under pressures that they knew nothing of. Let it go. We'll meet later.'

Pancholi invites Sadashiv Bapat to present his thoughts on art and how they are reflected in his work. As he rises, he begins to swell and colour. His body sparks with an electric charge. He finds it difficult to keep still. He raises his hand dramatically, a sign that he is going to make an important statement.

'I wish to speak today of a quality in art that was once inherent to it but about which now a sepulchral silence prevails. Today the world has turned its face away from that virtue in art, the virtue of *beauty* which is or ought to be the soul of painting. Beauty in art is refinement, compositional unity, rhythm. The root question an artist must ask himself is what is it that art, my art, must give the viewer? For the last fifty-five years we have been running amok like wild horses reined in by neither thought nor skill. I believe it is called multiculturalism. We have been trying to liberate ourselves from the true responsibility of the artist by raising slogans of freedom of expression. Artists, critics, collectors, art merchants are all complicit in this plot. That is why the vital link between art and the lay people sitting before us today has snapped. We are hacking away brutally at our old, integrated, harmonious cultural dialogue. The first to bring the axe down on our art traditions were those artists of the fifties who went by the name of the Progressive Group and looked to the West for scraps of praise. They were responsible for infecting our art with mange. We see the litter of that diseased generation all around us today. The worm has eaten into the very heart of who we are. These people have trampled over the glorious legacy of Raja Ravi Varma, the true father of Indian modern art. Please note, I did not say "modern art in India". I said "Indian modern art". He was wise enough to adopt the techniques and materials of Western painting and use them to produce art that sprang from and nourished our emotions, sentiments, culture. But that great artist has been flung on to the scrap heap today. Why? Because he painted for the people—people like you. Because he was popular.

'Have those who fly the flag of modernity ever given serious thought to the word "beauty"? Modernity cannot emerge as a healthy movement if it rejects tradition outright. Real modernity lies in making art that advances and enriches our tradition. A painting should possess the lustre and delicate scent of flowers; it should sing with the ache of a musical phrase; it should have the simplicity of women's songs and the vivid colour of the rangoli patterns they make in their courtyards. Such a painting and only such a painting can serve the ultimate purpose of art. That purpose is to give the viewer the experience of sublime beauty. These are my thoughts on art and this the purpose of my art.'

Sadashiv Bapat's light-skinned face, red when he started, has simmered down to shades of pink. He casts a glance of intense pride at his acolytes in the audience. He raises his hand to acknowledge the applause, flicks up the back of his kurta and sits down spaciously in his chair.

A murmur rises in the auditorium. 'How can he say we haven't thought . . .'

'. . . scent of what?'

'He's right. Modern paintings are . . .'

'The colours of rangolis . . . ayyoyyo . . .'

Suresh Pancholi puts up a hand to silence the buzz and invites Ashutosh Sen to speak.

'I'm going to make just a couple of brief points. In my opinion, there are some similarities between the time my generation picked up their brushes in the eighties and the generation that has turned its back on painting today. There was no demand in this country for our art in those days. Similarly there appears to be no demand in our country for the installation and video art that young people are producing today. Our feet were firmly rooted here, but our eyes were fixed on the West as we tried to relate to world art. I see that happening today too. About the charges made against the Progressive Group by the last speaker, I have only this to say. The years in which the Progressive Group was trying to find its language were a time of momentous transition. New paths were being sought in every field. The Bhakra Nangal dam was under construction. Le Corbusier had been invited to design Chandigarh. Bimal Roy's *Do Bigha Zameen* had turned up the exploitative underbelly of our society. A little before that, Uday Shankar had made *Kalpana*, the film that gave dance a new language and status. The Progressives faced the challenges of the times and in many ways cleared the path for us who came later. In Bengal where I belong, Abanindranath Tagore and Jamini Roy had represented the two sides of the "genuine" Indian coin. But it was not a currency that was available to us. We couldn't find ourselves in their work. I would like to assert that none of us rejected tradition. We merely moved it out of sight for a while to see ahead a little more clearly. We needed to destroy in order to make. This is true of all creative work. The artist stretches himself to almost breaking point to go beyond what is known and done. It is only when he does so that he is in a position to look back and examine what he has left behind, the traditions of art that took birth, grew and declined in this soil and the new traditions that are about to be born. He is in a position then to search for and determine his own creative space between then and now.

'This calls for continuous effort. It cannot be a one- or two-day affair. It is an effort that occupies an artist's entire life. My generation dived into these choppy waters. Some reached golden shores. Some continued to struggle. Some moved into the shallows and compromised. Some simply put down their tools. The challenge we faced was not only about art or the need to connect with society. It was about moulding the way society looked at art. It was a society to which only realism was acceptable, the mode of art that had been inflicted on us by the British but which had already become stale when they left. The middle class refused to recognize what we were doing as art. We received nothing but ridicule from them, our potential public. It was not, in any case, a time when paintings got sold. Recently, when we read with pride about the work of a painter, not amongst us today, being sold for Rs 99 lakh, we needed to remember that the first painting he managed to sell, at the age of thirty-two, had fetched Rs 200. The buyer was not one of us. He was a collector from the West. We also cannot forget that the artist whose works we now claim as Indian was once told his work was not Indian.

'It was for all these reasons that we had to fight to keep our commitment to art and our honour as artists. We did that through mutual understanding and support. We drew our strength not from personal ambition, but from the deepest desire to be part of the change that would soon bring forth a modern India. Nobody can deny the work that my generation has done in this regard.'

Loud applause greets Ashutosh Sen's analysis. During lunch many of the college students go away, but an equal number stays back. The last speaker of the day, Kruttika Jathar, takes the mic after lunch.

'Let me first respond to what Ashutosh Sen has said about the similarities between his times and ours. He is right but only about superficial similarities. The goals of modernism are now history. He spoke of Le Corbusier's Chandigarh. Today we see it as deadly in its rigid grids, its colourless concrete public buildings and its complete indifference to the human aspects of living. Large dams were once proudly regarded as vital to the development of modern India. Today's thinkers are proposing other, more sustainable models of development. Big dams have submerged acres of land belonging to already-dispossessed adivasis. In a country where blood is shed over temples that were razed 700 years ago by alien forces, there is no outcry when adivasi gods are submerged by dam waters. These are our people, the original inhabitants of this land. When we drown their culture, their livelihood and their community life with impunity under the glorious name of development, it is then we know to whom this land really belongs.'

Sadashiv Bapat suddenly explodes. 'Why are you dragging politics on to this platform? I thought we were here to talk about art!' A stunned silence settles on the audience, punctuated by a few sniggers. Four hands go up as Kruttika attempts to close her jaw fallen with shock at the interruption. Pancholi signals to the audience for silence and nods to Kruttika to proceed.

Kruttika does so with a crooked smile. 'I was trying to analyse the context in which I and my colleagues are working. Today that context is predominantly political. Painters of Mr Bapat's school of thought revile the work of painters of Mr Sen's school of thought. But their works are similar in a major respect. They paint on canvas. They may argue about the purpose and principles of art, but they have no quarrel over the tools of art. Between us and both their schools there can be no dialogue at all because we have rejected canvas, paper and the picture frame itself. Mr Bapat's interruption is proof of the breakdown of dialogue between us and painters of his persuasion. They do not concede to politics a place in art whereas our works are themselves political statements. To reject the picture frame is not a whim. It is a political statement. In doing so, we are returning more genuinely than Mr Bapat can conceive of, to the traditions of our ancient artists. They didn't hang their works in art galleries. Their art was in public places. Temples. We look to museums for patronage because they are our public places. We wish to raise questions directly with the larger public about the world we live in. We might use everyday objects to raise these questions or the new media that have entered all our lives. But the tragedy is that the public whom we address through our work cannot see our work because museums don't buy our art. Instead, our works are displayed in countries which have nothing to lose or gain by the problems of our world. They display our art because they have the money and a tradition of promoting the new. We also have money. But our society promotes those who look back and walk along old tracks. Our society frowns on those who look for new paths. Our society makes traditional foods in microwave ovens and eats them with relish because human taste buds are not mediated by the human mind or social consciousness. The public has fallen into the decadent habit of pleasuring itself sensuously and emotionally. Because it is moved by beautiful musical phrases, pretty colours and honey-sweet voices, it patronizes artists whose paint brushes dip into the same rut.

'Our parents are part of this public. They defend their high-flying sons' and daughters' decision to live and work in America with the excuse, "Where is the scope here?" But they expect artists to live here flying the flag of Indianness and creating moth-eaten art. This changes when we are invited abroad. Then suddenly our work gains value. Not a single one of our parents has bothered to ask why we do what we do. How then can we expect you, the public, to do so?'

Kruttika returns to her seat. Her group and many of the college students applaud. So do Ashesh, Anima and a few other artists. It is time now for the invited artists on the floor to respond. Pancholi calls first upon Ashesh to speak. 'We are running out of time so this will be the only response from an artist before we throw the discussion open to the floor. Ashesh Joshi is not known to say much in public. Those who know him will be surprised that he has agreed to speak here.'

Ashesh stands up, studies the lines on his right palm, takes a deep breath, looks up and begins. 'A point was raised earlier about beauty. The idea of beauty has been of deep concern to philosophers in the East and the West. Although the art of the East is different from the art of the West, philosophers from both worlds have linked the idea of beauty with the idea of truth. We use the word beauty very loosely. We define it as a quality that pleases the senses. By that definition truth is not beautiful.

'The other word we tend to use loosely is modernity. We must guard against confusing this term with modernism. Democracy, a scientific temper, tolerance, liberalism, freedom of thought, equality, human rights, et cetera are expressions of modernity. As I see it, these are at the root of the work that Ms Jathar and her colleagues are doing. Modernism, as practised by Le Corbusier, belonged to a certain historical time and receded with that time. But while rejecting modernism as an outdated aesthetic, we cannot reject the works that modernists produced. They have contributed enormously to our culture.

'Lastly, I wish to make a statement about the responsibility of the artist. A single line from the *Dnyaneshwari* puts it succinctly: "Our dialogue is with ourselves." We forget our responsibility when we conduct a dialogue with the market and copy ourselves to keep our place there. This risk can present itself to the artist at any point of time in his career. He must see the risk and be prepared to question himself all over again. Who am I today? What do I want to say today? Do I have the language and the tools to say it? If his answers to these questions suggest a new path, he must have the courage to follow it. To do that is to be an artist.'

The floor now explodes with questions and opinions. Pancholi finds it difficult to control the transactions that follow. He allows the audience and artists to address each other without mediation till finally he calls for silence. 'We have crossed our time limit long ago and we must stop this discussion here. The organizer has requested me to sum up the day's discussions. I shall try to do so as briefly as I can.

'Two main schools of thought have emerged today. One sees art as a part of history, in conversation with the prevailing sociopolitical conditions. The other sees art as timeless and universal in its practice and purpose. That both these streams flow side by side, tells us once again that we are a society that lives in many ages and at many levels. In our history of several thousand years, many alien powers marched into the land and ruled over it. We marched into each other's kingdoms and ruled over them. The borders of culture are porous. If the West had not received the idea of zero from us through Arab scholars, they would not have made the technological progress they did. Cultural pride and the national ego should not be allowed to obstruct the give and take of new ideas. We must define ourselves by how we use what we take from others. In the old days under royal patronage, artists were obliged to flatter kings in their work. Today the artist faces the public, its new patron. How she or he deals with this relationship is for every artist to decide. In the course of this discussion, we have seen the different ways in which they do so.

'This seminar was intended to be a forum for the expression of multiple views on art. It is for you, the audience, to decide what the discussion has given you. On behalf of Mr Vikram Shah, I thank today's speakers and this remarkable audience that has sat patiently through the discussion and responded so enthusiastically with questions and comments. Thank you.'

As people pour out of the auditorium, they gather once again in groups. Bapat breaks into Ashesh's group to say, 'The point you made about beauty is unarguable. We must talk about beauty at leisure some day. May I introduce my student Abhijeet? He's not exactly a student. He comes and sits in my studio, tries to understand my ideas, thinks about them for himself. He does good work. I'd like you to see it some day. He needs guidance. Only a thinking artist like you can give him that. After all I am a traditionalist. Only the common man likes my work. It will always be ignored by critics.'

Abhijeet squirms. 'Why do you say that, sir? I am so grateful for your guidance. You know that, sir.'

'You will continue to get my guidance. But for the first time you have attended an important seminar. You heard many opinions. You are young. Your mind is bound to be stirred.'

'No, sir. I see my future in following your path.'

Bapat executes a modest smile, reassured. Ashesh has not said a word. Bapat lifts his hand in farewell and moves on, his hand resting in fatherly fashion on Abhijeet's shoulder.

'What was all that about?' Anima asks. Ashesh shrugs.

'Never mind. What are we doing now? I'm not interested in Mr Shah's cocktails and dinner.'

'Let's go to the Udipi's. Feroze said he'll join us.' Anima looks at Janaki. Prakash is hovering behind her. Deeply embarrassed, she introduces him to Ashesh. 'Prakash would like to show you his work some day.'

Ashesh, liking Janaki's husky voice, says, 'Certainly. Any time.'

Prakash is encouraged. 'I was wondering . . . I mean if there's nothing private . . . in the sense all these things we heard, I'm confused . . . could I ask . . . I mean while things are still fresh in my mind?'

'We are about to have a snack-dinner. Do you want to join us? But I only listen. I don't give advice.'

'I'm so sorry.' Janaki is now totally crushed with embarrassment. 'I didn't mean to inflict . . .' But how can she complete the sentence when Prakash is right there. Just then Feroze, who's been talking to the senior queen, hurries over. 'Saala Ashesh, you spoke today. We must celebrate. I'll stand you bun-maska.' He slaps Ashesh on the back. Feroze has never grown a moustache. But looking at him, Anima thinks a moustache would make a perfect line between his hooked nose and his well-shaped upper lip. Feroze turns to Prakash. 'I don't know you; but Sumitraben wants you to call her. Here's her card.'

Prakash falls into a state of total confusion. He doesn't know what to do with the card that's been thrust into his hand. He changes hands then changes them again. The card falls. He picks it up. He looks at Feroze, stutters for a while, then asks, 'Who's she?'

'It's on the card. Now put the card in your pocket,' Anima suggests softly. Prakash stuffs the card in his pocket without reading the name. They look at him. 'I don't know her,' he explains.

'You will. Just call her. Don't worry. She is a dedicated patron of promising new talent. She'll ensure your future. Call her without fear. Who's for bun-maska?'

'We're going to the Udipi's. You're coming with us,' Anima says firmly.

'Udipi? Boring. But in a democracy . . .'

The procession of five sets off. At the Udipi's they have idli, dosa, vada, sambar and an incendiary chutney along with Prakash's confusions. While everyone eats, Prakash stumbles over the critical crossroads he finds himself at, now that he is out of art school and in the big, wide world of art. He is particularly disturbed by what Kruttika has said. If this is what young artists are doing, or are supposed to do, how can he continue to paint?

Feroze sighs. 'Confusion is an artist's permanent condition. We are always standing at a crossroads. Right, Ashesh?'

Prakash is silent for a moment. 'But I have only just started painting. How can I start doing video art and all? Won't I need special training for that?'

'Why should you do video art? Just paint.'

'But what about the political context and all that? I don't think about politics much. I've never thought of painting like that.'

'Forget all that. Do what you most feel like doing. Your paintings must be your truth. Nobody else besides you has experienced that. Just look into yourself and believe what comes out of there.' Feroze has had his say. Prakash swallows.

A silence falls on the table, shredded only by the waiters' shouted orders. Anima has been watching Feroze with some admiration. This man's goodness of heart is infinite. Janaki turns to Ashesh. She has been waiting to say something to him. His eyes turn towards her at the same time and an unexpected spark passes between them. Ashesh looks away and Janaki bends her head to gaze at the lemon-coloured laminate of the table. When the waiter brings the bill, Ashesh puts his hand over it. A sharp desire to place her hand over his leaps in Janaki's heart. She makes herself turn towards Prakash who is saying, 'But that will be even more difficult for me, sir. To look inside me . . . How do I do that? And how will that tell me about painting? I once tried to meditate. They say that's how you can reach into yourself. I'm not sure if I reached in but nothing came from inside. It was all dark.'

Feroze is exhausted. He nods to get through this one. But Prakash's eyes are still fixed on him, full of faith and hope. Janaki would like to be swallowed by a dark pit. 'Please, Prakash,' she begins. 'No, no, that's all right.' The milk of human kindness spurts once again in Feroze's heart. Ashesh eyes him with amusement. 'What our young friend says is right. When you enter a dark room all you can see at first is darkness. But when you stay put, you begin to see lines and forms and shades. Darkness has many shades. Ask Ashesh how often we've found ourselves thrashing around in the dark.'

'Still doing it,' Ashesh smiles ruefully. The waiter brings the change. 'What's this? It was supposed to be my treat.'

'Next time.' There's quiet mischief in Ashesh's tone. His quietness tugs Janaki's eyes back to him. 'Let's go,' he says. 'Each one to his own darkness.'

Janaki quickly blurts out what's been on her mind. 'I've recorded what you said back then. I hope you don't mind.'

'Recorded? No, why would I?'

'I might want to quote you later. I'll call to take your permission.'

'Good heavens, such conscientiousness! Journalists don't do that kind of thing.'

Ashesh's eyes shine with mischief. Janaki's eyes respond warmly. Their eyes remain connected for a while.

'Come on, get up,' Anima calls. 'They'll sweep us out with the crumbs. Udipis are Punekars in spirit. The only difference is they don't put up signboards saying, "No chatting at tables. Eat and quit."'

As they rise, Prakash dives unexpectedly at Feroze's feet. Feroze nearly trips as he moves back. 'Please don't ever do that.'

Prakash pleads, 'Please, sir, let me do this much. You are such a big artist but you gave your time to a small man like me. Your advice . . .'

'Advice? You're a fellow artist, damn it . . . I was only sharing experiences.' Feroze is still moving backwards. Anima puts her hand out just in time to save him from falling off the edge of the pavement. 'Mr Jadhav, please don't . . .' Anima begins, but meanwhile Sanjay has brought Feroze's car around and Feroze is making a run for it without pausing to ask, as he normally would, 'Lift, anybody?'

15

Just as Bachchu Kaka is entering Home on one of his routine visits, Dr Bhaskar is coming out. They greet each other warily. Dr Bhaskar had left India for postgraduate studies in the USA when he was twenty-four and stayed on afterwards. He lived in American style—spacious house, two cars in the garage, front garden, mowing the lawn on Sundays. But he also worshipped his motherland. So, while he made money hand over fist in his adopted country, he sent a percentage of it every month to a volunteer organization in Thane district which was working amongst adivasis, or as his cultural organization preferred to call them, vanavasis. In this he was following his revered guru's orders.

This much of Dr Bhaskar's history is general knowledge. What Bachchu Kaka would like to find out is why he suddenly decided to return to his motherland. His declaration that it was to enable him to take care of his ageing parents and also provide free health care to the poor of the district must be a cover-up. Question two. Why, being an allopath, does he prescribe only roots and herbs to his poor ill brothers? The question etches itself on Bachchu Kaka's face each time he sees the doctor.

'If you're looking for Sindhutai, you'll have to wait. She's just gone for her bath,' Bhaskar says as he walks out of the gate. Bachchu Kaka wonders at the intimacy of the tone as he watches the doctor's straight, slim back disappear down the dusty road. Frowning slightly, he walks slowly into the compound and settles down on the bench in the krishnakamal arbour. A memory has begun to stir at the back of his mind which embarrasses him.

Shankar and Sindhutai had just shifted into Home. Sindhutai had been deeply upset about entering the new house without performing the griha puja and Shankar going away on work soon after. When Bachchu Kaka dropped in on a routine visit, she had burst into tears. 'He goes away for days at a time. It's just me and these two little ones. What use are the Warli servants? And the townspeople won't look our way. If something evil happens who will . . .'

'What evil do you think is going to happen?'

'Anything can. We didn't appease the land before building on it, and we haven't appeased the spirits of the house before entering it.'

At that very moment, something had crashed in the kitchen with a loud clatter. Startled, Sindhutai had gripped his arm. At first it was the grip of a frightened woman. But as the echoes of the crash faded, his body was responding to it very differently. For a split second, she was female and he male. But before Sindhutai sensed the change, he had freed his arm and was hurrying away, only saying as he left, 'There's no need to feel scared. We're all here for you.'

This was the first time Bachchu Kaka had realized that even his body, controlled as it was by his mind, could unexpectedly do something independent of it. Or perhaps the first time he admitted to himself that it did and that it had its own needs. That might have been why he allowed his friendship with the land-reform activist Saguna Rao to go its natural way. Their enormous respect for each other's work, commitment and integrity had prompted them to confine their relationship to friendly meetings whenever they could spare the time from work. Then they were taking time off to travel together. Soon they were eating and sleeping together.

One such night was to be the last time Bachchu Kaka saw Saguna Rao alive. She was murdered the day after. The builder-developer who had been grabbing adivasi land for years had begun to find the court case she had filed against him too bothersome. He had enough clout in that part of Thane district to have her killed and to ensure that the land-grab case against him lingered in police files till it died a natural death. Saguna Rao's murderers were never traced.

For a month after her murder, Bachchu Kaka had locked himself away in his room. Only Anna was allowed in. When he emerged from this period of intense mourning, he had put behind him the most joyous time of his life.

Sitting under the krishnakamal creeper now, Bachchu Kaka recalls the mornings when he and Shankar would sit together on this bench having a late-morning cup of tea. Before him is the Gandhi mandir that Shankar had so lovingly built. It is a small, shoulder-high cube topped by a chhatri, with four niches in each side containing the Bhagwad Gita, the Quran, the Bible and the Granth Sahib. When Ashesh's friend Feroze had visited Surgaon he had asked in mock anger, 'And where is our Avestha, hunh? Our Dadabhai Naoroji worked with Gandhi, and no Avestha in Gandhi mandir?'

Where's Gandhi now, Bachchu Kaka thinks. Great men are great in their times, made great by their times. The poet Mardhekar hoped:

'Let another age pass and another Mahatma be born.' But such a hope is futile, a sign of weak minds. Gandhi gave the nation a dream that was born of his times. He gave them the weapon of peaceful resistance which he was shrewd enough to see would work with the British at that moment of time. There was only one dream that the nation could have at the time, the overthrow of one single enemy. No man, however great, can give this country of disparities a single dream today, not even a Gandhi reborn. And yet, for forty years after his going, his followers had lived with the idiotic conviction that he had bequeathed us a nation founded on peace, equality and communal tolerance. They did not possess the eyes to see what actually lay underfoot, nor the ears to hear the furious bubbling of hatred, envy and lust for power that lay just below the surface. When the volcano erupted, snapping them out of their rosy dream, all they could say was: 'This is not the land of Gandhi.' These people should have taken the other line of Mardhekar's more seriously.

We must see ourselves once more
With our glasses off our noses.

It was too late for some to take off their glasses then. So they kept them on and continued to walk the mouldy rut they had made for themselves. Some dusted the mould off and stood up to confront the newly revealed forces. Some went with the wind. A few true idealists like Shankar were shattered. The last dyke in his mind to spring a hole must have been Siddharth's murder. It was surely not a coincidence that he disappeared within two months of that tragedy. A lump rises to Bachchu Kaka's throat.

Sindhutai comes out of the house to pluck flowers for her puja, catches sight of Bachchu Kaka and halts on the veranda, taken aback. Recovering, she laughs and says, 'Where were you all these days? It's like the sun rising in the west. Would you like to come in? I'll make tea.'

'No thanks. It's lovely out here.'

Sindhutai comes down the steps and begins to pluck mogras, which are in full bloom now. Without looking at Bachchu Kaka, she asks casually, 'Been to Mumbai recently?'

'A while ago.'

'Did you meet Ashesh–Nima?'

'No. Went in the morning, back in the evening. I'll meet them on the next trip. Why?'

'Oh nothing. Anima was here. She didn't mention you, so I thought she'd forgotten. You go every month, don't you?'

'Can't do that now. Also there's less work.'

Sindhutai's little basket is filled with flowers. 'Why don't you come in? It'll get quite hot out here.'

'I'm a man of the sun. I'm not afraid of its heat. I'm more afraid of people.'

'I too. You never know when people will betray you. They disappear on a whim. No worry or concern for those they leave behind.'

'That's not true, Sindhutai. Shankar was more than concerned. He practically forced you to sign for a joint account so he could put everything he had into it.'

'Only money. What about loneliness? Does money make that go away?'

Bachchu Kaka has no answer. He sits looking glumly at the Gandhi mandir. The early morning sun shows up the fine spiderweb that is strung across the niche in front of him, making it shimmer. 'The mandir looks uncared for.'

'Who's to care for it with Rama gone?' Sindhutai demands angrily.

A light breeze blows an old, dry leaf off the peepul tree. It drifts down to rest on Bachchu Kaka's lap. He stares at it for a while, then sets it down beside him on the bench. He gets up, takes the handkerchief from his pocket and gently winds the spiderweb around it. Sindhutai watches him with cold eyes as he does the same with the other three niches. He picks up the holy books one by one and wipes the dust off their covers.

'Why this sudden love for holy books in the atheist's heart?'

'My friend wasn't an atheist. The love is for him. Why has Rama stopped coming?'

'You know the answer.'

'How would I know?'

'Because you have informers all over the padas.'

'I hardly go there any more. Others have entered the field.'

'You may not go to the padas, but the padas come to you.'

'Your network of informers seems to be stronger than mine. But never mind. My informer told me Dr Bhaskar abused Rama.'

'That's an outright lie.'

'That's why I asked you for the true reason.'

'Rama is old. Probably just a few years younger than *him*. He would have been eighty this year.'

'Will still be.'

'You call yourself a rationalist . . .'

'I believe what I see. I will say Shankar is gone when I see his body. Till then he is somewhere. So Dr Bhaskar didn't find Rama a nuisance? Rama's devotion to Shankar wasn't becoming bothersome? He didn't abuse him in order to provoke him to leave?'

'How would this nothing creature, this misnamed Rama, come in the way of Dr Bhaskar's work? He went because he's old.'

'Did he tell you that?'

'Why should I bother to even ask him? If a Warli doesn't want to talk he doesn't. The day after he left, Dr Bhaskar brought two Warlis in his place.'

'Then why does the Gandhi mandir look like this?'

Sindhutai clamps her lips tight.

'Never mind. May I take these books?'

'No need. Nima will take them. I don't have the strength now to look after this sprawl.'

Sindhutai looks defiantly at Bachchu Kaka. Bachchu Kaka shows no reaction. 'Please give a thought to just one thing, Sindhutai,' he says as he gets up wearily. 'Consider it my request. Just remember all those families who rejected your marriage proposal because you were born under Mars. It's not a harmless belief system.'

Sindhutai's face is aflame. 'Sure, sure. Your friend did me a big favour by marrying me despite Mars. But he abandoned me too. His belief system wasn't harmless either. Whatever you may say, today I have a life because of Dr Bhaskar.'

Bachchu Kaka shakes his head. 'I've done my duty by warning you. It's up to you to think about it.'

Bachchu Kaka leaves on tired legs.

16

Feroze has sent his car for Anima. 'Why send it all the way? I'll hop into the local train and zip down there in no time,' she had protested. He said, 'You're coming for my work. I will send you the car.' That was it.

Sanjay calls to say the car's there. She is wearing a white and green Pochampalli that Siddharth had given her years ago. She picks up her handbag, slips her feet into her chappals and is about to leave when she suddenly thinks how hot it is. May heat. The sky broods sullenly over the city, hinting at rain which is still a month away. Anima runs into her room and tears the Pochampalli off. Leaving the sari in a heap on the bed, she gets into a light handloom salwar kameez. 'Phew! That's better.' Long live the salwar kameez. Siddharth has not seen her in these togs. When he was alive she wore saris to look beautiful and trousers for convenience. He used to call the salwar kameez a 'messy muddle'.

As always, when she leaves the house, she remembers the routine of early days when Anisa lived across the landing. She would leave the house key with her when Siddharth was on shore duty because you never knew when he would return from work. When she suggested he carry his own key, his face would look like she had asked him to climb Mount Everest without oxygen. A man who regularly carried thousands in his wallet found a key too heavy to carry. In Surgaon the doors of his house were kept wide open in the day. He had never outlived the habit. Should she have recognized it as a sign when he had volunteered

CROWFALL   111

to carry his key that day? He had winked mischievously at the sight of
her astonished face. He had not needed it that day.

Down on the road, Anima can't see Sanjay anywhere. The five
o'clock sun pierces her eyeballs. She shades her eyes. There he is, right
across the road, smiling, holding the car door open for her.

'What's the news on your jhopdi, Sanjay?' Anima asks as soon as
she settles down. Giving her a deep-dimpled smile in the rear-view
mirror, he says, 'I've built it.'

She gapes at him in the mirror.

'I got the money, bought the stuff and built it overnight. Sunday.'

Sanjay had bought a plot of land in the marshland on the east side of
the city where once salt pans had existed. The political party in power
in the municipal corporation had advised its corporators to encourage
a few prospective voters to reclaim the marsh and build their homes on
it for free. Once a few shanties went up, others were bound to crowd
in like ants around jaggery. These new settlers had to pay the party
ten thousand rupees per plot. Including bribes to the police and to the
municipality for electricity and water connections, every family that
wanted shelter had to raise roughly forty thousand rupees, plus costs for
four truckloads of debris to reclaim the plot and building materials. The
shanties had to be built overnight. The bribed municipal workers and
police would find it difficult to turn a blind eye to the illegal building
work if they saw it in bright daylight. Once a shanty was built, it became
a fait accompli. Nobody could touch it after that. The task was beyond
anybody's capacity to complete single-handedly. It was therefore an
unwritten rule in the community that the older residents would turn
up in full force to help new settlers. A cousin of Sanjay's had persuaded
him to buy a plot and Sanjay had put all his savings into it. He had
needed twenty thousand more for bricks and bribes.

'So where did you find the money in the end?' Anima asks anxiously.

Sanjay grins widely. 'Sahib gave it.'

Anima is relieved, but also sad. Poor Feroze of Altamount Road. He
had been shocked out of his wits to hear about the marshland housing
scheme. 'I could give you twenty thousand this minute,' he had said,

shaking his head when Sanjay had asked him for a loan. 'But this is illegal. This is corruption. We shouldn't be part of it. You don't lack anything here. Stay on, no problem.'

Blushing up to his hairline, Sanjay had confessed that he was getting married. How could he continue staying in the garage with his bride? 'Good, good. Getting married. That's good.' Feroze was thrilled. 'Then why an illegal jhopdi? We'll get you a pucca room. Legal.'

Feroze went into rapid inquiry mode. A brick-and-mortar room in a legal block out in Kandivali would cost three and a half lakh rupees. Feroze didn't have that kind of liquid cash to give. But they could apply for a partial loan from a bank. But no bank would give a home loan to anybody who could not produce a 'salary slip'. Feroze told his bank he would give Sanjay salary slips for every month of the seven years he had worked for him and stand guarantee that he would repay the loan promptly every month. He was told that would not do. Feroze was neither a company nor an establishment. He was a mere individual. Neither his word, his guarantee, nor his salary slips held any value for banks.

Feroze applied to his banker friends for help. They too confessed helplessness in helping Sanjay. By now Sanjay was feeling sorry for his sahib. 'Don't worry,' he said to Feroze. 'I'll manage.' He had planned to borrow from a moneylender.

'Sahib knew that borrowing from a moneylender meant a lifetime of paying back, Tai.' Sanjay smiles wryly. 'He was very upset. One day he said, "If an honest man like you can't get a loan for a legal house, I'll give you a loan for an illegal house." He gave me the money there and then, Tai, interest free. It was sad for him. But I have a room. I needed only two truckloads of debris. Ten neighbours helped.'

'So the bride will come into a spanking new home.' Anima smiles. 'Have you found one?'

Sanjay ducks his head shyly and grins, fit to split his face.

The car winds uphill to Altamount Road and turns in at the wide gates of Windermere. The gulmohrs along the drive have shed every leaf but are thick with flowers. As Anima steps out of the air-conditioned car, the afternoon slaps her like a blanket steamed in a furnace. She stands still for a while with the red-hot gulmohr burning into her eyes. 'Please enter, your ladyship,' Feroze calls out from the bay window on the ground floor. He opens the door himself. Behind him stands a smiling Jijabhau, hands folded in a namaskar.

'How're things in Chakan?' Anima asks him as she enters.

'Everything's fine by Lord Vitthal's grace,' Jijabhau answers, his smile widening.

As soon as Feroze and she have settled down, Jijabhau comes in carrying a tray of nankhatai biscuits and patrel. Tea will follow. On a side table sit eleven fat volumes of the unabridged Mahabharata translated into Marathi. Feroze picks up the volume on top, opens it at a flagged page and says, 'This is where I want you to start reading.' After a pause he half closes his eyes and says, 'I'm planning something really big. Something I've never attempted before.'

Anima looks at the page he has opened. It's in the sixteenth book of the Mahabharata. She weighs the volume in her hands. She must read slowly and clearly because Feroze's acquaintance with Marathi is casual. They drink their tea first, wordlessly. The tea at Feroze's house is flavoured with lemon grass. Anima doesn't always enjoy it. But it seems pleasant enough on this hot and humid afternoon. She does not have a nankhatai or a patrel, nor does Feroze. Both have a sense of urgency, knowing they are about to start on something solemn and significant.

'I don't want the entire thing read,' Feroze instructs her as she glances over the page. 'I know what happens. The events. What I want to hear are the descriptions. Of all those omens that foretell the end. What Yudhishthir saw, what the people of Dwarka saw—all the colours, the sound, the magic.'

Anima begins to read.

In this way the Vrishni and Andhak clans made attempts to turn away the great calamity that was about to strike them. But even as they were doing so, Death was visiting their homes. His visage was terrifying and his accoutrements menacing. His body was black and bloodless. He would appear in the homes of the Vrishnis to observe them and disappear as suddenly as he came. The moment they spotted him, the finest archers of the land would send a shower of arrows in his direction. But he, who had the power to destroy the entire human race, was hardly going to be destroyed by their arrows.

Now, every day, terrifying storms blew that made people's hair stand on end. They heralded the annihilation of the Andhak and Vrishni clans. Rats multiplied in such numbers that they spilled on to the streets and ran amok. They made holes in cooking pots and nibbled away hair and nails as people slept. Mynahs screeched in Vrishni homes without a second's peace, having forgotten their honeyed call. Under the influence of Death, white-winged pigeons with red claws flitted in and out of Andhak homes. Cows began giving birth to asses, mules to elephants and dogs to cats . . .

Feroze's face is still with intense thought. His eyes are closed. 'Yes please. Go on.'

The Lord of Fire began whirling his flames in fury. Sparks flew from them, sometimes blue, sometimes red, sometimes purple. The finest and cleanest food cooked in the kitchens would come alive with millions of maggots even as it was served. When the holy men of the land sat reading from the scriptures, people would hear the sound of invisible feet, running hither and thither.

Feroze's fingers are tapping out a light rhythm on his knee. Anima stops reading. 'That's the end of the ill omens. The next bit is dreams. You want them?'

Feroze shakes his head without opening his eyes. He is no longer listening to the meanings of words. He is listening to their sound, to the form and colour of the sound. 'Go to the disarming of Krishna.'

One day the Sudarshan chakra, gifted to Krishna by the Lord of Fire himself, flew out of his hand into space before the very eyes of the people. The four incomparable steeds that drew his dazzling chariot also bucked suddenly and galloped right over the ocean and disappeared, carrying the chariot with them. Two flag posts, Taal and Suparna, most sacred to Krishna and Balaram, were also lifted straight out of the earth and carried away into nothingness by heavenly beings.

'Krishna's rage and annihilation, please.'

When Krishna saw that Sattyaki and his son had been killed, he was filled with rage. He uprooted a clump of grass. It turned into a massive iron pestle. Using the pestle, Krishna began to kill everybody in sight. Then the men of the Vrishni, Andhak, Bhoj and Shaineya clans began killing each other with iron pestles. Sons killed fathers and fathers killed sons.

Intoxicated with liquor, none of them had enough reason left in them to ask why and whom they were killing. They fell upon each other like moths on fire, unable in their inebriated state even to run away from the blows. Knowing this to be a sign of the wheel of time spinning backwards, the powerful Krishna attempted to intercept the pestles that flew thick and fast around him, but in vain. In that chaos, Samb, Charudeshna, Pradyumna and Aniruddha also fell, enraging Krishna again. His rage became uncontrollable when he saw Gud fall. Then he himself killed those that remained. Babhru and Daruk said to him, 'Lord, you have killed everybody now. Let us see where Balaram is.'

'I can see Balaram so vividly,' Feroze mutters. 'He sits under a tree, deep in meditation. Out of his mouth emerges a white, thousand-headed serpent, as large as a mountain. In a trice Balaram melts into thin air and Sheshnag disappears into the ocean. This is so fascinating. The serpent emerges from Balaram and Balaram is the serpent.'

Anima sits absolutely still. She sees Krishna before her, now all alone. His death has been foretold. Only the prediction remains to be fulfilled. It is a moment of waiting. What goes on in his mind in that brief time between life and death? Turmoil? Regret? Grief? Fulfilment? What is he just then? Man or God? The great poet Vyas is silent on this. But it is this moment, empty but potentially packed with drama, that invites the artist to fill it in with his imagination.

Feroze says without opening his eyes, 'Yes, this is beautiful. The silence after the massacre. In time there will be colour again and the world will fill with the strange and terrible sounds of a new beginning.'

Feroze opens his eyes. 'You remember *Macbeth*, Anima? Before Macbeth commits his ungodly deed, an eagle, soaring high in the sky, is swallowed up by an owl. The king's horses break their tethers and run amok. That's it. No more signs of what is to come. Perhaps two ill omens suffice in that cold and grey land. But look what we have here. A bounty of inauspicious signs. I want to make it all happen on my canvas. If I can. I am so grateful to you, dear heart, for bringing the whole thing alive.'

Feroze says nothing for a long time, his gaze far away.

'Shall I leave?' Anima asks softly.

'What? Leave? No. Wait a bit.'

Something stirs in the dark at the back of the room. Jijabhau turns on the lights.

Anima is startled. 'Were you here all this time?'

He nods. 'I have never heard this story of Krishna. We always hear about Radha and the milkmaids.'

Anima notices that Feroze's eyes have become unfocused. He will not speak now. He will continue looking at her without seeing her. He will continue to smile this smile. He will shift an object from here to there without intention, and then from there to here. But he will not bring himself to say he wants to be alone.

Anima picks up her handbag. 'Shall I tell you how I feel?'

'How?' Feroze pretends interest.

'Like a man must feel once the seed is sown. The woman's body will now go to work on it, exiling him from the magic of creation. I'll be off.' Feroze protests, but weakly. He gets up from his chair to see her out. Sanjay is waiting outside. She signals him to drive down to the gate. Feroze's gardener has just watered the plants. She fills her lungs with the fragrance of warm, wet earth as she walks slowly to the gate, the pebbles under her feet crunching with every step. She leaves behind her the unnatural happenings of the Book of Pestles. Out here, at least for the present, the gulmohr bears gulmohr flowers and the mango tree, mangoes.

17

Ashesh puts the last mark on the fourth painting in his Artists series. All four are the same size, rectangles of one and a half by two feet. Each carries a hint of a lively new colour amidst the browns, dirty greens and blue-blacks of his regular palette. There's golden yellow, kumkum red and turquoise—the favourite colours of the old miniature painters, made from leaves, flowers, fruits and stones.

The series had come to him as a seed idea a year ago. His old school friend, Vasant Gupte, had gone away to America after college to study business management and never returned. He had found a job there, married, had children, got promotions, become vice president of a multinational corporation and been recently appointed head of the South Asia region, which involved making frequent visits to Mumbai. It was on one of these visits, when he had stopped over for just one day on his way to Colombo, that he had called. 'Come to the office. We'll have lunch together.'

Ashesh had put away all work and headed for Churchgate. Vasant was still in a pre-lunch meeting when he arrived. He had waited in the anteroom to his cabin, happy to let his thoughts wander. Vasant's secretary cast a sideways glance at him. Ashesh was not occupying himself with anything. He hadn't picked up a magazine from the stack on the side table. He wasn't speaking on his cell phone. He was just sitting there, urgently in need of entertainment. Vasant's secretary was glad of the opportunity to provide it.

He cleared his throat and said, 'He's such a fine man—Gupte sir. Brilliant.' Ashesh started and stared. 'He should have been made president of the company long ago. But of course he's an Indian. Americans are pukka racists. Actually, our people are cleverer than any of them. I've heard they can't even spell simple words. And they count on their fingers, it seems.'

Ashesh bore a fixed smile on his face. The secretary changed gears. 'Mumbai's weather has gone to the dogs. Bound to, with slums multiplying.' Once he had shredded slums to his satisfaction, he lowered his voice confidentially and came to the point. 'Sir, I am also an artist, you know. I compose ghazals.' As he let this purring kitten out of his bag, Ashesh had noticed his hand sliding towards the second drawer of his desk. It was a clear sign that Ashesh was going to be subjected to pain-filled love songs. But just then, Vasant had walked out of his cabin. The secretary's hand had dropped to his side as he stood up to attention. Vasant's eyebrows had come together over his nose.

'Sonpatki, how often must I tell you that I'm not the national flag?' Sonpatki had buried his head in his shoulder bone and giggled. 'Can't help it, sir. It is how we are brought up in Bharat.'

'Brought up to lick boots,' Vasant had muttered as they left.

Sonpatki's whispered secret had lingered in Ashesh's mind. The five words—I am also an artist—carried more meaning than their number suggested. Sonpatki was in fact saying, 'I am not a mere yes-sir no-sir man. There's something hidden in me that makes me different from others, something of value. You and I belong together to a very special group of human beings called artists. That is why we recognize each other on sight. The two of us are alike. The only difference is that you exhibit your art, while mine lies hidden in the drawer of my desk.'

Within a few days, the secret ghazal composer had faded from

Ashesh's consciousness. What he had left behind was the idea of the hidden artist revealed in the daily life of those who were not seen as artists. Around this idea had gathered innumerable people he had seen and heard, with skills in their hands, vision in their eyes, music in their throats, that brought joy to the daily struggle of life. He remembered the seller of fresh green gram at whose flamboyantly decorated handcart he had seen a mustachioed police constable aggressively demanding his weekly bribe; the typist outside the post office, whose fingers danced on the keys of the machine till the end of the line, then rose in a graceful parabola after he docked the carrier with a click; Reshma who for years had rolled out chapattis as soft as silk in deft strokes of metrical perfection; and the white-haired, bare-torsoed man he had seen in a crowded neighbourhood of squat cheek-by-jowl buildings, who sat out on the narrow ledge of a dark upstairs room amidst a lifetime's junk, playing an old guitar while the traffic roared by on the street below. These men and women had prompted him to do his Artists series of which he has now completed four works.

Ashesh has time to relax for a bit, read, listen to music, snooze. Perhaps catch a film in the evening. After a leisurely lunch, he stands on the balcony looking out into the midday sun that has robbed the world of colour. A sharp ray of light ricochets off a windowpane across the road and pierces his eye. He shuts his eyes in pain. Behind his eyelids blue and purple shapes swirl, electrified ants run and scatter.

Not a single leaf of the peepul tree stirs. Nothing in Ashesh's mind stirs either, except for the drops of sweat that seem to move sluggishly through the very folds of his brain. He decides to sit under the fan and listen to Siddheshwari Devi. But as he is about to turn indoors, he hears a magnificent voice ringing out from the end of the street. It rings so loud and clear that God in his heaven must hear it too. It is the call of the woman who exchanges brand-new steel utensils for old clothes. 'Bhaand-eeyo,' she calls in a voice purified through rigorous practice, like gold in fire, every note imprinting itself sharply on the air. Starting on 'sa', it moves up the octave to the nishad, gives the note a little vocal click, and feather-touches the dhaivat in a perfectly controlled glissando as she descends to 'sa'.

Ashesh leans over the veranda railing, twisting his neck to get a glimpse of the source. He knows the woman will not enter his street. But he also knows that she will stop briefly at the corner to call once again before moving on. There she is and there is the call again: 'Bhaand-eeyo'.

Her sari is a deep magenta, her blouse pure turmeric. She carries a basket of glinting utensils on her head and a large bundle of old clothes slung over her shoulder. When she turns to face Ashesh's street, her eyes search the upper floors and balconies of the buildings. It is siesta time for homemakers and no answering call comes from them. She turns to move on but stops. Under her feet is a thick scatter of peltophorum blossom. She glances up at the tree from which they have drifted down. Even as she does so, one delicate yellow blossom comes to rest at her feet. Balancing the basket on her head and the bundle on her shoulder, she bends her knees without bending her back, stretches out her arm to the full, picks up the flower, holds it to her nose and walks on. Her call becomes a strong, flexible arc in Ashesh's mind, giving birth to an image which he hastens indoors to sketch. The arc of the woman's call gives shape to her body. A sandy desert stretches to the horizon. Her right hand is raised to her ear. Her basket is in the sand beside her, filled with dazzling utensils that look real enough to touch.

The cartoon for the fifth painting in the Artists series is done.

18

F for Fake
Janaki Patil

It is a well-known fact that the art world is booming. Works by some of India's most reputed painters have been selling in international auctions for unheard-of sums of money. When prices of products soar, fakes are never far behind. This is as true of art products as of any other products. Artists who have acquired high levels of mimic skills rule the fakes market. Choosing high-selling painters with clearly defined signature styles, they produce works so identical in subject matter and style to theirs that the difference might escape even the expert eye.

It is alleged that some collectors and galleries work hand in glove with the copyists, helping to grease their products into the fakes market. The modus operandi goes thus. They buy the fakes at modest prices and sell them at exorbitant sums to the new breed of collectors who buy works as investment with very little interest in or knowledge of art. In a recent event that has caused a major stir in the art world, the original artist has got embroiled in a totally unexpected way in the fakes market. Here is the whole murky tale. Quite appropriately, it happened on All Fools Day.

An acrylic-on-canvas work, *Woman with Flower*, by the prolific and popular painter Ranjan Khanna, was scheduled to go under the hammer at an auction held in Delhi on 1 April. It now transpires that Khanna had himself informed the concerned auction house that the work was a fake. However, the gallery that owned the painting and had now put it up for auction, asserted that they had bought it directly from the artist four years ago, that is, in the year 2000. How then could it be a fake? It was a question that only the artist could have answered. Unfortunately, by a tragic coincidence, he suffered a massive stroke the day after he informed the auction house about the fake and is reported to have lost his speech.

The concerned auction house has stated that it operates under rigorous regulations that do not permit it to sell a work that has come under even the smallest shadow of doubt. Accordingly, they have withdrawn *Woman with Flower* from the auction. However, this does not mean that the work is, in fact, a fake. There is a question mark against it and it now stands in an area of greyness between the artist's word, which has been silenced, and the gallery's, which holds no value without the other.

Jasjit Sandhu, assistant to Khanna till a couple of years ago when the two fell out, said, 'We must have painted at least two or three works with minor differences here and there titled *Woman with Flower*. I seem to remember painting one of these versions entirely on my own. If the gallery happened to have bought that one from Mr Khanna, it was genuine at the time. But Khanna sahib probably regards it as a fake now.' Sandhu sounded amused at the idea. Then he added, 'If Khanna sahib is calling that painting a fake, then he would have to declare all the works he painted till two years ago fake to a greater or lesser degree, because I had a hand in all of them.'

The art world has expressed misgivings at Khanna's revelation. Some artists say he has cut off his nose to spite not only his own face but the face of the art market itself. Hereafter, a collector desirous of buying any works, including Khanna's, will think many times before doing so for fear of discovering it is a fake. It is, after all, the idea of that elusive thing called an 'original' that makes the art market go round.

It is not a secret that popular artists from the last century, like Jamini Roy and Raja Ravi Varma, appointed assistants to help them fulfil the increasing demand for their art, a practice that continues with some leading artists even today. It is also not a secret that these guru–disciple pairs break up at some point owing to ego clashes or differences. However, gurus take great care that the practice is not revealed, particularly since they themselves have trained their disciples to copy their style. Against this background, Ranjan Khanna's act of taking the lid off a carefully maintained silence is likely to create ripples in the art world for some time to come. Every collector will henceforth be besieged by doubts about any work he plans to buy. Was this done by the artist or his assistant?

At a time when artists are making more money than ever before, some of them now find themselves in a situation that is likely to rob them of sleep.

19

Ashesh reads Janaki's article and remembers his quivering hand again. He had met Ranjan Khanna just five months ago on a visit to Delhi. They had had dinner together and talked into the night. Now he was in hospital, unable to speak. Things like that happen without a warning. So if you have had a warning, it's stupid not to heed it. Ashesh's hand had danced that night. That was a sign, surely, that something was wrong? Had Ranjan ignored some small symptom like that? Strokes are said to transmit minor messages before a full-on attack. Perhaps doctors can tell an attack is imminent by the condition of your functions. Or can't they? Anyway, it is finally your life. If you're stupid enough to believe that you're specially protected against disease, you end up in a sweat in the middle of the night and then in hospital. Much smarter to go to the expert at the first symptom and let him assure you you're okay; and if you're not, here's how to stall what's coming.

This is not the time, with black and grey shades whirling around in my mind like dervishes, to take risks. I must get back to that canvas, chase that image that flashed bright and clear out of the darkness and disappeared into it in a blink. I must coax it back. The show's round the corner. There's going to be stress. I have to be totally fit in body and mind. There's this respite now. I must have a full check-up done. But the Padmini is being serviced. So what? Take a bus. Can't wait for everything to come together.

Ashesh calls up his old school friend Haresh Pounda. Haresh says reassuringly, 'What you're describing is probably just an essential tremor. But if you're anxious, come to Lilavati this evening or Jaslok tomorrow morning.'

It is five in the evening. The appointment with Haresh is at six. Ashesh knows it's idiotic to go to him. He's an oncologist. But you want to start with old friends. Wait a moment. Start? What's that supposed to mean? There's going to be nothing after this start. You're only being cautious, because you don't want tremors, essential or otherwise, to get going in the middle of the night.

Ashesh walks round August Kranti Maidan to get to the main road, then turns left and walks briskly towards the bus stop. The sweat, dripping out of his hair on to his neck, trickles down under his shirt collar, tickling his back. Ashesh resists the impulse to wipe it. You start wiping sweat, you can't stop because there's more coming. Everybody has their own technique for dealing with summer heat. Haresh had perfected his, while still at school. He would wear two shirts one over the other when he left home in the morning. When the heat became absolutely unbearable, he would peel the top one off. 'Try it,' he would say. 'It's like switching on the air conditioner.' He would do the same at night. Cover himself with a thick quilt then kick it off. It was all cool inside. 'It's the same theory that keeps water in a clay pot cool.' Not true. But who was going to argue with him?

Waiting at the bus stop, Ashesh fixes his eyes on the sky for somewhere to look. Not a speck of rain cloud. The sky is like a vast tin cauldron inverted overhead while the world below bubbles like a stewpot on the boil. Human bodies, suffocating in its steam, stare open-mouthed at the cruel sky, like a many-headed chatak bird, breathless for rain.

The old man standing beside Ashesh under a large umbrella says aloud, 'In the old days pre-monsoon showers would have fallen by now.' Ashesh glances at him. All shrivelled up, he looks particularly lonely under his large umbrella. If you blew on him, he would waft away. The old man looks Ashesh up and down through the thick lenses of his glasses. 'Are you Marathi or something else?' There's suspicion in his voice.

Ashesh mumbles, 'Marathi,' but warily.

'That's lucky. Mumbai's no longer ours. Everything has changed.' The old man sighs dramatically. He is lonely in many ways. The time is not his, and no longer is the place.

'Brahmin?' the old man asks, once again looking Ashesh up and down. Ashesh is confused. Can he answer this grandfather's question with Anna's 'if we want to break the caste system, we must first forget our caste'? Haridas would have said (who knows whether truthfully or not), 'My mother was from the barber caste, my father was born a Mahar but converted to Christianity.' If Anima had been in Ashesh's place she would have deftly sidestepped the question altogether and asked the old man a series of solicitous questions about where he lived and which bus he wanted to catch. But Ashesh, being Ashesh, is tongue-tied and pretends he has not heard. As proof, he fixes his eyes in the far distance.

A little time passes. Then the old man taps him on the shoulder. 'Where do you live?'

'Close by.'

'Meaning exactly . . . ?'

'Behind Mani Bhavan.'

'Mani Bhavan? You mean where that charlatan Gandhi lived? Ruined the country and became a saint. Stuffed fifty-three crore rupees into those landyas' throats. Now they are claiming rights over Kashmir.'

Grandpa's wrinkled, fair-skinned face has gone red. Ashesh looks at him stunned. The old man asks him grouchily, 'What is your occupation?' His voice is full of reproach. Who can tell what a man who lives near Mani Bhavan could be doing? Trying hard to keep his voice light, Ashesh says, 'I paint.'

'That's okay. But what work do you do?'

Ashesh thinks of Haridas again. People think painting or writing poetry is a hobby. Spending eight hours in an office and three in local trains is work. The activity you engage in to qualify for the cheque that comes to you at the end of the month is work. What a contractor does is also work, though others do the work. We rip our arses working on a single painting. They take a month just to push a file from one desk to the next. But theirs is work, ours just a hobby. So why even talk to them about our work? When Haridas is asked what he does, he says very seriously, 'I kill flies' or 'I'm a coolie at Mumbai Central.' If he's totally pissed off with the prying, he might even say, 'I pimp in temples' or 'I supply young girls to old politicians.'

Ashesh hasn't answered, so the old man makes himself clearer.
'What I meant was, what do you do for a living?'
    'I paint pictures.'
    'Pictures?'
    'Yes.'
    'Who prints them?'
Ashesh's lower lip drops helplessly. He looks around to see if an
answer will appear from somewhere. He catches sight of a bus heading
their way. He doesn't care where it is going. He wants to get on to it
and leave Grandpa far behind. But 'There's my bus,' says Grandpa,
turning Ashesh giddy with joy. He gives the old man an eager hand
into the bus, steadies him as he totters on the footboard and even yells
at the conductor, 'Can't you wait?' when he notices his impatient hand
reaching for the bell. The bus lurches forward and is off. Ashesh takes
a deep breath and smiles.

It has been a long time since Ashesh has been on a bus. He stands
squashed between two hefty men like chutney in a sandwich. That
was always his way, even at college. Haridas's way was to push his
elbows into his neighbours' ribs to make enough space for himself to
breathe. Haridas said to Ashesh back then, 'If you allow yourself to
become chutney in people's bread, they will naturally gobble you up.
If someone gives you one, you must give them two back. Didn't your
Pa teach you?' The visual before Ashesh was Anna spinning every
morning on his charkha. He smiled and shook his head. Then asked,
'You got it from your Pa?' The question was just a bit of teasing designed
to bring on one of Haridas's special quips. But Haridas had tossed his
head contemptuously instead and spat out, 'Middle-class shit. You're
assuming I have a father. I mean he's there, somewhere.' He had left
it at that.

It was twenty-two years ago that Ashesh had unwittingly stumbled
into Haridas's private life. He had never done it again. Later he had
heard Haridas concoct all kinds of tales about his birth, place of birth,
parents, home, using his remarkable imagination to colour the stories
differently each time. This had created an aura of mystery around him

which the media had lapped up. Perhaps it was because Ashesh had respected his privacy that on a dry and empty night, when the two young men were walking on the Marine Drive promenade, Haridas had said apropos nothing, 'People want to know your full name, parentage, caste, so they can fit you into a docket. Don't give them any idea of where you come from and you remain yourself. And free.'

Ashesh had looked at him with wonder. In a culture where, if you asked somebody his name, he would convivially tell you his life story, how could this man hide his roots so successfully and live unattached? The wonderment was part of the first years of their friendship. Later he lost his curiosity.

Although Ashesh is squashed between the two hefty men, he has not lost the old skills that will free him from the bind. He still has his bus-riding wits about him. From the moment he has boarded the bus, his eyes have grown sharper. He appears to be standing erect, but psychologically he is bent over like an athlete waiting for the pistol to go. The moment he spies someone stirring in a seat to left or right ahead of him, he will be off the block. The bus player must have that degree of concentration if he is to win a seat. A little before the stop after Nana Chowk, the bony Bohri in the left-hand seat of the third row stirs. In that very moment Ashesh shoots forward, pre-empting his bulkier neighbour's rather more sluggish move, to stand proprietorially over the Bohri. As soon as he lifts his bottom off the seat, Ashesh pushes his in. He squirms his way into the seat even while the man is still halfway into the aisle. It is only after he settles in that he feels abashed. He is no longer a student. He is an established artist, for God's sake. He glances around surreptitiously. Nobody in the bus knows him. Relief.

Blocking his view of the road ahead is a massive back with a Terylene shirt with tiny blue pinstripes stretched across it. The shirt is so tight that the owner of the back is obliged to raise a shoulder and an arm every now and again to loosen its hold in the armpits. Every now and again he also looks out of the window on the right or the left and touches his forehead, chest and lips with the fingertips of his right hand. He does this at least half a dozen times between Nana Chowk and Haji Ali. When he turns his head, Ashesh follows his look. Twice he sees street-side shrines, but the other eight times he sees nothing. Which invisible gods is the man paying homage to? At Worli Naka, the man's neighbour and friend is truly and properly annoyed. 'Now which god was that?' he rasps. Ashesh eavesdrops shamelessly because he too must know. 'There's a cross down that street and one of the houses in there has a Ganesh plaque on the door.'

'That's your problem. Mixing your gods.'

'Yeah, well, I'm a fool. So?'

'Not a fool. More dangerous than that. Do they bow before our gods?'

'Why not? In Zaveri Bazaar . . .'

'Forget it. Do what you want.'

Massive Back laughs and again raises his fingers to his forehead, chest and lips. Ashesh continues to count. It's twelve up to Portuguese Church. Evidently there are that many dargas, crosses, churches, Ganesh plaques on doors, Shiva idols in niches, Sai Babas in tree shrines and stones smeared with sindoor tucked away in all those lanes and alleyways; and Massive Back knows them all.

Ashesh thinks back to the gods of his childhood—the needle-peaked Mahalakshmi Hill and the broader-peaked Pestle Hill next to it on the way to Surgaon. Mother and father to the local Warlis, these two hills had stood in his mind like guardians when he did his earliest paintings. The Warlis had turned the stones that had rolled off those hills into their goddess. They had gathered the stones in a pile, smeared it with sindoor, placed a mask on it and wrapped a sari around it. Gods reside even in stones. So this was their goddess. Not so the Kolhapur Mahalakshmi. The two goddesses shared a name but nothing else. That one was fair-skinned with large eyes and a chiselled nose. She was the goddess of Raja Ravi Varma's paintings.

Massive Back and friend get off at Portuguese Church. Ashesh looks at the man. He has a paunch and a bulbous nose. His eyes are bright, smiling. Ashesh feels drawn towards him. The man takes his place amongst others who fill Ashesh's memory.

Ashesh alights at Shivaji Park. He will have to take a cab from here to Lilavati Hospital. The air around Shivaji Park still stirs vague feelings of guilt in him even after all these years. This was where he had dreamt of another future. The daily walk from art school to Flora Fountain with Nasreen, the hope that their bus would come late, the ride on route 84, the welcome traffic jams that extended the sweetness of the journey and the inevitable end that always seemed to come too soon. They would get off at the Mahatma Gandhi Swimming Pool bus stop, downhearted about the coming parting. He could not have gone all the way to Bandra with Nasreen. Bandra was chock-a-block with her family, friends and neighbours. The slightest whisper in her father's ear about him would have led to her being withdrawn instantly from art school and married off.

After graduation, Nasreen would meet Ashesh in Anna's flat in Gamdevi whenever she could get away. But their dream was coloured now by reality. Finally it was here, in Shivaji Park, that Ashesh had hung his head and announced its end.

'It's all right. I understand,' Nasreen had said. Just that. She had never said much. It had been a survival strategy with her. Speak little. Don't create a disturbance. Don't draw attention to yourself. Keep a close eye on Father's moods. When the time is right, ask in a soft voice for what you want. Remain alert enough to step back if your request is not granted and still do what you want with the aid of expert lies. The strategy was in her blood. So when Ashesh went back on his promise of a future together, for vague reasons that he knew weren't convincing, she needed only four words to draw an unfussy curtain over their two years of happiness. A month later she had moved to London permanently, on money borrowed from friends. It was an alien land and an alien culture where she knew only one person, Sunil De from their class, whose father had just been transferred to London. Nasreen had not been angry with Ashesh. She wrote to him occasionally. When she visited Mumbai they would even meet. She could do this because she had instantly accepted the finality of what she had always known would end.

Then there was Yogesh. He had killed himself in a house across the park.

Sitting outside Haresh's room, Ashesh sees the unfairness of his presence there. Around him are a young woman with her young son; an elderly man with his wife, son and daughter-in-law; and a girl of twelve or thirteen, her head in a scarf, her legs pulled up and her chin resting on her knees. Beside them are large bags full of X-rays and blood reports. Once in a while they steal inquiring, sympathetic glances at each other. The expressions on their faces reveal their extreme vulnerability. They are waiting in the hope that the doctor will somehow negate their worst fears. Ashesh has no right to take up Haresh's time for his idiotic fears. He is about to tell Haresh's secretary to knock his name off the waiting list, when Haresh walks down the corridor flanked by his assistants. 'Come on in. Let me get rid of you,' he says, throwing his arm around Ashesh. 'You're looking fresh and fit, nothing the matter.'

As they enter his room, the young woman follows them in.

'Sorry, I didn't see you. How are you, Mrs Narayanan?' Haresh looks intently at her as if there is nobody else in the world who can claim his attention at that moment.

'I'm fine,' the woman says. 'How do I look to you?'

'Fit as a fiddle. No need at all to worry.'

She grabs Haresh's hand. 'Thank you so much for everything, doctor. It's your healing touch.' She pulls her son close to her, her eyes swimming with tears as she turns to go.

Back in his chair, Haresh says, 'Eight years ago, just after this child was born, she was diagnosed with uterine cancer in a pretty advanced stage. We had to remove her uterus and both her ovaries. Secondaries were a more or less foregone conclusion. But they didn't happen. She's still free of the disease.'

'Remarkable! How did that happen?'

'Difficult to say. Our prognostications are based on statistics. But the human body is a miraculous organism. Each body is unique. She says my healing touch did it. But my surgery only accomplished the first and necessary part of the healing. There was chemotherapy after that and finally radiation. Through it all, it was her body that was doing the most important part of healing. But she puts her faith in my touch. All I can do is feel humbled. Now tell me what the hell's the matter with you.'

'Nothing more than what I told you over the phone, Harya. Just that. It seems so trivial now. The way my hand trembled that night really shook me up. It's frightening when the body does something that's outside your control.'

'You're just fine. I can tell by simply looking at you. But we're in our forties, so it's a good idea to have a complete check-up. Why don't you see Dr Janorkar at Opera House? He's an excellent physician, close to your place and interested in your arty-farty stuff.'

The crowd outside Haresh's room has increased. The patients sit patiently. They look at Ashesh with interest as he emerges. Has he been given good news or bad? Then their glances transfer to Dr Pounda's door where their future is to be decided.

Ashesh descends to the lobby by lift. Visiting hours have started. The visitors' lounge is packed. It is a whole new world for Ashesh. He sits quietly in a corner watching the ebb and flow of the crowd, its gestures and its expressions.

20

'You've got it,' Sharada says. Then urgently, 'Hold on to it. Don't let go.' Janaki is panting. She has never heard this voice before. It is so raw and sharp that she gapes at her guru like Eliza at Higgins, but for the reverse reason. Eliza shed her natural voice for an artificial one. Janaki has shed her artificial voice for her true one.

Sharada laughs out loud at the despair on Janaki's face. 'Find your own voice strange? Wait till we've worked on it. It'll lose all its edges.'

The search had begun a month ago. Janaki had sat before Sharada, tanpura in hand, lesson after lesson, completely winded, throat dry. One day Sharada had taken the tanpura from her and slid it into its cover. 'You want desperately to sing. You are trying hard. Working at it. In a sense, you're even singing. I can hear that. But . . . you're too tense. Your voice simply isn't coming through.'

Sharada had sat looking thoughtfully at the covered tanpura before her, then picked it up and stood it in its corner. Janaki was filled with fear, embarrassment, despair. What was she supposed to do now? Sharada had sat down again and pulled the harmonium towards her. Uncovering it she had said, 'Let's try one last thing. It's like this. An actor chooses one of two paths to find his way into the character he is playing. The first is from the inside out, the second from the outside in. If he takes the first path, he enters the emotional space of the character. He builds up the character with the aid of his own life experience. Once he "becomes" that character, his body moves in consonance with the character's mind. So that becomes the character's body language.

'If he chooses the second path, he endows the character with external attributes, that is, he creates a body language for the character and decides that it expresses what the character is. We've tried the first path till now. Let's try the second.'

Janaki didn't have a clue to what Sharada was saying, but she had listened intently to every word. 'For now, let's forget all about teaching and learning singing. Let's just search for your voice. Your physical voice.'

Sharada had pressed a key. 'This is the "sa" in your key. Sing it. Not from your throat. That voice has no depth, no truth. Expand your diaphragm and let your voice come up from your belly and try and hit this note with that voice. This is a boring exercise, but it's the only way to do it.' Sharada's expression was serious. After that, twice a week for an hour at a time, Sharada would press that black key on the harmonium and signal to Janaki to catch the note with a belly voice. 'No, not from your throat, your navel,' she'd say. 'Sit up straight. Right. Now take a deep breath. Hit this note.' Today Janaki had hit the note with this raw, new voice.

Janaki laughs with Sharada. 'Gosh. It's really taken the wind out of me.'

'What did you think, singing is like eating channa? There's a lot of work before us, Ms Patil. But enough for today.'

Sharada has no engagements after the lesson. Shekhar is at his mother's with Shantanu. His mother's not well. In the extra time she has, Sharada wonders if she can work on her new composition. 'Wait if you have the time,' she says to Janaki. 'I'd like you to read a poem. By Indira Sant. I have an idea for a new bandish based on it. I'm not sure I can pull it off.'

Sharada draws a sheet of paper out of her notebook and hands it over to Janaki. 'Read it while I make tea.' Janaki reads Indira Sant's 'Alone'. The protagonist of the poem is a single woman. Her neighbours are consumed by curiosity because she lives alone. Where does she go when she goes out? Who are those visitors? What do they talk about? Why does she laugh so much? Their questions—full of unease, doubt, suspicion—pierce her closed door like arrows. What troubles the world is not whether she is rich or poor, but that she is single and lives alone. The world would love to see her dishonoured for daring to be what she is. Her success is reason to mourn.

Sharada comes back with the tea. 'I've never had to live alone. You've almost always been alone. You think this poem is a poem about you?'

Janaki laughs. 'I have so little to do with my neighbours here. Who has the time in Mumbai? But people watched me closely when I was in Kolhapur and even more closely back in my small home town. Every woman was watched. My aunt once fell off her bike and hit her head against a stone. Lots of blood all over. There was a Sikh shopkeeper in the town who knew our family very well. We called him Sikh as if that was his name. He was passing by on his motorbike. He saw my aunt and instantly put her on his bike and rushed her to the civil hospital which was miles away in the taluka town. By the time he came back to tell us of the accident, the village was abuzz with the story that Kunda Patil had eloped with Sikh. Even after Kunda Aunty came home with a huge bandage round her head, people continued to whisper about her. It made things very difficult when the family was trying to find her a match.'

Janaki laughs bitterly, her eyes clouding over. 'Sometimes I do feel very alone here. But nothing compared to how lonely women like us get in our small towns and villages.'

'Like us?'

'Who want to make something of themselves. Live differently. Respect themselves, won't take injustice lying down, even if it's your father who . . .'

Sharada looks at Janaki, startled.

'I once planned to take my father to court.' Janaki smiles awkwardly. 'But my relatives stood by him and got rid of me instead.'

'Take him to . . . ? Sorry, I don't want to intrude.'

Janaki turns her eyes away. 'I don't mind telling you. I've been waiting to tell someone. It's lonely to keep these things to yourself.' Janaki fixes her eyes on the tanpura in the corner. Her voice is a monotone. 'My father was . . . is a reputed lawyer. Our family is highly esteemed in the town. I call him Father, not Papa or Baba or any of those affectionately respectful names. I can't. His reputation extends over the whole district. He has been generous to the family. He's helped poor relatives educate their sons and stuff like that. But he beats my mother and then rapes her. When he's away from home he has fantasies of her infidelity. My mother is very beautiful but totally docile. She takes the beating and the assault without complaint. I'm an only child.' Janaki takes a deep breath. 'That's the background. One day the man comes home late from a tour. I am studying. It's my graduation year at college. He sits looking at me. I begin to get uncomfortable. I get up to go to the kitchen. He stops me. "You, girl," he says. "Who's your father? Come here. Here. Who's your father?" I am taken aback. I say, "You." He catches my arm, drags me into the bedroom and asks my mother, "Haven't you told the girl who her father is?" My mother begins to tremble as I have seen her do time and again before. I feel revolted by her. I shake off his grip on my arm. In the scuffle my sari pallu falls off my shoulder. He gets hold of my arm again. He stares at me. "Just like her mother," he says. "Ready to drop her pallu before any man." A red-hot something pierces my brain. I slap him, so hard that he stumbles back and falls. My mother rushes to help him up. I stare at her in horror. I run to Salunkhe Aunty next door. She fears my father but keeps me for the night. Mother comes next morning. "Come home," she pleads. "Tell me first who my father is," I demand. She sobs, "He is, please. He is." "So then? He throws these filthy things at you and me and you swallow them and ask me to come home? You think I'll come? Just see if I don't take your husband to court." That does it. Mother runs to all the relatives' homes in town and lies to them. "He just gave her a light slap because she wasn't studying hard enough and she's threatening to take him to court." I don't think I've ever felt as alone as I did when I heard that story.'

Janaki's eyes stream with years of repressed tears. Sharada can only stare at her, stunned. 'Then?'

'Then things happened fast. That night my uncle physically shoved me into a train and took me to another uncle's in Kolhapur. I did my BA under Uncle's strict guard. Then I did my master's in English. Had I been in the village, I'd have been married off immediately after graduation. Uncle wrote home to say I had got my master's. Two scrappy notes came back. One was from Mother to my aunt. "Buy her a nice sari on my behalf." The other was from Father to my uncle. "Ask her what she wants to do next. Money is no problem." I wanted to be a journalist. I had this great belief in the power of the pen. I also wanted to move away from Marathi people for some time. I did journalism from a media college in Chennai and joined *The Hindu*. I travelled to many places, heard and reported many stories. I saw how lucky I was compared to some of the women I met during the course of my work. I got this job in the *Mumbai Observer* on the strength of those two years of experience.'

The two women sit in silence. Sharada takes the poem from Janaki's hands. 'I can't put your story to melody and rhythm. You might fervently believe artists should not live in ivory towers, but every art form has its limitations. The nayikas of our music and dance suffer, at most, separation from their lovers or their infidelity. That's it. Taking that tradition forward, we can at most show them angry with their lovers.

Properly angry. Not mock angry, ready to forgive at the end of the song. But you and your mother simply can't be the nayikas of our classical compositions. Even I will not take that liberty. But I think I can fit Indira Sant's "Alone" into the mould.'

As Sharada mulls over this thought and Janaki watches her preoccupied face, the key turns in the lock and Shekhar enters with Shantanu sleeping on his shoulder. Janaki gets up instantly. 'Sorry. I took up all your time with my story.' She's already slipped her feet into her chappals. Sharada touches her shoulder. 'Your story was important. It helped me sort out my thoughts.'

A line from a song begins to hum in Sharada's mind. '*Pag ghungroo bandh Meera nachi re.*' Meera tied bells on her ankles and danced alone. She danced without caring for the world. She danced even more fervently when her family and society rejected her. She danced all her life. If I sang Meera's aloneness, would I not be singing the aloneness of Sant's heroine, of Janaki, her mother and of the thousands of other women who must live alone in themselves? Sharada finds the answer to this question as she feeds Shantanu his curd and rice. No. Meera was never alone. Her dancing feet, her ankle bells, her ecstasy—all belonged to her eternal companion, Krishna. She and he were entwined—devotee and God.

Dinner over, Shekhar reads. Sharada watches her son with doting curiosity. He is completely absorbed in trying to pick a small scrap of paper off the floor between thumb and forefinger. It takes a lot of trying. Finally he has it. He goes round the room triumphantly, holding it up like a trophy. Then he drops it and tries to pick it up again. The game has been going on for a long time. Shekhar too puts his book aside and smiles at Shantanu. Sharada turns to him.

'How's Mamma?'
'She says she's fine. But she looks tired.'
'Fever?'
'Still low grade.'
'Did you give her my message?'
'I did.'

'So?'

'She made the usual answer: "When I feel I can't manage by myself, I promise I'll move in with you."'

'It would be enough even if she cut down on her social work. She doesn't have to go to that stuffy office every day to listen to women's tragic tales. Just doing that could give people a fever.'

'I said all that, but she'll do what she wants to.'

After a moment, Sharada says, 'I don't think I would stop singing if someone thought it would be good for me.'

Shantanu has picked up his scrap of paper again and is waving it in the air, shouting, 'Baba, Baba.'

Shekhar claps. Shantanu runs round the room, stumbles, falls, gets up and is back with his scrap of paper.

'It's not just women she listens to.' Shekhar laughs. 'She was telling me about a man and his love marriage. Before marriage his wife was a fun person. But the minute they were married she transformed herself into this weird woman who put sindoor in her parting, served him his dinner first and ate after him, and brought him his shoes when he was getting ready to go to work. He found he simply couldn't stand this ideal Indian wife. He'd lived alone for eight years, had done and enjoyed doing everything for himself. He was an excellent cook. He loved being in the kitchen. But now his wife wouldn't allow him to even step in. He said he was scared she'd pray for seven lives of togetherness when she did the Vat Savitri puja.'

Sharada looks at Shekhar with a mischievous laugh. 'You're welcome in my kitchen any time, darling.'

Shekhar gets up, holding out his hand to her. 'I don't know about the kitchen. But I'd do the Vat Savitri puja any time to have you with me for seven lives.'

Held secure in Shekhar's arms, Sharada thinks of Janaki's mother, feeling momentarily guilty for her happiness. Her head resting against his chest, Shekhar wonders if he should give her today's bad news and be done with it. She feels his body tense. She lifts her head. 'Something wrong?'

Shekhar lets go of her and picks up the book he's been reading. Slapping an impatient hand on it, he says, 'Every other day a new management guru surfaces in America. It's like your gharanas. Some lay stress on beat, some on melody. Some will champion one kind of taan, some another. But finally there are only seven notes and twenty-two microtones. You can't do much beyond them. This guru has just discovered that man is the most valuable resource in business. Take care of your people and they'll take care of your business. So what's new?'

'Maybe this isn't what you wanted to tell me?'

Shekhar's heart thumps. He looks into her eyes. 'Haridas called today.'

Sharada's face grows taut. Her voice is flat. 'Called you? Why?'

'Invited us to dinner. Next Saturday. He said he didn't call you because you'd have asked me before replying anyway, so why not call me directly. He has specially requested me to come. Everybody'll be there. The occasion is to be a surprise.'

Sharada doesn't say anything. Shekhar fixes his eyes on her. 'You're free to go of course. You know that.'

'Not without you. You know that.'

'I refuse to come.'

'Then that's that.'

'Let him know.'

'He called you. You let him know. If he'd called me I'd have said no there and then.'

Two parallel lines crease Shekhar's forehead.

Shantanu comes to Sharada rubbing his eyes. 'Sleepy, Ai.'

Sharada carries him to the bedroom. Shekhar paces the floor outside, livid and confused.

21

Ashesh lifts *Artist 5* off the easel. He has five oils and last year's watercolours with five months to go for the show. Now he is going to concentrate on black. He must chase it, consume it, fill his head with it. Subjects will follow. But that's not how it is. Black is chasing him and consuming him. He must find a way to confront and command it. He must prepare himself to take the kind of risks he has not taken for a long time.

Ashesh leaves the house. It is not his time for a walk. The traffic must be crawling nose to tail on the main road. But he wants to walk. He feels the need for physical movement. He wants to tire himself out. Fatigue will drain away yesterday's stale thoughts from his mind. He needs an uninhabited mental space in which the black seed of that elusive image can grow.

Ashesh tramps down lanes and streets from Gamdevi to Opera House. Returning from Opera House along Hughes Road, he notices a simple name plate amongst the dozens nailed to the front of a building on the corner. It says Dr P. Janorkar. He was the giver of the good news that Ashesh's reports were absolutely clear. He had nothing to worry about. His dancing hand had been what he termed 'a minor episode'. He had shrugged and admitted that doctors did not necessarily know the cause of every passing event in the human body. After which he had turned to art, confessing he was a small-time collector. Ashesh had visited him again one day to give him one of his small pen-and-ink drawings.

Ashesh crosses the road from this warren of doctors and enters Sukh Sagar for a plate of idlis. There is food at home, but he would rather have this than eat alone. For a moment Ashesh feels sorry for himself. He is alone, by choice of course, but still alone. So is Anima. More than Ashesh because it wasn't always so. Feroze too is alone. But he never looks it. Haridas too, never. Does he? Do people look at

him and think, here's a man who is alone? Perhaps not. But he is, and
there are times when he feels it.

Back home after his marathon walk, Ashesh's body feels light, his
eyes heavy. Perhaps he can nap. Just as he is falling asleep, two lines
from an essay that Mr Pisolkar had once read out in class fade up in
his empty mind like lights on a stage. The essay was called 'Meditation
on Black'. The lines he remembers went: 'The silence of black is the
silence of death. Red is the denial of black. Red is life.'

Red is raucous. It tears through the silence of black. You don't exist,
red screams. Yet black exists, unmoved.

Ashesh sees Yogesh flat on the bathroom floor. The cut on his wrist
is as fine as a filament. The blood from it has coagulated on the floor. By
the time Ashesh reached Yogesh's uncle's house, it had turned black.
But some red still gleamed through. By the time the police arrived that
too had darkened. The blood that had flowed through Yogesh's veins,
singing of life, was now a dark dirge on his death. Ashesh had stood
beside this body the previous evening, erect and alive then with red
blood. He had sat before this body that had leaned urgently towards
him. He had drunk tea made by these hands.

It was a day in April, quite like today. Ashesh had parked his Padmini
at the south end of the park in a by-lane. He was going to take a brisk
walk to Yogesh's uncle's house on the other side, to compensate for the
walk he had not taken that morning. Stepping out of the car, he had
felt the stored heat of the asphalt shooting into the soles of his feet.
But once he started walking, the sea breeze had played around his face,
picking up beads of sweat from his forehead like a soft brush lifting paint.

As he walked towards the park he was thinking about Yogesh—
the quiet-faced youth he had first met in art school when Yogesh had
been a freshman. Much later, he had heard his work spoken of with
excitement. Ashesh had gone to the Jehangir Art Gallery to see his first
solo show. There were some fifteen to twenty paintings there, big and
small. They were complex works, done in layers, without their meaning
being overtly peddled. You had to look long and hard to comprehend
what the colours, lines and imagery were doing. Ashesh, who had kept

his relationship with brush and paint alive through the changing times, had been intrigued by Yogesh's use of computerized and photographic material to create those layers. In one or two works, the negative space was covered in a shower of short white lines suggesting it had been captured directly off a television screen.

One work was covered entirely with blow-ups of body parts tagged by text in elaborate lettering reading 'The nostril' or 'The inner ear'. Ashesh was fascinated by the work. He had seen Yogesh sitting at a table in the corner with two friends—a young man and a woman. Ashesh had stopped by to say a few words before leaving. As he approached the table, Yogesh had half risen with nervous anticipation. Ashesh had placed a light hand on his shoulder to reassure him. 'It's an enigmatic show,' he had said. 'Some of those pictures might haunt me.'

Yogesh's face had brimmed with joy. 'Thank you, sir, thank you.'

'I'd like to see you some time. Talk about your technique.'

Yogesh's fine features had lit up like a child's. His large, black eyes gleamed with gratitude. 'At your place, sir?'

'Why not,' Ashesh had said without a moment's hesitation. 'Call first.'

The young woman next to him had said, 'I'm Shilpa. I'd love you to see my show too. It's video installations. I'm showing at the Max Mueller. May I send you an invite? I have your address. I made Yogesh's list and sent out the invites.'

Shilpa's rapid-fire chatter had made Ashesh nervous. Although he had nodded vigorously in agreement to everything she said, he was looking at the door for escape. Descending the wide, curved steps of the Jehangir, Ashesh had realized this was the Shilpa who was supposed to be Yogesh's girlfriend from college days. He wondered how they could possibly be a couple, being so unlike each other.

Ashesh had suddenly felt old, far away from this generation of artists with their new media and new techniques. His world was still flesh and blood. Theirs seemed to be air waves and signals. They lived with such supreme confidence in the virtual world where he could never be the host, nor perhaps even a guest. Yogesh did not show the same hard, crackling confidence as Shilpa. He was tall, very good-looking, but Ashesh had seen a shadow of vulnerability in his eyes. Yogesh and he had met a few times after that—at Ashesh's place, at a cafe, in galleries. Ashesh had found a young friend in Yogesh. He read poetry, saw films, listened to music. You could exchange ideas with him but also dive into yourself and keep your silence. Yogesh had never brought Shilpa to any of their meetings. Ashesh thought this showed sensitivity.

Soon after, both Yogesh and Shilpa had won fellowships to go abroad. Yogesh had gone to London for a year and Shilpa for six months to Amsterdam. Yogesh had returned after that stint, but very quietly. Nobody realized he was back. Nobody had heard from him or seen him until out of the blue one day Ashesh had got a call from him. 'Can you please, please, come to see my new work today, sir? I've been working on it ever since I got back. Tomorrow my uncle and aunt return from America. I'm not sure where I'll be after that. Or the work.'

Ashesh had just completed a large canvas. He had some ideas for the next one but they would take a while to form. Meanwhile, he had the time.

Ashesh had reached the wide entrance to the park, his head down. Just as he was about to step into the park, the end of a gun barrel had appeared before him. He had looked up startled. The barrel had swung a little to the left. 'That way,' said the voice behind the barrel. The man was young, his face expressionless. 'Why not through?' Ashesh had inquired, mildly.

'Order.'

'Whose?'

The young warrior did not answer, merely pointed his gun once again to the left. An old man passing by had said with pride, 'Haven't you read the papers? Army exhibition next week. Parade, cannons, tanks, rockets, helicopters—they'll all be here, in our park.'

Ashesh saw then that the low parapet round the park, usually crowded with people out to take the air, was covered with a barbed wire spiral that extended all the way round it. Even the hardiest souls respect barbed wire. You can't slip through unless you want to be flayed both by the wire and the authorities. Ashesh submitted to the order. The old man had been mistaken. This was nothing like 'our park'. It was enemy country.

Yogesh had looked strained that evening. The skin seemed to be stretched abnormally tight over the fine bones of his face. 'I didn't do an inch of work in London,' he had begun without preamble. 'Just couldn't. Back here I was like crazy. Had to get it all out. Sorry, sir, water? Tea?' He led Ashesh to a chair.

'No, thanks.'

'Work wasn't expected. But a whole year doing nothing? It has never happened to me before. I felt weird out there—that weather, that light, the way people moved, spoke . . . so totally alien.' Yogesh fell silent. His gaze became withdrawn. 'Shall I show you the work?' he asked, coming out of his reverie.

In the room that Yogesh led him to, Ashesh was rooted to the spot. Before him stood an enormous, horizontal triptych. The background carried blurred bits of a soliloquy from *Hamlet*. On closer view, some lines were visible: 'What a piece of work is man'; 'how like an angel'; 'the beauty of the world'; 'the paragon of animals'. The first part of the triptych was the right profile of a large male head. The middle was a frontal view of a torso and upper arms. The third was the left profile of male thighs, the member upright. Wound around these central images was the wild growth of a black creeper. On it crawled caterpillars of all sizes, colours and shapes. The muscles, hair and nails of the male body were meticulously drawn in realistic detail and painted in vivid colours to create a crowded world of natural life.

Ashesh had stared in stunned silence at this adoration of man in life and life in man. He had felt Yogesh's eyes fixed on him as he gazed at the painting. Then, as if at an unspoken signal, both turned away from it and stepped out into the living room. Yogesh had left the room abruptly, without a word, returning later with two mugs of tea. Ashesh didn't know what he was going to say to Yogesh about the work except that it was stupendous.

'As I was saying, I didn't do any work there. But I saw a lot.' Yogesh had broken the silence. 'I literally lived in museums and galleries. What amazing work the old masters have done. Looking at Turner's seascapes, what storms, I thought this is the ocean from which our fourteen jewels were churned out. Those waves, the ships poised between sailing and keeling over, and that light pouring down from some divine source, right in the middle of every painting. Would anyone dare label his work "realistic" or "nature study"? The paintings are pure vision. Don't you think, sir, that the artist is looking beyond the ocean and the ships to tell us something about life?'

'I do,' Ashesh had replied eagerly. 'But the physical phenomena themselves are solidly there, whatever abstractions they may point to. In that sense and that sense alone, Turner painted observed life. But I saw something in the Tate that took you beyond observed life. It was a work by Anish Kapoor. Its impact almost erased the memory of the Turners I'd seen earlier. It was a huge, flattish stone on the floor, comparatively low in height but nearly four feet wide. It was covered in Prussian-blue pigment, textured like fine rangoli powder. The colour was so luminous you felt every grain was infused with individual light. There was a hole carved into the boulder at the top. When you looked in, you saw nothing. The inside was sheer black. Who knows how deep the hole went. It was infinite like the zero. I couldn't stop looking in, thinking that if I looked hard enough, I'd see into the womb of the earth.'

Yogesh had grown restless. He had got up, sat down, fiddled with a mug. His hand shook. 'I felt lonely,' he muttered. 'Cold and alone.' His eyes grew wet. 'I could never relate to the work others were doing—personal memorabilia and stuff like that . . . I went to Amsterdam to see Shilpa. She has taken to the place. She has lots of friends. She's doing wonderful work. She's staying on. She's got an extension on her fellowship. I saw her friends' works. Hers. Some of it stirred me. But then again the unease, the distance. What was I to do?'

Yogesh's hands were trembling so badly now that Ashesh laid his own spontaneously on them. Yogesh made a sound in his throat and gripped them hard. His eyes were filled with appeal. Ashesh's hands began to struggle like birds in a net. His body shrank away from the scream that he could see forming in the young man's heart. He did not want to see it or hear it. A fear rose in him that Yogesh's loneliness had the power to devour him whole. Yogesh hooded his gaze. He could hear Ashesh's eyes, hands and body telling him something. He listened intently. Abruptly he let go of Ashesh's hands. He had been leaning forward urgently in his chair. He sat back now. Then stood up.

Guilt had hit Ashesh hard. He had said quickly, 'There are times when we feel desperately alone. But your work . . . that's something else you know. Nothing like . . .'

Yogesh was watching him with eyes drained of light.

'No, truly. Why else would you have got that fellowship? Painting still has a place in art. It will always have. You've shown that with this work. All kinds of practices and techniques will arrive, grab the centre for a while, then fade away. But painting will always remain. It's taken centuries for the language to develop and grow rich. Artists will never stop speaking in it . . .'

Yogesh had made a show of listening but Ashesh saw he was elsewhere. He sat down again. Looked at his nails. Said, 'Yes, sir', and again, 'Yes, sir'. He had lifted a mug to his lips. There was no tea in it. Then he had said with unexpected violence, his voice coming from some hollow cavity within, 'I cannot live without painting. Everything that I see is colour. I desire the tactility of paint. I want to smear my body with paint. I want to be red and black. You look purple to me. That's your inner colour.' He stood up. 'Will you have tea?'

'No, thanks, really. I think I should be going.'

At the door Ashesh had said, 'But I wanted to say something about this work of yours. It held me. But it also disturbed me in a way I can't put my finger on. Perhaps . . .'

'I could see that, sir,' Yogesh had cut in.

The following day Yogesh had cut his wrist open. He was in the bathroom when his uncle and aunt returned. They rang, knocked, called to him. They realized that they had been locked out.

Back home, Ashesh takes these memories to bed and in his restless sleep dreams of an unending black tunnel. Waking up with a heavy head, he goes through his morning routine mechanically, goes for a walk mechanically. When he returns, he mounts a new canvas on the easel, mechanically. Suddenly he is no longer lifeless. In the next ten days he paints two new works. In one a naked man with a face cut out of stone stands on a white polished floor, hands outstretched. From the splayed fingers of one drips a stream of black, from the other a stream of red. The colours collect at his feet in two separate glossy pools. The background is filled with vegetation. The second work is a huge sideways shadow cast by a puny helmeted jawan. His back is to the viewer. He stands guard over spirals of barbed wire that stretch all the way to the horizon.

Ashesh sits very still for a long time after he finishes the second work. Then he lifts the phone, but puts it down again. He has done this a few times recently, lifting the phone, then telling himself not to be a fool and replacing it in its cradle. But finishing the painting has made him euphoric. He wants to be foolish. He lifts the receiver off the hook again and dials Janaki's number.

22

The front room in the twenty-first-floor flat of Himalaya Apartments is totally altered. Prakash gapes in stupefaction at the walls. The Husains, Tyeb Mehtas, Laxman Shreshthas, K.G. Subramanyams and Bhupen Khakhars have disappeared. Their place has been taken by ceiling-to-floor silk scrolls covered with Sanskrit shlokas. The veranda at the other end is thick with tall potted plants. A two-foot-high platform has been raised against this dense green background. A throne stands at the centre of the platform. It is covered in red velvet, its arms are gilded and its feet carved in the shape of tiger claws. Leaving a respectful space from the platform, soft mattresses with spotless white sheets cover the floor almost up to the entrance. In every corner of the room stand tall, three-legged stools of carved wood on which are placed enormous silver agarbatti holders with many arms. The scent of sandalwood agarbattis wafts in squiggles of wispy smoke and fills the air. A recorded male voice chants mantras in some unseen quarter of the house.

Prakash stands uncertainly at the door. Sumitra Jhunjhunwala emerges from a distant door dressed in a finely spun sky-blue cotton sari embroidered with delicate white tracery. She wears her signature string of large pearls, diamond-studded bangles and huge solitaires in her ears. Her earlobes flash when she turns her head. When she lifts her hands to fold them in humble namaskars of welcome, tiny multicoloured sparks fly off her wrists.

Sumitraben makes a slight eye movement to invite Prakash in. Even after slipping out of his chappals, he doesn't have the heart to step on those pristine white mattresses. He has had a bath before leaving home but he wonders anxiously if he has scrubbed the soles of his feet, particularly his heels, hard enough. It would be too mortifying to leave a trail of smudgy footprints behind him. He looks surreptitiously over his shoulder. The sheets are still white.

Sumitraben casts her eyes over him and says, 'You are beautiful.' Prakash's brain does a somersault. He is wearing a white kurta pyjama and has combed his hair neatly. The lady doesn't look as if she's teasing him. She doesn't look as if she ever teases anybody. But she is gazing at him as an art lover gazes upon a painting. She takes his sweaty palm in her cool marble hands. He thrills to the touch and lowers his head in shame. She stands erect and says to him in a mellow voice, 'A beautiful body is God's gift, Prakash. You must learn to celebrate it.'

Sumitraben drops his hand gently and glides to the door. She stands there greeting each guest with deep humility. The room gradually fills with men in churidars and silk jhabbas with wives in finely spun saris of pale cloudy shades and deep-necked cholis. Some of the couples are accompanied by girls in salwar kameezes and boys in jeans. As they take their seats, servants come out bearing silver trays of sherbets in crystal glasses—watermelon juice like melted rubies, litchi juice flooded by moonbeams and khus with the sparkle of pale emeralds. Prakash sits in a corner, his body squeezed small, waiting nervously for what is to happen. The light buzz of conversation passing between the guests suddenly stops. Sumitraben is escorting Shivanand Swami into the room. She requests him, bending very low, to ascend to the throne. The swami is dressed in a long robe of white silk. He wears pearl ear studs, a string of rudraksha beads around his neck—each as large as a grape—and a large, orange mark on his forehead. He sits down and, in a single sweeping glance, takes in the gathering of devotees, his eyes resting briefly on every face in the hall. The middle-aged woman next to Prakash exclaims 'aah' as if a sharp, sweet pain has shot through her body. The swami closes his piercing eyes and sits for a while in meditation. The air grows heavy with the devotees' collective bated breath.

When the swami opens his eyes there's an audible hiss. The swami claps lightly. The recorded chanting of mantras that has continued until this moment stops instantly. Four young men—the swami's disciples—emerge from an inner room. Three are brown, the fourth a white Caucasian. They are dressed in dhotis and sleeveless tie-up jackets. The arms of the white man bear huge tattoos. On the right arm is the image of Shiva and on the left, Parvati. The four disciples now hang a large painting high on a stand behind the swami. At the centre of the painting is a red circle. Around it are concentric rings of black, like sound waves. The swami closes his eyes again and chants a mantra in a low voice, enunciating the Sanskrit in rich, traditional cadences. When the shloka ends, he opens his eyes and explains its meaning:

That word which all the Vedas declare
That word which all the ages speak of
That word for which the desirous adopt celibacy
That word I will tell you in brief is . . .

The four disciples chant 'aum' in unison.
As their chanting fades, the swami says, 'I will explain the sound

symbols that form this sacred word which is not so much word as sound. The first symbol "a" stands for the waking state, for the self as universe and for Lord Vishnu. The second symbol "u" stands for the dream state, illumination and Lord Shiva. The third symbol "m" stands for the state of deep, dreamless sleep, the intellect and Lord Brahma. The ultimate reward of chanting "aum" is knowledge of Brahma which is creation itself. To tread the path to the ultimate reward while managing our worldly duties is extremely difficult, indeed impossible. However, it is possible to acquire some self-knowledge through the chanting of "aum". Let me explain how "aum" is to be chanted.

'You must close your eyes when you chant "aum". But it is not enough to close your eyes if your mind wanders. If you do not concentrate, you cannot enter your innermost self even with eyes closed. I would advise you to fix your eyes on the bindu behind me to help you concentrate. The bindu is one of Lord Shiva's powers. The bindu is the knowledge eye of yogis. We are about to enter ourselves using the concentration we acquire by focusing on it.

'Those who can sit in the lotus position, please do so. Those who cannot may cross their legs in the normal way. Now fix your gaze and mind on the bindu. When my disciples and I start chanting "aum", close your eyes and join in the chanting. All the ancient philosophies of the world have seen blindness as opening the door to another kind of sight. The one who cannot see the material world begins to see that which is without substance and without form. I will tell you a short story in this regard. Our guru-brother Prasadanand went suddenly blind in one eye. He did not weep over the loss. He accepted it with joy. Only those who accept their blindness rise to the higher level of sight. My guru-brother did not need anybody to tell him this. He said to his disciples, "I see with one eye what everybody sees. But with the other I see what is hidden from others, what does not exist in the outside world."

'To close your eyes is to accept temporary blindness, to cut the visible world out of your sight in order to begin the inward journey to find your soul. If you are successful in reaching your goal, you will see the visible world itself in a different way when you return to it. You will find you have shed all the anxieties attached to it. You will be surrounded by a space of extreme serenity created from within yourself. You will experience in yourself the existence of an infinitesimal part of divine power. It is time now to sit in the lotus posture and concentrate on the bindu.'

Prakash is awed by the swami's sermon. As he crosses his legs for the lotus position, he glances surreptitiously at his neighbours. Many are finding the lotus posture difficult to assume. The youngsters, and even some of the grown-ups, giggle at their failed efforts, while others wear masks of gravity.

Prakash fixes his eyes on the bindu. After a while his unblinking eyes begin to burn and water. The swami has said nothing about whether blinking or wiping your eyes is permissible. Prakash shifts his gaze momentarily from the bindu to check what the others are doing. The woman next to him has closed her eyes and is swaying. The man beside her is blinking rapidly. Prakash steals a look at the swami. He is busy instructing one of his disciples and pays no heed to these two. He pays no heed to anybody. Perhaps his inner eye can see all. He is hardly like Gunde teacher at the Shingne primary school whose eagle eyes were always open to catch pranksters who would then be beaten up. Here is a guru of all forms of knowledge—inner and outer.

Prakash quickly wipes his eyes and returns them to the bindu. After a while, the red spot appears to pulsate. Light waves begin to rise from it. Prakash grows light-headed. His eyes close automatically. The bindu is now behind his eyelids. He begins to feel its power seeping into him. He is filled with joy. The swami's disciples begin to chant 'aum'. Prakash joins the chanting in a sonorous voice. His head feels even lighter. He wants to tell the world of this experience. He will soon enter his inner world. He will paint everything that he sees there. His paintings will be unique, different from anything anybody else has ever done.

The swami's voice now intrudes from what seems like a huge distance. He is saying, 'Now, without stopping the chanting, try and pull "aum" gradually into yourselves so that it is no longer uttered but continues to resonate within you. That's right. Now open your eyes slowly. Entering the outer world from the inner can sometimes cause shock. You might experience a visual explosion akin to the sonic boom of a supersonic aircraft. So be very careful to open your eyes gradually.'

Everybody's eyes are soon open. A youth says to a girl in a loud whisper, 'Did anything happen to you? I toh fell fast asleep, yaar.'

The girl says, 'Shut up! It was a beautiful experience.'

The boy says, 'Bullshit! I hope the food is good.'

The girl says, 'It's vegetarian.'

The boy says, 'Shit, yaar! Why did you bring me here?'

The girl says indignantly, 'I did? You wanted to see me. I told you I was coming here. You asked to come. And I agreed. So how did I bring you here?'

The boy says, 'That's right. You didn't. But what about joy, and about all anxieties going away? After your beautiful inner experience, how come you argue with people from the outer world like me?'

The girl clamps her lips shut in disgust. The boy laughs out loud. That breaks the silence that the devotees, now lining up to touch the swami's feet, have so far maintained. It releases everybody's tongues and the room fills with a low buzz of chatter. Some people even laugh. Sounds of cutlery and crockery issue from a distant room.

All the devotees have now touched the swami's feet. Sumitraben comes out bearing a silver thali with silver katoris filled with delicacies for the swami. Someone places a low stool before his throne. She puts the thali on it along with a silver, lota-like tumbler and another silver tumbler brimful of cold almond milk. She stands before the swami with folded hands till he has taken his first mouthful. Then she glides back to the inner room to look after her guests. The room is set with a long, food-laden table that runs down its middle. Prakash stands in a corner with a silver thali piled with food. Should he have heaped so much on his plate? But did he have a choice? There were so many bowls and tureens on the table with different preparations, that even a spoonful or small piece of each had added up to the bounty before him. He applies himself to it now, with the hope that he might be able to demolish the whole lot before anybody notices. But he is less than halfway through when Sumitraben's voice interrupts from very close at hand.

'Meet Prakash Jadhav,' it says. 'A very fine painter. Just starting out, but very powerful work.'

Prakash's fork drops. He stares wide-eyed, first at Sumitraben and then at the spectacled man to whom she has addressed the above. The man nods gravely. A bearer materializes from somewhere, bows low and presents Prakash with a new fork. Prakash looks down quickly. The fallen fork has disappeared. Sumitraben puts a hand on the spectacled man's arm and leads him towards the food-laden table. She returns to Prakash and says in a low voice, 'I'm going to introduce you to a couple of other people—all collectors. Just smile, don't show surprise.'

She makes solicitous inquiries of her guests, a word here, a word there, gliding through the crowd like a silken serpent. Prakash returns to his plate, shovelling food fast down the hatch. Every bit of it is beautiful to look at and subtly flavoured; but his eyes and palate are in no state to appreciate its refinements. His tongue is dry, his intestines knotted.

'Meet Prakash Jadhav.' Before him stands a middle-aged, ravaged-looking woman with a huge red tika on her forehead. The woman's eyes are on the jalebis on her plate over which is piled a large mound of rabdi, but she makes her mouth smile. She is clearly not interested in who or what Prakash is, but such is Sumitraben's power over her, that she forces her gaze to rise from the jalebis and take in Prakash. 'Prakash has a very interesting background. I must tell you about it one of these days. Coming from such a background, the spirituality of his paintings is astounding. Of course, they are still a little raw, but that's part of their power. I've bought one already.'

Sumitraben looks at him with a faint smile and urges him with a light touch on the arm to return to his food. Later she introduces him in different ways to two more people. Each time Prakash puts his entire will into not registering surprise. Suddenly Sumitraben deserts his side and disappears. The swami has risen from his throne. She stands before him with folded hands.

'Where is that young artist of yours?' he asks in a stentorian voice. Everybody stops talking. Sumitraben makes a sign to Prakash. His limbs answer her call promptly but he has no control over their trembling.

He stands before the swami, quaking; bends to lay his head on his feet, quaking. The swami extends his right hand, palm upturned. A disciple places a rudraksha mala on it. He puts the mala around Prakash's neck and lays his hand on his head in blessing. It is a sight filled with such divine power that the guests watch in awe. This is not some common or garden swami. He is guru to some of the mightiest men in the country. He travels all over the world spreading the message of Shivashakti—the power of Shiva. He drives around India in a custom-made car gifted to him by an American disciple. Equipped with a powerful air conditioner, it has six doors and a body plated with gold. Prakash is overwhelmed by the idea that he has now entered this aura. He remembers his grandmother. She used to tap her forehead with her forefinger and say, 'When a man has this on his side, he can reach any height without doing a thing.' She would say it in the context of his father who was clever enough to have become a Supreme Court judge but remained an advocate in Shingne because he didn't have that thing in the forehead on his side.

After blessing Prakash, the swami moves. He is ready to leave. 'I shall see your work at leisure,' he says. 'There is an increasing demand for spiritual paintings here and abroad. I have left some books with Sumitraben. Simple books, easy to understand. Read them. They will give you spiritual guidance in executing your work.'

Prakash has not the faintest notion of what this is all about. But he nods all the same as though he has understood every word. Once the swami leaves, there is an exodus of guests. Prakash is all set to leave with them when Sumitraben's eyes hold him back. They signal him to sit down. As he lowers himself on to the mattress, his hand goes to the string of rudrakshas round his neck. 'Don't take that off,' Sumitraben whispers, addressing him for the first time in the familiar singular. She closes the front door on the last guest. She goes around the room switching off all the lights except one. She touches a panel on the wall across the room. It revolves slowly. The scroll with Sanskrit shlokas disappears and a mirror hidden on the other side appears. Sumitraben goes down on her knees behind Prakash.

'Gaze upon your beauty now,' she whispers. 'These eyes, these long lashes, these delicate nostrils, these bow-shaped lips . . .' Sumitraben touches every part of his body with her cool fingertips, as she names it. 'This chest.' She runs her fingers under his kurta. 'These arms.' She unbuttons his kurta. Prakash swivels his head around to look at her, petrified.

'Why do you look like that? Nobody will disturb us.' She laughs. Her fingers caress his chest. 'If you desire to go beyond the body, you must first enter the body, get to know the body. When you are released from the body you are free to go in search of your soul. This is Swamiji's teaching.'

Prakash's kurta is now unbuttoned. 'Look at yourself. Know yourself,' she says. He can't. She rises and slowly, methodically sheds her clothes. Prakash lowers his eyes in embarrassed confusion. 'No, you must not deny this knowledge.' She laughs again. 'You can only know your body through another body. That too is unavoidable.'

Sumitraben stands before him completely naked. Even in his confused, embarrassed, deeply ashamed, yet excited, state Prakash notices that there is not a single wrinkle, scar or blemish on her body. She kneels before him, lifts his face and says, 'Look, how beautiful my breasts are.' She lifts his hands and places them on her breasts. 'Your hands are burning. My breasts are cool. Your body is trembling. Mine is still. This is the result of knowing your body. When you know yours through mine, you too will reach this state.'

Sumitraben begins to undress Prakash. He forgets himself little by little. All the upbringing that has come with him from Shingne, falls to the ground with his clothes.

'Now you are pure male and I am pure female.' Lowering her mouth to his ears she whispers, 'You are Shiva and I am Shakti. You are Purush and I Prakriti.'

His body is utterly bewildered. It can't find its way to her. She takes him in hand and leads him in. As he enters her, Prakash understands what it is to be male. He is no longer Prakash. He is simply and purely an enormous, spontaneous force concentrated in one organ of his body. The force explodes. Flames lick up into his entire body. For a few seconds then, he is nobody, nothing. He is some unknown creature divested of all strength and will. When he returns to himself, when he recognizes Prakash's feet and Prakash's hands, his stomach churns, pushing vomit into his throat. He stands up trembling, pulls the first garment that comes to hand over his nakedness and turns his face to the wall.

'That's my sari.' Sumitraben laughs. 'See how difficult it is to know and accept your body. The soul is not even in sight.'

'I don't want to know anything. All this is filth. You're like a mother to me. I'm going.'

Prakash throws off the sari as though it were a burning coal and gets into his own clothes. He hurries towards the door without looking at Sumitraben. She watches him with a mild smile. 'Take the books that Swamiji has left for you. Read them carefully.' He turns around. She is still naked. For a moment he wants to refuse the books. But she says, 'Come tomorrow at five o'clock. We'll discuss your work then.'

'Work?'

'Swamiji wants three paintings by the end of the month. Small ones. He wants to take them to America. He wants you to paint the subjects he has suggested.'

'But . . .'

'There's plenty of money in this. You must also cultivate an image now. Grow your hair a little. Swamiji has suggested a dhoti-jhabba-shoulder-cloth get-up.'

Prakash's mind is in a whirl. He mechanically takes the books from Sumitraben's hands, executes a formal smile and rushes out.

There's a strong wind blowing from the sea. It buffets Prakash from behind, pushing him to the end of the road before giving up the chase. Prakash has no idea where he is going. He walks blindly, the string of rudrakshas swinging from his neck with every step he takes.

23

She has just put the mixture of gram flour and buttermilk on the gas burner when the doorbell rings. 'Just the right moment,' Anima mutters and continues to stir the mixture as though she hasn't heard the bell. It's done in a minute. She takes the pan off the flame and spreads the batter thin on the back of a steel plate, so thin that the metal shows through. The bell rings a second time. Anima wipes her hands on a kitchen towel and hurries to the door. It is Bachchu Kaka.

'How long? Were you sleeping?'

'Sleeping, Kaka? Haridas is throwing a party. Something special, he said. So I was just . . .'

'Water first. Then talk.' Bachchu Kaka throws himself into a chair.

'Oops! Sorry.' Anima runs into the kitchen.

'Lovely. You've put khus in it.' Bachchu Kaka downs the whole glassful in a series of quick gulps. 'Now you may tell me about that sex maniac. I hope he's not troubling Marli and Girji. You never know . . .'

'For heaven's sake, Kaka!'

'Heaven's sake? Why? But never mind. Let's hear his praises.'

'I wasn't praising anybody. Just saying he's asked me to bring suralichya vadya for the party.'

'And you're making them.'

'Can I say go to hell I won't?'

'Of course you can't. Women love dancing around that kind of man. The more intelligent and capable they are the more giddily they dance.'

'He's a fine artist, Kaka. Everybody has their faults. He likes women.'

'Likes? We like women too. But that doesn't mean we . . . never mind. So you're making suralichya vadya. How long will that take? I have to catch the Flying Ranee from Bombay Central at 5.55. I want to have a few words with you before that.'

'Why a few? Have hundreds of words with me. The vadya are not important.'

'Oh? Well, well. The old man gets ranked above the evergreen playboy.'

'The vadya can wait because once the batter's spread, the stuffing, cutting, rolling and tempering can be done later.'

'Is there no limit to your honesty? I gave up telling your father that. Never mind. Sit here and listen. When was the last time you went to Surgaon?'

'Last month.'

'Did you notice any change in the way your mother spoke or behaved?'

'I did sense something, but couldn't put my finger on exactly what. Why do you ask?'

'She's completely under Doctor Bhaskar's sway.'

'Whose sway?'

'Dr Bhaskar.' Bachchu Kaka takes a deep breath. 'First understand what kind of creature this Bhaskar fellow is. I've felt uneasy about him from the time he came to our district supposedly to work for the Warlis. I began to make inquiries. I've managed to trace him back to where he comes from. America. He was a doctor in a hospital in the town where our Sandesh Siddhapure lives. Sandesh has given me the complete picture—front view, side view, everything.'

Bachchu Kaka has a coughing fit. Clearing his throat, he says, 'Would you happen to have honey in the house?'

'Of course.' Anima gets up.

'Where are you going? First listen. One teaspoonful of honey in a glass of warm water.'

'Kaka, let me get you tea.'

'Get me tea when I ask for it. Now I'm asking for warm water and honey.'

Sipping from the glass of water and honey, Bachchu Kaka continues, 'So this doctor is extremely intelligent, focused, capable and ambitious. Sandesh guesses his children have left home as they do in America. His wife was a classical dancer. She used to teach the Indian girls in the neighbourhood her style, whatever it was.'

'Was?'

'She's dead. Died at the end of 2001. Murdered.'

'Oh my God!'

'At first the police thought this was a classic hit-and-run case. But investigations threw up a different possibility. The only eyewitness to the incident said the whole thing had happened so fast, he hadn't had time to note the registration number of the car. But he remembered clearly what the occupants had shouted as they sped away. "You black bitch terrorist. Go home." Clearly a post-9/11 thing.

'Apparently his wife's death and the thought that her murderers were driving around free, made Bhaskar go berserk. He began to say wild things to his white colleagues. Things like "You'll come licking our feet when we are masters of the world." And "Let's see how your 300-year-old civilization stands up to the power of our 5000 years." There was menace in his voice. Gradually his work began to suffer. His hard-won reputation hit rock bottom. The other Indians, who were first sympathetic, soon began to find his ramblings embarrassing and even dangerous. They began suggesting he return home. "India needs you," they said. "That's where your real work lies." When his local guru said the same thing, Bhaskar began giving it serious thought. The guru finally commanded him to return to the motherland and serve her poor children. He told him that his fellow NRIs would support his work.

'That's how he returned to his village. His cover story is that he has come back to look after his aged parents. For one year, he lay low. Then suddenly he was everywhere. He became known as a social worker. Our fields and forests are wide open to doctors who want to give away free medicines. We have such an abundant supply of the poor who can live or die for all our government cares.' Bachchu Kaka's voice drops to a self-questioning whisper. 'Our adivasis are still the poorest of the poor. My party set them free from bondage, fought for their rightful wages, brought them to a certain stage of education and good health, but couldn't take them further. We left the field open to these Bhaskars to barge in with their free medicines and a free place in the fold.'

Bachchu Kaka slaps his thigh and laughs out loud. 'So there he is, Dr Bhaskar, flitting in and out of your house, influencing your mother.'

'Sounds odious. But what do you mean influencing her?'

'Wish I could say. Something's happening in that house, I don't know what.'

'Ai has given Dr Bhaskar Anna's room for his clinic. Is that what's bothering you?'

'No. That's old news. There's something bigger going on.'

'Bachchu Kaka, I have a feeling you know what it is. Why are you behaving like a character in a thriller, dropping clues and then clamming up?'

Bachchu Kaka removes his spectacles, draws a handkerchief from his pocket and wipes them carefully. He lifts them to the light to make sure they are free of dust and settles them back on his nose. Clearing his throat, he says, 'I'll have tea now. Make it really light with just a bit of sugar.'

Bachchu Kaka gets up and hobbles to the window. Earlier, it was only the right knee that bothered him. Now the left one has decided to play up. Next month I will be eighty, he thinks. If Shankrya had been alive, we'd have gone together to the beach to celebrate. Spent an hour watching the sun go down. Gone over our histories for the nth time—the hows and whys of events and where we had gone wrong. Why did ninety per cent of our population not become free when the country did? Is idealism always defeated by its own people? Are ideals by their very nature sacred only to a few, while the rest pay lip service till the opportunity for self-service offers itself? We would have sighed together over these questions and agreed, as we always did, that we couldn't set ourselves apart from 'the others'. We were lips and teeth in the same head as the saying went. The thought would have silenced us. But Shankrya just upped and left, the coward. And here I am, alone. I always was, but it's not romantic to be alone at eighty. It's a bit pathetic . . .

'Kaka, tea.'

'How fast this neighbourhood is changing! Last time I was here there was a large open space next to your building. We could see the sea beyond.' Bachchu Kaka turns from the window and sits down. 'A builder's trying to gobble it up. Imagine, this used to be a jungle once. Listen to this story. In the plague of 1896, eleven Parsi families are said to have sailed across the sea from Bombay to escape the epidemic and found themselves in this safe haven. They built eleven bungalows, seven here and four farther down. That's where the names Seven Bungalows and Four Bungalows come from. Only one of the original eleven is still standing. Once that gets sold and the developer bulldozes it, the last landmark of nineteenth-century Versova will disappear.'

Bachchu Kaka sips his tea, his eyes fixed on the opposite wall. 'Is that Ashu's work?'

'Yes, one of his old ones. He didn't want to sell it or give it to me though I wanted it very much. I suspect this is Nasreen. Then suddenly some time ago he said if you still want that painting, you can have it.'

'What exuberant colours! I hear he sells quite well.'

'True. Some collectors are pretty keen on his work.'

'Shankrya had art in his fingers. He didn't value it. Paint can't do what words can, he used to say. Everything he did was to awaken people. What does this painting say? Anything of use to society?'

'Not of use in the way you mean. But you've been staring at it. Why?'

'Because it's there!' Bachchu Kaka lets out a loud laugh. 'My dear woman, I was also a lawyer like your father. Don't try and catch me out. But you are right. The painting is forcing me to look at it. I can't say why.'

Anima looks curiously at Bachchu Kaka. His shining bald head is ringed by fine white hair, lit up now like a halo under the rays of the slanting sun.

'Kaka, you look like a Christian saint. So you're going to tell me in simple words what's going on with Ai.'

'No, I'm not. I'll tell you why. Because I've begun to think you two don't value your heritage as much as you should. You come once a month, that too in the evening, and are off again next morning. I think you should spend more time there if you want to see what's happening.

If you don't do that, it means you're happy letting things take their course. I don't need to worry about it then. We did what we could in our time. Now you must take over.'

Anima feels suddenly alone. It's as if somebody has whisked the roof off her head and the sky above is empty. There's deep disappointment, even a touch of bitterness, in Bachchu Kaka's voice. She has displeased him. The thought hurts Anima.

'Kaka, you tell me what we should do. Ai was Anna's wife, yes. But you know they were as far apart in ideas as in age. But the fact is, Anna has left his entire property—the house, the orchard, everything—to her. If we question her even mildly, she says she has the right to do what she wants with it. We must grant her that right, mustn't we? How can we interfere? As far as she's concerned, I'm irresponsible because I married Siddhartha, a shippie from a lower caste, when there were any number of well-educated Brahmin boys I could have married. So my opinions don't count. Even Ashesh had shown his irresponsibility by getting involved with "that Mussalman girl". But he's better than me because he gave her up when Ai opposed the match.'

'Ashesh never gave that as the reason. He simply got cold feet.'

'I think she suspects that, and it makes her angry. When he wouldn't even look at the matches she suggested to him, she decided he too had no sense of responsibility. His only interest is in slapping paint on paper she says. So there's no point asking him for his opinion on serious matters. Ai thinks she's terribly unlucky to have produced two irresponsible children like us. I haven't been able to budge her even a fraction from her complete mistrust of me. Ashesh doesn't even try to do that. So what can we do to prevent whatever's happening in Surgaon from happening?'

Bachchu Kaka wipes the sweat off the top of his head. 'You're right. I've never understood why Shankar had to give Sindhutai sole rights over all the property. We believe we know our loved ones. But they suddenly throw us a googly that leaves us stumped. Oh well, I must leave. If I get to the terminus early enough I might beat the crowd to a seat. Crowds scare me now.'

Bachchu Kaka gets up and stands still till his knees loosen. His eyes are on Ashesh's painting.

'Kaka, you've said nothing specific about what's worrying you. I'm going to Surgaon next week. What do you think I should do?'

'Don't make it a rushed visit. Keep your eyes peeled and ears pricked. Then decide for yourself what you have to . . . or can . . . do.'

Bachchu Kaka is still staring at Ashesh's painting.

'Ashesh doesn't play with colour these days. Is he disturbed?'

'No more than an artist should be.'

'If he has an old unsold painting like this one, please tell him I'd like to have it. My room looks bare now.'

'Why? Where're the books?'

'Given away. Getting ready to depart.'

'Depart? Where are you off to?'

Bachchu Kaka points to the floor. 'To that place reserved for atheists.' He's still laughing as he leaves.

Anima goes to the kitchen. She finishes making the suralichya vadya in an uneasy state of mind. She tastes a roll. Smiles. Her mind is uneasy but her hands have done their work. The roll is silky smooth, bright yellow and flavourful, the tempering of asafoetida and mustard seeds crackling between her teeth.

In the living room, she wonders what heritage of Anna's Bachchu Kaka was referring to. Is Ai all right? She didn't appear too well when Anima saw her last.

The doorbell rings and all questions fly out of her mind. It's Vaishali. Then Mangesh and Rahul arrive. Finally Radha. Radha is very excited. 'I have something wonderful to show you.' She sits at the dining table. The others gather around. From her tan leather tote bag she draws out a small jewel case covered in royal-blue velvet. She shoves the hair out of her eyes, opens the case and pushes it to the centre of the table. The others bend over it. 'It's a dragonfly,' Mangesh says laconically. They gaze upon the iridescent blue, purple, green and silver of its gossamer wings and its two huge eyes that meet on top of the head.

Radha whispers, 'I was at my computer when I heard a little plop on the table next to me. It was this beauty. I thought it would fly away, but it lay absolutely still, its wings spread out, the colours vivid and the eyes wide open. Much later I realized it was dead.' The others continued to gaze in wonder at this lively form of death.

'What's the Marathi word for dragonfly, Bai?'

'Chatur, I think.'

'That's what Ai said. But Baba said "bhingri".' Radha laughs. 'Ai told him that must be his village word. Baba said, "I'll ask Arvind." He called up Arvind Kaka. Arvind Kaka said, "Let me look it up in my English–Marathi dictionary." He came back with "patang". Ai said, "What rubbish! A patang is triangular and dusty brown. It throws itself at flames and dies."'

'I think it's "chatur",' Anima says, but tentatively.

'Ai asked Arvind Kaka to look up "chatur" in his Marathi–English dictionary. There was no "chatur" noun there. Only "chatur" adjective. So Baba asked him to look up "bhingri". It was there but the English for it was beetle. Ai insisted that dragonfly was chatur and proved her point by singing a nursery rhyme which went:

Oh you gullible little chatur
Playmate of my childhood

Baba said, "Rubbish! Chatur means clever. How can a chatur be gullible?" Ai said chatur as in dragonfly refers to its four wings. Chatur is four. Baba slapped his forehead and gave up the argument. Ai turned her face away from him and went "hrmph". I sat in peace looking at this beauty. Where could it have come from?'

'From North America or Japan,' Mangesh offers.

As a general rule, nobody doubts Mangesh's general knowledge. But this time Rahul thinks his suggestion is too, too far out. So he runs to the computer and googles 'dragonfly'.

'Mangesh could be right,' he says, half disappointed. 'Listen to this. Japan's second name is Akitsushima—Dragonfly Island. Japan is home to the greatest variety of dragonflies in the world. They have a sanctuary for them. Oh my God! Listen to this. These insects have been in existence for 300 million years. They migrate every year but nobody knows why or where to. They can fly at a speed of forty miles an hour. And listen to this last thing. Lines from a poem by Tennyson.'

'Oh no, not poetry please,' Vaishali pleads.

'Okay. Not the whole poem. Just one line. The poet describes the dragonfly's flight as "a living flash of light".'

Anima gets up to switch on the light. The dragonfly's wings look even more radiant under the glow.

'What shall we do with it?' Mangesh wonders.

'What do you think?'

'Throw it out. Into some bushes.'

'It's so alive.'

'Don't be stupid. It's dead. What will you do with it?'

'It'll attract ants if you put it back in your box.'

'Bai, shall we bury it in the planter outside your door?'

Anima smiles assent. Radha puts the dragonfly on the open palm of her hand. Mangesh rakes up the top soil in the planter. Radha buries the dragonfly. Then everybody comes in and sits down silently.

'It's so sad,' says Vaishali.

'What?' Rahul asks.

'But isn't it fascinating? That it looked as beautiful dead as alive? It died yesterday.'

'They say beauty doesn't last.'

'I don't know. I attended a lecture where this man couldn't stop talking about inner beauty which lasts.'

Rahul is back at the computer.

'Baba said they used to catch bhingris in the village, tie strings to their legs and fly them. That's why I said it's so sad.'

Rahul turns around and says, 'We're not as beautiful as dragonflies. But there's something that we share with them. Dragonflies are sometimes part of a swarm but sometimes all alone. Listen to this translation of a Japanese haiku. Sorry, Vaishali. But haikus are only three lines long.'

'As if I didn't know that.'
'Then listen to this one.

'Lonesomely clings the dragonfly to
The underside of the leaf.
Ah! The autumn rain.'

24

The way to Haridas's house is through an inconspicuous by-lane. In the old days his directions to newcomers were: 'Go straight past Siddhivinayak temple, take the first left and the second right. Go straight down this road till you hit a garbage container. My house is in the wadi opposite. It's a tiled cottage called Le Chateau.'

Two months ago the garbage container disappeared. The MR Party had opened an office nearby. The party workers began to find the stench of the garbage unbearable and had the municipality remove the container. Haridas was upset about the loss of this important landmark; but Ramprasad gave him a piece of happy news. The MR Party, keen on local votes, was planning a urinal in place of the garbage container.

The urinal was built before you could say piss. The heavyweights of the party were happily available for its inauguration and so it went on stream in style. When the inaugural ribbon was cut, ten strapping, hand-picked locals were lined up to pee in the urinal. They were paid a handsome fee. Their only regret was that, given the nature of their services, the press had published no pictures.

With the urinal in place, Haridas began directing newcomers to his home thus: 'Second right. Walk down the road till you hit Shri Maibhoomi Rashtriya Paksha Ablutions Complex No. 11. The wadi opposite that is where I live.' A few days later some public-spirited local youth improved on the MR Party's idea of social service. Taking into consideration the linguistic inadequacies of the common man, they painted 'URINAL' over 'Ablutions Complex No. 11' in big, red letters. Nobody knew why the MR Party workers had decided urine was less offensive, as stinks go, than garbage. The garbage had kept more or less to itself. But you could smell the urinal all the way to the end of the street. In fact, Haridas often tells people now to 'turn right and follow your nose till you hit . . .'

Anima enters the wadi, managing the container of suralichya vadya carefully so they don't go to pieces. Children of all sizes are playing on the mud path leading into the wadi. Men have rolled up their vests over their stomachs to let in the air. Women in maxis fan themselves with squares of folded scrap paper and make soft shooshing noises to feel cooler. They sit untidily in the doorways of their squat, tin-roofed, single-room homes, half their attention on the noisy children and half on their dinners cooking on improvised three-brick chulahs fired with wood shavings. Rice bubbles and crackles on one chulah, dal on another. A young girl in a salwar kameez angrily beats dough into large, thick bhakris and slaps them on to an iron griddle on a third fire. In the split second that she allows her attention to wander to the gold border of Anima's sari passing by, the tip of a finger gets seared on the griddle. 'Oh shit!' she spits out. Anima looks back startled. A woman sitting in a nearby doorway howls with laughter. 'Her father's put her in an English-medium school, see? But her mother's in hospital so the fancy miss has to make bhakris.' The girl throws the woman a venomous look and beats out the next bhakri with even greater fury. The eater of that bhakri is going to end up with a stomach ache, Anima thinks, and stubs her toe on a stone.

'Watch it,' a voice emerges from the dark shadows on the right. Ramprasad clicks his tongue sympathetically from his seat under the banyan tree. 'This is the exact place where a coconut this large dropped off that tree on a visitor's head,' he says, speaking in his UP Hindi. 'That was in '55 when there were three times as many coconut trees here than you see now. Fellow died on the spot. He was right there where you are, standing one minute, down the next.'

Anima makes yes-yes noises and slips away, with Ramprasad's voice in hot pursuit. 'There was no electricity in these parts then. The wadi was full of Bhandaris' huts, toddy tappers . . .'

Anima rings Haridas's doorbell. That is, she pulls at the rope hanging by the door releasing a rich, melodious tinkle within. Haridas has had the bell cast by a Bastar tribal in bell metal. Marli opens the door. She's dressed in vivid colours—a salwar kameez of large floral print, shiny, coloured clips in oil-slicked hair tied with a bright-pink nylon ribbon bow topped by three clusters of blazing gulmohr flowers. Marli's face is a wide grin as she steps aside to let Anima in. Anima gives her a playful pat on the head and hands over the suralichya vadya to her.

Haridas moved to this cottage when his work started fetching good prices. He was utterly charmed by its tiled roof, its spacious, light-filled living room and its unexpected French name. He had not only paid the price that its East Indian owner had asked for without bargaining but had presented him with a painting as well.

The design of the cottage is traditional. There's a covered veranda in front and one at the back, with a sprawling living room in between. On one side of the living room is the kitchen and a small room where Girji and Marli sleep, and on the other, two rooms—one of which is Haridas's studio and the other his bedroom, equipped with a mattress on the floor.

Anima follows Marli into the kitchen to ask after Girji. Girji shows her blackened teeth in answer to her how are you. Marli giggles. She has spent ten of her twelve years in Mumbai but it never fails to amuse her that people should ask her mother how she is. How is a mother supposed to be?

Returning to the living room, Anima notices that the wall facing the veranda door is covered with a kalamkari bedspread. Haridas winks in response to her raised eyebrows. 'My surprise,' he says, then adds with a smirk, 'Shekhar's coming.'

Anima's expression is neutral. Haridas pretends not to know why Shekhar finds him so unacceptable despite his having moved out of Sharada's life long before she married him. Haridas has adhered strictly to his principle of never messing with married women. Sleeping with women should be a straightforward matter. When he comes across a woman who is both interesting and unattached, he might say to her over coffee, 'I'd like to sleep with you. How about it?' It is entirely possible that the woman has never heard such a direct statement of interest from a man before. This might cause her to feel a little confused, even embarrassed. But she owes him a response. A straight answer to a straight question. If she is attracted by his polished dark skin, his mischievous eyes, his straight gaze, the bhikbalis in his ears and the aura of fame around him and if, as he has rightly gauged, she is far from being a prude, she might say, 'Why not?' So the woman of the world and the man of the world get together. When either has had enough of the other, they part as good friends. Later, if the woman marries, her husband too becomes Haridas's friend.

Sharada had turned out to be different. She had replied, 'I'd rather just be a friend.' He hadn't minded. 'Being friends is also not a bad idea.' But then Sharada had fallen in love with him and slept with him out of love, despite knowing that he was not in love with her.

'I said Shekhar is coming,'

'I heard you,' Anima says. 'Who else?'

'All the others and a new girl from the *Mumbai Observer*.'

'Janaki?'

'You know her? Oh God! Of course. She was with you at Sharada's concert.'

Anima looks at Haridas with narrowed eyes. He grins. 'Don't worry. I don't find tense women attractive. The types who weigh every word they speak and smile once a month.'

The doorbell rings. It's Feroze. 'Late. You're forgetting Mummy's lessons.' Feroze smiles, gives Anima a tight hug and pecks her on both cheeks.

'How's it going?' she asks.

'Going.'

'Your magnum opus?' Haridas asks.

'What's this?' Feroze points at the covered wall.

'The reason for the party.'

Ashesh comes with Ramprasad's question still caught in his smile. 'Sa'ab, why haven't you brought your missus along?' Like everybody else, Ramprasad finds Ashesh's attachment to his old car amusing. But Ashesh has begun to find driving too stressful. 'Where's Mrs Padmini?' Haridas asks, echoing Ramprasad. 'Didn't hear her grumbling and coughing.'

'Bet he's left her at home,' Anima says.

'How can he do that?'

'He's become a Gandhian. Travels by public transport, rubbing shoulders with the likes of us.'

Ashesh turns to Anima. 'I came by cab today.' His face glows at having scored a point over her.

'My brother looks pleased,' Anima says to Feroze, her eyes resting curiously on Ashesh's face.

'Work must be going well,' Feroze murmurs.

Sharada, Shekhar and Janaki arrive together. They smile stiffly and look for places to sit. Silence descends on the room. It's the first time after Sharada's marriage that Shekhar and Haridas are face to face in the same room. It's hot outside, but the temperature inside has dropped. Shekhar looks stern, deliberately so. Sharada's face is blank. Ashesh's eyes avoid Janaki's. Janaki's avoid Haridas's, but turn repeatedly to Ashesh. Haridas looks nervous. Anima watches everybody in turn, conscious of the drama that is playing out silently. Only Feroze is relaxed. The ins and outs of complex human relations are beyond him. Since nobody says anything, he says to Janaki, 'Your friend Prakash calls me all the time. I should have stuck to using my mouth to eat dosas that evening. The last time he called he wanted to know if he should accept Sumitraben's invitation to a satsang. A satsang, for heaven's sake!'

'What did you tell him?' Anima asks, while Janaki looks at the floor mortified.

'I think I said go.'

'Poor boy. Straight into the lioness's jaws.'

Now everybody starts talking all at once. Haridas says to Janaki, 'Who's this friend?'

Sharada says to Feroze, 'Who's Prakash?'

Shekhar says to Ashesh, 'We haven't met for years. I believe your show's opening soon?'

'Not all that soon,' Ashesh answers. 'Twenty-eighth September. Between Ganapati and Dussehra.'

'By the way, meet Janaki,' Haridas announces. Everybody bursts out laughing. 'Oh God, of course. You were together at the great seminar. What about you, Shekhar? Do you know Janaki?'

Shekhar's eyes turn into two quick-frost ice cubes. 'She is learning music from my wife.' The emphasis on 'my wife' amuses Haridas. He turns to Sharada. 'You didn't tell me.'

Sharada reddens. 'Did I need to?'

Anima says, 'Really, Haridas. You expect us to keep you updated on everything that's happening in our lives?'

'Plain human curiosity,' Haridas says.

'That could be my problem too. So tell me, which lucky woman are you making divinely blissful these days?'

Several pairs of shocked eyes turn to Anima. She, the epitome of good form, has broken an unwritten rule. The women in Haridas's life are to be left out of conversations unless he brings them in. Ashesh's eyes warn Anima to keep off. But Feroze puts his arm around her shoulders. Anima doesn't shift her gaze from Haridas's face. Haridas rubs his cheek dramatically. 'That stung. But you're right. Why should I want to know who Sharada's students are? Anyway, take my advice, Janaki. Don't learn those new things she's composing.'

Ashesh moves over to Janaki's side.

'Why not?' Sharada asks coldly. 'Do artists have a monopoly on experiment?'

Haridas looks at her gravely. 'That's almost how it is. Our language is global. It is not bound by traditions like yours. Tradition's your anchor. Throw that away and you lose everything. Any wind from anywhere can toss your boat around.'

'Did Kumar Gandharva's boat get tossed around?'

'Are you Kumar Gandharva?'

'As much as you are Picasso. But nobody denies you the right to experiment.'

'The tradition of art itself is about constant experimentation and change. Nobody practises "classical art" like they do classical music and classical dance. We don't touch our ears in apology to an unseen guru every time we make a mistake.'

'And yet you make monumental mistakes. Your installation of white sheets hung all over the place was one. But it was important for you to try it out. Because artists have to keep pushing back what they've done successfully to discover what else they can do. An entire gharana in classical music was born out of rejecting known raags for newly composed, unknown ones. Who composed them? Wasn't that experimentation?'

'But your bandish that day . . .'

'. . . might have failed like your white sheets. But I learnt a few things from composing and singing it.'

'So did I,' Janaki comes in. 'The words and the music together hit me straight in the gut.'

A heavy silence descends again. Sharada stares defiantly at Haridas. Haridas gets up from Janaki's side, gazing appreciatively at Sharada. 'Touché. You've shut me up . . . at least for the moment.'

The atmosphere lightens. People shift in their seats. Anima moves over to Janaki's side. 'Why have you deserted me, Anima?' Feroze calls out melodramatically, hand on chest. Ashesh gets up and moves away. 'Come sit here,' Janaki says and smiles at Feroze. From where he is standing, Ashesh has Janaki's three-quarter profile in view. The pearl drop in her ear catches the light. Ashesh holds his breath. Vermeer's *Girl with a Pearl Earring*. He smiles. Haridas catches the smile. He winks. Ashesh frowns at him and turns to study the Gaitonde on the wall behind him.

Shekhar comes over to him. 'Can't stand him. How could you be his friend for so many years? You are poles apart.'

'They say opposites attract.'

'He's constantly performing.'

'He's a wonderful artist.'

'Does that absolve him?'

'Absolve? We all wear masks to protect ourselves from the world. His is a little exaggerated, that's all. I've never gone into why he's like that.'

'You mean he might have had an unhappy childhood and all that? Makes no difference. He's got his eyes on Janaki now.'

'What rubbish!' Ashesh realizes his voice is louder than necessary. 'Sorry,' he tries to compensate. 'I don't think she's his type.'

'Does he have a type? Never mind.'

Ashesh touches Shekhar's shoulder in a spontaneous gesture of empathy.

Haridas emerges from the kitchen. Feroze growls, 'Ei, you jungli! Where's the daru?'

'It's coming. But not to get sozzled on. It's to celebrate what's behind that bedspread.' He points to the covered wall. Looking around, he continues, 'I think it's only right that the newcomer in our midst, Janaki Patil, should unveil it. Ms Patil, please do the honours.'

Janaki is thrown. She shakes her head vigorously. She looks at Ashesh. He fixes his eyes on Haridas, asking him to lay off. Haridas refuses to meet his eyes. 'To introduce Janaki Patil briefly, she kind of took off my chuddies in a little piece she wrote on me last month. After that she did a serious analysis of the clay objects made in Dharavi's Potters' Colony as objects of art. If she continues to write stuff like that, she'll be thrown out of her paper. Ladies and gentlemen, Janaki Patil.'

Janaki sits frozen in her seat. She resents impositions. Her eyes shoot arrows at Haridas. His thick skin deflects them. Anima says, 'Just get up and pull that cover off. Two seconds' work.' Feroze says from the other side, 'Go on, heave.'

Janaki refuses to move. She will not submit to Haridas's whim. Ashesh gives her a close look, then says to Haridas, 'I object. I am the seniormost artist in this room. I think the honour should be mine.' He looks around the room. 'I shall feel very hurt if my right is ignored.'

'There's no senior and junior amongst friends,' Haridas deliberately takes Ashesh's words at face value. 'Janaki's our guest today. The rest of you are family.'

'I don't think family should be ignored for outsiders.' There's a round of applause. Haridas bows his head, touches his ears and says, 'Forgive me, guru. Come this way.'

Ashesh flicks the cover off in one deft movement. The wall behind is covered by a Warli painting. Everybody is stunned.

'Girji made it,' Haridas whispers. All eyes turn to the kitchen doorway. There is nobody there.

'She's sitting in there. She will not come out. I'd been after her for years to paint something on this wall for me. Suddenly she did this.'

'Warli women never paint on order.' Ashesh's voice is thick with emotion. 'They paint their own walls for their own rituals. This is amazing.'

Haridas pops a bottle of champagne. 'Let's toast Girji's art.' They raise their glasses towards the kitchen. Marli is now in the doorway, twisting the curtain around her hand. She giggles when they raise their glasses and runs in.

Sharada stands before the painting. There's a whole world there, quite unknown to her. Janaki stands beside her, looking closely at the motifs worked in white lines on a plaster of geru. The space, almost five feet across, is filled with human figures. Each figure is two triangles, meeting at the apex. The meeting point is the waist. The upper triangle bears the arms, the lower one, the legs. There are many species of trees around, some with frond-like branches. They have leaves like jagged teeth or spotted sprays. There is a sun in one corner of the sky. Its dazzling light is represented by four concentric circles and six short, pulsating rays. A crescent moon hangs in the opposite corner, surrounded by twelve cool rays made up of tiny dots. In the left-hand corner at the bottom are a tiger and a peacock. In the right-hand corner is a line of eight men. Before them on the ground lies a body.

Janaki looks at Ashesh. 'What's happening here?' Anima takes her by the hand and leads her to the kitchen. 'Let's ask Girji.'

Girji sits with her back against a wall, her legs drawn up to her chest.

'It's a beautiful picture, Girji,' Anima says. Girji looks at Anima with clouded eyes and draws her legs tighter against her chest.

'What is it about?' Anima asks.

Girji does not answer. She looks down and rubs one foot against the other.

'This lady is going to write about your picture in her newspaper. How did you think of it?'

Girji continues to look down but mutters, 'Just like that.'

'Who is the woman on the ground in the corner?'

'Bhutali,' Girji says.

'Bhutali?' Janaki asks as they return to the living room.

'A bhutali is a witch,' Anima answers.

Janaki doesn't get it. There's a sun, a moon and trees there. And a witch? She must find out what it means. Haridas stands behind her. 'What do you think of it?'

'Can't get it. I'd love to write about it.'

'If your paper publishes that, then I'll know for sure.'

'What?'

'That your editor is in love with you.'

'Love my foot! He's shit scared of orders from above.'

'It's his skin he's scared for. Now instead of writing about Warli paintings, if you wrote about my mysterious past . . . Do you want an exclusive?'

'That'd be like killing the goose that lays all those golden eggs every other month.'

'Goose? I am interviewed for the greatness of my work. But I'm offering you a golden egg. "Haridas Unplugged"!' He laughs. Janaki joins in reluctantly. He catches Ashesh's look over her head. 'Guruji doesn't like our frivolity.'

Janaki turns so suddenly that Ashesh has no time to detach his eyes from her. He goes red.

'I don't know about your editor,' Haridas murmurs. 'But this man's a goner. This is a scoop. If I were your gossip columnist, I'd have written you a juicy snippet about Mr Bachelor being clean bowled.'

Janaki says coldly, 'I'm hungry.'

Marli has arranged several bowls and dishes of steaming food on the table set against the kitchen wall. The aromas wafting out lure everybody in. It's a colourful spread. There's a white chicken curry in coconut milk, a red cauliflower–tomato gravy preparation, a curry of black gram with Malvani masala, a pale green salad of cabbage, cucumber, green peppers and raw mango—all made by Haridas. Then there are Anima's soft, plump vadya. Everybody attacks the food. The world is silent.

Later, Feroze offers to take Anima home. But she's staying at Ashesh's in Gamdevi. 'Why don't you see Janaki home,' Ashesh suggests. 'She's on your way.'

Shekhar and Sharada sit stiffly in their car, separated by a wall of fire. 'Never again,' Shekhar growls. Sharada stares ahead without a word. 'He talks of only one thing. Himself. And talks incessantly. Courtesy and good form are so middle class, aren't they? He's the great artist. How could you bear to be with him for two whole years? I know love is blind and all that. But deaf as well?'

The road is quiet. A gentle breeze blows through the car window. It stirs the loose wisps of hair around Sharada's face. She undoes the knot of hair at the back of her head, pulls the wisps back in and, with two twists of her wrists, reties the knot. Looking at the curve of her neck, Shekhar says through clenched teeth, 'And what did he finally want? Just the body. You were thinking love. The way he looks at you even now. Men have a certain way of looking at bodies they have known. You're busy arguing experimentation in art and he's gobbling up your body with his eyes.'

Shekhar steers the car in through the gates of Ganesh Krupa.

'You've decided to say nothing. It's an old strategy. You have to demonstrate how unfair and idiotic I am and how long enduring you have to be. There's enough life in your relationship with him for you to argue heatedly with him. But why bother to argue with me?'

Shekhar gets out of the car and slams the door shut.

'Shall we walk on the beach for a while?' Sharada asks.

'Why? Let's go upstairs and relieve Ai of our son. She's getting on after all.'

'But if she sees you like this, she won't sleep the whole night.'

'What does "like this" mean?' Shekhar squares his shoulders.

'Upset.'

'She knows the reason.'

'She used to. She thinks you got over it after Shantanu came.'

Shekhar kicks at a stone near his foot. The stone somersaults into the gutter.

'Then you go up. You aren't saying anything anyway. I'll go for a walk.'

'Alone?'

'Why not? I was alone in the car. I'll be alone on the beach. What's the difference? If I have to talk to myself, I might as well be by myself, so I don't fool myself that I have a companion.'

Shekhar strides off without looking at Sharada. Sharada's body is heavy as stone. She drags it up three floors and opens the door with her key. Ai is pacing the floor with Shantanu on her shoulder.

'Good heavens! Isn't he asleep yet?'

'No. Aji, let's do this, let's do that, and where's Mamma and where's Baba.'

Sharada takes the drowsy Shantanu from Ai.

'Where's Shekhar?'

Sharada fumbles around in her mind for a fib. She glances at Ai. Won't wash.

'You've had an argument.'

'He's made himself miserable.'

'I thought he had got over that. He has to try and let it go.'

'He still can't.'

'I expect you said nothing as usual.'

'Yes.'

'Why?'

'What do I say? Whatever I say turns out wrong.'

'But you should still say something, dear. It makes people feel less alone.'

'I've said so much already, Ai. Tried so hard to convince him that this me is a different person from that one. Even I wonder how I could have been in love with that man. But I can't deny that I was. We have to learn to live with that, don't we?'

Ai says nothing. Sharada goes in to put Shantanu in his cot.

'Even simple things become complex at times like these. Question— what do we do now? Pretend nothing has happened? Go to bed? Or do we stay up till he comes back? If he's still upset he'll say, "See, she's gone to bed." If he has calmed down and we're awake he'll say, "Why did you stay up?" Makes me feel guilty.'

Ai and Sharada sit still. Then Ai says, 'I'll go to bed. You stay up. Face whatever's coming.'

Shekhar returns after an hour. Sharada stiffens when she hears his footsteps on the stairs. He lets himself in. He looks at her, opens his mouth to say something. Closes it. But then he opens his arms. She flings herself into them. Her eyes are streaming. His arms tighten around her.

'I'm going to put myself through this test again. And I'm going to win. But not too soon.'

Sharada is gazing up at him from the comfort of his chest.

'Your lower lip is very tempting.'

'The whole of you is very tempting.'

25

Painting Walls

Girji, a Warli woman, has done a traditional painting on a wall in artist Haridas's home in Prabhadevi. Janaki Patil writes about the painting in the context of Warli art.

Twenty-five years ago, Mumbai's art world discovered Warli art. Till then these pictures, attractively etched in simple white lines on cow-dung-plastered walls in the dark interiors of Warli huts, had not been seen in the outside world. Warli paintings are auspicious signs marking rites of passage. They are invitations to the gods to attend events like weddings and births. They are never painted outside this ritualistic framework.

The painters of the pictures must be married women. In a typical painting, the deity's image occupies a central square. The space outside the square is figured with natural phenomena like men and women, the sun and the moon, snakes, tigers and trees, all drawn in keeping with traditional conventions of representation that are held sacred.

It is not known who first brought this art out of its traditional space into the space of Mumbai's art galleries. But when it happened, there was great excitement in certain sections of Mumbai's art world. When Mumbai is excited, thoughts of commercial exploitation are never too far behind. How were Warli paintings, trapped in ritual and tradition, to be turned into commerce? Gallery walls did not lend themselves to being plastered with cow dung. Nor could wall paintings be sold.

The answer was textured paper in place of textured walls. If women were unwilling to work outside tradition, men could be persuaded to do so. They were not bound by tradition because they were not the traditional painters. However, they knew how to do it because they had grown up watching their mothers and wives paint. Even then, men living within the community might be difficult to persuade for fear of censure.

A solution was found in Jivya Soma Mashe, whom circumstances had separated from family and community. He lived away from his pada, scratching drawings into the earth to express his sorrow through his art. He was willing to shift to paper. He had the talent, imagination and skill to add new motifs to the old, deploying them in new ways. Jivya Soma Mashe thus became the first and most famous Warli painter on the urban circuit.

Meanwhile Warli women had continued to paint their auspicious drawings on the walls of their huts.

It is against this background that the picture painted by Haridas's maid Girji on a wall of his house assumes significance. Girji has been working in the house for several years, but had thus far disregarded all of Haridas's requests to make a painting on his wall. He has no idea what prompted her to change her mind. But the result is a large painting done in conventional motifs. There is a crescent moon, a dazzling sun, trees and animals. Along with these regular motifs, an intriguing, even disturbing event has been recorded in the bottom right-hand corner of the work. (See picture.) A female figure lies prone on the ground before a line of men. This figure is a 'bhutali' or witch, a practitioner of black magic.

When there are sudden, inexplicable deaths in Warli padas, when epidemics strike, or when somebody's illness refuses to respond to traditional medicine, the pada begins to buzz with the word bhutali. The bhutali is always an inhabitant of the pada and often turns out to be a destitute widow. The village exorcist is called in to discover who she is. He makes a pretence of reading a scatter of rice, but with his ear to the ground, he knows whom the villagers suspect or hold a grudge against. As soon as the exorcist declares her to be the bhutali, the men of the village drag her out of her hut, or wherever she may be cowering in fear, and take turns to beat her with sticks till she . . .

'Busy writing, hunh?'

Janaki looks up startled and stares open-jawed at the person standing before her.

'Prakash?' Her voice sounds like a bleat.

'May I sit down?'

She nods in a daze. He lifts his white robe a little to prevent it from catching the dirt off the floor and sinks into her visitor's chair, settling his silk gold-bordered shoulder cloth firmly on his shoulder. His hair flows down to the neck of his robe. The gold links in the string of rudrakshas he wears glint in the light.

'What's all this, Prakash?'

'Prakashanand.' He beams. 'I've been granted deeksha by Swami Shivanand. I am now with him.'

'And your painting?'

'It's taken off in a big way. I do spiritual paintings. Bindu, chakra, kundalini. Those things sell like hot cakes abroad. Once I do my solo show here, I'll start selling here too. Feroze sir advised me to go to Sumitraben. I touch his feet in my mind every day.'

'You're having a solo show?'

'Sure. That's why I'm here. I had to meet your editor for pre-publicity. I told him you were the best person to write about me. Your owner is Sumitraben's cousin, you know. Sumitraben is sponsoring the show. So now you can write about me without any problem.'

Janaki doesn't know what to say.

'Why don't we have a cup of tea somewhere if you're not too busy?'

'No, no, no,' Janaki protests. 'I have a deadline to meet in an hour.'

'So I shouldn't eat into your time, right? No problem. We'll meet for the interview. That'll be some time next month.'

'Who was that?' Suryakanta asks, hurrying over to Janaki's desk.

'Prakash Jadhav, artist on the make.' Janaki leans back in her chair, shaking her head.

Her cell rings. Ashesh. Janaki's hand goes instinctively to her hair to tidy it. How stupid. He can't see her. Ashesh sounds excited. 'Are you writing that piece about Girji's work? I've just found my book on Warli art which has a painting by Balu Dumara. It shows bhutalis being chased by an exorcist with a whip. The interesting thing is that these bhutalis' hair stands up around their head like sunrays. But Girji's bhutali . . .'

'. . . has hair like all the other women, sticking out at the back of her head like a tuft.'

'Correct. Now, if we're saying Warli paintings are bound by strict conventions of representation, think what this departure might imply.'

'That the woman who's being lynched is not a bhutali at all, but innocent, like the other women in the pada.' Janaki's voice is excited.

'That's it.' There is a long silence as Janaki mulls over the possibility.

'Want me to hang up?'

'Why?'

'Then continue in silent communication?'

'Sorry.' Janaki laughs. 'Prakash was here just now.'

'Whatever for?'

'Who is this Sumitraben?'

'A wheeler-dealer. They say she likes young men.'

'She likes Prakash all right! He's become the disciple of some swami. He wears a robe and does spiritual paintings.'

'Ahah! That's clever. There's nobody in the spiritual slot right now.'

'She's sponsoring his show.'

'He'll go far. Remember Feroze was urging him to look into himself? But he did better. He looked around himself. Good for him.'

26

Haridas drops in unexpectedly. He sits for a long time without saying a word. Haridas has always had first right on opening conversations between them. Ashesh has rarely appropriated that right. Since Haridas is silent, so is Ashesh.

At last Haridas says in a low voice, 'You're still with black, are you?'

Ashesh says, 'Yes', knowing full well that is not what Haridas has come to ask him.

'Show me. I'll look. You make coffee.'

Ashesh turns his latest work around for him and goes to the kitchen. Haridas looks at the painting. When Ashesh returns, he is sitting down. Ashesh pulls a peg table forward and places two mugs of coffee on it.

'There's nothing more left for you to say in black. You've done death, you've done the individual and you've done the power of the state. What else?' Haridas's voice is transparently concerned.

Ashesh looks at Haridas, startled. Are his black and grey works about those things?

'I'm not sure I'm out of black yet,' he murmurs tentatively. 'Or maybe I am.' Again Haridas is silent. Then he bursts out, 'I find the idea of the finality of black unacceptable. As Feroze says, black is alive with countless shades. I was looking at Girji's painting. She plastered the wall with red earth. In the rust red were hidden not only all imaginable shades of ochre but, if you looked deep enough, even a hint of purple.'

He looks at Ashesh with ravaged eyes. 'That's what I wanted to tell you,' he says and falls into silence again.

'What?'

'Girji and Marli went home for a wedding. They haven't returned.' There is a silence.

'They'll come,' Ashesh says at last. 'They don't keep to days and dates. You know that.'

'But they went home only recently for the Mahalakshmi fair. Why should Soma fetch them away again? He muttered something about a wedding. But the wedding season's nearly over.'

'They'll come, don't worry.' Ashesh doesn't sound convincing even to himself. 'Do you want me to call Bachchu Kaka?'

'How the laburnums have bloomed. I came that way just to see the trees. Some of the trees in Girji's painting look like laburnums, with clusters of leaves instead of flowers hanging from the branches.'

Haridas sits still. 'Let's wait for a couple of days, then . . . yes, please ask Bachchu Kaka.'

The doorbell rings. 'That must be Janaki.'

Haridas's face changes. Mischief replaces cloud. 'Good news?'

'She wants to interview me.'

'That's even better news. I'll be off. I'm sure you won't press me to stay.'

Both go to the door together. Ashesh is about to open it when suddenly Haridas hugs him very tight. He raises a hand to greet Janaki before he walks out.

'A very grave Haridas?'

'Girji–Marli went home and haven't returned.'

There's a line of worry on Ashesh's face. Janaki too is silent. Both think of Girji's painting.

Janaki sets up her recording Walkman. The interview has to go off well. The editor had turned his nose up at Ashesh's name. 'A middle-class artist from Gamdevi, for heaven's sake. Can anything be duller? Why should our readers want to know anything about him?'

She had said, 'We're running out of spicy artists. We need these types to fill space once in a while. We're putting Shilika on top of the page. It's about her new film. She's in a bikini.' That cheered him up.

Ashesh watches Janaki's every move with interest as she checks the Walkman. Looking up, she smiles. 'I'm going to ask you basic questions that you might find difficult to answer.'

'You're scaring me.'

She bubbles with laughter at the mock fear on his face. Ashesh thinks if I were a portrait painter that laughter would give me a key to her spirit. He picks up the coffee tray. 'Tea or coffee for you?'

'Nothing right now, thanks.'

He looks at her for a second, smiles to himself and goes to the kitchen. When he comes back, she's looking at the red-and-black work that he'd turned around for Haridas.

'This painting is a terrific start-off point for the interview.'

'Why?'

'It answers my first question.'

'Which is?'

She reads from her notebook. 'For several years, your palette has been limited to a few sombre colours. Some critics say you are loath to leave your comfort zone. What would you say to that?'

Ashesh wonders for a moment why he should have anything to say to that. The readers of the paper don't give a damn what colours he uses and why. They'll flip the page as they sip their tea. Then another thought breaks in. Janaki is interested. She wants to know about his work and he wants to talk to her about it. Very much.

'Well, what can I say?' he begins. 'There's a time in every artist's life when it may not be apparent that he's doing anything different. That might even be true on the surface. He is still doing what he has been doing before but that could be just to keep his hand in while new ideas stir within him. They take time to form. It's like soil. After you've had a few good harvests, you must let it lie fallow for it to regain its strength. A critic might see this fallow period as a comfort zone that the artist is trapped in. It is a time when even the artist might secretly wonder if he has dried up. Finished. But he's also wary of doing something "new" to quell his doubts. What is new? The new is not the novel. The new is something fresh and true. Something that connects the artist's being with the being of the world outside. These are complicated processes which the artist himself doesn't fully understand.'

'Your fallow period, as you call it, has lasted about ten years. That's a long time. During this period are there links in your work to events in your personal life?'

'Only to the extent that everything the artist does relates in some way to what's going on in his life and in the world at large. Those are the sources he draws upon. But the truth of a painting doesn't lie in biographical detail. The artist himself isn't conscious where his ideas come from. A series of purely aesthetic concerns comes into play in the very act of painting, carrying the work further and further away from the personal event that might have triggered it. If you go hunting after that personal event, you lose the work.'

'With your latest work, you appear to have moved out of your alleged comfort zone. Do you agree? And if so, can you say what accounts for the shift?'

'No, I can't. Not with any certitude. I am not at a sufficient distance from my present work to see it objectively and explain what is happening or why it is happening.'

'But do you at least feel that this is the beginning of a new period in your work?'

'Yes, you might say it is. I had never used black in my work. One day it accidentally entered a painting I was contemplating. I wasn't sure for a long time whether I wanted to accept its presence or reject it. When I decided to accept it, I realized I had entered another world. The world of black.' Ashesh presses his finger tips together. 'I don't think I've come out of it yet.'

Janaki watches him, as he sits before her with head bent, thinking. She murmurs a soft thank you and switches off the Walkman. He looks up as she rewinds the tape and switches on the play button. Ashesh goes into a panic. He doesn't want to hear his own voice. Let the tape be blank. Let it not have recorded a single word. 'Well, what can I say? There's a time in every artist's life . . .' His voice? Good heavens! No inflections, no modulations. Dull, boring, flat. Ashesh gets up. 'That's enough, don't you think? It's all there. Will you have something now? Tea? Coffee?'

'Love some tea.'

Ashesh is at the cooking counter.

'Who cooks for you?'

He turns around startled. It's a simple question. But it tends to have undercurrents when a woman asks it of a single man. Whether his answer is, 'I do it myself' or 'I have it catered' or 'I have a cook', the expression on the woman's face is almost always: 'Poor chap. No wife.' After years of experience, Ashesh answers curtly, 'Reshma cooks for me.'

'Oh,' Janaki says. Ashesh swings around to look at her. She doesn't look as though she's thinking 'Poor dear'. Totally relieved, he asks, 'What about you?'

'When I'm at home, I eat with Mrs Khanna. Lunch is in the office cafeteria.'

That's about it as far as food as a topic of conversation goes.

Janaki takes the first sip of tea and murmurs, 'Hmmm.' Ashesh feels as happy as he would be if the appreciative sound was directed at one of his paintings. Janaki lets the liquid touch every part of her tongue before swallowing it.

'My association with tea is clouded,' she says, taking a second sip.

'A grain of sugar more or less, temperature a degree cooler than boiling, and my father would thrash my mother.'

'He what?'

Janaki observes the disbelief on Ashesh's face. 'He would thrash my mother.'

There is complete silence after this, while Ashesh recovers. Janaki waits without saying another word. Tea drunk, she gets up. 'Our photographer will call you for an appointment.'

'What?' Ashesh leaps out of his chair. 'Don't be funny.'

'Funny? We need pictures to go with interviews. He'll do some of you and some of this painting.'

'Let him do the painting, but not me. You think I'm going to pose for a picture?'

Janaki looks at him helplessly. The vein near his temple is jumping. She puts her tote bag down. 'May I stay for a while?'

He sits down, his lips clamped tight. She doesn't sit down. She goes round to the back of his chair. 'Excuse me, but I'm going to take a liberty with you,' she says and begins to press his temples gently with the tips of her fingers. Ashesh contracts his body. 'No need to be tense. There's as little of the personal in what I'm doing as there is in your paintings. I am doing this with zilch emotion. So relax.'

As she presses Ashesh's temples, the tension of the interview gradually melts away. His mind is still wary, but his body begins to respond to Janaki's touch.

The doorbell rings.

'Stay put. I'm leaving anyway. I'll get the door.'

Janaki hurries to the door. It is Haridas again. He looks at her and then at Ashesh and says, 'I'd say you've had a good interview.'

Ashesh smiles limply. Janaki calls out to him from the door, 'The photographer will call tomorrow.'

Ashesh glances at her, but then lets his shoulders drop in resignation.

Haridas says, 'I didn't go home. I'd like to sit here for a while if I may. Hope you don't mind.'

27

Rain chokes the sky. Ashesh and Anima stand in the back veranda of her fourth-floor flat, gazing at the horizon where leaden sky meets leaden sea. As hard as they look, they see no other shade to nuance its monotony. The grey seeps into their spirits as Anima finishes telling Ashesh about Bachchu Kaka's visit.

'Perhaps I should go there.'

'As soon as you can. I don't like the sound of it.'

A terrifying explosion cracks the sky beyond the sea. Its reverberations come rumbling to the shore, crashing over their heads. Lightning zips through their eyes. A wind rises over the sea and roars across, taking everything that comes in its way into its erratic embrace. It snaps off branches, swings windows and doors on their hinges. It is a monster gone berserk. Then suddenly it subsides, not to die, but to take a deep breath. In that brief silence another sound rises on the horizon and sweeps across the sea, its angry swish growing louder by the minute. The wind pushes it relentlessly on. The sky rips open and hard, fat drops of rain thrash the earth.

The Mumbai monsoon has been inaugurated. Anima closes the sliding doors of the veranda. They will remain closed for the next three months. The wind howls round the building, finding its way in through cracks. It rams into the gulmohr tree, whipping the last flowers off its branches. The flowers twirl helplessly in the air to fall sodden and exhausted on the ground. Ashesh leans out of the window to feel the wind on his face. There is already a large pool of water in the narrow yard below. Thumb-thick raindrops dance on it. A postman wades through the pool to enter the building. His umbrella serves no purpose. His trousers are drenched up to the knees.

Anima comes out with two mugs of steaming tea. 'Ever heard of our postmen going on strike?' Ashesh asks.

'No, now that you ask.' Anima shakes her head in surprise.

'We should honour them, not take them for granted.'

'Why postmen all of a sudden?'

'One just entered the building.'

The doorbell rings.

'That's probably him.'

The handwriting on the envelope makes Anima frown. 'It's from Ai.' She tears the envelope open and quickly runs her eye down the page. 'But it's not her handwriting inside.' She reads some of it a little more carefully. 'Not her words either.'

'Will you read it out, not just mutter to yourself?'

Anima reads.

Dear Nima and Ashesh,

You will be surprised to see a letter from me and even more surprised to read its contents. You may not have realized it on your occasional visits, but Surgaon is no longer the quiet town of your childhood, surrounded by chiku orchards and scented with mogra flowers. We no longer see the quiet, long-enduring people of the old town. The winds that are blowing over the rest of the country have touched this town too.

It has been many years since that stipulated period of seven years after your father left us has elapsed. He was then legally assumed to be no more. What had been mine already in accordance to his will, then became mine by legal right.

Over recent years I have found it increasingly difficult to look after the house and property. It is no longer easy to find reliable servants. When Bachchu Kaka visited a few days ago, he asked why the Gandhi mandir looked so uncared for. It made me angry that he should ask. He knows many people in the Warli padas. It was he who found the mother–daughter pair for one of your friends in Mumbai. But not once has he offered to find me a replacement for Rama and his wife.

However, it doesn't matter any more. Dr Bhaskar has come to my aid like a messenger from God. He does a lot of social work here. Part of his work is looking after the elderly, living alone like me. I will not list here the many things he has done for me and others in the town after he came.

Dr Bhaskar is steeped in the knowledge of Hinduism. He admires Gandhiji as your father did, but believes that, despite being himself a good Hindu, he took Muslims and Christians to his heart for political ends. When a Hindu shows a preference for people of other religions over his, flames of anger are bound to leap up in the Hindu heart and violence, which he abhorred, is bound to follow. Dr Bhaskar believes our religion is tolerant. But that does not mean we will accept proselytizers luring our people to their religions. Tolerance is not to be mistaken for cowardice.

Dr Bhaskar, who thinks and speaks with great clarity and a complete grasp of today's reality, says what Hindustan needs today is not Gandhi but Shri Ramachandra. Lord Ramachandra forms the very foundation of our culture. He was a king committed to one wife, a king who was bound by his word, a king who stood for truth. He honoured his father to the extent that he endured fourteen long years of exile in forests, exposed to rain and sun, to honour his word. He was a true democrat before we had even heard the word democracy. It was on the word of a subject, a dhobi, that he abandoned his beloved wife. Only this avatar of Vishnu can show our westward-bowing young generation and our forest-dwelling brethren, who convert to other religions for money, the path of truth. Unlike Gandhiji, Lord Ramachandra found it unnecessary to indulge in outlandish experiments to arrive at truth. He was himself Truth incarnate.

The people of Surgaon have been deeply stirred by Dr Bhaskar's speeches. I am completely convinced by how vital Lord Ramachandra is for our country and our people today. Therefore, I had no hesitation in agreeing to Dr Bhaskar's suggestion that the dilapidated Gandhi mandir should be demolished and a splendid marble Ram mandir built in its place.

The first hammer fell on the Gandhi mandir today in the

presence of a huge crowd of townspeople. I cannot deny that I
felt a twinge when I heard that sound. But Dr Bhaskar calmed
my doubts by reminding me that only the destruction of the old
can create space for the construction of the new. When your
father himself felt no qualms in abandoning his Gandhi mandir,
why should we have qualms about letting this empty symbol of
his faith and ideals go?

The inauguration of the Ram mandir is planned for Dussehra.
Stone carvers from Rajasthan are working day and night in our
backyard, on large slabs of marble. The atmosphere is alive with
joy. It is Dr Bhaskar's wish that the temple be inaugurated by
a Warli from one of the nearby padas and not some powerful
political leader. This will be in keeping with your father's ideals
which Dr Bhaskar respects deeply.

I hope you will put aside everything to attend the
inauguration. It is still two months away. You have plenty of
time to plan your work accordingly. Ashesh, you spend all your
time painting pictures based on Western ideas which nobody
understands. It would do you no harm to offer a day of your time
at the feet of Shri Ramachandra who is the very foundation of
our culture. Nima, Bachchu Kaka visits you often. Perhaps he
misleads you with his slant on my life here. You don't have to
believe everything he says. Remember one thing only. He does
not believe in God. Your father did.

Your loving Ai

28

Shekhar looks up at the clear sky and says, 'Just as I thought. When
the Met Office says it'll rain, leave your umbrella at home.'

'Don't do that. Shantanu has a cold. What if the weather changes? The umbrella can stay in the car.'

Shekhar makes a face, picks up Shantanu and his umbrella and leaves for his mother's. Sharada's Sunday mornings are for working students. Shekhar takes Shantanu off her hands so she can get through the lessons undisturbed. Shantanu's minder, the feisty Karishma, takes what she calls a 'hoff' on Sundays. She goes to the movies in the afternoon with her friends. Her real name is Kunda. But once out of school, she changed it to Karishma, after the reigning superstar of Hindi cinema.

Karishma had once said to Sharada, 'You have such a sweet voice. Just like Lata's. Why do you sing those boring aaaooo aaaooo songs? Don't you know any of ours?' 'Ours' meant playbacks that were presented by Karishma and Govinda, Salman and Madhuri on the silver screen. Looking for some respect from Karishma, Sharada had belted out a stanza of '*Chhaiyya Chhaiyya*', and then, at Karishma's special request, the whole of '*Aati Kya Khandala*'. Shantanu had dropped his toys and danced to the song with Karishma. When the song was over, Karishma had stared at Sharada with awe. 'I swear upon my mother, what a voice! You should sing for films. You'll have them all at your feet.'

Including Guruji, Sharada had thought wryly. Karishma couldn't stop clicking her tongue over the tragedy. She simply couldn't see why anybody would want to ruin themselves like this. After that day, she had listened to Sharada's aaaooo aaaooo songs with even greater sadness.

Sharada waves to Shantanu from the veranda. If it rains, her first student will most likely not turn up, Sharada thinks, setting up the room for her lessons and feeling guilty that the thought pleased her. When she comes out on to the veranda again, the sky has changed colour. It is about to stage an epic drama. The lights have dimmed. Curtains of cloud have descended. In the wings, a wind growls.

Kishori Tamhane emerges from the house next door. Her husband doesn't live here. He has a job in Sharjah. She lives alone, handling home, children, illnesses and homework. She looks up at the sky as she steps out of the building. A plump drop of rain falls on her face. She

smiles and jerks her head to shake it off. She looks up again to gauge
whether she needs to open her umbrella or if this is just a light drizzle
that will pass. The sky isn't all cloud yet. A thin ray of sun struggles out
to land at her feet. Kishori shrugs and walks out briskly. But she has
barely gone ten paces when the few blue streaks in the sky disappear
and the rain comes slanting down. Within seconds, her hair is plastered
to her head and drops of water are streaming down her face.

Sharada recalls a bandish in Malhar that Guruji had once sung at
a private concert. It had given her goosebumps. It was one of those
evenings when the rain had lashed at houses, people, trees, insects,
everything. People had come to the concert drenched. Guruji's opening
notes of Miyan Ki Malhar, low and resonant, merged with the bass of the
rain outside. Guruji was in a leisurely mood, caressing every note into a
rounded, luminous presence. The listeners were keyed up, wondering
which bandish he would sing. It was the way of his gharana to introduce
the bandish as soon as the introductory notes of the raag had been
sung. It was different that day. Guruji continued to explore the notes,
delving deeper and deeper into them. Sharada was accompanying him
on one tanpura and Madhavrao on the other. They exchanged glances,
wondering what Guruji intended to do. There was something about his
voice that they had never heard before. It was as though the rain had
seeped into it and made it moist and soft. Elaborating on the notes of
Malhar, he gradually climbed up the scale. When he reached nishad,
he spent a long time swinging gently between the sharp and flat note.
He was completely entranced by the two faces of the note and was
striving to touch on every facet of their relationship. The listeners were
no longer keyed up. They were swaying to the delicate swings Guruji
was executing between the two nishads. Every time they thought he
was preparing to touch the upper shadja, back he came to play around
a little more with them, discovering for the listeners microtones they
had never heard before.

At precisely the moment when the listeners' desire to hear the shadja
had reached its very peak, he slid into it quietly, without the usual
drama, and almost instantly zoomed down with a taan like a streak of

lightning to the lower shadja. He paused, then sang the opening line of the bandish. It was not one of the most sung bandishes in Malhar, though the sentiment it expressed was the usual. The nayika says to her absent lover, 'See how the clouds wrap themselves around me. How I fear them. My eyes too stream like the sky. Why are you not with me?'

Watching Kishori disappear down the street, Sharada thinks of that terrified woman, alone in the rain, calling out to her beloved. And here's Kishori taking the rain in her stride while her husband is away in a foreign land. She must miss him acutely, but she is not afraid. Her eyes had laughed at the rain, not streamed with tears. Conventional poetic conceits make it so easy to sing of separation and yearning. The feeling Guruji had put into the words had sent thrills of sensuous pleasure through the audience. Mightn't I be able to put just as much into the quality of Kishori's aloneness and her laughter in the face of the rain?

Sharada plays around with lines that could sing of Kishori. There she goes alone, wrapped in clouds, the rain upon her; she laughs at its touch. Why can I not sing that in Malhar? Why should Malhar always be sombre? If there is any possibility of laughter in it, I could explore it with this song. Sharada wonders, have I stumbled upon a way to sing Indira Sant's 'Alone'?

The telephone rings. Anjali isn't coming. Sharada doesn't ask why. She rushes to the music room, uncovers the tanpura, tunes it and starts singing Malhar. Will the words find themselves in the melody? Can a musical relationship grow between the two? Will they make natural companions? Her struggle to discover the answers through the music itself continues till Janaki arrives for her lesson.

Janaki's singing is now pure and clear. Her true voice has matured. Although every note still emerges as a discrete, regimented sound, it is without doubt a true note. Janaki feels confidence licking at her heart. She grows careless, lets her attention wander and at once loses two notes. Sharada gives her a sharp look. She shakes her head and repeats them. She's back in control. She is singing a very simple bandish in Yaman. If she gets the melody right, the beat slips. If she concentrates on the beat, the melody slips. She tries over and over to get both right

and finally manages. She smiles happily at her guru, savouring the magic
of arriving perfectly on beat at the end of the line. Sharada bursts out
laughing at her expression. 'There are times when you pass the test.
When the voice produces exactly what your mind has directed. You've
arrived at base camp. But if you want to climb higher, there's only one
way. Practise, practise, practise. You have to find the time somehow . . .'
    'Time is not a problem. But the minute I open my mouth, Mrs
Khanna frowns.'
    'Change your place. You've decided to settle in Mumbai, haven't
you? You have a good job, a good salary. Take a loan. Invest in your
own place.'
    'The salary looks good, but I'm on contract. There's a permanent
sword hanging over my head. The minute they think I've stepped out
of line, I'm out.' Janaki makes a wry face. 'But a room of my own would
be something.'
    'Think about it. I feel like a cup of tea. You?'
    'It's time for Shantanu to come back. Shouldn't I leave?'
    'Let's forget about timetables for once'.
    Sharada makes tea. Janaki asks hesitantly, 'Have you been to see
Guruji?'
    'Hm.'
    'You've been?'
    'Hm.'
    'Animatai says he refuses to teach you. Just keeps you sitting.'
    'Hm.' Sharada pours the tea and they come out again.
    'Aren't you hurt?'
    'I come home and weep.'
    'Then?'
    'I decided long ago I wouldn't let anything he says or does hurt me.
I love his style. I want to master it. There's no place for egos here.'
    'But he's blocking your growth.'
    'One day he'll see that the bandishes I compose and sing are rooted
in his gharana. Composing them is not a sign of disrespect. It is exactly
the reverse. I'm confident he'll start teaching me again and give to me

as generously of his knowledge as he has done till now.'

Janaki examines Sharada's face above the rim of her cup. She is a proud woman. How can she willingly take this humiliation?

'I wouldn't have taken this treatment.'

'It's not easy.' Sharada smiles wanly. 'We are very far from his times. In those days the guru's word could not be questioned. Perhaps it was easier for Guruji not to question his guru. But we are full of questions. We believe it's our right to ask. I am happy when you ask me a question. If I don't have the answer, I try to find out. But if I ask Guruji and he doesn't have the answer, he flies into a rage.

'He has thought deeply about music. He has explored it, arrived at his own individual way of singing his tradition. You can hear that for yourself. But point this out to him and he'll say he sings exactly as his guru taught him to. The claim is simply not true. But he will not assume the responsibility of being who he is, in the tradition and yet a forerunner, carrying it forward. He wants to show he is Gandhari, blindfolded in his tradition, refusing to look beyond what is prescribed.

'You can't blame him, Janaki. Music is his life. In those days people didn't equip themselves with a college degree, just in case things didn't work out and they needed a job. He didn't. He couldn't have afforded an education anyway. His guru and the training he gave him were the only guarantee he had of a future. If he missed a note even by a microtone, his guru would throw a tuning hammer at him. The musical note was God. To dishonour it was sacrilege. Guruji would continue to sing even if his blood was flowing. That is how he commands every note of every raag he sings. These are the stories old masters tell. They lived in a different world from ours. We must try and understand their world, not expect them to understand ours.'

Sharada puts her cup down. 'There's a new bandish forming in my mind today. I want to set it to Malhar. That's supposed to be a sombre raag. Deep and grey. But I want to sound out its playful aspect. I don't believe the mood of a raag is fixed in stone. The mood has to change according to the mood of the bandish. Even the exquisitely disturbing Marwa can be sung merrily. I want to try this out with Malhar.'

The door opens. Shekhar enters softly. As usual, Shantanu is asleep on his shoulder. Shekhar puts him in his cot and comes out. 'Please carry on.' But Sharada says, 'We're through,' and puts an arm around him. Janaki feels like an intruder. Saying a quick goodbye, she leaves.

'I said carry on because I have to pop into the office for a bit.' Shekhar gives Sharada's hand an apologetic squeeze.

Sharada's face falls. 'I know what "for a bit" means. It means the whole evening. So when do we see *Taking Sides*? Feroze loaned us the film two weeks ago. Why do you have to go? It's not fair.' She is upset.

'I have to go because the American boss says so. He refuses to understand that the work culture he's trying to introduce into the company after the takeover will not be effective right away. We have to give it time. We discussed the problem threadbare in the conference. But the man isn't satisfied. He's going back to America tonight, and still has some last-minute questions.'

'What's so difficult or different about this work culture?'

'Our parent company has a bunch of idealists at the top. They want their employees to have total freedom, to come and go as they like. They can decide when and how to do the work they've been assigned, as long as it's completed by the deadline. Meanwhile they can play video games or work out in the gym. When they introduced the system here, I said let's go slowly. They didn't and now they've fallen flat on their faces. They want to know why money is being embezzled, why people are making fake taxi vouchers, why people aren't coming to work for days on end, why they spend entire days playing video games.

'At the conference the staff told this man frankly, "Tell us what you want us to do, when and how. We want pukka rules. That's what we are used to." See, Sharu, there's a basic rule that companies who want to work in alien cultures must take the trouble to follow. They must understand the culture of the place. This man says to me, "What culture are you talking about? There's only one global culture now. My son wears jeans, drinks Coke and eats burgers. So do your teenagers." How do I get through to him that dress and food are only superficial signs? Belief in hierarchy goes deep. We find it difficult to be free in the way they are. Our caste system is all about the high and the low. If people in high positions begin to treat subordinates like equals, it upsets our world view. If they don't make strict work rules and show their authority, we are lost. We don't know how to be the boss's equals without being disrespectful. I've been trying to tell him these things. He just needs to trust me. We'll learn to balance freedom and individual responsibility. But he wants to change the world with a snap of his fingers. He will try to force his ideas down our throats and fail. So fine. Go to hell.'

Shekhar is truly upset. Sharada swallows her disappointment and puts her hand over his. 'Go, since you have to. We'll see the film after you come back. A late-night show.'

By the time their late-night show ends, it is midnight. It has been a tense two and a half hours watching two men engaged in a fight to the finish. A quiet, cultured, utterly bewildered, world-renowned music conductor on one side and on the other an American army major appointed to grill Germans suspected of having supported the Nazis. The major is rude, aggressive, and sees the world in black and white. He has only two questions for the man of music. If you were opposed to Hitler as you claim, why did you not leave the country as other artists did? And if you stayed back, why did you not do anything against the gassing of thousands of Jews?

Sharada is shaken. It is an enormous and ancient question that the artist has had to face time and again. How is an answer to be found within the framework of the major's two-plus-two-makes-four scheme of things? How can you even begin to talk to a man who holds music and musicians in total contempt? How can the conductor answer the question why he conducted a concert held to celebrate Hitler's birthday? The conductor says Hitler was all-powerful. He invited him. He had to go. But he didn't bow to him. That was the only sign of opposition in his power to show. Was such a subtle sign of opposition visible under a flag bloody with genocide? The major hates music but he is a good man. Hitler loved music, had an excellent understanding

of it, but he was a monster. How is this to be comprehended? Hitler
planned to annihilate an entire race of people while listening to music.
How can one believe then that music has the power to elevate one to
a spiritual level? Forget spirituality. To the level of humanity? If as a
singer I can't do even that, then why do I sing? For my pleasure alone?

Sharada's mind is in turmoil and Shekhar is livid with the American
major. That afternoon his boss had snapped his fingers and told him,
'You have to change, my man. The world is changing. Take this as a
challenge, Shekhar, and let's see results today, not tomorrow.' When
he left for America, he thumped Shekhar's back in a friendly man-to-
man gesture.

'America needs somebody else to rule over them for a while,'
Shekhar says coldly. 'We'll see how they respond to a cultural takeover.
Let's hear them snap their fingers then.'

Sharada looks at him with a grin. Snapping her fingers, she says,
'Get up, Shekhar. No sitting around on your arse, man. Working day
tomorrow.'

Shekhar laughs. Pulling Sharada to him, he says, 'Let me finish
some pending work here.'

29

The autorickshaw turns a sharp right-angled corner on to the Versova
approach road; Bachchu Kaka yells above the noise of the traffic, 'Stop!'
In that right angle where the land slopes to the sea, a crowd of some ten
people is in heated argument with four men. Anima is amongst them,
her salt-and-pepper hair glinting in the midday sun. She is impatiently
pushing her glasses up the sweaty bridge of her nose.

As Bachchu Kaka approaches the knot of people, Anima notices
him. She smiles and signals to him to wait. He waits. And watches.
Anima's side of the skirmish shouts, 'We will not allow it. We're ready

to take the case all the way to the Supreme Court.' The four men on the opposite side shout back that the government has sold the land to their company. Houses can't be built unless the mangroves are cut. One of them adds sarcastically, 'Your houses were also built on mangrove land.' Anima's side says, 'Sure, but it won't happen now. We are a registered residents' body. Tell your boss to talk to us and our MLA. The government has no right to gift this land to your company or anybody else.'

The four men look undecided. In the normal course, their orders would be to start beating up the protesters. But the protesters are well-to-do people and include a couple of popular television actors. The boss has warned the men not to mess with these types. There are other ways of dealing with them. Yet how can they retreat before this unarmed bunch, of which six are women? The men stand their ground, chests stuck out, while the enemy waits silently for them to go away. They can't hold out much longer. They must go, and they do, but not without shouting a menacing threat over their shoulders, 'Wait till the police sort you out.' The Advanced Local Management members disperse. Locking horns with the developer's men is only the first round of the battle. Who knows what machinations the developer will put into motion now? But win or lose, they are primed for battle.

Back home, Anima froths at the mouth over the whole corrupt conglomerate of politicians, the builders' lobby and the police. Bachchu Kaka remembers Saguna and his heart feels utterly empty. 'Get us some hot tea,' he says, his voice thick. 'Maybe that'll cool you down,' he adds and tries to laugh. Anima runs to the kitchen, all apology, while Bachchu Kaka's eyes turn once again to Ashesh's painting. The more he looks at it the more he feels he must have it, surprising himself. He has never been acquisitive. There are few possessions he wants to keep. The old wooden chair in his room in Chopade's Chawl is one of them. That chair is a part of his life. The others make no difference. But he wants intensely to possess this picture. It's a simple picture of a woman sitting astride a brown bicycle against a background of speckled green. The front wheel of the bicycle is turned a little towards the viewer. The woman's body is hunched, her neck stretched. She concentrates every ounce of energy on getting where she wants to go. The loose end of her turmeric-yellow sari is tucked firmly in at the waist. Her minutely detailed red print blouse has slipped a little off her right shoulder.

When Anima comes back with the tea, Bachchu Kaka says, 'You think that idiot will give me a picture like this? I'll return it to him in my will. Won't let it fall into anybody else's hands.'

'Why don't you take this one, Kaka, since you like it so much.'

'You mean that?' Bachchu Kaka's eyes light up like a child's. Anima is moved. What is it in this picture that this man, so devoid of material temptations, finds so compelling?

Anima observes Bachchu Kaka as they sip their tea. 'There's something on your mind,' she says. 'What is it?'

'You said you'd come to Surgaon soon. You haven't been. You have no idea what's going on there.'

Anima looks down, locking her hands together. 'We don't have to come there to know what's going on, Kaka. Ai has written to tell us what's going on.' She gets the letter for Bachchu Kaka to read. 'It's our childhood home, Kaka. Don't you think we'd want it to stay the way it is forever? But our hands are tied. You know that yourself. I can argue with people till my last breath. But I simply don't have the language to deal with Ai who thinks only emotionally. I must confess I have failed that test. Ai's letter was very depressing. It left us stunned. Then we thought is the house Anna's only, or even his real, legacy? What Anna has left us is a way to think and live. He has set us an example of equality. We've tried to build our lives on that foundation, Kaka. If we can make even a smidge of a difference around us, isn't that the best way to cherish Anna's legacy?'

Bachchu Kaka nods. 'Yes, my little one. You are doing that. But the world doesn't give a rotten fig for your individual values. It has to be fought more actively.' He puts his cup down with a trembling hand. 'Those people have killed Girji.'

Anima's heart plunges. 'What? Who? When, Kaka?'

'They killed her.' He stares at the floor. 'Her own people declared her a witch and killed her. Three children in the village had diarrhoea. They called the bhagat. He is Dr Bhaskar's man. He got the villagers to line up all the widows. He said, "It's not one of these. It is someone who stays far away from here. Her son is here. Who is it?" Everybody turned to Soma. "Get her," the bhagat ordered. Soma brought her. They beat her to death. Then they went home. But Soma noticed she was still alive. He slung her over his shoulder and ran all the way to the Mission Hospital. While she was under treatment a mob gathered outside carrying sticks and axes. They broke the doors and windows of the hospital. They dragged all the patients out, except Girji. They poured can after can of kerosene on the building and set it alight. With its old wooden flooring, it burst into flames. The mob disappeared into the dark shouting slogans against missionaries. By the time we got there, half the hospital was ashes. The flames were devouring the rest. The sky, the tops of trees were red. The crackling of the flames was deafening. Things collapsed with loud thuds every now and again. The bunch of us just stood there watching, our tongues and limbs useless.'

Bachchu Kaka speaks as if he is seeing the scene again.

'But why?'

'In Soma's pada everybody, except a few like him, are eating Bhaskar's food.'

The vein in Anima's forehead dances with rage.

'Both of you were born in that hospital. The Brahmins of the town refused to go there. It was really for the Warlis, and they have destroyed it themselves. Now, what Bhaskar gives them is medicine, what he sermonizes is dharma.'

Bachchu Kaka sighs. Anima takes the tea things in, mechanically.

'The nurses went to the hospital the next morning to pick out whatever was saved. Not much. Just odds and ends.'

'What was Soma doing? How did he allow this to happen?'

'He knew what was coming when the people of his pada went to the next pada for the bhagat. That pada celebrates Dussehra these days. They get brand new clothes from the people of Surgaon. They burn Ravan's effigy with loud celebrations. Half the ten faces of Ravan are made up to look like mullahs and the other half like padres. Soma alone in his pada has objected to the celebrations. He was asking for something like this to happen. It has. A stick was thrust into his hand too, to beat Girji. That's the custom. He didn't touch it. By custom this meant he was an accomplice in Girji's witchcraft. He knew they would soon find a way to kill Marli and then him. So he absconded with her the night he took Girji to the hospital. He came to me. I've found him a safe home for the moment. But they can't hide there forever.'

'I don't suppose the police showed their faces while Girji was being beaten,' Anima asks bitterly.

'They came after. They'll file a case. The village has decided who is to confess to the killing. It has also decided that nobody will bear witness against him. Our laws are built on the floating foundation of individual freedoms and rights. Our real foundation is tradition, where the clan calls the shots. Individuals are nothing without the clan. How are the two ideas to meet?'

Bachchu Kaka joins Anima for a simple lunch of poli-amti-bhaji. Anima says, 'Let's go.'

'Where?'

'Don't ask. Wherever it is, I'll get you to your train in time.'

'Do you have saunf or something?'

Anima holds out a small jar of pounded masala supari.

'Is this from Sindhutai?'

'Last year's.'

'Meaning?'

'She didn't have any made this year. No supari and no banana flour.'

'She's lost interest in these things.'

'She looks tired.'

'Can I have a nap?' He settles down immediately on the floor.

'Kaka, please sleep on the bed inside.'

'Rubbish. The floor's good enough. We'll go wherever you want to take me in twenty minutes.'

Anima sends an SMS to Haridas. 'Can I bring Bachchu Kaka over for a little while?'

He replies immediately: 'Of course. But the old bastard hates me.'
'He does. But he has news for you. Try not to go out of your way
to shock him.'

Bachchu Kaka is up in exactly twenty minutes. 'Where are you
taking me?'

She looks him in the eye. 'Haridas.'

'Have you gone mad?'

'He must know what's happened to Girji. He has been very
disturbed.'

'You tell him then.'

'What if he wants information that I don't have? Also, Girji has
painted a picture on his wall. You must see it.'

'Rubbish. These women don't go painting other people's walls.
He's fibbing.'

'I've seen it, Kaka. The party he had last time you were here was
to celebrate the painting.'

Bachchu Kaka says nothing. When Anima changes and comes out,
he follows her with a stiff face.

'How are you, madam?' Ramprasad asks, doing a humble namaskar.
'You've not been for some time.' The aerial roots of the banyan tree
frame him. The concrete platform around it is patterned with crow
shit. Ramprasad's expression is of a man relaxing in the gracious living
room of an old-world mansion. His eyes turn to Bachchu Kaka. 'May
I know his good name?'

'He's my uncle. He's from my home town.' Anima hurries on but
can't stop Ramprasad from shouting out the latest news. 'There's some
white madam staying there.'

Bachchu Kaka bristles. 'Don't expect me to be polite to him and
all that. Or you go give him the information. I'll have a chat with this
whiskered fellow. He looks interesting.'

'Kaka, you are free to talk to Haridas any which way you like. I only
want you to tell him about Girji.'

Haridas has fixed his art-camp horn to his door. Children blow it all
day as they come and go. Ashesh says it must be fun for the children,

but what about his neighbours? 'Neighbours?' Haridas smirks. 'They'll
soon give me synthesizers for Ganapati, drums for Navaratri and
double atom bombs for Diwali. This is my humble contribution to the
environment.'
   'But what about you? Doesn't the horn bother you?'
   'Me? I'm a true-blue son of the soil. Our inner-ear systems are
different from other people's.'
   Haridas's door is ajar. Bachchu Kaka steps in and stands rooted to
the spot. The wall before him is covered with Girji's painting. He is so
stunned, he doesn't hear Haridas say twice, 'Please sit.'
   Finally he mutters, 'I can't believe this.'
   'I'd been asking her to do one for me for years. She only smiled. One
day she said, "I'll make a picture." And she painted this.'
   'I can't understand how she could have known.'
   'Known what?'
   'That they were going to kill her.'
   'They? Who? They what?'
   'That bhutali at the bottom.'
   Bachchu Kaka then tells Haridas the terrible story. Haridas sinks
to the floor. 'What witchcraft? Girji? Our Girji?' His voice is dry, his
tone harsh.
   'Did Soma visit her before she made this?' Bachchu Kaka is still
staring at the bottom right-hand corner of the picture.
   'I think so. A month or so ago. He used to come and go so quietly,
I didn't ever know.'
   'He must have told her what was happening in the pada. She must
have heard the warning in his voice.'
   They are silent.
   'And Marli?'
   'She's with Soma in a safe place.'
   'They can come and live here for as long as they want. Will you
please tell them that?'
   'I'll send a message.'
   The door opens. A tall, slim woman, with hair the rich brown of

tamarind seeds, enters. Haridas signals to her to join them. 'I'll be with you in a minute,' she says and hurries indoors.

Bachchu Kaka stiffens. 'Let's go.'

'Please have tea. It's your first visit.'

Bachchu Kaka looks in the direction in which the woman went and says a pointed 'No, thank you.'

Haridas grins. 'That's Maya. She's half Dutch and half Tamil. Her mother used to live right here, in Matunga. Maya and I are doing some work together. By work I don't mean . . .'

Anima sees what's coming and warns Haridas with a sign.

But Haridas persists. '. . . we're sleeping together. Not yet.'

Anima looks at the floor in despair. Bachchu Kaka goes red. 'I have no interest in knowing who you work or sleep with.' He gets up and dusts down his clothes.

'Why don't you stay a bit then?' Haridas presses on shamelessly. 'I'll make us some great tea. It's our teatime anyway. Afterwards I'll show you my work.'

Haridas speaks with such casual warmth that Bachchu Kaka stands nonplussed. Taking advantage of the pause in hostilities, Haridas disappears into the kitchen. Bachchu Kaka is left pacing up and down near the door in helpless anger. At last he sits down. His bald head is covered in a burst of sweat. He scrubs it roughly with his handkerchief, then fists his thighs to calm himself down. Haridas emerges with the tea. His eyes are red. 'The kitchen is not merely empty. It's dead.' The grief in his voice is so deep that even Bachchu Kaka loses some of his pent-up steam. Anima has seen Haridas's face in many moods, but never like this. Bachchu Kaka doesn't know what to say so he says, 'Don't worry. I'll find you someone else in Girji's place. There's no shortage of destitute women in our padas.'

'Bachchu Kaka, Girji was Girji.' His voice is edged with pain. 'I know you don't expect me to feel this way. You have only contempt for me. But I'd like to put you right on some things while we have tea. I didn't marry because I knew I couldn't have dealt with marriage. And my wife would have found me difficult to deal with as a husband. I have relationships only with women who know what they want. They are mature enough to choose lifestyles that suit them. I wouldn't know what to say to submissive types who think husbands are gods. Physical relationships are clean. I strive to give women as much pleasure as they give me. We remain friends after the relationships end because nobody has deceived anybody. I don't understand why you and others like you have a problem with how I choose to live.'

Haridas has returned to his normal state. 'Please try not to see me as a sex maniac, but as a man who is trying to live without causing anybody pain.'

Bachchu Kaka has listened to the monologue with a neutral expression. He says calmly, 'You are free to live as you like. You don't need to justify your ways to me. Equally I don't need advice from you on what I should think about whom.'

Bachchu Kaka gets up. He is at the door waiting for Anima to join him. Haridas's voice is humble again. 'I don't justify my choice of lifestyle to anybody. I did so to you because I respect your life and your work. And because you brought Girji and Marli to me. They've gone, but I have this painting.'

30

Janaki sits at her computer, eyes closed. She had two stories to do. She has just finished one—a pre-publicity piece for the Habib Tanvir festival scheduled to be held in the city. Briefing Janaki, Mr Singh had explained that the old story about Tanvir and his troupe being attacked in Madhya Pradesh during the performance of *Ponga Pundit* would suffice to create the necessary buzz for the festival. All she had needed to do was tell that story in 300 words.

Background: The play—for which the eighty-year-old theatre man had had eggs, chairs and whatever else thrown at him—had been written seventy years ago by two folk actors from Chhattisgarh.

Point number one: *Ponga Pundit* was not a new play when it toured Madhya Pradesh. It had been performed hundreds of times before.

Point number two: All Indian folk plays mocked those in power. They had been granted the freedom to do so by tradition. If *Ponga Pundit* satirized the double standards of a priest's religious transactions, that was as it should be.

Incentive to attend the festival: *Ponga Pundit* is one of the five plays that will be featured in the forthcoming Habib Tanvir festival.

Three hundred words over.

Janaki is now persuading herself to write the second story. Two years ago, in 2002, Tyeb Mehta's painting *Celebration* sold for a crore and a half rupees at a Christie's auction in New York. The owner of the *Mumbai Observer* has let it be known that he would like an informative piece that traces the impact of this event on the contemporary art market, perhaps even on contemporary art itself. She has found all the information she requires on the net, but there's a resistance within her to the material. Her mind is like a mule. Won't budge. The art market is an aspect of the art world she cannot muster enthusiasm for. It's a middle-class thing, she knows. The romantic view of art that wants to keep it safe from the touch of filthy lucre. But she must chew on her resistance and swallow it. Five hundred words shouldn't be difficult.

Indian art has finally found its place on the international map. The big event that marked its arrival was the record price that Tyeb Mehta's work *Celebration* fetched in 2002 in New York at a Christie's auction. Contemporary Indian art has not looked back since. In March this year, in New York again, the iconoclast Francis Newton Souza's work, *Mystic Repast*, sold for a whopping lakh and thirty thousand dollars in a Sotheby's auction. Twelve more auctions are scheduled to take place during the rest of the year. The Indian art market is expected to see a turnover of eleven crore dollars in this period. This expected turnover will be fourteen times more than that during a similar period in 1996. Speaking only of Bengali artists, a Rabindranath Tagore work fetches 5343 rupees per square inch, an Abanindranath fetches 4903 per square inch and an A.R. Chugtai fetches 3518 per square inch. Despite these dazzling figures, experts are of the opinion that Indian art has . . .

'Madam, the boss wants to see you.' The editor's peon, Raghunath Uttekar, is standing at her desk fiddling with her stapler. She completes typing the sentence: '. . . miles to go before we can say it has arrived.'

'What's up now?' she asks Uttekar.

'Don't know. There's a woman there and a swami baba in a long robe.' Something goes ting in Janaki's head.

Janaki knocks on Mr Singh's door. 'May I come in?'

His voice booms from inside like a drum. 'Yes, yes.'

Sumitraben and Prakash sit facing him, their backs to her.

Mr Singh says, pointing towards Prakash, 'I believe you know each other since childhood.' Janaki nods and smiles.

'Please sit down. Sumitraben is planning a truly novel evening. You arty-farty types are always accusing the media of not encouraging new talent, only doing celebrities. We say give us something newsworthy and we'll cover it. Sumitraben is about to do just that. She's planning a one hundred per cent newsworthy evening. Pandit Omkar Mishra has evolved a new form of music. He calls it Shlokabandish. Which is, er . . . why don't you tell her, Sumitraben?'

Sumitraben speaks a melodious, highly Sanskritized Hindi. Prakash looks at her open-mouthed. 'There is a treasure house of shlokas in our sacred literature which can be a source of immense spiritual support for people today. Panditji has gone deep into this literature and turned half a dozen shlokas into bandishes. He has set them in popular raags like Des, Bageshri and Kedar. He sings them as chhota, not bada khayal. He makes the music so light that it appeals even to people who've never heard a phrase of classical music before. They feel instantly uplifted by it because it is classical music after all. But they are not bored because the khayals are almost like Hindi film songs which they have grown up with.'

Mr Singh is almost dancing in his chair with excitement.

'That's not all,' he says. 'Sumitraben means to include this young friend of yours in the novel experiment. You probably know he's a spiritual artist. Now, listen to this. While Pandit Mishra is singing, your friend will express his spontaneous response to the music in paint there and then, before the very eyes of the audience. There's more. There's a third aspect to this plan. At the end of the singing and painting experiment, the paintings will be auctioned to raise money for Swami Shivanand's residential school for Sanskrit studies. You'll never guess who the students at this gurukul are going to be. Sumitraben will give you a brochure later, but, briefly, the school will teach Sanskrit to Dalit students. Imagine. Education, empowerment and progress for those who were once outcasts of society.'

Janaki has been looking fixedly at Prakash. His face glows with a new lustre. He nods, smiles to himself and keeps shooting secretive glances at Sumitraben. His fingers sparkle with auspicious nine-gem rings and the front of his robe with tiny diamond buttons.

'So now, Janaki, you and Prakashanandji set up a date to talk. Interview format please. That's pre-publicity for his *Geetichitra*. Song pictures. Sounds good, doesn't it? Then we cover the event itself. And after the event, an interview with Swami Shivanand about his ashram. Someone else will do that because that's not art. By then all our readers will have heard of Prakashanandji. No problem then in covering his solo show. When is it?'

'The date's not fixed yet. But we'll let you know in good time.'

'Great. Terrific.' Singh sahib rubs his hands. 'Please carry on.'

Prakash slips a visiting card towards Janaki. It is saffron with gold lettering. Inclining his head slightly, he says, 'Call me after eleven o'clock any morning. I meditate till then.'

'And when do you paint?' Janaki asks making her voice deliberately casual.

'Whenever I feel inspired. Even at night . . . all hours.'

Janaki sits before her computer with a bitter mouth. Her mind is alive with negative thoughts. I have turned into a circus clown here. A thwack on the backside with a new split stick every day and a pay cheque in return for handing over my backside to them. Come, Prakash dear, be my guest. You turned out smart. Found out in double quick time in which direction to wag your tail.

Janaki's nose now picks up the fragrance of khus that had earlier filled Singh sahib's cabin. Sumitraben must have wafted out. Janaki closes her eyes quickly pretending to be in very deep thought. But when the fragrance begins to billow around her and does not move on, she is forced to open them. The woman and the man stand before her.

Sumitraben murmurs in her honeyed voice, 'It is not our way to interrupt meditation. We would have waited,' and does a very humble namaskar. 'You will come for the big event, I hope. You really must.' Then like a kathak dancer, signalling towards Prakash with her eyes without moving her head, she says, 'We will be waiting for you.' The 'we' carries notes of warm intimacy.

Looking at their retreating backs, Janaki grins to herself. Singh sahib, I have a really spicy story for you. Shall I write it? But of course, she knows that the whole world (or the part of it that matters) knows what's going on and, equally, that none of them would want to see the story printed. Singh sahib is only a very small fish in Sumitraben's net. Seen beside her in page-three photographs are personages of the stature of the supremo of the MR Party, sundry CEOs of giant multinationals and one permanent fixture—a majorly corrupt, majorly womanizing joint police commissioner who is supposedly a lover of art.

Janaki swallows the bitter taste in her mouth and gets down to work. If she takes care not to grumble about interviewing Prakash, she'll be able to slip in Ashesh's interview without Singh sahib protesting. With this thought in mind, she ends 'Indian Art in the International Market' with a flourish.

Janaki leans back in her chair, then eagerly picks up the phone. 'This is an exhausted Janaki speaking. I see a good chance of being able to publish your interview Sunday after next. I will pay the price this weekend.'

'What price?' Ashesh sounds horrified.

'Tell you when we meet.'

31

'There's a well-known theory that colours evoke smells and sounds. You think it's a lot of bosh. But then you experience it and you sit up.' Ashesh and Janaki are on the veranda. He is looking at the peepul tree in front of the house and she at his eyes. She notices that the last light of the monsoon day has tinged the whites of his eyes with blue. Ashesh turns to her. 'Black meant nothing at all to me till it took over my life. Now I think about it constantly. When I hear the English word "black", I hear a faintly screechy sound with a sour taste. When I hear the Marathi word "kaallaa" with the retroflex "l", I hear burbling water and imagine the taste of a fully ripe, sweet-tart jambhul fruit.'

Ashesh looks at Janaki to see if he is making sense to her. He thinks he is. Encouraged, he continues, 'It's the sound of words. Otherwise black and kaallaa mean the same thing. To me black sounds like the shooting of a bolt. A final sound. Because of the way the "a" is pronounced. It's not the laid-back "a" of father, but the sharp "a" of fat or bat. That's followed by the consonant cluster "ck" which forces you to cut your breath and stop sound. Now take kaallaa. Apart from the soft retroflex "l", it ends with a long vowel that allows you to extend the breath. Even the graphics of the consonant suggest continuity—two plump circles hanging on a short line. Like a figure of eight, it makes continuous movement possible. The sound of the retroflex "l" must have seduced the poet into writing "Pushkallaa". It's a homage to the consonant.'

'I don't know the poem.'

'Oh? Then you have to hear it. It's meant to be heard not read.'

Pushkall anga tujhe
Pushkall pushkall mun
Pushkallatli pushkall tu
Pushkall pushkall majhyasathi.

Bughtana kiti dole pushkall tujhe
Bahu galyat pushkall, pushkall oor
Pushkallatli tu pushkall kalavanti
Pushkall pushkall pushkallnari. *

'Now try and translate that into English. Without the retroflex "l", it loses all meaning. It's the sound that conjures up the voluptuous woman of the poet's imagination. It is that sound I hear these days when I think of black. I want to get that sound into my work.'

Ashesh glances at Janaki, wondering if he is boring her. She is listening and nodding her head. 'There's another woman that the sound paints. Saint Namdeo's milkmaid.'

The night is black, the water pitcher black; black too are the waters of the Yamuna, oh mother
My head-shawl is black, my crystal bracelet black; black too are the pearls round my neck, oh mother
I am black, my choli is black, black too is the drape of my sari, oh mother
I must not come to the water alone; send the dark god with me, oh mother
Vishnubhakt Namdeo's goddess is black; and blacker than all is Lord Krishna, oh mother.

---

* Bountiful your body
Bountiful bountiful heart
Most bountiful of the bountiful
Bountiful bountiful for me

Gazing, how bountiful your eyes
Giving, how bountiful your lips
Bountiful arms around my neck,
Bountiful breasts

Most bounteous of the bountiful
Bountifully bountifully bounteous.

Ashesh looks at Janaki, eyes dark with excitement. 'Do you see a flat, final black in this picture? Look at the shades and textures of black we have here. And the different densities of her crystal bracelet and her pearl necklace. Her choli is one texture, the clay water pitcher, another. It is endless. Will you sit for me?'

Janaki starts. 'Sit for you? To do what?'

He leans forward and puts his hand on her knee. 'Please. If I can manage to paint this picture, it'll free me of black. I'll have said everything I want to about the colour. I don't know what form the painting will take. It could be a portrait. Please . . . I can't do this without a sitter . . . you.'

Janaki knows this work he is thinking of is not about her. She mustn't think it is. It's a painting about a colour. So why is she feeling embarrassed? She nods slowly. He is ecstatic. He pulls her off the chair and takes her in his arms. She rests in his embrace for a few minutes. Then they forget the world, flow into each other and merge.

The doorbell rings. Ashesh reluctantly disentangles himself from her, muttering, 'That must be Anima. I'll get the door. Will you make tea?'

His compact body is bursting with energy. He walks to the door on springs. He throws an affectionate arm round Anima's shoulder. The sight of his happy face brings a smile through the worry on hers. Janaki comes out with tea which they sip in silence. Anima looks at Janaki. The buttons of her shirt are in the wrong buttonholes.

'Ai is not at all well,' Anima says. 'Bachchu Kaka called.'

'Shall we go tomorrow?' Ashesh asks promptly.

'We really should.'

The leaves of the peepul tree rustle wildly and soon it is raining hard.

'Do you have a picture of your mother? What is she like?' Janaki asks.

'Beautiful,' says Ashesh.

'Was,' Anima says sadly. 'She's very thin now. The last time I saw her, she looked terribly frail. She didn't say much. Didn't make any of her regular complaints. We should bring her here, Ashesh. Let Haresh see her. Or the doctor he recommended to you.'

Ashesh is silent, thinking. Then Janaki says, 'Who is Bachchu Kaka? Not your blood uncle, is he?'

'He's a monster,' Ashesh says, making a face.

Anima laughs, looking at her brother in surprise. 'Don't let him put you off. Bachchu Kaka's a lovely person—warm, sharp, strong, extremely dedicated and wonderfully eccentric. He's mellowed now. He had lunch with me some time ago. I said, "Sorry, it's all vegetarian." He said, "That's all I eat now. Meat doesn't suit me."'

'What?' Ashesh's eyes almost pop out of his head. He and Anima exchange glances and burst out laughing. Janaki is an outsider to the joke. Ashesh notices her face, controls his laughter and brings her in.

'Bachchu Kaka once dropped in after one of his tours of the Warli padas. We were having dinner. Ai asked him if he'd join us. He said he'd just eaten in one of the padas. Ai wrinkled up her nose and said, "Shee! You'll catch some terrible disease eating with them." That riled Bachchu Kaka. So he set out to annoy her. "Disease? It was delicious. They killed a rabbit for us. Sometimes we have to make do with insects. But even they are fine when roasted. Snakes too." Ai got up from the table and rushed out to throw up. Anna told Bachchu Kaka off for upsetting her. "Why should she be upset? I am upset. One doesn't turn down people's hospitality. We eat what the Warlis can offer. Some Budhibai in rags shares her meagre meal with you. Her food is something that she's dug up or killed or torn off a tree. It's enough to fill just one corner of her stomach so she can keep her skin and bones together and work and live another day. But she offers us a little bit out of that. Do we turn up our noses and demand dates and cow's milk instead?"'

'After that, every time Bachchu Kaka came back from a tour, we'd ask for a list of the things he had eaten,' Anima says. 'I could barely take it. But this fellow . . . He'd listen to the list as if it was a fairy tale. Didn't you feel revolted, Ashesh?'

'Of course I did. I'd just pull my stomach in and stay put. I tried to control my instinct to run and puke. If Bachchu Kaka could eat those things why couldn't I hear about them without feeling queasy? That too would be an insult to the Warlis. What depressed me though was why our people were forced to live like that. One day I overheard a conversation between Anna and Bachchu Kaka. Anna was pacing up and down muttering, "What's to be done?" Bachchu Kaka was watching him with a cold face. "We can't mend everything that's wrong in one lifetime. We make our choices. You give them free legal aid. I organize them. That's all we can do." "But people still grab their lands. Pay them a bit of compensation. They've never seen even that paltry sum. They are happy. They go on a drinking binge and sink into worse penury than before. They don't file cases. So what use is legal aid?"'

Ashesh looks at Anima. 'That's the kind of thing that would depress me. It still does. But as Bachchu Kaka said, we make our choices. Anna chose work that came as close as he could get to making a difference. Yet he felt depressed. I think he went away to challenge this common-sense rule of one lifetime, one choice. To do something else in his lifetime that made an even bigger difference.'

Anima stares at Ashesh. In the terrible days that followed Anna's disappearance she and Bachchu Kaka had tried endlessly to guess why he had gone away. But Ashesh had never offered a single conjecture. And now here he was with a pretty plausible theory.

Anima looks at Janaki. 'So that's our Bachchu Kaka. By the way, Ashesh, I gave him the painting you'd given me.'

'*Woman on the Bicycle*? Why?'

'He was very keen to have it.'

Ashesh's eyebrows shoot up. 'Good heavens. Bachchu Kaka wants one of my works? I must have made the right choice after all if it makes a difference to him.'

32

Ashesh has never taken umbrellas seriously after he gave up his association with them at college. When he's out and it rains, he steps into the nearest shelter. If it looks as if it isn't going to let up, he nips into an Udipi's and sits watching the rain over steaming cups of coffee. These are rewards that come to those who have made the right choice in life.

Anima, on the other hand, is deeply attached to umbrellas—the classic blacks with hooked wooden grips. The problem is that people's taste for new designs has pushed this umbrella out of the market. If you get a black at all, which is rare, it has one of those short, thick, cylindrical grips with which Anima's hand fails to form a relationship that could be called comfortable. She realized how worrying her plight in the modern world was when she forgot her twelve-year-old umbrella in an autorickshaw last year. Versova is a comparatively newly developed area where it would have been foolish even to ask for a replacement. So she had headed straight for Girgaum, where you could rely on some shops not having moved ahead with the times. Sure enough she had found her umbrella in a moth-eaten cavern of a shop near Prarthana Samaj. It was clear that the shopkeeper, being Marathi, had no interest in change. It was equally clear that he was not interested in commerce. He watched Anima laconically as she peered into the dark interiors of the shop for what she wanted. There they were—black umbrellas from ancient times gathering dust on a wooden shelf at the back of the shop. She asked to be shown them and picked one, upon which the man warned her in a funereal voice, 'Lady, lose this one and you may not get another. They don't make them now. I've been using this one of mine for forty years. My father used it for twenty before me. It's British made. Look at the stem. And the spokes. Strong devils. Sixty monsoons have poured on this cloth and look at it. Not a hole.'

He had danced his eyebrows at her, inviting her to touch and feel the umbrella. She had accepted the invitation and confirmed his claims about its virtues. She had put on an expression which said such an umbrella had never been and would never be again. Finally, to show how seriously she had taken his warning, and how much she appreciated the merchandise, she had bought two umbrellas in place of one.

By the time Ashesh and Anima step out of Surgaon station, the sickly drizzle that had started as the train pulled in has turned into plump raindrops that will soon merge into a blinding sheet of water. Ashesh lunges for shelter, but Anima grabs his shirt sleeve. 'If you want to be fancy-free and not carry umbrellas, get wet. We'll soon find a rick.' Sliding her umbrella open, she pulls him in. The next moment the wind gets under the umbrella and blows it inside out. The slanting rain attacks them viciously. 'So much for umbrellas,' Ashesh says happily.

As he climbs into an autorickshaw, Ashesh remembers the Gandhi hater at the bus stop in Gamdevi. Imitating his squeaky voice he says, 'In our times the rain didn't fall diagonally like this. It came down straight. That Gujarati baniya changed not only the map of Hindustan but the rain as well.'

'There has to be something wrong with you, Ashesh. You're positively light-headed.'

'Janaki and I are getting married.'

Anima gapes. Of course she knew something was on, but this is sudden. She reaches out for Ashesh's hand, embarrassed that her eyes are moist.

'She's a bright girl. Sensitive,' she says.

'I'm nervous. There's a big difference in age.'

'Shouldn't be a problem. She's mature and you're getting younger.'

As they get out of the autorickshaw, the sound of hammer on brick explodes in their ears. In Shankar Joshi's front yard, three labourers are taking turns to bring down the Gandhi mandir. Sweat mixed with rain runs off their skulls into their eyes. Dr Bhaskar stands on the front veranda supervising operations. The men may not stop in their labours even for a second to wipe their eyes. That would break the rhythm of the work. Half-blinded, they bring their hammers down turn by turn on the mandir, accompanying every blow with a 'ha' and a 'hai'.

Anima and Ashesh have turned to stone at the gate. Anima's eyes stream with tears. She makes strange sounds in her throat like someone struggling to scream in a nightmare. Ashesh grips her hand tight. Dr Bhaskar notices them but, for some time, only stares without reacting. Recovering from his confusion, he calls to them more loudly than necessary, 'Oh hello! It's you. When did you arrive? You should have told me you were coming. I'd have sent the car for you.'

Anima and Ashesh walk numbly towards the house. 'Ai?'

'Come in, come in. Your mother's resting upstairs. Come.' His spectacles glint as he turns. He must be in his mid-sixties but his stride is of a forty-year-old.

'We'll be fine. Please carry on with your work.'

'My work? It's our work. Everybody's work.' He gives them a self-deprecating smile as he takes off his spectacles and polishes them.

'Whatever.' Anima's voice is sharp. 'These days many people think "I" is "everybody".'

Ashesh studies Dr Bhaskar with great curiosity. Then he sniffs the air. Some scent is missing. He looks around.

'The trees have gone,' Anima says, following his gaze.

'The bakul?'

'Looks like it.'

Dr Bhaskar bows them upstairs. The doors to all the upstairs rooms are shut. One of them opens. A young woman with a cell phone stuck to her ear steps out. 'Yes, sir, yes, sir. They're here, sir.' Her physiognomy is unmistakably Warli, but her dress is urban lower middle class.

'Yes, come in,' she says leading them into the room.

Sindhutai Joshi lies before them on a bed covered in a spotless white sheet. Her face is as white as the sheet. Ashesh's hands turn to ice. He moves quickly to her side, sits on the edge of the bed and takes her hand in his. It is warm.

'Close that door, Sandhya,' she calls out feebly.

The young girl goes to the door.

'Please go out and close it,' Anima says. Sandhya stays where she is, stone-faced.

Ashesh gets up and bounds downstairs. 'Will you take your flunkey off our back?' he says coldly to Dr Bhaskar. 'We want to be by ourselves with our mother.'

'But of course. Certainly. I only thought in case you needed something . . .'

'We'll help ourselves, thank you. It's our house.'

Sandhya is instructed to leave the room. Anima and Ashesh sit on either side of their mother.

'I can't bear this sound, Ashesh dear. I close the door, plug my ears but it won't stop. Another two days he says.' Sindhutai's voice sounds as if it's floating up from a deep well.

'But why are you in bed?' Ashesh asks.

'Look at my sleeves,' she says absently. 'So loose. I was walking around fine. Used to get a little tired. Nothing to worry about. But after Rakshabandhan . . . did you tie him a rakhi, Nima? I can't count the number of people I tied rakhis to. I was wearing one of my nine-yards. I've kept them from the old days. I'm going to wear my mother-in-law's nath for the inauguration.'

'Ai, you are ill.'

'Just a little tired. Bhaskar has prescribed a herbal tonic. He gives it to me himself. I'll be fit as a fiddle by then.'

'Do you have an appetite?' Anima asks anxiously.

'Of course I do,' Sindhutai says, but looks away quickly, avoiding Anima's eyes.

'Will you come and stay with me for a few days?' Ashesh asks.

'With you?' For a moment Sindhutai's face lights up, then crumples. 'How can I, in this state?'

'Don't worry. I'll take you by car. A comfortable car.'

'Oh dear. I wish I could. But it's too late now. I can't live for a moment without Bhaskar.'

'Ai?' Anima's eyes widen.

'He cares for me.' Sindhutai casts a bitter glance at Ashesh. 'The world thought no end of your father. But he didn't touch me after your birth.'

'You weren't well, Ai,' Anima says quickly. 'He was only being considerate.'

'And after I recovered?'

Anima is silent. The thought that their mother was a woman, is still a woman, shocks her and Ashesh.

There is a long pause. Then Ashesh pulls himself together and says, 'Dr Bhaskar can come with you. I have space.'

'Leave his work and come?' She shakes her head.

Suddenly Ashesh springs up and throws the door open. Sandhya is leaning against it, dozing. 'Tell your boss to come up.'

'Ashesh,' Sindhutai calls out in a cracked voice. 'What did you tell her?'

Ashesh says nothing, just strokes her forehead. 'Where was the love in your hands all these years, my pet?' Her voice breaks. 'How you'd cling to me as a child. And she to her father. She never loved me the way you did.'

Anima smiles wanly.

There's a light knock on the door. 'May I come in?' Sindhutai tidies her sari and looks eagerly at the door as it opens. 'Isshya.' She smiles. '"May I come in?" A doctor doesn't need permission to see his patient.'

A shiver of revulsion runs down Anima's spine. How Anna had hated that coy exclamation 'isshya'! Every time Ai said it, he'd rebuke her mildly with a 'Sindhu!' She had stopped saying it in his presence, but it is back.

'Who's the patient here? You?' Bhaskar says gaily.

'I'm a patient only when my healer isn't holding my hand.'

Dr Bhaskar cannot hide his confusion. Anima takes brief pleasure in seeing his face go red. 'It's all right, doctor. Don't we all distinguish between private and public behaviour?'

'Why don't you sit down, doctor?' Ashesh suggests.

Dr Bhaskar sits down but on the edge of a chair. 'You asked me up.'

'Yes. Because we want to know what's wrong with Ai.' Anima's voice is deceptively soft.

'She gets tired. And there's some loss of appetite.'

'Those are symptoms. We were wondering about your diagnosis.'

'Nothing to worry about.'

'That's not a diagnosis. Have you had any tests done?'

'Tests? We don't believe in that kind of hocus-pocus. We diagnose by checking the pulse.'

'Is that how you treated your patients in America?'

'Are you cross-examining me? I'm not submitting to this kind of questioning.'

'Right. Then we'll take our mother with us to Mumbai to satisfy ourselves.'

'That's your right. The noise bothers her anyway. A change might help her recover.'

Sindhutai's eyes are like a dog's when it is kicked by its master. Ashesh's heart fills with compassion for her. He sits beside her, gently stroking her forehead. Bhaskar recovers his composure. 'Akka, go if your children want you to. You'll feel better. I'm telling you as your doctor. We're not going to be stubborn now, are we?'

Another shiver runs down Anima's spine.

'Can we take her today?' she asks.

'Sure. Why not?'

'Right. Then we'll see about hiring a car,' Ashesh says briskly and gets up.

'What are you saying? What's my car for if it isn't to take care of my dear sister?'

'No thanks. You need it for your work.'

'I don't use the car for my work.'

'But I don't want to leave you and go,' Sindhutai interrupts, now near to tears.

'Akka. You must listen to your doctor.' He turns to Ashesh. 'Please hire a car since you insist. I'll make sure she comes.'

He can make sure she comes. She's putty in his hands.

Anima and Ashesh walk down the road briskly without speaking. Then Anima says, 'Do you recognize the symptoms, Ashesh?' Her voice breaks with a sob. 'Have we neglected her? Should we have forced her to come earlier?'

'We couldn't have forced her, Anima. You know her as well as I do. But we should sue this doctor. Would he have dared hang a patient's life on pulse examinations in America? I'll call Harya right away for an appointment.'

Bachchu Kaka's room is in the old town, in Chopade's Chawl. He points to the wall as Anima and Ashesh enter. 'How does it look?'

Ashesh's painting has brought light into the dim room, but Ashesh barely looks at it.

'How was the meeting?' Bachchu Kaka looks at them with concern. 'She's really ill.'

'Was she sitting up or . . . ?'

'Lying down. Looking like nothing on earth. We're taking her to Mumbai, Kaka. Can you arrange for a car?'

'Give me just a minute,' he says. 'Meanwhile keep looking at the picture. If you have another one like it, I'll return this to Anima.'

Bachchu Kaka goes out. In five minutes he's back. 'The car will be at Home at four. You'll be home before dark. Where will she stay?'

'With me. Anima will be there of course and . . .'

'And?'

Ashesh looks at his feet. Bachchu Kaka gives him a sharp look. 'Don't tell me you've got secretly married.'

Ashesh laughs awkwardly and tells Bachchu Kaka about Janaki. After exclamations of surprise and pleasure, Bachchu Kaka says, 'What is this age difference you're harping on?'

'Nearly thirteen years.'

'What a coincidence. Shankrya was that much older than Sindhutai. Good. Good. Now you can give me a painting as your wedding present.'

'Done, Kaka. A clown. Bright, multicoloured costume. I have a joker series in mind. The clown removing his make-up will be yours.'

Anima glances at her watch.

'There's still time. I sent Rama a message this morning. He wants to see you,' said Bachchu Kaka.

Rama is unrecognizable. His hair is quite grey and his chin is covered with a three-day stubble. He's wearing his customary pair of loose shorts and oversize shirt hanging out. Anima and Ashesh smile at him but don't know what to say beyond how are you. Anima gets up, takes him by the arm and sits him down in a chair. Next moment he's up and standing.

Shifting his weight from foot to foot, he says, 'Annasahib was talking to madam all night. Went away in the morning.' Rama lifts his right shoulder and wipes his eyes on his shirt sleeve. Then he stares into space.

'Talked all night? You never told me.' Bachchu Kaka is alert.

Rama shakes his head.

'Did you know about this?' he asks Anima and Ashesh. They look blank.

'He wrote this chit. She threw it away.' Rama takes a piece of crumpled paper from the pocket of his shorts. Unbelievable that he has kept it for ten years without showing it to anybody.

Anima takes the paper from his hand. Her heart pounds. It is Anna's scrawl. Just a few lines. Anima reads them out in a trembling voice.

I thought long and hard about our conversation last night. I realize now that I was wrong to expect you to understand why I needed to go away. Our ideas never did match. I tried to impose mine on you. That was unfair. Last night, once again, I tried to do the same. Your decision not to go with me is right, for you. But I know if I continue here in my present state of mind, I'll be more trouble than help to those I love. Please forgive me but I must do this. I have settled all my affairs. All my money is yours. The house is yours. I don't know how things will go for me, but I may never come back. Please explain to Anima, Ashesh and Bachchu why I'm doing this. They will understand.

Rama has gone. Anima is weeping soundlessly. Ashesh holds her close. 'That's enough. Enough.'

'No, it isn't. I want to scream. Don't come with me.'

She rushes out. She's on the beach for a long time. When she returns, she is as quiet as the seabed.

Bachchu Kaka has engaged a large van that will allow Sindhutai to travel lying down. She weeps as Dr Bhaskar settles her into the van. 'He has cared for me like a . . . like a real brother, and I'm going away when he needs me most.'

She is silent throughout the journey. When they arrive in Gamdevi, she says, 'If something is to happen to me, let it happen in Surgaon.'

Harya has ordered several tests. Sindhutai has to be coaxed and pleaded with to go through them. The sonography shows it clearly—the mass in the colon. Haresh looks at the images and reports carefully. 'Metastasis in the liver. Looks bad.' To Sindhutai he says, 'Aunty, I'm going to put you on your feet in no time. I will have to, because I want to eat your delicious puran polis.'

'I know I'll be fine.' Sindhutai puts extra energy in her voice. 'All this is to satisfy my children. You must also come to Surgaon on Dussehra day. We're inaugurating a magnificent Ram mandir in front of Home.'

Later Haresh tells Anima and Ashesh nothing much can be done for Sindhutai. 'I could operate, but there's always some risk in that. If I felt sure it would give her a couple of years at least of normal life I'd have advised you to take the risk. But with the metastasis . . . I'll prescribe some painkillers for later, but right now coax her to eat as much food as she can take and she must have lots of rest and happiness. Of course, I could operate if you want me to.'

That night Ashesh tries to explain the situation to Sindhutai. He and Anima have agreed that she must have the chance to decide whether she wants surgery or not. But she refuses to believe them. 'There's nothing the matter with me. I was feeling fine with Bhaskar's medicines. You forced me to come here.'

The following morning Anima asks her in a casual voice, 'Ai, did Anna tell you why he was going away before he left?'

'Why are you asking me this after all these years? Who's been telling you things?'

'Nobody. We just needed to know. It was so unlike Anna to just up and go.' Ashesh's voice is carefully mild.

'He said all sorts of things.'

'Like?'

'Why are you tormenting me?'

'We aren't, Ai. Tell us only if you can bring yourself to.'

'Bring myself to?' Sindhutai smiles bitterly.

Ashesh leans forward and takes her hand. 'Ai, we've been in the dark for ten years. We never dared to ask you about it because you were so angry with Anna. But now you are doing what you want to do with the house and the Gandhi mandir. Now you can tell us if you know, or can guess. Why did Anna go away? Where did he go?'

'How do I know where he went? He was selfish, that's all. Always did what he wanted to.'

'That isn't true, Ai. You know that. He did so much for others.'

'Others. But not for me or you. Weren't we his people?'

Sindhutai is short of breath. Anima gets her a glass of water. She rejects it.

'He went off to live for strangers. "I can't do what I want to unless I break away from my attachments," he said. He asked me to go with him. Ridiculous.'

'But he did ask.'

'Was there any sense in it? Just something to say. He himself didn't know where he was going. And I was supposed to go with him?'

Ashesh and Anima exchange glances. 'Why didn't you tell us about this?'

'Why should I? Why didn't he tell you?'

Somebody's car horn gets stuck down the road. It bleats helplessly, on and on. Sindhutai closes her eyes, exhausted. Anima laughs soundlessly.

Sindhutai lies in bed every day, staring at the ceiling or weeping silently. Ashesh and Anima wonder whether there's any point keeping her in Mumbai. They ask her if she would like to go back to Surgaon. For the first time since she came to Mumbai, her face breaks into a smile. She even comes out to the sitting room that evening. She is sipping tea when Janaki drops by as planned.

'Ai, I'd like you to meet Janaki Patil. I am going to marry her.' Sindhutai starts as if a bomb has fallen at her feet. She looks at Janaki, her forehead creasing vertically. 'Patil? What is that?'

'You want to know her caste, Ai?' Ashesh asks.

'Why would I want to know her caste? Patil is Pachkalshi or Maratha. But it makes no difference. You want to marry her, so go ahead. It's fine by me.'

Janaki signals a question to Anima. 'Shall I touch her feet?'

Anima signals back, 'No.' Janaki continues to stand awkwardly. As far as Sindhutai is concerned there is nobody besides herself in the room. 'Perhaps I should go,' Janaki murmurs at last.

Sindhutai looks at her now. 'Why should you go? I'm the one who should go.' She struggles to get up. Anima helps her. Steadying herself, she says, 'You might as well touch my feet, girl. Let me bless you. I may not be around for your wedding.'

33

Sharada and Janaki enter the spacious sea-facing auditorium at the southern end of the city. Sharada is late. She had been listening to Abdul Wahid Khan sahib's Darbari Kanada as she got dressed for the evening. She had been so lost in the leisurely pace of his singing that Karishma had had to call out twice to say she was taking Shantanu for his evening stroll, before she had heard her. The Kirana gharana maestro had teased out incredible variations on every note of the raag as he moved grandly up the scale. By the time he had arrived at the top with a sharp, precise shadja, she had stopped all pretence of getting ready. Raag Darbari was all around her, filling the room. She had allowed herself to be cocooned in its sombre notes, only half-conscious that she was getting late for her date with Janaki.

There was no point wondering why musicians no longer sang at Wahid Khan sahib's pace. History could not be denied. Speed was the mark of the age. Those who resisted its temptations only did so because they mistook slowness for substance. They ground out every note with repetitious phrases and ended up making tedious, joyless music.

Janaki stands outside the main gate of the auditorium, shifting her weight from one foot to the other. Coming straight from work, she has had barely enough time to wash her face and comb her hair. Her lack of interest in the evening's programme is clearly written on her face. It's a boring extension of her work that is taking her away from what she'd rather be doing—sitting for Ashesh. As she waits for Sharada, she smiles to herself with the memory of his tapering fingers, their precise movements, the sprinkling of grey in his fine hair and the incline of his neck as his searching gaze fixes first on her and then on the canvas.

The auditorium is fairly full by the time they enter. Janaki cranes her neck every which way to catch the action. She has been briefed to begin her piece with a succulent description of the scene, meaning who was there and what they were wearing—handbags, watches, footwear included. Next she must devote space to an admiring account of Sumitraben's mist-like sari and her signature pearls. She must also give her piece a negative edge by commenting snidely on the East–West clash of rosewater sprayed on guests and the sophisticated perfumes they are wearing.

She realizes there is a fracas taking place up front. She quickly jots down details. The front row is filled with special invitees whom Sumitraben has personally welcomed and ushered to their seats. Now Kamaladevi, the empress of classical music, arrives, flanked by her sons, supporting herself with a walking stick. She never attends concerts, but not to invite her is an unforgivable sin. Her appearance here is not for the love of music, but to find fuel for an old fire.

Pandit Mishra always makes a point of naming her as the guru to whom he owes everything that he is. Many years ago, he had been her favourite disciple. But they fell out. The ill feeling has grown and festered to such an extent that she has recently announced to her inner circle of sycophants that she will no longer tolerate being named his guru. She has come today to make sure he does not and to create a scene if he does.

Kamaladevi stands before Sumitraben as an urgent seating problem.

Swami Shivanand notices Sumitraben's embarrassment and whispers
to his disciples to give up their seats. They instantly slide down like
shadows to sit on the floor at his feet. Sumitraben smiles graciously and
leads the empress and her sons to the vacated seats.

While this drama takes place, Sharada fills Janaki in on the details
of the quarrel between guru and disciple. Ten years ago Kamaladevi
was invited to sing in Gwalior at the Tansen Music Festival. She had
declined the invitation on account of ill health. She had expected
the organizers to press her to come despite ill health, offering to do
everything in their power to make her comfortable, asserting that the
festival would be no festival at all without her presence. But they had
promptly accepted her regrets instead and invited Pandit Mishra to
sing in her stead. This was logical given that he was her seniormost
disciple and an established performer. But the mortified Kamaladevi
accused him of having engineered the whole thing. When this came to
Pandit Mishra's ears on the ever-obliging grapevine, he retorted to the
grapevine, 'How could I have wangled Kamaladevi's bad health and
her consequent turning down of the invitation?' Kamaladevi had had
no answer to this riposte when it came back to her on the grapevine.
She had exploded with anger.

After this exchange over the grapevine, a lot of gossip about
Pandit Mishra's private life had begun to circulate in the music world.
Everybody knew where the stories were coming from. Some people
licked their lips over the possibilities of the situation and got busy
whispering nourishment into the ears of both parties till the rift became
unbridgeable. Sharada concludes her tale with a sigh. 'She's come with
some drama in mind, I'm sure.'

'That'll be manna from heaven for the piece I've been asked to
write.'

Pandit Omkar Mishra walks on to the stage. Sumitraben must have
warned him of who is in the front row, giving him time to prepare his
strategy. Descending from the stage, he goes directly to Shivanand
Swami, apparently seeing nothing else in the vicinity. He bows low to
touch the Swami's feet for his blessings and returns to the stage. He

sits down in the lotus position and closes his eyes in meditation. His disciples enter and sit around him. A while later, Pandit Mishra opens his eyes and says in a voice that is touched by the ethereality of what is about to happen, 'The music I'm going to present before you today has not come to me from my guru. I have dared to create it because my spiritual guru commanded me to. My inspiration and the words of my songs both come from the rich treasures of our ancient literature. Performing with me will be my young fellow seeker of the spiritual path and one of the foremost painters of his generation, Prakashanand. He has lived twenty monsoons less than me but the maturity of his work is astounding. My performance is with words and music, his is with paper and paints.'

Prakash has entered the stage on cue, his hands humbly folded. He wears a light saffron kurta and a gold-bordered Bengali-style dhoti. There's a drizzle of applause at his entry. Both artists now walk to the edge of the stage. Pandit Mishra says, 'Our guru Swami Shivanand is before us today. We will prostrate ourselves before him for his blessings and begin this auspicious programme.' The swami rises and raises both hands in a generous blessing.

Pandit Mishra and Prakash sit down again in the lotus position, and again close their eyes. Then, at the same moment, on the same note, in perfect unison, they begin to chant 'aum'.

At this point Kamaladevi rises with a dismissive swish of her whole body. Snorting loudly, she fixes her eyes on her favourite disciple of long ago and says in a loud voice to her sons, 'Get up. We're going.' Although she comes from Sangli, her public language is Hindi. 'If we stay any longer, this tamasha will make us ill.' Having delivered this sentiment, she walks out, tapping her cane angrily. Sumitraben bows low with folded hands as though Kamaladevi's going away in a huff is the most natural thing to happen. This pretence of everything being just as it should be enrages Kamaladevi further. Spewing contempt on 'people of no culture', she leaves with her son Giriraj, while Jairaj stays back in order to give her a blow-by-blow account of how the evening proceeded.

Pandit Mishra opens his eyes and, for the first time, looks at the audience with a gracious smile. Prakash stands behind him, a carved walnut-wood Kashmiri stool beside him bearing tubes of colour. On the wooden screen at the back hang four medium-sized canvases, one per bandish.

Pandit Mishra's disciples sit in a semicircle around him, leaning a little forward to catch every word and note he sings. Two senior disciples, who will accompany him on the tanpura, tune their instruments. All the disciples are dressed in pearl-coloured kurtas, embroidered at the neck, with white churidar pyjama trousers. Each one has a black, gold-bordered Kutchi shawl covering his feet.

The tanpuras are tuned. Their deep resonance fills the auditorium. Janaki whispers to Sharada, 'I could listen to just the tanpura forever. It is so hypnotic.'

'I might agree with you today. All this shloka stuff sounds a little suspect to me. But Mishra has a wonderful voice.'

That voice now merges with the tanpura. Pandit Mishra sings a couple of notes and then stops while the tanpuras continue to play.

'Namaskar. I beg your leave to present before you four shlokabandishes composed in raags Bageshri, Kedar, Mand and Khamaj. The shlokas invoke the four elements—earth, water, ether and sky. They are in Sanskrit so I shall explain their meanings first. The shloka addressed to Earth says: "Let your grace be upon us, you who bear the human race upon your back. Please give us joy." The shloka to Sky says: "All the elements emerge from you and return to you. You are the final resting place of all things." To Water: "Darkness was the first to come into being. Then everything was filled with you who have neither shape nor form." To Air: "You are beautiful, self-contained, thousand eyed. Your radiant chariot is drawn by a thousand stallions."

'My friends, I will begin with "Earth".'

Pandit Mishra closes his eyes, sings the opening notes of Bageshri and moves straight into the bandish. The audience feels ennobled by the sacred sounds of Sanskrit. But Sharada groans as words, melody and beat fight against each other in the composition. Prakash has picked up his brush with a flourish and is painting a Parambindu Yantra with the bindu located within a large triangle. He makes a circle to touch the three sides of the triangle and, beyond it, concentric circles in black moving to the edge of the canvas like sound waves. He rapidly inscribes the words of the shloka at the bottom of the canvas, finishing exactly at the moment that Pandit Mishra sings the last note of 'Earth'.

The audience bursts into applause at the split-second coordination of the act. 'That was perfectly rehearsed. Sumitraben is nothing if not a perfectionist,' Sharada whispers to Janaki.

When Pandit Mishra begins to sing 'Sky', Prakash starts off on another Parambindu. Only this time the concentric waves around the central bindu and triangle are in light blue, with the shloka inscribed at the bottom of the canvas in black.

'Shall we leave?' Sharada asks. 'We aren't getting any music here and even less art.'

'Can't.' Janaki sounds rueful. 'I'm on duty. But you carry on.' Sharada moves quietly to the back of the auditorium and leaves. A few others take courage and do the same. Pandit Mishra sings 'Water' in Mand and 'Ether' in Khamaj. Prakash produces two more Parambindus surrounded by midnight-blue waves for water and grey waves for air. Every time the music and the painting end together as on a sam. The audience is so excited by this phenomenon that they can't stop clapping. When the last song is sung and the last painting painted, they stand up as one to give the artists a standing ovation which the artists receive with humbly folded hands.

Sumitraben escorts Swami Shivanand to the stage. The artists fall at his feet. Swamiji puts his hands on their heads and raises them up. Sumitraben takes the mic. Speaking in lilting English, she says, 'I thank you, the audience, from the bottom of my heart for honouring our invitation and blessing us with your presence on this occasion. I can see that you are as overwhelmed by what we have heard and seen today as I am. I have no hesitation in saying that the artists have together touched the highest peak of spirituality. [Applause.] You have already acknowledged their rare talent with your applause. I now hope you will also respond in a more material way. You already know that these four

paintings are to be auctioned here and now. Sharmila Parekh, ex–Chief
Director of the Indian branch of the world-renowned auction house
Sotheby's, has flown down from Delhi especially to be with us. We are
profoundly grateful to her for agreeing to conduct today's auction. I
will repeat that the money collected from the auction will go towards
funding a new and novel project planned by Swami Shivanand. He plans
to build a gurukul where he will teach Sanskrit to Dalit children. He has
graciously agreed to accept our humble contribution towards his work.
May I now invite Sharmila Parekh to the dais to conduct the auction?'

Ms Parekh, the toast of Delhi's party circuit and popularly known
as 'Shums', dresses in Western designer outfits as a rule. On this day,
however, she is draped in a red-and-black Orissa ikat sari, accompanied
by chunky, oxidized-silver jewellery. She sways up to the dais. When
she turns to face the audience, they notice the coup de grâce of her
look for the day. A line of sandalwood paste is etched from the middle
of her nose to the parting in her hair in imitation of the Vaishnavs of
Manipur. This is in honour of Swami Shivanand who is said to have
come to the plains from the hills of the North-East. While Sumitraben
introduces Ms Parekh to the audience in hyperbole, Ms Parekh stands
with head bowed, blushing modestly. When the introduction is over,
she descends from the dais to kneel before Swami Shivanand and lay
her head on his feet. Janaki makes rapid notes.

Bowing and blessing over, the auction begins. The base price for
all four paintings is declared. One lakh rupees. Shums takes in the
audience with a sweeping glance and begins the auctioneer's chant.
'Who says a lakh and a half? Do I hear a lakh and a half? Who said a
lakh and a half?'

Initially, nobody responds. They watch each other awkwardly to
figure out what they are supposed to do with the paddles that have
been thrust into their hands. A hesitant paddle goes up somewhere. 'A
lakh and a half! Do I hear two? Who says two?' Another paddle goes
up. 'Two, two, two . . . I have two lakhs. Do I hear two and a half?'

The race is getting exciting. The quality of the paintings is no longer
important. What is important is to show you have two lakh rupees to

squander against your neighbour's one and a half. If your neighbour
has two, you have three and a half. Sharmila eggs the audience on with
reminders about the great cause to which their money will go. Finally
Earth goes first, for three lakh, followed by the other primary elements
for three and a half, three and a half, and four lakh.

The auction will give Prakash the stamp of saleability. No matter
what the critics say about his work, he will have this fourteen lakh
made in an evening to vouch for its quality. It will not be long before
Prakash has his own flat and car.

34

Janaki gazes intently at the canvas. It is still on the easel, set up at an
angle near the door to catch the cross light. Under that light Ashesh's
play with textures comes alive.

The woman in the painting is, and is not, Janaki. The viewer who
does not know that Namdeo's milkmaid is one of the inspirations behind
it will not see a milkmaid there. Nor, for that matter, Pu Shi Rege's
'Pushkallaa'. It is perhaps to Janaki's disadvantage that she knows the
genesis of the work. She would like to see it without that knowledge,
but knowledge cannot be thrown out at will. Under the circumstances,
she must try her best to look at the work objectively.

The work shows the bust of a woman, her head turned to look at
the artist. The face is neutral. One hand, ornamented with a thick,
smooth bracelet, rests easily on the cheek. The hair is coiled on top of
her head. The contours of the figure are made with myriad little marks
in grey. This softens the edges, allowing the substantiality of the face to
merge with the background in a fluid relationship. The background is
painted in shades of grey that flow into each other cloudily with thin
slivers of black with hints of blue showing through. The whole is bathed
in a mellow light that appears to come from a hidden moon.

Janaki finds herself drowning, resurfacing and drowning again in its greys and blacks. Ashesh watches her nervously, trying to gauge her response. She feels a strong urge to touch the tactile surface of the painting. 'May I touch it?' she asks.

He smiles. 'Sure, but lightly.'

'It's erotic.'

'That's the effect I wanted. You think I've succeeded?'

Janaki nods, moves towards him and lays her head against his chest.

He looks down at her untidy hair, strokes it lightly, then sits her down in a chair. He has things to say which must be said now.

'Look, Janaki, I'm nearly thirteen years older than you.' His voice is studiedly neutral.

'So?' She raises her eyebrows quizzically at him.

'I have all sorts of fears. I might go suddenly blind. Things like that.'

'Everybody has fears.'

'But there's one fear in particular.'

'Which?'

'That I might suddenly decide to disappear.'

'Because of your Anna? Disappearing is not hereditary.'

'There's a story about my grandfather too.'

'I said it's not hereditary. But tell me.'

'We had some land in a village called Arsal in the Konkan. We were fairly prosperous. At some point my grandfather began to hear strains of the flute and he took off in the middle of the rice-sowing season, without saying a word to anybody. Grandmother saw him go and, because of the look in his eyes, knew he wouldn't return. So she put Anna on her hip and followed him. Anna's uncle tried to stop her but she wouldn't turn back. Every few hours she would ask my grandfather where they were going but he kept walking not saying a word. Grandfather wandered restlessly from place to place, halting for the night then moving on again. One night they halted at Surgaon. As always, they slept in the village temple. When they woke up in the morning, grandfather looked around him in a daze. He said to my grandmother, 'I can't hear the flute. We've arrived.' So they sat there waiting. The villagers were astonished to find a Brahmin taking shelter in their temple. The temple priest had died only the previous night without heir or disciple. My grandfather told them he had been called to serve the Lord. That's how he settled in Surgaon.'

'Villagers sit under peepul trees and spin yarns to pass the time. In time the stories become more and more bizarre. You don't believe in this one, do you?'

'Thinking rationally, I don't. But I've heard it so often since I was a child that it's become part of my history. Anna too must have heard it from the time he was a child. Could our minds be suggestible? Anna followed his urge because his father had followed his? Myths work at deeper levels than true stories.'

'If you go, I'll go with you, like your grandmother.'

'But I may not tell you. Anna didn't tell us.'

'You'd have stopped him.'

'Because he had responsibilities.'

'The two of you had your lives and he had provided for your mother. I've always wondered how she knew that he'd moved all his money to her account. How she knew where his will was. He must have told her. And why did he tell her? Because he was going away. She must have known he was going away.'

'She did. We've only just found out. I'll tell you about that later. Right now I want you to know that I have all these fears. Another thing you must know. If someone tries to molest you, I'm not sure I'd rush to protect you. I'm not one of the world's chest-thumping men.'

'Don't worry. I'm capable of looking after myself. I have only one question for you. Are you gay?'

Ashesh is taken aback. 'Janaki, you know I'm not. You think I'm play-acting when we are together? People say these things about single men. It's just gossip.'

'People say you didn't marry Nasreen for that reason. Since we're airing fears, let me air mine.'

'Nasreen and I may not have flaunted our physical relationship but we did have one. I didn't marry her simply because I got cold feet. I wasn't sure I could handle marriage.'

'Are you sure now? I'm not. Let's just do it and see?'

Ashesh smiles at her, feeling more relaxed.

'What was Nasreen like?'

'Let me show you.' Ashesh goes to his room and comes out with a large photograph. Janaki looks at it intently. She sees a woman with shoulder-length hair hanging down straight on both sides of her face and gold-rimmed spectacles with round lenses. She sits cross-legged on the floor, looking straight at the camera.

'Nasreen at twenty. She hasn't changed much over the years.'

'You've met her recently?'

'I met her when I went to London. We meet when she comes here. She's doing extremely well. Her work is highly regarded there.'

'Are you still emotionally involved with her?'

'I admire her. She lives alone. She has never betrayed herself, never made compromises in her work. She's an independent, spirited woman. Ai would have rejected her even if she'd been a Hindu. She could never have dealt with Nasreen's kind of spirit. She can't deal with Anima.'

'Is your mother very traditional?'

'Yes. I've always been her favourite because I'm male and I'm light-skinned, like her. Anima is a girl and dark-skinned like Anna. Ai must have loved her but didn't show it. Ai's rejection of Anima worked to Anima's advantage. She attached herself to Anna who loved her and didn't restrain her from doing any of the boy things she liked doing. She'd fling her leg over a bicycle and ride off to the market. She'd leap into the well for a swim. She'd play tops with the neighbourhood boys. I stayed at home, under Ai's protection, and grew up to not be "a man amongst men".' There's a pause. 'Will I do?'

'Do? I want you. I've known one "man amongst men"—my father. And that one's enough.'

'What about your mother? You don't meet her much, do you?'

'No.'

'Don't you feel any sympathy for her?'

'Perhaps I do, now. I didn't then.'

'What will it be like with us? Are you sure we'll be good for each other?'

'Look, Ashesh, I don't just love you. I like you. And I love your work. That should be enough to go on from my side. You've never told me your side. But you don't have to. I feel it.'

'Shall we not be afraid then? Shall we jump in?'

The following morning, Ashesh allows Janaki to make tea, introducing her to his ritual. 'What would you like as a wedding gift?' he asks as they sit with their tea on the veranda. 'I don't understand jewellery and stuff like that.'

'I don't either.'

'Oh good. So what would you like?'

'There is something I want desperately.'

'What?'

'A tanpura?'

'I know nothing about tanpuras either.'

'Sharada does.'

'I'll paint out here and you'll practise in there. Sounds good.'

'When I get time from the job.'

'Give up your job. Freelance. Money's no problem. My work sells moderately well.'

Janaki grins and shakes her head. 'Be careful, Ashesh. "No need for you to work" is a man's first step towards becoming a husband.'

Ashesh slaps himself on the cheek. 'Damn! I've failed before I've begun!'

35

Dear Asheshji,

I am still in Amsterdam. I had planned to return this winter. But I've got into something else unexpectedly. My boyfriend, Jan, has been offered a handsome scholarship to work in Japan for a year. He is very keen that I should go with him. I was in two minds about it. But I've decided to go. It's going to be a great year for us with two weeks in Korea thrown in. You know what a lot of good work is happening there. But this letter is not about me. I've been waiting to tell you about something that's been weighing on my mind. I'd expected to do it face-to-face, but since I'm not coming back just yet, I'm forced to do it by letter. I hope a handwritten letter will carry some of the warmth of a personal meeting.

This letter is about Yogesh. It is two years since he died. He had come to meet me in a very disturbed state of mind before he left for India. He stayed with me for a week and just before he returned to London he came out to me. We, his close friends, had suspected for a long time that he was gay. I don't know how you'll receive this, but he also told me that he was deeply in love with you. In fact, obsessed. Perhaps his hopes in that regard might have been kept alive by the whispers all of us had heard in the art world about you. Naturally, it was through this prism that he saw your words, looks and gestures. There were times when he came to meet us after he'd met you, his face glowing with joy. At other times he would look so depressed, we didn't know how to bring him out of it.

When he came to Amsterdam, he told me he'd written several letters to you from London, but torn them up. He was extremely lonely there. One night after he returned to London, his room-mate called me in panic. Yogesh had tried to commit suicide. Fortunately he was rushed to the hospital in time and he survived. We were all terribly worried. We called him every day to talk to him, but he wouldn't say much.

When he was back in Mumbai, he seemed to be a changed person. He called us cheerfully about the large work he was doing. All the hopelessness that had filled him in London seemed to have vanished. He was working feverishly. He kept emailing me about the work every day. He said it was something in praise of Man. He wrote his last mail before he completed the painting. I am enclosing a printout of it. Please let me know if he called you, and whether you saw the work. I want to bring a closure to this terrible thing that happened to my lovely, gentle friend, though I will always feel guilty that I didn't tell you about him before it happened.

If you could confirm the email ID I have for you, I'd love to email some of my work to you if you'll allow me to. You used to look at us young people's work with a lot of interest and respond with rare generosity. I would be very eager to know what you think of my latest work. My email ID appears on this letterhead.

Sincerely
Shilpa

Hi Shilpa,

The picture's done. Or almost. Last touch-ups, that's all. It is H-U-G-E. I'll email a pic once I photograph it. I'm going to invite him to see it as soon as it's done. Feeling terribly nervous. Don't know if he'll come. Don't know if he'll like it. Don't know if he'll give me a sign. How will I have the courage to call him? What should I say and do when he comes? I don't know. I'll mail you.

Yogi

Ashesh's hands tremble violently as he passes Shilpa's letter and the printout of Yogesh's letter to Janaki. He sits looking at the stamp on the envelope with blank eyes, his face drained of colour. They're beautiful, he thinks—the stamps. Vivid colours. Janaki finishes reading the letters. She takes the envelope that's hanging limp from his hand and slips them into it. He gets up.

'I'll go for a walk.'

'May I come?'

'No.' He turns to look at her. His eyes are hollow. He whispers, 'Yes, please.' The guilt of Yogesh's death lies unbearably heavy on his shoulders. He will have to live with it. He grips Janaki's hand tight.

36

For years now, Ashesh has held a solo show once every three years in September in the Jehangir Art Gallery at Kala Ghoda. He likes the human traffic that comes and goes there. He likes to listen in to what people are saying about his work. Their outspokenness keeps him grounded. He remembers most vividly the UP man who came one year trailing his veiled wife and four children behind him. He was showing off the glories of Mumbai to the rustics just up from the village. Looking curiously at his work, the woman had remarked from behind her veil in a thick UP accent, 'What kind of pictures are these? No god-goddess, no buffalo-cow, no trees-flowers.' The man, bred to the city, had cast an apologetic glance in Ashesh's direction and scolded her. 'Shut up, you village piece of nothing.' Then added for Ashesh's benefit, 'These pictures fetch more thousand rupees than you can count.' A high-pitched exclamation of astonishment had issued from behind the veil, after which there was silence. The wife had dutifully walked behind her husband like a docile cow. When they were leaving, she had whacked a child on the back for grinning at a painting.

Most of the unkind remarks he had heard belonged to his 'abstract' period. One year a group of municipal clerks had turned up to see his show. He had gathered that one of them had just treated the others to lunch at a nearby restaurant. They had sauntered over to the gallery afterwards, presumably to satisfy their cultural appetite. Not realizing Ashesh was the artist, they had stood right beside him exchanging brutal views on his work. One had said, 'You know what? If we stuck paper on our stairwell walls we'll get stuff like this by the evening.' Another had said, 'We could call the series "Spitting Image 1, 2" etc.'

They had slapped each other on the back and neighed in amusement. Ashesh smiled at having his knickers pulled off. Their reaction was understandable. How did his games with space, line, form and light touch their lives?

But this year is going to be different. A businessman settled in the UK has opened a gallery called 'Sanket' on the ground floor of an old colonial building in the Fort area. Before the inauguration, the man's Mumbai manager, Manjeet Kapoor, met artists who were not already bound to established galleries. Ashesh was one of them. After two decades of organizing his own shows at the Jehangir, he was beginning to tire of the tedious work it involved—printing invitation cards, chasing over-busy writers to deliver promised essays for the catalogue, biting your nails till they did, dealing with the printers. It would be a relief to have that burden and the weightier burden of talking prices to buyers taken off his back. When Manjeet Kapoor called, he was more than ready to meet him. It was a successful meeting. Ashesh was free to paint while Kapoor took care of everything else. The date for the opening was set—28 September, the day after Anant Chaturdashi.

Ashesh can think of this date now with something like pleasure. Most of his works are ready to go. One remains to be done. *Joker*, the last in this show, heralding a series for his next. He sees it in bright hues in complete departure from his recent blacks and greys. The flip side of being with Sanket will mean an all-out, no-holds-barred opening.

'Anna had a client,' he tells Janaki, 'who'd raise his finger and shout "give them an opening" when he heard we were unwell.' Ashesh laughs at the memory.

'Opening?' Janaki is lost.

'Castor oil. For us Hindus, the bowels hold the key to good and bad health. If the bowels are clear, the body is healthy. If the body is not healthy, clear your bowels.'

'What's castor oil?'

'There it is. The difference in age. Castor oil was the bane of children's lives. You were supposed to take it once a month and spend the day clearing your bowels. For you it's history.'

The worst thing about openings is the presence of the media. Kapoor is busy wooing them ardently while Ashesh hopes most won't turn up. The second worst thing is that an opening will compel his friends and well-wishers to come on the day. At the Jehangir they could drop in any day that suited them. There was time then for him to sit and chat with them. A couple of his collectors would even come home before the show and ask him to reserve works they wanted to buy. The prices on his list would make Haridas click his tongue and shake his head. 'Too low, way too low. Why don't you let me be your dealer?' Twenty-eighth September is going to be different—stuffy and crowded with no time to spend with friends. It is good he has decided to take them out for dinner afterwards.

Feroze sees danger in his arrangement with Sanket. 'Make sure you're not taken for a ride. This fellow could be a fly-by-night crook. These new galleries are crass business ventures. The youngsters are savvy—business, media, networking. But, you saala, you're a Warli.' Feroze has been with one of the oldest private galleries in the city. It's a little lackadaisical in business but above board. There's a mutual love–respect relationship between him and the gallery owner. Most importantly, the owner understands and loves art.

When Ashesh enters Sanket, he feels he is in someone else's home. The walls on which his paintings hang are brash, unmellowed by memories. The Jehangir walls felt warm in a very personal way. His paintings looked right there. When he stood around in that gallery, he never felt like an exhibit. He could create a fiction about being a passer-by who happened to have dropped in casually like others did. He was free to stand and stare without being attacked by false smiles and routine reactions.

At Sanket, Kapoor and his assistant are all over him. He is to be looked after, made much of. 'Hasn't Miss Patil come?' The inquiry is unctuous not because Janaki is his friend but because she is the media.

Kapoor smiles all the time. 'Everything is under control,' he assures him. Except me, Ashesh thinks. There's a huge ball of something heavy rolling around in his stomach. It's like the first day of exams. He relaxes only after Anima and Janaki come.

On the wall directly opposite the entrance hang the four paintings in black, *People*, *Soldier*, *The Red and the Black* and *Woman*. Haridas has seen the first three. He now stands looking at *Woman*. He narrows his eyes. The skin on his cheeks trembles imperceptibly. He walks over to Ashesh, puts his hand on his shoulder, looks at him for a couple of seconds, nods and moves on. Ashesh is filled with joy. Janaki watches from a distance, envious of the silent exchange between the two old friends. Ashesh notices her look. He moves to her side in two quick steps and puts an arm lightly around her waist.

Ashesh feels surprisingly comfortable as the evening proceeds, chiefly because the press photographers are not interested in him. They flash their bulbs at the celebrities Kapoor has invited to the show. Neither are the press reporters interested in him. The English-language press is there because it's a 'do' that will go into the gossip columns of their newspapers. They stare at the celebrities, chat with them, honour the wine served by the host and hurry away. The Marathi- and Hindi-language press pick up copies of the catalogue from which they will extract a few lines for their reports.

Amongst the old critics who no longer write because art has been forced to retire from the public gaze is Som Parikh, who has seen Ashesh's work from his earliest days. He has seen all his shows, and he is here again. Ashesh is happy to see him in the crowd, not socializing, but looking carefully at the paintings. He looks at each painting from close up for its texture and from a distance for its composition. Having gone around, he returns to the four works in black.

He comes to Ashesh with his customary smile that is warm without being cloying. 'So the *Joker* takes you out of black. Is that the beginning of something new?'

Ashesh nods. 'I've been static for too long. I want to travel now.' Parikh shakes his hand warmly and says goodbye.

Meanwhile Sumitraben and Prakash have arrived and are posing for the press. Prakash, thrilled with the attention, smiles his recently developed swami smile. He says a few words to Janaki, introduces Sumitraben to Anima, then floats over to Ashesh and intones, 'Sir, it's a great show,' taking Ashesh's hand in his own soft one and pumping it up and down.

The opening has been a success. Kapoor's face is wreathed in smiles. The only fly in the ointment is Ashesh's insistence that he will not go to the post-opening dinner. He wants to have a private party with his friends. Kapoor cannot understand this. Is this man mad or crazy? He wants to pass up this great opportunity to network? He wants to shoot himself in the foot?

Ashesh is full of apologies but firm. 'I'm sorry but I'm useless at small talk.'

Kapoor nods sadly. 'I understand,' he says, but his face makes it clear that he is completely bewildered.

The first-floor restaurant is an old haunt. Tables are joined. Ashesh is flanked by Janaki on one side and Sharada on the other. Opposite them are Anima, Feroze and Shekhar. At one end, on a chair dragged up from another table sits Haridas, the arrangement ensuring that Shekhar need not see Haridas at all throughout dinner.

Liquor flows, the food is good and everybody is in high spirits. As the plates are cleared away Anima says, 'I think Ashesh has something to say to us.' Ashesh is a little annoyed at her for jumping the gun. But he also sees this is the right time for it. He gropes for Janaki's hand under the table and stutters out four words. 'I am getting married.'

'Alone?' Haridas laughs.

Ashesh reddens and holds up Janaki's hand. The friends break into loud applause. Champagne arrives. Haridas raises his glass. 'To the great institution of . . .'

Shekhar cuts in, raising his own glass. 'Shut up, Haridas. You have not earned the right to speak about that institution. At this table I'm the only one who has the right.' Sharada, who has stiffened, relaxes. Shekhar is laughing happily. He clears his throat. 'You are entering the great institution of marriage hand in hand. We hope—no, we are confident—that you will continue this wonderful journey hand in hand. People make institutions. Institutions don't make people. Make of your marriage what you want it to be. You will encounter ups and downs, but if you respect one another you will conquer all. Here's to you, dear friends!'

As the levels in the champagne bottles dip, the joy on the friends' faces spills over. 'This is the stuff the gods must be drinking,' Anima says to Feroze. He nods happily. 'The Yadavas must have drunk something quite different. You're not going to throw pestles at me on this, are you?'

'There's no drink on earth that will make me hurt you, Feroze.'

Feroze takes her hand in his and squeezes it. 'Shall we also get married?'

Anima pretends to think hard. Then smiling sweetly, asks, 'What for?'

Feroze nods wisely. 'Yes indeed . . . what for?' But he keeps her hand in his.

37

This year Dussehra is in the middle of October when the post-monsoon heat blocks your breath in the chest. The afternoon sea breeze offers the only reprieve from the layer of sweat that otherwise clings to the skin. As Anima climbs into Ashesh's Padmini, she regrets their decision to travel by road. Trains are crowded but they have fans. Even if a couple of them are in working order, they stir up the air. The train tracks are not dusty and potholed. And trains don't have to follow in the wake of tankers and trucks belching clouds of poison from their exhausts. If you can bear the stench of human excreta around the tracks as you enter railway stations, the rest of the journey comes quite close to being comfortable. Of course, Ashesh's point is well taken. If the inaugural ceremony becomes unbearable at any point, a car sets them free to return home immediately. Ashesh, fed up of driving, has only recently engaged a driver. The only Padmini in the country that is chauffeur-driven. Thus said Haridas. Ashesh sits next to the driver and Anima and Janaki in the back.

The mahurat for the temple inauguration is at six in the evening. That is the time when the idol of Lord Ram will be ritually installed. Only a few select guests have been invited. Once the inauguration is over, the entire town will come for the celebratory dinner. Dr Bhaskar's local guru, Swami Satyanand, will chair the occasion and his senior devotees will look after the general organization. The earlier idea of asking a Warli to inaugurate the temple has slipped off the agenda at some point between the lips and the will.

It is four o'clock when the Mahalakshmi Hill looms up before them. In gut reaction, Anima hears the monotone of the tarpa, sees young men and women dancing, half in a trance, to its accompaniment. The coloured clips and ribbons in the young girls' hair and the sweat trickling down the midriff, bare between choli and tightly wound half-sari, gleam under the moonlight.

'I must have been around nine,' she says to Janaki, 'when I pestered Anna to let me come to the fair with Rama. Remember, Ashesh? I sat on Rama's shoulders to see the dancing. Ai was livid. "They drink all night. How did you trust Rama? He's as much of a Warli as the others." "I trust Rama more than I would trust my brother if I had one," Anna replied quietly. Ai didn't speak to Anna and me for four days afterwards.'

'Why do the Warlis worship Mahalakshmi? They have their own gods, don't they?' Janaki asks, puzzled.

'This is their goddess, not to be mixed up with the Kolhapur Mahalakshmi either in form or powers. This one's no more than a pile of stones with a goddess mask on top. It is possible she was called by some other name in the early days, who knows? The story goes that this idol used to dwell in a cave on top of the hill. The Warlis had to do a very tough climb to worship her. She was known to grant babies to infertile women and bless the fertile. A pregnant woman once felt a strong desire to worship her, but couldn't climb the hill in her condition. That night the goddess appeared to the priest in a dream and commanded him to carry her to the foot of the hill and install her there. We don't know if the Warlis improvised a temple for her in place of her cave. But the one you see now was built by Gujarati merchants. The temple business is now in their hands, but the priest is still a Warli.'

Janaki is struck by the fluid fusion of religions and cultures that has been going on in the subcontinent for centuries. As they enter Surgaon, it becomes evident that the inauguration of the Ram mandir has become a public celebration. Flags, pennants and posters of Lord Ram are everywhere. The posters show a resolute, even stern, Ram, standing erect, raised bow in hand, unaccompanied by Sita, Lakshman and Hanuman in their designated places beside him and at his feet.

When Ashesh, Anima and Janaki reach Home, there is still an hour to go for the auspicious moment of idol installation. The drone of loud chanting issues from what was once Anna's study. People in dhotis and shoulder cloths fly around busily in different directions. The three new arrivals stand in the midst of it all, staring in dumb astonishment at the enormous marble Ram mandir that occupies the whole of the huge front yard where once a garden bloomed with mogra, roses, an arbour of the purple-blue krishnakamal creeper and a massive bakul tree. The well, from which the outcasts of the town once drew water and in which Anima swam with such heady joy, has been covered. A small Sita mandir now stands on top of it. None of this belongs to them or their father. The thought plunges like a dagger into Anima's heart. They are mere observers, as much as Janaki is.

They move forward gingerly to peep into the temple. There are eight carved pillars inside and an idol of Lord Ram, gleaming in the dark of the sanctum sanctorum. Above the sanctum is a large mural depicting his coronation in Ayodhya.

'Done by local artists on traditional red-earth plaster,' a voice offers. 'Local customs must be respected. It's a foundational principle with us.' Dr Bhaskar stands behind them, eyes sparkling with pride and pleasure. 'The concept of this painting came from our brother devotee Shyam

Sarpotdarji. The fantastic thing about it is,' and here Dr Bhaskar's eyes take on a brighter shine, 'the positive-energy vibrations that it communicates. Feel that? You see, the secret is . . .'

'Who did you say has painted the mural?' Ashesh asks.

'Some local artists.'

'I meant their names.'

'Oh that. You'll have to ask brother Shyam. He's here somewhere. Anyway, the secret behind the positive-energy vibrations—Brother Shyam had a mind-blowing idea. He went to Kashi. He visited all the old bookshops there, looking for old manuscripts of the Tulsi Ramayana. After days of ferreting around, he stumbled on an exquisite manuscript and bought it on the spot. But not for his pleasure. You'll never guess what he did with it. He tore the pages one by one and got our workers to paste them on this wall . . .'

'The pages of the exquisite manuscript?' Ashesh is aghast.

'Yes, yes. Then he got the local artists to lay their red-earth plaster over them. It gave the plaster a special texture and if you look closely, you'll see bits of the old manuscript peeping through the plaster where it is thin. See? Obviously you can't read those bits, but what the sacred words are doing is setting up this flow of positive energy. It will enter the bodies, minds and hearts of the devotees who come here to pray. We believe it will bring them an osmotic understanding of Lord Ram that no amount of teaching or reading will give them.'

Dr Bhaskar watches their faces for reactions with a gracious smile. The expression reminds Ashesh of a folk tale in which the king would come into his court, sit on his throne and say, 'We are now ready to receive your gifts.' Dr Bhaskar notices that they are not as impressed as they should have been with either the temple or his words and begins to move towards the house. Gesturing towards Janaki, he says, 'We haven't met.'

'Janaki Patil,' Anima says, putting all her will into not sounding noticeably uncivil.

'The journalist? Yes. Akka has told me about her. I believe she is now part of the family?'

Dr Bhaskar raises his eyebrows archly. Ashesh clamps his mouth shut. Dr Bhaskar addresses Janaki. 'We have only just begun this work, thanks to their mother's generosity. But in time, young lady, you will see things here that will make exciting stories. This temple is going to attract devotees from all over the country. It is set to become an important place of pilgrimage.' Flashing a smile, he adds, 'One day you will tell your friends and relatives with pride that you were here for the inauguration.' Dr Bhaskar folds his hands and points them to the staircase leading to Sindhutai's room.

Ashesh and Anima climb the stairs with dread in their hearts. Janaki follows, wondering what she is doing there. Sandhya steps out of Sindhutai's room and leads them in. Sindhutai is sitting in a chair, her head lolling to one side. The skin on her neck hangs loose. Her arms are like sticks. The sleeves of her gold-embroidered choli of magenta and green shot silk look empty. But her stomach bulges out under her green nine-yard sari. She senses their entry, lifts her head a few inches and opens her closed right fist. 'I won't wear this just yet. It's too heavy.' In her palm lies an opulent nose ornament studded with pearls, emeralds and rubies. She doesn't recognize them nor, in a sense, do they recognize her. They need to tell themselves she is their mother and they her children.

Janaki wishes she hadn't come. Ashesh's mother looks terribly, terribly ill. But why is she dressed up like this? Something really bizarre is going on here and she wants desperately to laugh. She steals a look at Ashesh. He stands there, lost for what to say to his mother. Anima too is rooted to the spot. At last she asks the redundant question we ask acquaintances for the sake of good form. 'How are you feeling, Ai?'

'Who's there, girl?' Sindhutai asks and begins to gasp immediately.

'Your daughter, son and daughter-in-law.' Sandhya giggles. 'She forgets.' At which Sindhutai rasps, 'I don't forget. I can still remember old songs.' She begins to sing a Manik Varma love song in a weak, tuneless voice.

'I swear upon my life dear heart . . .'

She coughs, but goes on.

The cup of honey is at my lips
I have not taken a single sip.
Don't snatch it away from me so soon,
Don't betray me, oh please don't.

She leans back in her chair panting hard, her head lolling back. Anima rushes to her side with a sob. 'Please, Ai.' She kneels beside her and pleads with her not to strain herself. 'You must lie down, Ai. Ashesh, tell her.'

There's a light knock on the door and Dr Bhaskar comes in. 'Sindhutai.'

She can barely open her eyes. 'So you've come at last. I've been waiting so long for you.' She raises her right hand and struggles to screw the nose ornament into the hole pierced in her nostril. With a mighty effort of will, she succeeds. Dr Bhaskar puts one arm under her knees, the other under her neck and lifts her bodily, like a feather. Signalling to the others to follow, he begins to descend the stairs. The invitees are gathered in front of the veranda, dressed in gold-embroidered, nine-yard silk saris and dhotis. A gasp of awe mixed with fear goes up when Dr Bhaskar emerges on the veranda with Sindhutai in his arms. When he sets her down in a chair, lumps rise to the women's throats to see her brilliant sari, choli and nose ornament. One woman whispers, 'She looks like a goddess, doesn't she?'

The rituals of installing the idol are completed in haste for Sindhutai's sake. The gathering is overwhelmed with emotion to see Lord Ram, their Ram, standing erect in the sanctum sanctorum. They chant his name joyously, over and over, transported that he has found this new home in their midst. Dr Bhaskar raises his hand to silence the gathering and invites Swami Satyanand to say a few words. He has not risen from his seat because he is supporting Sindhutai's head on his shoulder. Swami Satyanand rises. 'This is not the occasion for long speeches. You can see how ill our patron, Sindhutai Joshi, is. It has been her dearest wish to see Shri Ram installed in her front yard. It is a great day for us that we have been able to fulfil her wish. We have no doubt whatsoever that her health will mend rapidly now. I wish to express my gratitude to her for two things today. First, for the deep faith she has shown in our work. And second, for having willed this gracious home to us so we may continue our work in this district. Today, with you the eminent citizens of this town as witnesses, I solemnly promise Sindhutai and her son, who is present amongst us, to turn this temple into one of the most important places of pilgrimage in Hindustan.'

Ashesh and Anima cannot hear what he says after this. A thousand insects seem to be fluttering in Anima's ears and Ashesh's eyes have turned to cold marbles. Janaki glances anxiously at them in turn. They glare at Dr Bhaskar who is watching over Sindhutai with tender care. A few moments later he whispers in her ear. She brings her trembling hands together in a namaskar. The audience breaks into thunderous applause. Sindhutai's head lolls back. Dr Bhaskar rises in a hurry. 'My sister is exhausted with all the excitement. With your leave I will carry her upstairs.'

Tutaris and conch shells are blown outside the gate. Bright orange jhendu flowers are thrown in the air. Photographers run forward. Buttons click, cameras flash. Dr Bhaskar raises Sindhutai's right hand. Then once again, he puts one arm under her knee, one under her neck and lifts her up bodily. Somebody whispers in Anima's ear, 'It's over. Come home.'

She turns to see their old playmate Shantaram whose father's farm used to be their picnic place. They spent entire days gambolling around it, plucking succulent vegetables off their creepers and eating them raw. When mango blossom turned into plump green fruit, they would bite into its crisp flesh dipped in salt and chilli powder, the sourness setting their teeth on edge. Anima nudges Ashesh, touches Janaki's shoulder. All three rise and follow Shantaram. A barbed wire marks off his farm from the Joshi property. They bend under it as they always did to cross over to the other side. Shantaram's wife brings them tea. His daughter and son lean against the door jambs and stare at them. A puff of breeze brings in the warm smell of cow dung and milk. A buffalo moos resonantly.

'I've given up the old dairy business,' Shantaram says as he slurps his tea. 'I've kept just one buffalo for our needs.' He jerks his head towards his children. 'They aren't interested in carrying on. The farm is there while we last. He can do what he wants with it afterwards.'

The boy listens with an expressionless face. 'Our days are over, eh, Ashesh? Everything changed after Anna went away.'

'Anna went away because everything was changing.'

'Don't know about that. If he'd stayed, the well would have remained open for everybody. These people closed it saying the missionaries had poisoned the water. No news of Anna, no?'

Ashesh shakes his head.

'They say he has brought water, electricity and trees to a small village Satara side.'

Many such tales have made their way to Surgaon and nearby villages since Anna's disappearance. Whenever a news item appears in the papers about some maverick do-gooder, he is instantly rumoured to be Anna. There is a strong belief that he will return one day as suddenly as he left, and everything will be as it was.

When Ashesh and Anima return to say goodbye to Sindhutai, Janaki asks if she may be excused from going up.

Sindhutai is peacefully asleep in her silk choli and her nine-yard sari. Ashesh calls out to her. She doesn't move. 'She is very tired.' Dr Bhaskar sits beside her. 'But she'll be just fine tomorrow.'

'I assume you read the reports we sent you,' Ashesh says in a tight voice.

'So you know what the diagnosis is,' Anima says coldly.

'Doesn't worry me. We've asked a miraculous ayurvedic doctor from Vapi to visit. He'll be here tomorrow. Even people in America have his medications flown to them.'

'In America, you'd have been sued for not treating a patient with regular drugs.'

Dr Bhaskar laughs drily. 'Let's not talk about America. I spent twenty years there. So I know what a rotten society it is. But you don't worry. I will personally bring her to Mumbai for your wedding. You'll see.'

38

There are moments when Anima is off guard and the memory of Siddharth sears her gut like a red-hot skewer. She has got off at Charni Road station and is in a cab that's playing a tape of old film songs. Right now it is Mohammed Rafi's song of lost love, '*Din dhal jaaye haai . . .*' The days pass, the nights will not go. You do not come to me but your memory tortures me so. Anima wants to tell the driver to turn off the song but cannot. Rafi's voice is deep and gruff with grief. He is not complaining. He is neither angry nor resentful. He is just pure pain and the acceptance of pain.

A whole gaggle of them saw *Guide* in the ramshackle Poonam cinema hall in Surgaon. Anima was fifteen and Siddharth seventeen. In the confusion of who was to sit where, they had found themselves next to each other. As the film unreeled, in the secrecy of the dark, Siddharth's little finger had touched hers. Was it an accident? Her cheeks had burnt at the touch. A little later, his little finger had sought hers once again and, finding no resistance, had stayed, then tentatively hooked into hers. She had let it be. On the screen Dev Anand sat on the floor, leaning against a chair, abandoned, singing '*Din dhal jaaye haai . . .*' about past times while Anima's and Siddharth's fingers were divining the possibilities of a future.

Anima wrenches herself away from her pain by listening to the song objectively. It speaks of only one kind of separation, but there are so many others—temporary and permanent, natural and man-made. Elaborate rituals have been evolved to help us endure the permanent separation of death. But there are no rituals to help us overcome the disappearance of a beloved father. Or to help us survive when a civilized divorce by mutual consent becomes painful fact.

Anima remembers Vaishali's older sister Mridula. They were in a square room with yellow walls and grey file cabinets. The fans creaked high above them in drunken circles. Anima was there to give Mridula moral support. Mohan and Mridula sat next to each other, afraid to allow their eyes to meet. Mohan could not bear to see the sorrow on Mridula's face. She still wanted him, but he wanted another. Mridula had decided to step out of his way with the generous thought that it was better for one to be unhappy than three. Mohan had found it difficult to accept her generosity. He hated being forced to feel guilty. He had tried very hard to blame her for what he was doing. But she had refused to take on the guilt he was trying to offload on her. Why talk of who was at fault and who wasn't? He didn't love her any more so she was offering him a divorce by mutual consent. Her self-respect had hurt him deeply.

Across the room from them, another drama was unfolding. A young man in jeans and shirt was not prepared to give up on the thin woman beside him. Waving away a fly that kept settling on her face, he was pleading with her, explaining to her, trying to coax her into agreement. He pinched his throat several times pledging never again to do the thing that had driven them apart. His face was ready to crumple in tears. Hers, turned away from him, was like stone. He touched her hesitantly with the tip of a finger to get her attention. But her skin too was stone. What was his crime that had made her so unforgiving? This was three years ago, but she has still not forgotten the young man's pain-filled face. She sees it before her now, as Rafi's song ends.

'Have you been crying?' Feroze asks with instant concern when she steps into his house.

'Tears of joy.' She laughs. 'Because your painting's done and I'm the first to see it.'

'It is, it is, at last.' He sighs happily. 'You should also sign the work. I saw the entire painting in your voice, Anima, and your voice was in my ears as I painted.'

Anima stands before the painting, awed by its size and its detail. It is a narrative painting that tells the story of the Kurukshetra war. It begins in the top left-hand corner, takes serpentine curves diagonally across the triptych and ends in the bottom right-hand corner. At the top, Krishna is Arjun's charioteer. In the middle he reveals the universe to Arjun. At the bottom he stands helpless against the events that have been foretold, divested of weapons and all that has made him Krishna. The rest of the canvas is trees and flowering shrubs, wild and domesticated animals, hills and rivers with dead bodies strewn all around. Done in vivid colours and minute detail, the work, at first glance, seems to exude optimism. But then you notice the corpses. Krishna, a vivid blue at the top, is pale white at the bottom. There is not a stitch of clothing on his divine–human body. He is neither man nor woman. His body is on its way to attaining formlessness. The painting is entitled *Annihilation*.

Krishna is both the doer and the done to in this ultimate massacre. It is known that he will kill and be killed. There's no question then of his crying out for succour at the last moment, as Jesus Christ did on the cross. He can only wait for what is to be. An archer will come to the jungle and unwittingly shoot an arrow into his heel. He will thank the archer for releasing him from life and merge with the elements. God kills man, man kills God, man kills man and brings the world to a temporary end.

Jijabhau comes in with tea. He looks at the painting and says in a choked voice, 'Panduranga, what have we done to you!'

'This has been his chant since I completed the painting,' Feroze says.

'I see my beloved Vitthal every year at Pandharpur, and every year I feel this way. We have not been good to our gods.'

Outside, darkness has begun to pull everything into its belly. Only the windowpanes at the top of the twenty-three–storey building across the road reflect the pale rays of the setting sun. No wonder this time of day is called 'katarvel': time caught between two blades of a pair of scissors. Jijabhau switches on the lights. The blood-red roses in the clay vase in the corner spring to vivid life.

The doorbell rings. Jijabhau hurries away to open the door. Feroze frowns. 'Who the hell is it at this time? I'm really not in the mood to be polite.'

'Sahib, there are four men asking for you.'

'What four men? Who are they? Tell them I'm busy.' The four men have not waited for the return message. They have rushed in behind Jijabhau.

'Busy with your woman, eh, you landya,' one of them shouts, his moustache bristling. The others look around. They call out to one another, point to the painting in the studio. They run in. Jijabhau follows. Feroze freezes. Anima watches the men with dilated eyes. The men whip penknives out of their pockets and slash at the painting. Jijabhau holds one back. A knife cuts his hand. Krishna is in shreds. The cow standing beside him is stabbed in the neck. Her head falls limply over the bottom of the frame.

The men rush out of the studio. One says, 'Strip your Paigambar naked and sell him to the highest bidder. Don't touch our gods, you landya. Just watch out!'

'Landya?' Anima begins to laugh hysterically. 'The name's Feroze Banatwala.' But the men have disappeared.

Feroze is still motionless. Anima is still laughing. Tears stream from her eyes. Jijabhau presses the gash on his hand with the other. 'Please don't laugh like that, madam,' he pleads as his blood drips to the floor. Anima looks at the blood for a moment with blank eyes. Her laughter turns to horror. She howls, 'Siddharth!' Feroze comes to life. He throws his arms around her. 'Go, bandage that,' he tells Jijabhau, who tiptoes away. Anima sobs till she can sob no more. Feroze strokes her back, his cheek resting against the top of her head. They remain that way for a long time, slowly healing with the warmth flowing between them.

'What will you do now?' Anima asks in a trembling voice.

'Let's first see what they have done.'

'I can't.'

'You must. Come on, get up.'

They stand close together, hand in hand. Feroze lifts the cow's head gently, picks up pieces of Krishna from the floor. He puts them all on a nearby stool. A wave of excitement rises in him as he does so. He looks at the jagged strips of canvas on the stool. 'I've never attempted a collage before,' he says. 'But this might make an interesting one. I can stitch the pieces together, stick other bits in to fill the gaps, paint over them, and call the work *Annihilation II*.'

39

Janaki's article about the attack on Feroze's painting, and similar acts that have been on the increase in recent times, appears on the Sunday following the attack. Besides arguing for the usual freedoms of thought and expression, she has drawn attention to a fact that is specific to the case, namely that the attackers believed Feroze Banatwala was a Muslim. Admittedly, the attack would have been equally condemnable whatever his religion, but the error demonstrated, yet again, that fanaticism and ignorance were bedfellows that fed off one another.

To point out that such attacks are the products of a mindset of victimhood that has been politically engineered would be redundant. Behind each of these acts of vandalism stand politicians who feast on the gains of violence. This has become the signature of our age. There is today a systematic attempt, which politicians do not even bother to hide, to divide society into 'us' and 'them'. Its aim is to sow fear, contempt and hubris in the minds of the majority. As a result, the number of people in civil society who see such acts as justified is growing at a disturbing rate.

The article ends here because the subeditor has put his scissors to the discussion that follows. The excuse he has trotted out to Janaki is lack of space; but secretly he is in total agreement with the owner's view that the culture page in a newspaper is no place for serious writing.

The MR Party, whose members were responsible for the vandalism, is livid with the article because it exposes their gaffe in taking Feroze Banatwala for a Muslim. In a revengeful non sequitur, they have spread the party chieftain's word amongst his followers that the article is blatantly anti-Hindu. The chieftain and the owner of the *Mumbai Observer* have a long-standing friendship. The chieftain has called up the owner already. 'Our workers are going to riot outside your office.

I am holding them back on the assurance that I will force you to apologize to us on page one of tomorrow's edition. We will not put up with an apology that begins, "In case we have hurt the sentiments of Hindus . . ." That's your favourite trick. You hurt our sentiments and then pretend to be surprised but offer a generous apology. It will not do. You must state categorically that you have hurt our feelings and offer an apology.'

'Come on, man, we can't do that. The writer didn't intend to hurt your feelings,' the owner grumbles. 'It's a question of the paper's credibility. Why don't I turn your men's attention away from this? I can throw in some other kind of news for which your men can go on a rampage.'

'No, that won't do. Till now, Parsis have never made a fuss about such things. But there are hotheads in every community. If they decide to protest, public sympathy is bound to go to them.'

'Oh all right. But what must the apology say?'

'That you've hurt Hindu feelings. And put it on the front page. In bold. Tomorrow.'

'Okay, okay. It will be done.'

The owner calls up the editor. The editor calls up the news editor. The chief sub makes a draft of the apology. He shows it to the news editor. The news editor passes it. Singh sahib approves it and leaves the office for a keynote address he has been invited to deliver at a seminar on 'Religious Fanaticism and Democracy' at the Nanikji Mehta Arts, Science and Commerce College.

Singh sahib was once a lecturer in Delhi's famed St Stephen's College. In those days he used to lean left. In later years he tilted a little towards the right. By the time he entered the newspaper business, he had decided there was not much to be said for leaning either to the left or right. So he became flexible. He leaned towards the owners of his newspaper when he was in the office and allowed his leanings outside the office to be determined by whosoever was honouring him or paying him or entertaining him.

When Singh sahib delivers keynote addresses, he shows a

pronounced leftward incline because he believes, mistakenly, that students as a group tend to incline that way. But when he is dining with some of his wealthy, pure-vegetarian friends, he slips judicious soupçons of yeses into the rabid fare that comes to the table with ghee-fried delights.

Today he intends to assume a strictly secularist position. Briefly, he will posit faith and emotion against thought and reason, to show how the former militates against the very idea of democracy. He is also toying with the idea of referring to the attack on Feroze Banatwala's Krishna painting, with a not-too-deep or lengthy exegesis on the significance of Krishna, a subject he happens to have devoted himself to some years ago. This would, incidentally, give the audience a glimpse of his erudition. Sitting in his car, he goes over what he might say.

Who is Krishna? Is he to be identified by the plywood Sudarshan Chakra he twirls on television? Is Krishna his pitamber? Is Krishna his peacock feather? Is Krishna his flute? Is Krishna his milkmaids and their clothes hanging on a tree? Or is Krishna the very principle of life, of the universe spinning timelessly with its load of the good and the bad? Is Krishna not Death? Why have so many novels and plays been written on Krishna's last days? Isn't it because his end comes at a point where one cycle of time has ended and another is set to begin? Into that moment is gathered the very essence and meaning of the events of the past. In that moment Krishna's garments and weapons have lost meaning; his being a grieving king and a distraught father has become irrelevant. He is now preparing to return to his source. His journey from the body into formless universal matter has begun.

Heads of all religions, ours as well as others, have conspired not to allow even a hint of the sublime philosophy that is at the root of every religion to reach the minds of our common folk. They have, instead, been deliberately bound to the narrowest ideas of religion. Today politicians everywhere are reaping the benefits of this conspiracy. They know full well that it is not blind faith but questions, doubts, discussions and debate that have brought man this far on the path of spiritual enlightenment. But they turn a blind eye to this glaring truth.

Their unhappiness with democracy stems from the fact that it strives to make religion a private affair. That is why those who seek power through religious bigotry will always find democracy an obstacle.

Singh sahib is pleased with this neat tying up of religion and democracy. But there is a nagging uneasiness in his mind. There is bound to be some pest in the audience who has watched the latest news update on television and knows that the chief of the Maibhoomi Rashtriya Party has demanded an apology from his paper for its 'anti-Hindu' report on the Banatwala episode. How the electronic media messes up the lives of newspapermen! This pest is bound to ask, 'Sir, will you apologize to the MR Party?' Singh sahib must decide his strategy here and now. He mulls over the problem and decides to brazen it out. 'We will never apologize,' he will bark. The pest is hardly likely to come after him when he sees the apology in tomorrow's edition of the paper. He might at most write a letter to the editor taunting him for being such a coward. But it is in the editor's hand not to publish letters. You cannot be too rigid about ethical principles these days. That is how life is.

Singh sahib calls the news editor before he reaches the college. 'Has the apology gone in?' The news editor assures him that the chief sub has 'done the needful'. What he has actually done comes to light only the following morning. The chief sub is not a neutral conduit. He was angry that the apology was going to appear in the very space which the news editor had promised him for a personal favour. The daughter of a man to whom he owes much was the only girl from the city to be selected for an international student-exchange programme. He had promised the man that he would slip in a small news item about it somewhere on the front page with a tiny picture of the girl. He had to butter up the news editor to allow him to do this, and now that space was going to this damned apology. The news editor had asked him to push his little item to page five, still a good page. 'That's where it really belongs,' he had said. 'Tell your friend even that's a big favour we're doing him.'

It is not certain whether this complication or plain journalistic ineptness is responsible for what happens to the apology. But the apology does not appear the following day, not on the front page nor on any other page of the edition. Singh sahib goes over the front page four times. No apology. The owner will not be amused. Singh sahib steels himself for the inevitable. Meanwhile he mulls over the words in which he will ask the news editor what the f---ing hell 'doing the needful' means in his part of the country.

The MR Party goes berserk. Party workers burn thousands of copies of the paper in Chinchpokli. They stone M.F. Husain's house as a matter of course. They descend on the *Mumbai Observer* office and go on the rampage. Television cameras are invited to record the action. The police are also invitees to the show. Video clips of the riot are run on TV channels as a loop from noon onwards. They show a couple of constables walking around the place swinging their batons. A couple of senior police officers are locked in a discussion, their faces confused. Their confusion is understandable. They are not at all sure what their role in this particular riot is. They are caught in a trap described exactly by the saying, 'If you catch it, it bites; if you leave it, it runs away.' Free India has never made it clear to the police whether they are supposed to serve the politicians or the people.

In the afternoon the chieftain of the MR Party calls the owner once again. 'If you want us to halt the rioting, give us that apology on page one in tomorrow's paper. But that's not all. We now demand the dismissal of whoever was responsible for not carrying the apology today.'

The owner first heaps the expected abuse on the editor's head and then asks him to sack the news editor. The editor tells the owner it is not the news editor's fault but the chief sub's. The news editor tells the editor that however hot-headed the chief sub is, even inept and cantankerous at times, in the balance the man's on our side when there's worker trouble. The person who is really responsible for the entire mess, the root cause of the whole problem, is the one who should be thrown out. And you know who that is.

The editor sends for Janaki and hands her a letter of dismissal. She stands before him, her mouth hanging open. 'The owner is angry because it was your article that caused the riot. He was already unhappy about your intellectual writing. I had assured him that I was grooming you to become more reader friendly. But then you went and did this.'

'But you read the piece and passed it, sir. You even praised me for writing such a balanced piece on a sensitive subject.'

'I would still say so. But however balanced the piece of writing, if people don't see it that way, it means trouble. I've been warning you all along. Our readers don't deserve this kind of writing. Give them something that appears thoughtful but is nicely fluffy and we're safe. Anyway,' an arch smile breaks on his face, 'there's talk in the office that you're planning to get married. You don't need this job. With an artist husband who sells well, money won't be a problem. And with a home to take care of, you'll have your hands full. You can always freelance. I can sneak you in once in a while when things cool down.'

Janaki nails him with her eyes, raises the letter of dismissal like a flag, says thank you and walks out. She sits at her desk, emptying out the drawers of her table. The phone rings. Like a character in a Marathi commercial play, she looks at it as if it's going to bite her before answering it. If this is one of those persistent mediocrities asking for publicity, she'll happily tell him the arts section of the *Mumbai Observer* is dead and no amount of painting or singing will revive it.

It is Ashesh. 'Ai's gone,' he says. Janaki can hear the effort it costs him to keep his voice steady. 'Early this morning. Anima and I are going, so we can't meet this evening.'

Janaki's tongue goes dry. 'May I come?'

'You won't get leave.'

'I've been given permanent leave.'

Sindhutai's once well-formed body is now a skeleton. The disease has eaten away every bit of flesh. Her once-translucent, cream-coloured skin is now yellow-grey parchment. But her forehead is smooth. All the lines have vanished with the worries, resentment, bitterness and anger of a lifetime. Dr Bhaskar has made efficient arrangements for the funeral. Men and women that Sindhutai hadn't even known have gathered to touch her feet with respect. Their faces reflect feelings inspired by her story. A woman alone, abandoned by her husband. Nobody to look after her. Children as good as missing. Dr Bhaskar her only saviour. She is his akka—elder sister. She cares for him and his work. She wills her entire property to him for his sacred mission. The cloying fragrance of incense is everywhere. The mourners look elated. Dr Bhaskar's face glows with pleasure. Sindhutai has made everybody happy by her going, because she goes as a saint.

Anima tries to repress the sob that rises to her throat. It breaks despite her. She is indescribably sad for having lost touch with her mother. She is physically no more, but she had begun to withdraw emotionally many years ago, and neither Anima nor Ashesh had been able to stop the drift. They had failed her. The sobs rise and break, waves of sorrow that will not stop. Bachchu Kaka puts his hand on her elbow in commiseration.

They gather in Bachchu Kaka's room after the funeral. Silence fills the room, broken only by Bachchu Kaka's breathing that is becoming difficult. Anima notices that the lines on his face have deepened. 'You must come and stay with me, Bachchu Kaka,' she says, worried. He breaks into a false laugh. 'And do what? Help you make suralichya vadya? Or light a beacon for your student group? Who's this ancient bag of bones, they'll say. Lock him in a cupboard with mothballs.'

On the way back to Mumbai, Anima asks in a listless voice, 'Have you two decided where you are getting married? At the registrar's or at home?'

Janaki looks at Ashesh. 'The registrar's.'

'Witnesses?'

'You, Haridas and Shekhar's mother.'

'Shekhar's mother?'

'Yes. She called to say we must have an older witness. Somebody whose feet we can touch and be blessed.'

40

On the morning of 26 December, the foundation of the eastern world is shaken. At the tip of Sumatra, where the India plate slides below the Burma plate, the crust of the earth cracks. A crevasse 400 kilometres long and 100 kilometres wide rips through the surface at 10,000 kilometres an hour. The seabed rises, throwing up monstrous waves. They swallow up the coasts of Indonesia, Thailand, Sri Lanka and India. Ships, boats, men, women, children, animals, trees, homes, cupboards, beds, documents, letters, shoes, dolls, crutches—all go under and come up later transformed into junk. It takes only a few minutes for living habitations to look like pre-creation chaos.

Ashesh has switched on the television to stabilize his nerves before the wedding. He goes into extreme shock. His attention wanders idiotically to Janaki's tanpura standing in the corner of the room. It is safe.

He switches off the television but cannot switch off the pictures of waste in his head. He sits with hands pressed tight to his forehead. Fear pounds in his chest for friends living along the coast. How are they? Are they . . . ? Or are they not? The clock says it is time to leave. He stands up on numb legs. It is weird to be getting married when half the world has disappeared. His legs carry him mechanically to the door. Downstairs Padmini is where she ought to be. That is strange. His hands unlock her door. His eyes see the road running dizzily under the tyres. His forehead breaks into a sweat. The road to the registrar's office in Bandra seems never-ending. But it ends. The others are there already. Janaki, Anima, Feroze, Haridas, Shekhar's mother. Sharada and Shekhar will join them later. Their faces are alight with joy. None of them has heard the news.

Janaki is wearing a gold-bordered sari the colour of pomegranate seeds, a delicate gold necklace and small gold earrings of traditional design. Her hair is combed off her face giving her the look of a neatly groomed girl off to school early in the morning. Ashesh's insides do a somersault. Her future is in his hands. Can he handle the responsibility? She is so young. His palms grow damp.

'Come along, Mr Groom,' Haridas booms and slaps his back. 'Take your place in line.'

The registrar's room is bursting with humanity. An elderly fan stirs the air sluggishly. Not half a puff of breeze reaches the sweaty armpits of the silk-bloused brides. Some cast nervous looks over their shoulders. They must have eloped. Their prospective husbands stand with possessive arms thrown around their fearful shoulders. Ashesh wonders what he is doing in such a place. Perhaps they should have called the registrar home and done this private thing privately.

The registrar is tetchy. Why such a crowd? Why so many marriages? What a dreadful job this is. How many of these couples will one day move to the other side of the building, for the judge to part them forever? The registrar has no faith in the marriages he registers. It's frivolous to get married like this. Marriages must be solemnized before the sacred fire with the gods as witnesses.

Ashesh and Janaki's number comes up. Ashesh allows fear to grip him for the last time. His hand trembles as he signs the register. Janaki signs after him with a confident flourish. Ashesh looks at her in wonder. Isn't she nervous? Is this real? Are they now that thing called husband and wife? What does it mean to be that?

They emerge from the stuffy registrar's office into the cool, end-of-year air outside. Photographs are taken. There's a wedding brunch at home. As soon as they get home, Ashesh and Janaki touch Shekhar's mother's feet. She showers generous blessings on them. Sharada arrives. She and Anima remove the cover of the tanpura and proudly present it to Janaki on behalf of all the friends. Janaki looks at Ashesh with tears in her eyes. She mentioned a tanpura only once to him. But he has remembered. She doesn't know what to say. So she asks a pedestrian question. 'Who got it? From where?' Anima has been waiting to tell everybody the tale of the tanpura. Before she begins the last guest arrives. Shekhar. He has taken a little time off from work.

Anima begins the story. 'Sharada knows a tanpura maker in Miraj.

They call him Aba. He visits Mumbai once in a while to deliver orders. Sharada calls him to ask if he has an instrument ready. At first he says no. Then he says yes, but adds he wouldn't advise her to buy it and he will certainly not bring it to Mumbai. Sharada asks him why. He says there's a curse on it, that's why. Sharada covers the mouthpiece and says to me, "Do we give Janaki a cursed tanpura?" I say ask him if it plays. He says it's a beauty to look at and listen to. So Sharada says, "It'll do for us. A friend of mine will come to pick it up." He says first hear about the curse then let her come if she still wants to. Sharada says he can tell her the story when she gets there.

'I leave on a Friday night. The next day is my students' Saturday. I ask them if they want to join me to see the nuts and bolts of music making. They are thrilled. We take the night train, reach Miraj in the morning, wash, have our breakfast and go to Aba's workshop. It is a fascinating place full of the aroma of wood. Aba stares at us and refuses to show us the tanpura. "First listen to the tale of the curse," he says, "then I'll show you the instrument."

'And so begins the story of the curse. A German student of Hindustani music, Hans Engelbert, ordered a tanpura from Aba. The man who was to take it to Mumbai lost his wife unexpectedly so he couldn't go. Engelbert decided to come to Miraj himself to fetch it. While he slept on the train, his luggage got stolen. He arrived in Miraj minus passport, credit card and the money he had set aside for the tanpura. He borrowed money from Aba to return to Mumbai empty-handed. He didn't want to buy the tanpura on credit. He told Aba to sell it off.

'Aba challenges us with dire warning in his eyes. I say, "Right. Now show us the tanpura." He shakes his head in an "it's-your-funeral" way, and has it brought in from a corner of the shed at the back. He has been planning to burn it. We marvel at its beauty. It is terrible to think Aba would reduce such a thing to ashes. For some reason, Girji comes to mind. When we lift the tanpura, Aba's face is like he's seen a ghost. He won't even touch the money we give him. He asks us to put it on the chair outside. He will probably exorcise it before he lets it enter his home. When we get back, Sharada calls up Aba to assure him that the tanpura and its couriers have arrived safely and that we are all in one piece and haven't as much as stubbed our toes on the way.

'Now you must decide, Janaki. Do you want to keep it or shall we drown it in the sea?'

Janaki's answer is to run her fingers over its strings and strum them lightly.

Anima's mention of the sea hits Ashesh in the pit of the stomach. They still know nothing, and he can't tell them while they are still savouring the joy of the occasion. When everybody has eaten and their high spirits have come down a notch or two, he makes a clinical announcement that does not betray his emotions. 'An earthquake measuring 9.5 on the Richter scale has hit the seabed off the coast of Sumatra and entire coasts around the Indian Ocean have been annihilated.'

He switches on the television.

'It is difficult to assess at this moment how many people have died in the tsunami. The water has still not receded and aftershocks continue to be felt. We will be tracking this terrible catastrophe through the day. Experts are still not certain where the tsunami is likely to hit as it travels westward. It has already hit India's eastern coast and experts see the possibility of its hitting the east coast of Africa.'

Janaki holds Ashesh's hand tightly. The room is engulfed in a dense silence. The friends look at each other, stunned. The tsunami is doing its tandav, the dance of destruction, on the threshold of the country.

41

To: Haridas, Anju–Atul, Gieve, Shanta–Sudhir, Ashesh–Janaki, Anima

Subject: The Tsunami

Dear Friends,

Thanks for your kind inquiries. I am OK. But it was a terrifying experience.

On 25th December, some relatives and I were in Nagercoil for a family wedding. The place is half an hour's drive away from Kanyakumari which we wanted to visit. There were six of us—two children, their mother, her elderly parents and I. That morning we heard news of giant waves hitting the Chennai coast. When we reached Kanyakumari, we found the sea there behaving oddly. So we turned back immediately. On the way to Nagercoil our driver took a road that goes past the Suthavli coast. Since we had not spent time at the Kanyakumari beach, he thought we might want to spend some time here. There too the locals told us that the sea had been behaving in a peculiar fashion since the morning. The waves would ebb for a while and suddenly swell and advance. When we arrived, the sea had receded. We got out of the car, walked a little way but felt anxious and turned back in five minutes. The car was parked on a rise. The distance to it from the seashore was barely twenty feet. As we were walking towards it, some locals shouted, 'Look! It's a miracle!' We turned round to look. A monstrous wave had gathered on the horizon and was lunging towards the shore. I began to record the sight on my video camera. It was instinctive. None of us had seen anything like it before. I thought I could even make a short documentary on the phenomenon if I got enough footage. But within seconds the wave had expanded across the horizon and was advancing at a crazy speed. It was now as tall as a two-storey building. We started running towards the car. The driver managed to get in, but before we could reach, the wave had pounced on us. The car was tossed up into the air and shattered to bits. The wave pulled us into itself with a demonic force, tossing us around as it advanced. I held my breath. I was being dragged over some hard objects that I couldn't identify.

There was a moment when I thought this was the end. I was still holding on to my camera. Just then, I felt something hard and knotty, and grabbed it with my other hand. I don't know how long I held on to that thing, my body completely immersed in water and my head barely above it. At some point I felt the water around me being sucked back. My head emerged fully above the water and I saw I was holding on to the thick branch of a tree that had miraculously escaped being uprooted. The water was receding fast, leaving behind bits of human bodies that lay strewn all over the beach. Those who could use their limbs got up slowly and began to comb the beach for their loved ones. The children's mother from our group and our driver had disappeared. The others survived but are in a critical condition in the hospital. I honestly don't know how I was saved, but I came through without a scratch. I don't know yet if my camera has been saved. If it has been, it carries some incredible footage of the end of the world.

Shankar

42

Feroze puts the last touch on *Annihilation II* at three o'clock on the morning of 29 December. He has photographed the bits and pieces of *Annihilation I* in different exposures, screen-printed them on the canvas and painted an enormous stunted tree in one corner. He looks at the result now in high excitement. He has never done anything like this before. But he can now see unlimited possibilities in this way of working. He feels the urge to share his excitement with somebody, this minute. He'd like it to be Anima. But he can't wake her at this hour. Haridas then. He might be awake or he can be woken up, *saala*.

'Who is this?' It is Maya's sleepy voice at the other end. Feroze is all stutter and stumble at his goof-up. 'So sorry, Maya. Feroze here.'

Haridas comes on the line. 'Can't a man sleep peacefully in his own home?'

'Sorry, Hari.'

'Did you call to say sorry or do you have something else to say?'

'I've had an idea. We should all go to Matheran for New Year's Eve.'

'Right. Anything else?'

'No, nothing else. You can go back to sleep.'

'Much obliged.'

Feroze looks at the phone, thoroughly confused. What was all that about? How did Matheran get in? He was supposed to talk about his painting. Maya's voice threw him. But come to think of it, Matheran is a brilliant idea. Jijabhau can come along to help Pandurang with the extra work.

Feroze is lying in bed, still wide awake with no sign of sleep. He gets out of bed, sorts through his CDs and finds the one he is looking for. Years ago, a cousin had spent her own money to cut a disc of her self-composed ghazals and distributed copies to the family as New Year's gifts. Feroze had played it once to be fair to her and discovered there was neither throb nor pain in the songs supposedly about love. And had fallen peacefully asleep in his chair as he listened to it. When he woke up, he had put away the valuable CD carefully for future use. There it is now. He slips it into the CD tray, presses the play button on the player, switches off the lights, lies down on his bed and is soon fast asleep.

On 31 December, the friends leave separately for Matheran. Haridas is in his Mercedes with Maya beside him and a Nepali cap on his head. Maya has almost finished her work in Mumbai. She has been commissioned to make short films on ten of the world's most exciting cities, to document the changes they have undergone with globalization. Mumbai is now done. Maya has concentrated on what was once known as Girangaon, village of mills. This large expanse of land in central

Mumbai, where the city's textile mills once stood, has now been taken over by malls and high-end residential towers.

'You know something, Maya,' Haridas says. 'I'm about to give birth to a fantastic idea. Will you sell me copies of your stills? Or is the copyright with your sponsor?'

'No, it's with me.'

'Then let me buy a dozen or so of them please. I'll use them to make paintings. But I won't exhibit the paintings as paintings.'

'What then?'

'Listen. In the old days bioscopewallahs used to roam the streets of the city. Wherever they set up their bioscopes, eager children would crowd around to take a look. The machines were colourful with a toy monkey on top which played a pair of cymbals when it was wound up. For a couple of paise a piece, the children could put their eye to the eyehole and see pictures sliding by while the man sang descriptions of the sights. Why can't I have a bioscope made, fit it with magnifying lenses, paint the outside and show my Girangaon paintings on it? Go back to old media instead of forward to the new.'

Haridas whistles a happy tune although Maya has not agreed to sell him the stills and is even doubtful about the idea.

Feroze picks up Anima. Even this early in the morning, cars creep bonnet to tail in both directions along the city's arterial roads. Jijabhau takes the container Anima is carrying as she gets into the front seat. 'What have you brought?'

'Frogs' legs.' Anima laughs at Feroze's eager expression. Then says quietly, 'The latest estimate is 25,000 dead.'

'Anima, please. Can we not speak about the tsunami for this one day at least?'

Shekhar and Sharada are a little late in starting. Shantanu has not slept all night. The sudden chill in the air has given him a cold. They don't want to take him to Matheran. So Shekhar's mother has been called to babysit. She has had to hurry through her own chores before she can come over. Despite the late start, they are at the foot of Matheran a little before Ashesh's Padmini winds her way there.

Once all there, they set off on foot up the incline to Feroze's uncle's bungalow. 'Why did your Hoshi Uncle have to build a house at the other end of town?' Shekhar is already panting.

'He didn't build it. It belonged to a Britisher. Hoshi Uncle bought it from him.'

By the time they get to Sylvania, it is lunchtime. 'When I was a kid, this place was dense jungle,' Feroze tells Maya. 'By the time you got to the berry bushes your feet were in tatters.'

'What berries?'

'I'll show you if there are any left.'

She nods and strides ahead. Haridas shouts after her, 'Watch out for snakes and elephants.'

She turns around and says, 'I'll have them for lunch.'

In the evening Feroze takes them to his favourite 'point'. The road is long and difficult. When they finally arrive at the 'point', they flop on the scattered boulders, completely done in. The wind funnels up the valley, whistling. The sun is about to set behind the hills. Feroze wants his friends to watch the drama that is about to unfold. He puts his finger to his lips to hush them. As the sun dips, the shadow of one hill slides slowly across the face of the other. While gold dust still gilds the tops of the hills, their rugged rock faces are turning slate grey. The men and women on the boulders hold their breath as the rims of the hills dim, looming against the sky like monsters in black. An enormous shadow climbs swiftly up from the valley to hug their feet.

There is nothing left in the world that is not in shades of black. They get up one by one. Feroze lends Anima a hand. It is suddenly chilly. The wind roars behind them pushing them forward. Dried leaves crackle underfoot. Janaki throws her head back and laughs. Ashesh bends down quickly for a kiss. Their arms tighten around each other's waists. The climb is over. The road is flat now. They turn right. The wind lets go of their backs and whistles off into the night. The descent towards Sylvania is covered thickly with moist leaves on which their feet slip and slide. Maya laughs. They all laugh. Their laughter whirls up into the tops of the trees, echoes and fades away.

The spicy aroma of jhunka greets them at the gate. The aroma is so out of keeping with the colonial bungalow that Anima halts in shock at the door. The front room is furnished with heavy teak armchairs and old-style lights. The doors are veiled with frilled curtains. China bowls, plates and flower vases stand on the teak sideboard by the wall. And in the midst of all this Victoriana wafts the rustic aroma of jhunka.

'Why don't we eat in the kitchen, sitting on the floor?' Anima suggests. 'Then Shevantabai can serve us bhakris straight off the fire.'

Shekhar wrinkles his nose. He's wearing tight trousers.

'I can lend you a lungi,' Haridas offers.

There's a moment's silence. Then Shekhar smiles and says, 'No, thank you. Each to his own.'

Feroze too is unhappy with the floor idea. So he and Shekhar decide to sit at a small table that Feroze draws up to the kitchen.

As fast as Pandurang's wife Shevanta roasts the bhakris, they are walloped. Haridas points to Sharada and says, 'Don't give her any more. She is going to sing for us after this.'

'What are you going to sing?' Ashesh asks.

'If there's going to be singing, we're all going to do it,' Sharada answers.

They think the idea's a joke.

'How's guruji's temperature these days?' Anima asks.

'Down to normal. We've struck a deal. If I want to continue to learn from him, I am not to sing my own compositions for a year.'

'It could have been for as long as he is alive.'

'Gurus also need disciples. The embargo gives him the satisfaction of victory over my rebellion.'

'The embargo's a good idea,' Haridas chips in. 'Gives you time to polish your compositions.'

'Maya can't understand anything we're saying,' Janaki points out. 'Shouldn't we speak in English?'

'Why?' Haridas asks, putting his left arm around Maya. 'Do I understand anything when I'm with her Antoines and Francescas? All I can tell is whether they are happy or upset.'

Maya nods without understanding a word. Neatly filling the last piece of bhakri with jhunka and popping it into her mouth, she says to Shevanta, 'Buss.' Then looking at the others proudly, she says, 'I've picked up at least that word.' Then she says even more proudly, 'And matherchod.'

The room goes dead for a moment. Shevanta's eyes roll. When everybody bursts out laughing, she too hides her face in her sari and giggles.

At midnight they hug each other in sombre silence. What will the coming year bring them? Feroze will show in January. *Annihilation II* will be exhibited. Another riot? Janaki doesn't want to depend on Ashesh financially. The space for serious writing on the arts has all but disappeared. She can always find another job. But will the work be satisfying?

Sharada takes her drone box from the cloth bag Anima has made for it. 'I'm not in the mood to sing anything classical tonight. I want us all to sing. No, honestly. I'll sing an abhang of Tukaram. You can join in the refrain. Have you brought your cymbals, Jijabhau?'

Jijabhau grins and nods. Pandurang and Shevanta come in. Sharada clears her throat. It is the third quarter of the day but traditional songs are not time bound. Sharada presses the shadja on the drone box and begins.

Music is filled with the colours of magic,
It is your gift to us, my Lord,
Accept it back from us.
The love that fills our hearts never ebbs,
Says Tukaram, voice and speech are pools of nectar.

The power fails. The song continues in the dark.